GLOWROT
NO WAY OUT OF WONDERLAND

BEATRICE LEBRUN

CONTENT WARNINGS

This story contains themes that may be distressing to some readers, including:

Stalking

SA

Dissociation/self-distraction during SA

Doxxing

Fetishization of a NB person

Viewing pre-transition content of a NB person without their permission

Drug usage

Habitual smoking

Non-specific sexual content

Body dysmorphia

Eating disorder

Hallucinations

Sensory overload / overstimulation

Confinement

Sexual/physical contact during altered state

Please read with care. Your safety comes first.

If you ever need to step away, that's okay.

This story is already rotting, but it'll still be here when you're ready to return.

Soundtrack

Listen as the story breathes under your skin

Desafío - Arca

High On My Lows - Sawyer Hill

The Mad Tea Party - Michael and Spider

Little Dark Age - MGMT

Stalker's Tango - Autoheart

Otra Noche de Llorar - Mon Laferte

The Red Means I Love You - Madds Buckley

Sweet Hibiscus Tea - Penelope Scott

Apareces de la nada - Quelle Rox

Mad World - Gary Jules

Flamingo - La Vida Bohème

Further descent available here.

GLOWHOT

BEATRICE LEBRUN

GLOWROT

© 2025 Beatrice Lebrun

All rights reserved.

ISBN 979-8-9991162-0-8 (ebook) - ISBN 979-8-9991162-1-5 (paperback) - ISBN 979-8-9991162-2-2 (hardcover)

Cover design, illustrations, formatting, and layout by Beatrice Lebrun.

Edited by Danyelle Briggs, In The Write Dyrection

First edition, 2025

To those who looked for something to fill the void, and found it staring back.
To the ones who couldn't leave, even when the door was open.
To the girl who begged the world to love her back.
To every version of me that didn't make it out.

I made this for you, even if I had to give myself away to do it.

0
Danger, Do Not Enter

Mirrors are meant to reflect reality; at least, that's what you learn as a kid. They are the closest thing you could have to seeing yourself through your own eyes; even cameras have some distortion.

So, the monster They are looking at must be real, right?

The air conditioner runs at full speed, roaring like a beast—fierce and violent. It echoes loud music; They don't want to think about it right now but can't seem to stop remembering.

The hotel room is freezing, and yet They're still standing there, half-naked, poking at their skin in front of a dirty mirror They know they should have destroyed.

Beep, beep, beep.

What's the use of an alarm clock anymore?

"I'll be late!" With that sound, their eyes are no longer glazed over. Now it's time for the jittery hand movements, the desperate gasps for air. "I'll be late. I can't be late!" But even with all the effort in the world, their gaze can't stop staring.

Staring at the unnatural push their ribs have against their skin. At how they expand and contract until they inflate like balloons and then pop. At the bumps in their knees, shifting back and forth into balls of grease. The reflection bends towards the bed, but the skinny figure in the real world stays petrified until the one on the other side picks up a lighter.

A <u>white</u> lighter.

Their <u>white</u> lighter.

"I'm already late." They say to no one specific, or maybe to the one on the other side. "There's no use to trying."

GLOWROT

Even when They close their eyes, the reflection is still there. A hideous face, despite all the compliments they could receive on the street. Only they can see the truth, the ugliness that they truly possess.

Their mind is racing almost as much as their hands, contrasting with their feet' sluggishness. At some point, the suit that waited patiently in a chair falls to the floor and disappears between shards of glass of the mirrors of the past and plastic spoons.

"I have to, but I can't." But without even realizing it, they're lighting another cigarette and subconsciously glancing at the smoke detector they made sure to damage the first day of their stay at this hotel. Now the room's smell of lavender mixed with antiseptic welcomes the newfound scent, like a fucked up perfume that perfectly summarizes their mental state.

A scream tries to leave their throat, but the pain is too strong to let it. Gums bleeding, purple lips. It's all happening again, and there's no going back once it starts. No one else knows it as well as They do.

Memories, then, of a figure that moves like a snake on the dance floor. White, long hair stuck with sweat on their face, neon pink saliva trickles down their chin. It's the pull they've felt since the first time they found themselves in that place, back when it was all wonderful.
Perfect.

Like them.

"She can't see me like this," they speak again to the nothingness.

This time, the shadows in every corner respond. They start with a chuckle that crescendos until they transform into a cackle so vile the whole room trembles. They lean closer, twisting into shapes too similar to their reflection for comfort. Imitating the inflating and deflating, their limbs stretching and deforming, their movements jerky and erratic.
Beep, beep, beep.

Now the alarm is not coming from the phone, but from the walls. Like a ticking clock, like a beating heart hidden under the floorboards. It can't stop, not now. They're already late, after all.
They

are

always

late.

There's something else, something the shadows are trying to tell them.

They tug at them, desperate for attention. Scratch their back until the rabbit tattooed on it looks bruised and damaged. But the scream still doesn't come, it can't. It's too much at the same time.

Whoops, when did that cigarette fall to the floor?

Better be careful, they wouldn't want to burn the whole place down. Right?

Beep, beep, bzzzz.

Once again mutating, the sounds are no longer coming from the walls but from inside their head. It doesn't matter that They have no clue when they arrive at the bathroom, just that they can't shatter this mirror either because they'll have to pay for it, too. Their futile attempt at putting on some white eyeliner gets interrupted by another hideous reminder of their true nature.

Raised ridges on the skin of their arms that aren't going away no matter how hard their short nails scratch. With a close glance, they realize something even more horrific: dark veins glowing faintly beneath their thin skin. Pulsating, shifting like snakes, as if they were trying to escape. All the scratching in the world will not make them go away, not this time.

It's too late to fix it. To fix themselves.

Bzzzz, bzzz, bzz.

It's too much, it's unbearable. The light flickers, and in the second the bathroom succumbs to darkness; a neon outline surrounds them. And then dissipates as if nothing happened. The buzz still inside their head is too familiar, too much like the neon lamps that plague their nightmares constantly. And yet, are they really nightmares?

The sweet haze of oblivion, of being so detached from reality, their shape doesn't matter. The delightful sensation of not feeling hunger. The wonderful lullaby of a perfect world.

It couldn't have been that bad, right?

"Right," respond the shadows.

"Maybe just one more time, only one more." They say, picking up the <u>white</u> lighter and flicking it on. The only thing that seems real, tangible. Their ticket to *that place*. They flick it off now, and then on and off. The rhythm soothing their internal void.

Click, click, click.

Much better.

With a smile, They zigzag through the room like a wounded animal trying to run, get dressed, and sketch an attempt at makeup without staring at their reflection. The shadows are silent now, content. Every single one of them knows what's about to happen. It's what comes naturally, after all.

"I'll leave after just one drink. I won't even talk to anyone. Just one drink." The thought of the sweet flavor is enough to send shivers down their spine, and the <u>rabbit</u> tattoo is now decorated with goosebumps all around.

One arm, the other one, somehow that leather jacket always made them feel better. Their hands shake, and They still hold the lighter firmly, their only key to *that place*.

Right before exiting, one last glance at the mirror reveals a twisted, almost unrecognizable version of their true self. Their veins pumping neon venom to their heart, their eyes glowing like a specter. But they force themselves to look away.

And They leave. They leave the shattered glass on the floor, the spoons, the shadows living in the corners, the cigarette still on.

The hotel hallway is desolate; cobwebs start forming in the corners whenever they pass by, almost mocking the one they have tattooed under their eye.

It's curious how their steps don't sound, as if they were lighter than air. If only they truly were.

The world is empty.

The elevator was waiting for them.

The twins in the reception don't even attempt to look at them.

The door opens the second it senses their presence.

And then the rest of the world.

Click, click, click.

Neon city lights illuminate their path, casting distorted colors across their face. They walk without direction because they know this process way too well, and yet their back is straight, and their steps are small and quick. The glow that seems to be emanating from the lighter starts wrapping around them, guiding them, almost devouring them.

At least where they're going, they'll never be late.

1
NoExiT

The tip of my tongue caresses my upper lip, and I smile because I know the inside of my mouth is not bleeding yet. The night is off to a good start.

With a smile and my eyes closed, I slip into the crowd. Here, feeling things is much more important than seeing them.

Everything seems familiar and utterly alien at the same time. I can't remember how I got here, but I don't think it matters. For all I know, I could have fallen down a giant hole and ended up in the center of the Earth.

Things are different here; my body recognizes the sensations.

It's like I belong here.

My pores absorb the music around me like an echo drowned out by the movements of more people than there should be in such a small space. I am soaked, not only from the rain I vaguely remember but from the indecent amount of substances that shouldn't have ever touched my body.

Was my drink always this color?

MY TEETH TINGLE, so I smile because that's always the best way to scratch them.

Someone laughs, and I mimic it, even though I feel like a mirror without control over my actions.

The music threatens to burst my eardrums. Its lyrics matter less than the monotony of the tone. The hypnotic ticking of the words, one after the other, makes me go into a trance. My lips move as if I know what I'm doing. I'm just one more in the pile of bodies.

Yes, I belong here.

I need just a little more fuel, and I search desperately around me. My dry lips implore me for it. It comes as a little glass vial someone puts in my hand before I ask them to. "Drink me" is written on it, as it is in every glass in this place.

A few drops to finish emptying my brain, and my hips finally loosen up. My tongue travels to the outside of my lips and tastes the air in front of me. It tastes like pineapple juice with cotton candy.

Long live e-cigarettes for making even something as tasteless as air fun in places like this.

Almost there.

Finally, my mind begins to fog over, and I can stop battling the memories that try to remind me of who I am. Then I feel the salty taste of something that doesn't exist anymore.

Tears?

A scream rings out, and just like I was waiting for it, I start bouncing between the shoulders and elbows that surround me. I go from side to side without control over where the movement takes me. I let all my worries go because I'm not here to remember; the appeal is being able to escape.

It's the one thing we all have in common; we know it even though we have no awareness of who we really are. In this instant, I'm nothing more than a jacket tied around my waist, an amalgamation of movements and stomping feet, and the interesting guy I have shaking off sweat in front of me.

Salty.

Like what?

If I forgot, it's because it was never important.

A hand makes its way through the stacked bodies and holds a syringe with an electric blue liquid that calls to me and glows in tune with the silhouettes around me. The girl, more skin than clothes, takes me by the chin, and I obediently open my mouth.

I stick out my tongue as I make sure to drink the poison she offers me, and I try to detail her face, but she seems almost part of the furniture. It blurs every time I try to focus too much on it. When the syringe finishes emptying I can swear it vanishes, sucked through one of the walls of the club.

My tongue now tastes like grapes, and I feel an uncontrollable desperation to let the sweaty guy know.

GLOWROT

I grab his white shirt and pull him to me, claiming the sensation of his skin slapping against mine. Liquid dances between our mouths, and I feel his nails dig into my hips.

My body tenses, but I'm in no condition to refuse, not now. So, I run my tongue over the roof of his mouth. It tastes like glory, with cheap cologne in the mix.

The pace slows, and his hands travel down my back, then up and under my shirt. I'm panting, and every time I try to breathe, he kisses me more violently. My head slams against the wall behind me. Arching in surprise, I feel his groin press against mine. His lips finally release me, and the second they try to travel to my neck, I push him away with what strength I no longer have left.

Why?

He keeps looking at me, thirsty and desperate, a trickle of saliva slipping from the corner of his lips. There's something under his skin, neon blood pumping through his veins.

I try to make out his face, but his features change with every movement he makes. I duck and manage to break free of his grip, slipping through the maze of people.

Suddenly, I feel like going to the bathroom.

I squeeze through the soaked bodies, bumping into each other in hardly discreet ways. If I look up, I can see the four walls of the place. I know it is far from being big, but moving from one end to the other becomes an odyssey when I must avoid the crowd of people crammed together.

Every time I turn, I can swear I see shadows shifting for a split second, just out of reach. They grow and shrink with the music; they seem to be coming directly from the walls. But when I focus, there's nothing there, of course. It's my brain, already filled to the brim with things accelerating its decay.

After passing near the bar, I somehow know I'm close. When I manage to free myself from the tangle in which I was trapped, I smile at the neon sign indicating the restroom.

Because there are signs here for everything except the exit.

How do I know that?

I run to a cubicle, thankful there's no line.

MY SCALP IS ITCHING and the feeling gets worse with each gag. The more I get rid of the junk I've put into my body, the more I get back in tune with my surroundings.

Maldita sea.

Something sticky is clinging to my knees, making me regret kneeling in front of the toilet. It starts burning, prickling them. For a second, it feels like sharp claws trying to drag me through the floor, and the familiarity of the sensation makes me throw up even more.

It could be the pain in my chest I get every time I vomit or that I'm starting to get my feet back on the ground, but I begin to cry. And when I realize it, I hate myself for doing it. Then I cry harder.

No way, I'm regretting it.

The music, getting slower and slower, makes the situation worse. And I don't even know what time it is anymore. Then, against all my wishes, I start to remember.

I was right, assuming it's not my first time here, and it's always the same thing. My phone disappears, there are no clocks, and I can never guess how much time has passed. I'm not in control of when I'll leave; fuck, I don't even know how to get out of here!

It's the price to pay to fuck up my body and my brain, and I'm willing to oblige. I need it.

For some reason, the toilet paper I use to clean my lips tastes like cotton candy. It's pink, like everything in this place. Intoxicating.

Managing to pull myself together, I pull down the lever with one foot as I stumble out of the cubicle. The scratches on my knees hurt like alcohol was dumped on open wounds, throbbing with every step. I might be bleeding. But the droplets somehow come from my chin, too thick to be just sweat.

A hot, boiling sensation starts overcoming my face, from my nose to my ears.

My skin feels *wrong;* soft, pliable, like invisible hands are dragging it down. It's hard to breathe now. I feel my eyelids pulling downward, and the corners of my mouth drag with them.

No. No.

My face is melting, I know it.

I can feel it.

My fingers sink into my cheeks when I try to grab them; I feel the indentations they leave when I pull back. The gooey warmth starts strangling me, suffocating me.

Panic takes control as I run to the sinks and try to find a mirror, but a wall of neon flashes taunts me instead. Desperate, I try to claw at the empty space, and a couple of my nails start bending backward. The pain grounds me in place and helps me come back to whatever version of myself I am in the moment. I hear a faint hum behind the neon. It laughs at me; it loves seeing me like this.

Every faucet is turned on. The water seems luminescent and slowly hums a tune that makes me want to drink it. I soak my face, trying to stop whatever has overcome me; it tastes like cherries.

Of course, I just had to drink it.

So, I bend to the faucet and take in as much as I can in big gulps. It's freezing but calms the heat in my throat. I can breathe again; the slight lightheadedness confirms I'm returning to how I'm supposed to be: anyone else but myself.

Other people shuffle in and out of the bathroom, nothing more than humanoid shapes. I recognize their smiles; I smile back and join the shuffling group.

The two identical women standing guard give me a blank stare, black drool coming out of the corners of their mouths. I just shrug. I have absolutely no money, so no tip, I guess.

Maybe next time they can find someplace that isn't trashy to work at, or at the very least clean up some of the gunk on the floor that now adorns my knees.

Fuck, it still hurts.

As soon as I get out, I scream victorious. The wave of humidity slaps me in the face, but I jump up and down because I love the song playing, even if I can't remember the title.

Someone else comes out beside me, and I feel their arm around my hip. They start singing along with me. It doesn't matter that we're blocking the traffic of people desperate to get from one place to another.

They take my hand, and I let myself be led to a secluded corner of the dance floor, with couches lit by fluorescent lights that don't allow us to distinguish anything but silhouettes in highly saturated colors.

Their lips feel different from the others, softer, juicier. The tip of their tongue runs over mine calmly, and I slowly caress their tattooed scalp. I don't feel the pressure in my chest anymore, it's like I'm inhaling some designer drug.

I hear a moan leave my throat, and I end up letting myself go completely. Their breath sings along with mine, we laugh in unison.

1 NoExiT

It feels good, in contrast to the desperation and tactlessness of the guy from before. It feels like a decade ago, but I could swear it happened this very night.

I reach out my hand to the table next to the couch and take the first glass I feel. I sip the contents that taste like sour milk, and their lips drink the remnants that have spilled down my chin to my collarbones. Feeling their touch exploring my chest helps me lose control of my actions again, thankfully. I drop my head back, and their hands bind my waist. Suddenly, I'm lying on the couch and don't need to open my eyes to know what's happening.

It's the right amount of sweetness without being cloying.

And I want more, so much more. I let my hands roam their body too and slip into the minuscule space between the fabric and their skin. Their gasps cloud my senses. I can't speak, I can't think. In this instant, it's only our primitive instincts at work.

I'm trembling, and cling tighter to their body. I don't want there to be any space between us. But I have less and less strength.

I'm leaving, I'm leaving again, I'm losing myself.

I'M DISSOLVING

But no, I'm not ready, not yet!

Their hands are now clinging to me in what feels like an attempt to keep me there. They slip between the edge of my pants and my skin.

"A little more, just a little more," they whisper, biting my ear, their voice cracking. "It's the last time, I swear."

They're crying.

We are crying.

And I know it will end, and I will forget.

And maybe they know it too.

In those last lucid seconds, I'm sure I'll only remember the neon lights and the maze of bodies I was trapped in, with more limbs than there should be. I don't want to leave. I refuse to.

The last memory comes into my head as if taunting me. The certainty that those hands have traveled my body before, that this has happened more than once.

"This can't be the last time," I try to say, but I have no idea if the words are leaving my mouth. "This won't be the last time; I won't let it." I bite their lower lip; the metallic taste fills my mouth.

My hands try to hold on to each of their corners, their most intricate nooks and crannies. The sensation is warm and pleasurable but slowly fades away. I try to concentrate on how good the movement they are making with their fingers inside me feels, on their breath on me.

But I'm dissolving once more.

And I hate myself for it.

"Come with me," I try to whisper, but the words never leave my throat.

2

Out of Order

It can't be.

Coño de la madre.

Again.

I don't remember anything.

I feel so disgusted just by existing all sticky and so... fucked up. I don't think I can breathe; I forgot how to. *Where am I?*

I feel the world spinning still, the twists and turns it takes seem to have come out of the most absurd amusement park ever in the history of all—

Oh no.

Oh no.

My feet slip on the questionable liquid on the floor of wherever I am, and I don't know how I don't kill myself while running to the bathroom. How obnoxious to see the vomit didn't hold out a little longer, how disgusting to have to mop the floor right next to the toilet because my body is so insufferable I can't even aim properly.

The rays of light from the window confess to me that the night ended long ago. I rub my eyes to protect them from the intense reflection against the white walls.

So why does life keep spinning as if the only thing in my veins is alcohol?

Is that what I did last night? Did I go out drinking?

I want to crawl into bed, but I dig my fingernails into the wall and feel them cling to the indentations that were already there, filled with dried blood, from some other time when I also felt like dying.

But for very different reasons.

GLOWROT

A familiar chill runs down my spine, sharper than a knife dragging against bone. Fuck.

Not right now.

Not here.

I can't handle him right now.

The air thickens, heavy and damp, like something alive pressing against my skin. The temperature starts rising, suffocating me. Each one of my inhales now feels like it's being sucked out of my chest.

I scream and kick the air in a stupid attempt to push him away, even though I know way too well it's impossible to predict where he'll appear each time. There's obviously nothing there.

My legs don't hit anything, as expected, and I collapse backward. My head bounces off the bathroom tile, and a sharp, blinding pain blooms at the base of my skull.

I close my eyes. I don't want to see. I refuse.

But the sensation crawls under my eyelids, prying them open with cold claws sharp like needles. So, I try to cover them with my hands, only to have them pulled away.

He's here.

I know it.

His presence is so abysmal that I feel like he is stepping on me with steel boots.

I hate him, I hate him, I hate him.

But I shouldn't.

I don't.

He's so good to me.

He cares; I know he does. He just has a weird way to show it.

Then I see him. A shadow, stretching along the bathroom wall, bending closer and closer to me against all laws of physics.

A dot of light flickers, and then another one next to it, his eyes slowly forming, judging me. Then the slit starts expanding until it becomes the jagged, distorted smile I have known since I was a child. It's too familiar, almost comforting.

But now's not the time, and he knows it.

He doesn't care.

He knows best.

I want to cry, but the tears don't come. It's just frustration because I have no fucking clue what the fuck I did last night, and having to deal with him right now just makes things worse.

And in the blink of an eye, it's been seven hours, even though the clock says it's been seven minutes since the light blinded me on the phone screen.

When did I move?

An empty three-liter bottle is lying on the floor; perhaps it has contributed to the collection of watered-down liquids that, at this point, have mixed with my skin. My feet are dirty, and my clothes are torn; a single wrapping of a pack of ramen is lying in the corner.

"YouDidn'tGoOutLastNight,YouKnowThat," he whispers, his voice slithering through my brain like smoke.

Oh my god, I hate you so fucking much.

I don't, I don't hate you. You know I don't.

I'm sorry.

But I wish you would leave my life forever and never stand before me again. I swear, if you dare say one more word, I'm going to...

"GoingToWhat?

TouchTheUntouchable?

FightTheUnreal?

You'reAdorableWhenYouTry."

His voice reverberates against the walls; it vibrates in every possible direction, like one of those 8D sounds, the kind you play when you're getting fucked up because you don't know where anything's coming from, and it weirdly scratches your ears. It goes from right to left, top to bottom, front to back. My thoughts get tangled in between them.

"YouHateMeAndYouDon't.

YouWantMeGoneButHereIComeAgain.

Isn'tThatRight? BoWhoCan'tLetGo."

Por favor.

Ya.

Ya basta.

"YouThinkGoingBackToSpanish

WillMakeYourHeadStraight?

Darling,IAmTheOneThatDoesThatForYou."

He sounds concerned, sad, worried.

GLOWROT

"DoYouRememberWhatHappensWhenILeave?"

His smile widens with a chuckle, and his eyes fix on mine like he's waiting for me to admit he's right. My hands tremble, but I clench them into fists. I don't answer. I can't. I try as hard as I can to remind myself that I hate him again, but he digs one of his claws into my shoulder, and I smile because I don't really do.

It feels good.

Everything feels good.

Yes, I remember.

I'm okay now.

He approaches me, and I close my eyes. The light from his luminous sockets flickers right in front of my eyelids, and I know that if I open them, I will be met with that blinding, burning emptiness. I prefer to keep them closed and not risk him snatching my soul again.

Sometimes, I think he can't see, but he knows the precise moment to arrive and leave because he smells my fear.

He feeds on it, and on my nightmares, and on terrible things. He gobbles up the bits of fingernails still on the bathroom floor because I don't bother to pick them up, and no one else will see them there anyway. The claw digging into my neck makes me finally open my eyes and notice the TV in front of me.

When did I get here?

W sits calmly next to me on the floor without looking at me. Grinning again.

"You'reInYourApartment."

He whispers to me.

"YouHaven'tBeenOutInOverAWeek,Silly."

He hesitates for a moment and continues softly.

"OtherThanToBuyThatOneBottleYesterday."

He explains, pointing at it with a skeletal finger much longer than any person or semi-humanoid shadowy being could have.

"Didn't I go out last night?" I ask, and W shakes his head.

I forgot how to breathe.

Leaning back on the edge of the mattress, I stare at the ceiling and try to make him understand what I can't say. There are still images desperate to come to my mind, brushing against it the way words tickle the tips of your taste buds when they want to mock you.

2 Out of Order

I want to feel his claws again, not on my shoulders, but around my neck. His giant, bony hand closing in tighter and tighter.

I need to feel my eyes roll over until I see the inside of my sockets.

But he doesn't do anything; deep down, I know he won't. I feel his weight on the mattress right behind me. And his presence is enough, much more than his words, which end up being little more than an echo of something far away that once existed or will exist.

And even though my chest struggles to rise and fall to the rhythm of a breath that seems unreal, I smile.

Despite all the disasters I've gotten myself into, he's always there. And accepting it causes me to squirm in my place, so much so that I lie there, MELTING INTO THE GROUND.

I may be in absolute deep shit, but it's all good.

W will always care for me, and I don't need anything else.

That's why I haven't been out all week. The images trying to raid my thoughts must be nothing more than a drowsy hallucination from some late-night moment when I was surely watching a movie, too glued to the TV for my well-being.

It wouldn't be the first time.

GLOWROT

3

Open 24 Hours

I must stop doing laundry at ten o'clock at night, but that's my only free time.

Yeah, right.

It's not about free time; it's about how far down the food chain I've let myself sink.

Living in a hotel sounded glamorous at first, but I should have known it was too good to be true for my rent price. What was I expecting? Getting fluffy robes and dry-cleaned sheets like the guests?

The truth is, I'm here now because I've run out of clean underwear. Again. And I cannot stomach the thought of hand-washing my panties in the shower again, only to stay damp and clammy because the AC doesn't even work well on my unit.

Just another cycle I can't break out of.

Amazing.

Besides, at this time of night, there's hardly anyone left here. No one to look at me and wonder why I'm dressed like this or why my eyes are sunken in, let alone look too closely at the marks on my face or the scabs under my fingernails. At this hour, everyone is too tired to exist, myself included.

A man in a suit is pulling his clothes from the dryer. The tie dangling from his pocket says, "busy office guy," but the laundromat at this hour tells the truth: he's just another pretentious jerk stuck in the same grind, like me. Or maybe he's the sleazy car salesman type, flashing cheap smiles while pushing overpriced junk. His stupid haircut and sunglasses perched on his head at midnight confirm it. We're all poor fuckers stuck in the same cycle of garbage lives, I suppose. So pathetic.

Except for the girl at the entrance, I like her and she once helped me when the coin machine jammed.

Still, I cross my legs and smile at the sight of him. What will he think? That I'm a desperate girl looking for extra cash? His smile crawls under my skin, and nausea overcomes me.

What the fuck am I even doing?

I glance at the soda machine instead, its dim light flickering like a half-dead firefly.

Stupid.

Stupid.

Stupid.

Stupid.

It's absurd that I keep trying to feel pretty for a second. I should know better by now. I know it's better to stay out of trouble.

Except I can't stop looking for it.

Because I have suicidal thoughts every seven minutes.

Trouble makes my pulse race and makes me feel real, even for a moment. That's the reason for the skirts, the disheveled *but cool* look, the sneaky smiles, and sticking my nose where it doesn't belong. Little breadcrumbs I leave behind for whatever wolf or monster might follow them.

I've lost count of the ones that have followed through already.

But my body seems to remember well enough. The nausea, the shivers, the little bits of memories that remind me of the scars not so visible. All the things that have happened already since I came to live here.

I'm not brave enough to hurt myself directly, but no one said that's the only way to do it. Not looking sideways while crossing the street, making eye contact with strangers in the dead of night. My tiny screams into the void.

And yet, here I am, folding laundry like it's the most important thing in the world. Slow, deliberate, as if each shirt I smooth out could fix whatever's broken inside me. Thank heavens, these places run 24 hours straight.

Still, despite trying to convince myself that I'm begging for a bit of excitement, a little danger, I run out almost the second I see the homeless guy on duty cross the door's threshold.

There's something about the nauseating smell, but it's nothing personal. I just don't want to go through the "give me money, I don't have any" and the "me neither, so if you get some, share" dance that happens every time I meet one of them. Once, one even asked me to give him one of my blankets.

Like, dude, if I give you my blanket, what do I tuck myself in with? Haven't you seen me?

So, I run, even though no one even approaches me. I push the door with my shoulder, and it stings; my shoe gets tangled with a chain or something on the floor, and I'm close to eating pavement. It's hard to breathe and to focus my eyesight on the keys. Between juggling the bag of half-folded laundry and the rest of my stuff, I almost drop my phone, too.

And now I'm hyperventilating inside the car, as if I'm being chased, and this time they're really going to kill me. Because it's eleven thirty and I just remembered that I panic in the city at night. Somehow, I had convinced myself that the paranoia I'd lived with my entire life wasn't more than a minor occurrence.

I should have stayed home.

Or at least come way earlier.

The neon lights look so appealing, and now that I'm out, I refuse to go home. So, despite the drunks on the street, I decide to roll. With the windows up and the heater on to avoid the chills, I start to turn to whatever corner I like the most, the one with the brightest lights.

"LookAtYou.

LikeTheNightlyButterflies,

AttractedToTheMake-believeFlames."

W's voice reverberates against the windows.

He took a while this time.

He's in the passenger seat, but I do my best to ignore him. I know what he's going to say; he'll force me to go back home and be as far away from people as possible.

He's so possessive.

But it's for my own good.

The asphalt is navy blue, and the lights are multicolored; I don't know where I am, but I love the view. Time feels thick and slow, like moving through jelly. W watches me quietly, unnervingly still, like he's waiting for something. It doesn't sound like a crazy idea, after all, trying to make peace with him, just this once.

"Where should I go from here?" I ask, my voice cracking as if it's been caged too long.

"thatDependsOnWhereYouWantToGo,Bo."

His chuckle hums low and sharp, and his smile glows in the corner of my vision. The sharp teeth come into focus even though I don't look at him directly, more defined than before, like they're pushing through the edges of reality itself.

"I don't really care where—"

"thenItDoesn'tMatterWhichWayYouGo,

DoesIt?"

He cuts me off, taunting me, testing me. I know that tone too well. I slam the brakes at a flickering red light. It blinks, once, twice, so violently it feels like it's winking at me.

My thoughts race, but I go again.

And then the lights start dancing.

More and more neon lights surround the car, buzzing and flooding the street. They try to talk to me and tell me secrets I will never know. The vibrant colors, cool pinks, and electric yellows scream at me to go with them.

And again, I come to a sudden stop. So much so that I notice how W's head bounces back and forth. And even though I have parked the car terribly, no one is around to judge me for it.

"ShoppingForPleasure?"

He asks, but rather than being angry, I sense interest in his voice.

"YouKnowI'mAlwaysHereToHelp."

The first thing that catches my attention is a low hum from the neon sign at the entrance. It whispers, like the other lights on the street, but I don't understand what it's saying. They pulsate like beating hearts in the middle of nowhere.

Well, not exactly nowhere.

It takes me a second to realize where I am.

I'm supposed to be going home, and instead came to a stop at a *sex shop* on what I'm beginning to recognize as The Motel Street. That one exists in every city, like it's almost mandatory to have all the paper-walled slaughterhouses together.

I look around me; the streets are empty, but I feel watched. W is standing beside me, so I know it's not him.

And for a second, I want to run to the comfort of my car again, but

3 Open 24 Hours

I'm already here, and my feet are taking me inside, so I might as well enjoy the view for a little while.

I'm not awful, so I smile at the girl at the counter when I walk in. She's playing something on her phone, and I don't know if the sounds are moans or screams. I might be imagining things again.

Have I been here before?

I don't know why, but the place looks familiar.

I wander among the front clothes, costumes, and more conventional attire. I inspect them as if I have money or some excuse to use them, or maybe I already have. I see the masks and the corsets and slowly make my way to the back.

The stuffed handcuffs are tangled with the leather chains and whips and the low light makes me doubt for a second if they are really moving.

Oh, fuck.

Maybe I'm not crazy after all.

Maybe someone is still following me after the turns I took coming out of the laundromat.

It makes sense, right? That's why I heard the lights humming and felt someone watching me. But why? I don't look like I have money, so a robbery is probably out of the question. Is it just bad luck?

Is it something else?

Have I had a stalker all along, and I just never realized?

Is that why I can't shake this feeling?

Why I can't sleep at night?

Maybe.

Maybe.

THE AIR SMELLS LIKE COTTON CANDY.

The store is a maze that I wander through, feeling the fabric and plastic of everything I see with my fingertips.

Yes, I hear footsteps, but I still can't tell if they're inside my head or if W isn't the only shadow chasing after my heels.

There has to be someone else.

But every time I look around, they hide.

I try to ask W for help, but he just stares at me with vacant eyes; gradually, he starts fading until his smile is the only visible thing of his already incorporeal body.

And then he's completely gone.

GLOWROT

Fucker.

But he's probably doing it to help me; I just need to find out how this is good for me.

"Do you have a popper?" I ask the girl in the front when I have no more store to go around.

She plays with the diamond embedded in her cheekbone, picking up a small bottle from behind the counter. Her puffy lips smile tiredly at me, and I smile back. I want to bite them so bad.

"Are they new?" I ask without knowing why. I feel like I've seen her before.

"Yes!" A gleam of joy that only happens when a stranger notices something you've spent a lot of money on appears in her eyes, "I got them yesterday, they're still a little swollen."

"They look super cute on you," I whisper with the smile still plastered on my face, paying without taking my eyes off her, wanting to know how they would feel between my teeth.

"Here you go, enjoy!" she winks at me, and the tension dissipates as soon as I turn to leave.

Another missed opportunity.

> *Isn't that what this city is all about?*

Because that's how these things are, ephemeral like the twinge of pain you feel when you crack your fingers.

And the bell jingles as I leave, once, twice.

Here it comes again. That feeling. Like someone else has walked out right after me.

And my brain screams danger, but my body doesn't respond.

Fuck, fuck, fuck.

I walk as if nothing is happening, even though I'm clutching the baggie and have the car key between my knuckles as if that will make a difference. My entire body is shaking, and I want to throw up on the pavement.

Aquí fue.

> *Me voy a morir en el estacionamiento de una sex shop por pendeja.*

> *What a pitiful place to die.*

Somehow, I reach the car. Somehow, I lock the doors. Somehow, I'm still breathing.

When I start the engine, I see no one around me because no one was ever around, and I'm paranoid as fuck.

3 Open 24 Hours

Again, the neon lights are passing by me instead of me passing by them.

The fright makes me decide it's time to go back to what I'm supposed to call home, but the GPS is taking too long to load the connection, and the little paper bag on the passenger seat looks very tempting.

"no,NotWhileDriving"

Oh shit.

I should be used to him popping back up the least I expect him to. Still, even if his words feel like a demand, he doesn't force me to comply. So I stop at one of the motels and hold the tiny bottle in front of my face.

I just need to calm down a little so I don't crash the car.

And I'll go home, straight home.

I promise.

Blasting music on my phone just because I can, as soon as a male voice asks me to *choke him like I hate him*, I open the lid and inhale with the bottle under my nose.

Just a few seconds of absolute glory, with the lights taking advantage of getting inside my ears, and the TINGLING OF MY HAND makes me smile.

W digs his claws into my shoulders, extends his arms, and tries pulling me back.

Maybe he didn't think I would do it.

All around me, the walls talk, scream, and moan. I recognize one, two of those places, a glimpse of something I don't know if it ever happened.

How miserable does your life have to be to drive in the middle of this street and know you can't get into any of them because you have no one to do it with?

I move my head in circles, and I don't know how my body is acting logically, and I haven't planted myself flat against some pole. It's the lights, scratching at me with their toxic stingers and nagging me to keep moving.

The street is straight, and I feel it gets narrower by the second. I ignore the car I see in the rearview mirror because I don't have time to do anything but enjoy the tingling I feel in my body. And maybe this will finally be the day when my bullshit overcomes fate's will to make me want to go on living.

I hope so, at least.

I remember passing by here a million times, and I can swear this didn't exist the last time.

GLOWROT

What's this place doing propped upright at the end of it all?

I stop abruptly, and the effect wears off. My surroundings are still vibrating, but my mind is three percent less foggy.

It's not a motel, not entirely. Why do I feel like I've seen it before, though?

The sign at the entrance is neon, and the letters change color every time I blink. They shapeshift and rearrange, and yet it always comes back to the same three:

N I U

A car pulls up next to me, almost running me over. And my heart skips a beat when I react and finally realize who's getting out of it.

3 Open 24 Hours

4
ProceedWithCautioN

It's Them; it has to be Them.

Something within my brain reacts, the muscle memory of recognizing their slim shape. My dream suddenly willed into existence.

The thoughts of going home disappear in a second. The neon lights stop blinding me and look more and more like an invitation. Sweet, like cotton candy.

Sweet, like them.

Every single one of their movements is so delicate, almost to perfection. The subtle glance towards my direction without locking their eyes with mine, the quick flutter of their fingertips.

Everything is fine.

After their sudden pause, they skitter towards the entrance. A perfect invitation. I run toward them before they disappear behind the door.

The entrance hallway is dark and damp, and the ceiling drips over my head. I can see them turning a corner for a second; their tattoos start glowing in the darkness of the walls, constricting us slowly.

But once the hallway gives way to the rest of the place, their silhouette is soon lost among the others. The music, previously stifled by the entrance walls, knocks me down.

And I lose track of where is up and where is down.

I don't know if my head is spinning because of the popper I smelled again or the toxic smell of sweat in the air that seems to have taken up residence in my brain.

It hammers it, but I smile. I close my eyes, and the dizziness increases, my feet moving on their own even though I'm stumbling over a myriad of random bodies that seem even more off-balance than I am.

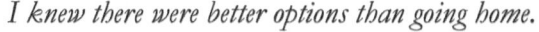

I knew there were better options than going home.
Can I even call that home?

My fingernails itch like something is picking at them from the inside out. After turning right, I turn left and sit on one of the steps most people are hopping on. Still with my eyes closed and yet knowing perfectly how many steps I have to take, when to stop, and when to move forward. My body tells me what I need because my brain is shutting down more and more.

I open my eyes.

I see bodies moving all around me, and my chest rises and falls. I want to join them; I need to.

The sea of cigarette smoke and other substances I can't name surrounds me like a dense fog that separates me from the rest of reality, from whatever is out there. Then I stand up on the same step I'm on and sway from side to side, letting my head fall by inertia.

And I laugh.

I laugh so hard that I get scared.

So much so, that MY GUMS START TINGLING.

This is my first time hearing this song, yet my lips move along with the melody. I bite my tongue as the speed of my breathing increases, more and more, and more and more. I stumble.

It has been a pleasant coincidence to have fallen into this guy's arms.

By complete accident, of course.

My mouth is dry. I take the glass in his hand and drink the contents with a grimace but smile in satisfaction because it tastes like mango with a hint of Tabasco. I don't look away when his gaze seeks my eyes, and I don't stop smiling, even though the liquid is spilling from the corners of my lips.

Why does he have my name written on his arms in neon colors?

For a second, I lose myself in his contact lenses, glowing in the dark, like an animal watching from the shadows. The letters on his arms pulse, their glow syncing with the pounding music, like they're alive.

As I come to, I realize that his hands are running down my body. They're cold and clammy and keep looking for my skin underneath my clothes.

GLOWROT

He keeps looking at me, and I can't look away. His sweat sprinkles my face, his stare telling me I'm the most important person in the world right now.

That I'm someone.

That I'm special.

Two fingers running down my back, one on my chin, three on my neck, and five in my hair. They clutch at me, grab and let go, caress my senses. I let myself be rocked back and forth and start letting them do their bidding, whatever it will be.

How many limbs are those?

"enough!That'sEnough!" W's voice is distant as if I'm listening to it from a broken radio. It crackles like static and starts fading like it's being ripped apart.

The only time I can close my eyes is when I allow myself to moan from the nails digging into my lower back.

And as soon as I open my mouth, I feel it flood with the intoxicating saliva of the anonymous man clinging desperately to my hips. If I keep this up, maybe I'll get lucky, and I can forget I exist and finally stop thinking.

I no longer care how many hands are touching me because, in this instant, I feel that the music has taken a back seat and I am the center of attention. I'm their queen. All eyes on me, too many eyes, devouring me as if I'm prey.

The whispers snake through my ears, each word cold and sticky. They wrap around my thoughts and strangle them.

It sounds like hunger.

And I want more.

More.

"nO", he manages to scream and whisper simultaneously. Far away and right next to me. There, but not there.

I am surrounded. One of them speaks to me in a forbidden language, and though I have never heard of it before, I know he says I am perfect. Wonderful.

And it feels good.

Here, in this corner, with my shirt half torn and teeth grazing my chest as if I were a work of art on display, I take another breath of air. And it's no longer cigarette smoke I inhale but a citrus perfume that detonates an explosion inside my brain.

4 ProceedWithCautioN

And I remember things I shouldn't because I know they never happened.

I shake my head and try to breathe normally again, but the sensations from my lower body distract me more and more. I no longer feel them looking at me, and before I can react, the edge of my skirt brushing against my navel tells me that maybe I don't have much of a clue what is happening after all.

Am I still The Queen?

Am I still perfect?

Am I still wonderful?

"youNeedToLetHimGo."

He commands me.

"letGo.NOW."

But it's not W's voice that takes me out of my trance.

A warm and delicate hand grabs my wrist, rescuing me from the vultures that were taking over my body seconds before.

I turn around to look at them one last time and watch as the one with my name tattooed on his arms runs his tongue full of a red liquid across his teeth.

Cherry juice?

Blood?

I've never been to this place before, yet I know exactly where I'm going.

I follow the pull on my wrist and walk to the front, kicking aside the bodies, trying to separate myself from the grip of the one who rescued me.

I lean forward and cough.

I regret it.

I want to cry.

But I continue walking, their pull too strong on me, magnetic. We stumble into the bathroom and, inside a cubicle smaller than my desire to continue to exist, I can finally see their face.

The spider web tattoo under their right eye and the countless moles that decorate their face slowly pulsate at the rhythm of the muffled music. I show them my teeth in appreciation and feel the first retch when I dare to approach their lips.

They take my hair in their hands, and I feel a deja vú that does not quite fit my situation. Memories of scenes similar to this flood my head as I expel the obscene amount of substances that have entered my body. I wonder how many of them I have been aware of.

I puke out my guts, maybe even what I haven't eaten yet. Until my stomach twists in on itself, and tears are all that's left.

I remain motionless, kneeling and useless.

Stupid.

A few minutes ago, I was the most important person in the universe. And now I'm back to being nothing more than a blur on the floor. Locked in the bathroom, afraid to come out because I have no idea of what has supposedly happened all night or how much time has passed.

At least I'm not by myself.

I feel like I'm living inside a cheap *indie* movie with a very stoned director who has no fucking clue what he's doing.

"noOneHereHasAnyIdeaWhatThey'reDoing,

BecauseThe'here'Doesn'tExist."

W says, almost cutting through the air. His words feel nearly tangible now, so close they can stab.

"that'sWhyNothingMakesSense.

You'reNotHere.

NothingHereIsReal."

But he has to be lying. The deep, black eyes staring at me are real. Their subtle touch while they wipe my lips. Their eyebags match mine.

Maybe if I don't move, I can find a glitch in reality and stay at this point in my existence forever.

Their fingers caressing my neck feels good, even better when they reach my collarbones. I close my eyes and imagine I'm back outside, and everyone looks at me. I smile and grit my teeth, so I don't ruin the moment with a second wave of half-digested liquid.

"Too long, too long," squeaks one of the dried-up women with calluses on her feet guarding the bathroom.

We stand silently, holding each other closer. I close my eyes, pretending the voice is not real, but everything else around me is. Maybe if we stay still, she'll give up. I just need to keep holding them a little longer, to keep feeling their heartbeat next to mine.

"Too long, too long!" she repeats, her voice crackling like broken glass.

I open my eyes and look down at her callused feet, shuffling closer underneath the cubicle door, leaving smudges of something dark and wet on the tile. The door shudders as her knuckles rap against it, too sharp and fast, like the clock ticking that's gone mad.

The door rattles on its hinges, her fists slamming harder and harder, the rhythm almost rhythmic, almost mocking.

"Come out! Come out!" she screams, her voice deeper, slipping through the cracks.

My first instinct is violence, to open the door, rip off my stiletto heel, and stick it between her eyes. But I don't move; I just can't. Coming to my rescue, the wonderful being playing with my senses takes my hand.

Their touch is grounding, but their eyes glow with something broken.

Like me.

They open the door and push it so hard I hear the woman's feet dragging along the floor. The second they turn their back to me, I see the head of a tattooed rabbit peeking from behind their jacket.

"Disgusting bitch," They mutter, flipping her off with such precision I think for a moment their finger might actually pierce her eye.

They pull my hand, and I follow, entranced by their strength.

But they looked so fragile a second ago.

The air conditioner I'd forgotten about slams cold air into my forehead, a sudden jolt back to reality, or whatever passes for reality here. My eyes catch the neon wall, mirrorless and taunting me, its flickering glow like a forgotten memory clawing at my brain.

Too familiar for comfort.

Like everything in this place.

I let myself be led, their grip pulling me past the woman, past the cubicle door. Her screaming fades, but I can still feel it vibrating in my skull. The corridor stretches ahead, lined with bodies and needles that slither like vines, trying to cling to my ankles, to drag me back.

"it'sNotSafe," W murmurs, distant and fractured, his voice spiraling around me like smoke.

A thousand and one endless doors scream in languages I don't know but understand perfectly. My feet move on their own, dodging each broken glass, with the memory of someone who knows them.

"you'reLosingYourself."

The words are not stabbing me anymore; they're slowly losing their grip on me.

GLOWROT

The mirror on the ceiling reflects our silhouettes, and I look up, detailing the tattoos on their scalp as we walk. They reflect the shifting hues of the neon lights that surround us.

They're so perfect.

What was their name again?

The spikes on the wall behind me threaten to tear the skin on my back, and I don't even flinch.

"it'sNotReal," W keeps talking, as if it will do any good. As if he hadn't lost control for more than a moment.

"it'sNot—YouNeedTo—BO.LEAVE.NOW!"

I turn to look at the stranger, my stranger. They feel more familiar than anyone I've ever met in my life. They look back and smile, their cheeks sunken in. Their eyes are darker than the nightmares I can never remember. A trickle of saliva slips past their lips as they stare at me, like a predator hunting, glistens in the darkness.

And then something else, their eyes become less and less clouded, and their expression transforms into something unexpected.

Hunger?

Pain?

Regret?

They step back and let go of my hand, their breathing quickening. I try to reach out to calm them down, but their horrified stare is enough to make me freeze in place.

"timeToWakeUp."

My sweet companion's cry of despair booms against my ears, thunderous and shattering, echoing into the spaces I thought were mine. Their voice lingers like a ghost in my chest, tangled with my own scream.

Until the darkness swallows us whole.

5

Mind the Gap

I think I slept, but the memories don't exactly line up.

The sheets feel like someone else's skin, clammy and unfamiliar. They get tangled with my fake nails, and I end up ripping off a couple without realizing it. I yawn.

A shadow stares at me from the corner of the room.

Of course, he does.

"GetUpBo," W's voice cuts through the morning haze. **"DutyCalls."**

One of the most excruciating things about living here has been, without a doubt, the reprogramming of my brain. I have never, not once, managed to get up late for work. It's that level of sickening anxiety that invades my senses, even more than my own desires to be irresponsible.

I may have a death wish, but that doesn't mean I want to live on the streets.

I'm shivering, and I don't know if it's because I

FEEL OVEROXYGENATED or the lack of rest makes me think I'm still sleeping.

The sun is not yet up, and I prefer not to turn on the lights; the phone screen is enough to make sure I'm not going to stab myself with any piece of broken glass of those still left behind on the ground.

And now the obligatory ritual begins.

Toothbrush, toothpaste, look anywhere but the mirror. Water, almost choking on the toothbrush and closing my eyes, about to fall because I don't know who told me it was a good idea to agree to work the morning shifts.

Maybe I'm the only weirdo who rinses her mouth with hot water, but I'm constantly fucking freezing, and I'm sick to death of having to get up so fucking early.

There are bruises on my arm that I don't remember being there yesterday. Was I having nightmares last night? It wouldn't be the first time I wake up with weird marks all over.

I grab the toothbrush and squeeze some toothpaste on it, my eyes dance between the wall and the sink. Anywhere but the mirr—

Wait a minute.

Didn't I do this already?

Whatever.

Rinsing my mouth with hot water is not that bad. At least I'm not freezing anymore.

I then look at the shower and hesitate, but my nauseating smell forces me to get in, so I almost boil myself in the stream that's nearly too hot for comfort.

The hot water hits my skin, scalding at first, then icy cold, then thick like syrup. I rub my arms, but the soap doesn't lather, no matter how hard I try.

This is one of my favorite parts of the day, at any time: pretending I'm a functioning person, taking a regular shower for the first five minutes, and then standing motionless with the almost boiling drops running down my skin until the temperature regulates and I can no longer feel anything.

My hands feel raw the more I scrub. Sometimes, I feel like my skin is not even mine.

I don't see him right now, his shadow creeping in from whatever direction he believes will give him the best seat.

But I know he's there.

He wouldn't miss the opportunity to watch.

To protect me.

From what? The fucking hot water?

Lately, W always watches me when I shower or bathe. It doesn't bother me; it's part of the same daily routine. He looks at me; he takes care of me. Most of the time, he doesn't really talk to me while I do it since I'm not doing anything wrong.

Because he only tries to communicate with me to criticize me.

It's fucking repulsive.

No, he's not; he's here to help.

What time is it? How long have I been here?

5 Mind the Gap

The time. The time. Check the time!

The scalding water was the only thing that soothes me, but now that's semi-frosty, it's too real for comfort. I hate it. It injects me back to life against my will.

Losing track of the passage of time is also usual, but that doesn't mean I'm happy about it.

I slip as I get out of the shower, and my phone falls into the garbage can, almost empty, thankfully. It's still early, and the screen full of antibacterial gel tells me so.

Makeup, the hair straightener.

The uniform.

Why is it that I don't leave things ready the night before?

Don't look in the mirror. Don't look in the mirror. The thought bounces off the walls of my mind; it gets louder with every bounce. I don't want to turn on the light, but I have to.

Turns out, I remember I hate existing, and I can't help but hyperventilate when I think about how I'll have to face yet another day of despair of smiling all the time because I'm too much of a conformist to find something else to do.

I want to die.

"everyMorningYouDoTheSameThing.
Breathe."

W's soothing tone brings me back to reality, and I realize the hair straightener is in my hand and has been on all along.

And I'm staring right into the mirror.

And for a second, the Bo on the other side blinks.

For how long did I space out?

I have my skirt and shirt on.

Funny, it's like I've jumped minutes into the future or if my body is moving on its own.

I'm sure that's pretty normal, right?

The light's on, I guess that's fine. By this time, I'd better force my eyes to get used to it because I know what's going to be waiting for me outside the front door.

My eyes dart back to the bruises on my arms, but I force them back to the mirror only because I know its necessary to make sure my hair and face were done right. **Perfect**.

GLOWROT

I bare my teeth in that customer service smile that everyone who knows me believes, and I hold back my retching, like every single morning, because my body hates me.

I should brush my teeth before I forget.

The kitchen is only steps away from my room; I see the heels lying on the side of the door and try to make a mental note so I don't go crazy looking for them later.

A banana will be enough for the moment, maybe even a yogurt. I don't even have the energy to open the microwave door, let alone make a sandwich.

I need the money because I don't want to be homeless or without subscriptions to services I don't use but forget to cancel. I'm a millimeter away from having to go to the bank again to ask for the loan I've already been turned down for once, and calling the credit card company to set up a payment plan makes me so anxious that I haven't answered their calls for months.

I run my tongue over the banana as I eat it. It's a little dark and melts on my lips as I push it into my mouth.

How long have I spent doing this?

The time, the time!

The heels! I run to get my purse and throw the sheets on the floor because I'm sure I fell asleep with it hanging from my shoulder.

I then rip the charger off the wall because my phone is begging for mercy and bolt out the apartment door, hoping with all my heart that I didn't leave the keycard inside again.

White.

The unbearable desire to fill the walls with red CLAWS ITSELF OUT FROM UNDER MY NAILS.

The light given off by LED lamps bounces all over the polished surfaces, burning my skin, and the sound of my footsteps almost running to the elevator blocks them.

There is no one outside, not yet. The others have already left or are still sleeping with no idea what happens in the world when their eyes are closed.

A white, cold world. Perfect. Impersonal.

Six o'clock in the morning is too early for tourists and too late for businessmen.

5 Mind the Gap

I live in the loop of discomfort that comes from knowing that more than half of the people I might run into in the elevator are forced to see me every day, in passing, and yet act as if I didn't exist.

I wish I didn't exist.

That would be amazing.

The doors open, and my heart beats harder than it should. But even here, there is no one. The silence presses in. I unnecessarily fix my hair for the twelfth time, as W's silhouette slips between the doors opening before closing, uninvited, unasked for, as always.

"ericAndNinaNowInTheMorning.
AndNovaAtNoon."

He hums, his voice sliding between my thoughts like oil. The words don't feel like reminders; they feel like warnings.

He speaks to me from the imprecise point in space where he's planted. His voice lingers too long in my ears like it's trying to settle under my skin. I know today will be one of those days. His silhouette becomes more solid by the second, more real.

"What did I do last night?" I take the opportunity to ask him while the miracle of him wanting to take on a more corporeal form lasts.

"YouDreamedOfRabbitsAndRot," he says, with a grin I can't see but feel.

"YouFellAsleepListeningToASubliminalMeditation
That'sWhyYourPhoneHasNoBattery."

I don't believe him. His words are too smooth, too convenient. But I'm too tired to argue. Instead, I press my back against the elevator wall, letting my reflection distort in the warped metal.

If he says it, it must be true. Besides everything my brain wants me to believe, there's no reason for him to lie to me.

Other than to protect me from something.

From what?

The watch history on my phone proves W right, and I can't do anything about it. Still, I feel the slight burning in my nose that tells me something doesn't add up in his explanation and dizziness that tries to scream something at me.

It all goes away when the doors open, and I nearly crack my head in two, crashing into Eric's forehead as he runs inside.

He smells so good.

GLOWROT

"HiIlefttheheadphonesupstairsI'llberightbaaaaaack" His words are drowned out as the elevator swallows him, and I walk to the front desk with the nastiest smile I have.

The one everyone loves.

"Good morning!" Nina's eyelashes are almost as long as the urge I have to run away. They flutter as she blinks, forcing her tired eyes to stay open, and the faint shimmer of yesterday's mascara clings to the corners.

I need the money, I need the job, and I can't afford to go to jail or get deported for assaulting a coworker just because I got up on the wrong side of the bed.

It's not her fault, after all. She's always trying her best, smiling and wanting to help, as if she didn't know we can hear her crying whenever she disappears into the lobby bathroom.

I glance at her hands as she organizes the desk. She's still wearing that awful chipped nail polish, the same pale pink she's been wearing for weeks. I think she likes the color because she believes it makes her look soft and delicate, even though her knuckles are always red, like her eyes.

"Did you sleep okay?" Nina asks, her voice gentle, like she knows I didn't.

"Yeah," I lie.

She smiles. It's a tired smile, stretched too thin, like warped plastic. She knows I'm lying, but she doesn't push. She never does.

Instead, she places a cup of coffee on the desk next to me. I didn't ask for it. She didn't ask if I wanted it. It's always the same.

"Thanks," I whisper while taking the cup.

She shrugs, paying too much attention to the papers that definitely don't need organizing.

But she's not my problem, and I hate that I feel that she wants to be it.

I hate that she makes me coffee and knows the type of chocolate that I like. That she's trying so hard, for what? It's not like I'm, I don't know, worth it or anything.

Taking another sip, I walk further away from her, trying not to get distracted by her long blue locks and teary eyes. She doesn't move, so I can go back to my misery.

What did I do last night?

I try to look for some mark on my body to suggest some answers, memories that are more than disjointed colors that have more to do with dreams than real life. There's nothing other than the bruises I decided to cover with a mesh long-sleeved shirt under my uniform. It's not a bad look; it makes me look edgy.

Maybe Eric will like it.

The air conditioning is freezing my senses, and I grab the leather jacket that I know so well, which still smells like him, hanging in the chair.

It's the perfect time to arrange the mail packages in the back room, Nina doesn't mind in the least because now she's playing on her phone, and on a Thursday at six twenty in the morning, no one is going to check in at a hotel like this.

It's time to close my eyes for ten seconds, breathe, and try to think.

Nine

I want to cry, but I know my eyeliner will get ruined, and my eyes will burn because of its lousy quality.

Eight

Only I can think of working in the same place I live, but at least I don't have to worry about driving and getting up even earlier.

Seven

Something in the back of my mind is imploring me to leave, the urge to vomit increases, and I don't want to open my eyes because something tells me I'll meet W's icy stare judging me. I don't think I can take it. Not right now.

Six

The bag of laundry lying on the floor this morning reminds me that at least that part of my night was real, that I did go and wash it. And then?

Five

Popper. Sex shop. Lips injected. The feeling that someone was following me. Motels. Lights, so many neon lights. Buzzing everywhere.

Four

The smell I adore so much now doesn't let me concentrate because there hasn't been a single moment in these last four months in which this jacket is not impregnated with seven liters of men's cologne.

Three

All those neon lights calling me, pulling me. A sign.

The brush of skeletal fingers along my waist makes my whole body tremble like I have ice fizzling under my skin. Something presses against my lips, hard, insistent, and the only fragile thread of memory I had unravels, slipping out of reach.

GLOWROT

I open my eyes, reflexively gasping, only to choke on the chewing gum he just shoved into my mouth.

Eric's cross-shaped earrings swing dangerously close, clinking like tiny warning bells in our dead silence. His breath hits my cheek, too warm, too close.

"Nina's busy talking to the guy with the rental cars. No one's watching," he whispers, his voice slow, deliberate.

The scent of his cologne lingers, sharp and metallic, mixing with the stale taste of the gum now dissolving on my tongue. My jaw tightens, teeth grinding against the rubbery bitterness. But my heart beats fast as if it had forgotten how until now.

I imagine biting his nose clean off. Tearing it away like a dog shaking loose a bone. The thought comes fast, and I clench my fists at my sides. If I start something now, at this hour, in this place, I won't be able to stop.

His fingers linger on my waist for a moment too long before he pulls away.

"Relax," he says with a smirk that never reaches his eyes. "You look like you're about to jump out of your skin."

6
Authorized Personnel Only

The cold is gone, replaced by the cloying scent of his leather jacket. Thick and sticky, like tar. I'm suffocating, drowning, even if it's no longer because of the belt tightening around my waist.

My eyes stay fixed on the door, unmoving, unblinking, even though I know it's locked.

I try not to make noise. I try to shrink, to fold into myself, but the walls press closer, and it's getting harder and harder to think clearly.

One of the things I like most about Eric is his hands.

His fingers trace invisible patterns over my skin, too familiar, too possessive. They leave no marks, but I feel them just the same. They've always been his way in: gentle enough to make me doubt myself, firm enough to make it clear I never had a choice.

I'm lucky I did laundry yesterday; if I'd brought the same underwear I've been wearing for two days, he would have killed me.

His lips brush against mine, and my pants are around my knees. It's an echo of all the times we have done this before. And it's not *that* bad, if it was, I wouldn't cling desperately to it every time we go too long without doing it.

He makes me lose my breath with each movement back and forth, each time he presses his fingertips inside me.

I can't stop shaking, and he knows it —of course, he does— because the fucker laughs as he forces me to bring my face close to his, to be the one to kiss him first.

And when the first moan escapes me, it dies inside his mouth, choked off as he rams his fingers harder, deeper. He holds my back so tightly it probably bruises and his grip feels like a brand burning my skin.

Like he's leaving his mark, carving himself into me.

Like he's making sure I can't escape.

Why would I do that when it feels so good?

I bury my hand in his hair, about to pull it. His free hand slides down my side, slithering like a snake. Before I can pull away, his fingers wrap around my neck in one smooth motion.

One that I know already too well.

His thumb presses under my jaw, cutting off air. My head slams against the wall. He licks my ear with a chuckle.

"Hey," his voice is soft, melodic. "We talked about this, didn't we?" he whispers, ramming me harder.

His knuckles crash against my tailbone.

If I open my mouth, the whole hotel will hear me scream.

But my mouth stays shut.

Because no one would listen anyway.

I smile, but I'm not sure I really mean it, then start breathing faster and faster. I take special care to make it noticeable, my chest rising and falling, my back arching. The whole world doubles and becomes a blur, and in a millisecond, I feel as if something inside me has short-circuited. The tiniest sensation of being electrocuted from head to toe.

My nails dig into his shoulders then, and I watch as he withdraws his hands from me, looking at me satisfied, only to insert the fingers he just tortured me with into my mouth without warning.

After all, I always said I like the taste.

I play with them, wrapping my tongue around them and trying not to look at the dark spot on the wall, the one that twists and stretches like a bleeding wound, judging me with its hellish eyes.

One of Eric's rings digs into my forehead as he forces me to my knees; I haven't finished closing my lips when I have to open them again.

A fair exchange, as always.

I run my tongue over the fabric of his underwear, tracing the outlines I've memorized too well. I look up at him, smiling. He pulls my hair even more, with a desperation that grows as much as his desires harden.

Now, it's my turn to pull his pants down to his knees. The fabric crumples around his legs like a collapsed puppet, and I hold my breath. I don't have time to lick because the thrusts now go all the way down my throat, and I have to unhinge my jaw to avoid scratching him with my teeth.

I feel each vein against my lips, pulsing like a second heartbeat, and I can't tell if it's his or mine.

A river of saliva begins to run down my chin until it reaches my collarbones, and when my lungs beg for prayers, I squeeze him hard with my right hand while licking the salty tip like a treat. I need to breathe, and he doesn't seem to be affected.

Thankfully.

He grunts, even though he knows Nina could be listening to us outside, even though anyone could walk in at any moment. It's the feeling of being about to be discovered that turns him on the most, I can taste it.

It's going to end soon, I know it.

"Almost there," he clears his throat as if he's reading my mind, and I open my mouth again.

"likeATrainedDog," W says inside my head.

Mierda.

I try to brush him off, at least until everything is done. None of the times he has been able to interfere with these moments have ended well.

I hold my breath again and choke down the torrent of Eric's whims without having the time or desire to savor it, getting rid of even the most insignificant droplet.

The water he hands me is cold but doesn't wash anything away. I drink half, open my mouth for a fresh piece of gum, bite his finger just enough to make him wince, and we both laugh.

Routine.

Like nothing had happened.

Then he leaves, and I'm back at the counter, sorting packages, the smile lingering on my lips like a phantom. It lasts maybe ten minutes. Maybe fifteen.

And then it's gone.

"Please don't keep the key with your credit card, it demagnetizes it," I ask for the third time to the woman who has come to complain about being unable to get into her room.

"I keep them separate! These shits are useless. So much modernization, and they can't do anything right." She says as she takes the fucking card out of her wallet along with the rest of the other cards because I look stupid, apparently. "I don't understand what it costs y'all to get real keys instead of this."

"Have a nice day."

I hate my job.

The headache I have is already bordering on unhealthy. Weren't orgasms supposed to help with that?

"youDidn'tEvenFinish"

W murmurs, his voice slides under my skin like an itch I can't scratch.

I drink more water, hoping the cold will shut him up. It doesn't. It never does. He always gets unbearable after my encounters with Eric, like he knows I'm already too fragile to push him out.

But he just looks so cute with his rings and curls falling over his ears that I just can't help but think how good it feels to sit on him from time to time.

It's already going to be eleven o'clock, even though seven hours ago it was ten-thirty.

The numbers on the clock mean nothing; they tick by in random, nonsensical rhythms that I can't keep track of.

My stomach wants to eat itself, and I feel like I deserve the cramps. I lose count of how many people I've seen pass by and how many are arriving or leaving. All the faces are the same, with blurred features and monotone, emotionless voices.

Because to the glorious guests of Cameo, I am nothing more than a robot placed on the first floor for them to complain about when they are bored of yelling at the pool bartender. Even if it's hypocritical because I live under the same roof as them.

Their mouths move, but I can't make out the words.

I don't want to.

The sounds fall flat, like a recording played on a loop.

"Welcome back. Enjoy your stay."

Over and over. Until it's nothing but static.

I blink, and W is closer now, perched on the edge of the counter with his legs crossed, engulfing everything in shadows that only I can see. His smile is slow, sharp, and knowing.

"How much money do I need for you to tell me which celebrities are staying here right now?" This new voice caught me so off guard that W disintegrates for a split second.

There's a guy in front of me, one that's actually trying to make eye contact. His gray eyes look at me with dilated pupils. Still, I'm too busy flicking my eyes between the dollar bills on the counter and the flamingo shirt that perfectly matches his pale pink bucket hat.

"What?" Customer service is history, I don't even know if I'm hallucinating more than usual.

"Famous people, queen. Where are they?" He puts a finger to his temple as if his behavior is entirely normal. "They're the ones who throw the best parties, obviously."

The idea of a party appeals to me for reasons that don't quite make it into my head. A party with neon lights in a bar with no exit signs.

"I think I saw Jasmine Fierce last week at the pool, but no idea if she's still here," I whisper.

He gestures in annoyance, fiddles with the keycard to one of the penthouse rooms in one hand, and points to the bills scattered on the counter. I pick them up and hand them to him with a shudder.

"Influencers are no good, they don't get real drugs." He chews on one of his necklaces and raises an eyebrow, pointing the bills at me, "Don't you want them? It was useless, but you told me something. Either I give them to you, or they end up in a stripper's panties."

I can't help but laugh, and he laughs too. To my right, Eric drops a box loudly; to my left, W approaches me like a predator, ready to attack at any moment.

"I can't accept them, if the cameras see it, they'll kill me." And since I can't help it because I'm a mess, I add: "But you can buy me a drink later."

His smile widens.

His smile widens!

"*Bueno,*" he responds, and I guess he recognizes my accent. "You'll have to look for me. But don't worry, I'm everywhere," he says, licking his lips and rubbing his hands together, "Martin. Nicholas Martin." He adds as if he's in a spy movie. "But you can call me Nick."

"I'm Bo," I smile, and he looks at me confused. "Just Bo. With a B, as in bitch."

Nick laughs and bows goodbye while juggling the suitcases, the keycard, and the bills he's trying to put in his pocket.

A fragrance lingers in the air for a second, but it disappears when he's out of sight. I start doubting if the exchange was even real; it felt too magical, too interesting to have occurred to me. But it had to be because I can sense how uncomfortable Eric is.

Good.

And as much as W reminds me how much he hates the guy's guts, he's acting very similar.

Posessive.

Just in case, I don't dare turn to either of my sides; instead, I search for the look of any other hotel guest, wanting to have them come to me with any cheap excuse to get me out of this mess.

I hate to attend to them, but right now, I'd prefer it a thousand times to have to deal with Eric's hints or W trying to punish me for getting out of line.

But what's wrong with me wanting to meet new people?

Nova appears out of nowhere, and her arrival is so sudden that it feels like reality glitched. For a second, I wonder if she really did teleport. It wouldn't surprise me.

"You've been staring at me for about ten minutes." She grins, wide and teasing, her teeth catching the light like she knows a secret I don't. "Is everything okay, or are you planning my murder?"

I shake my head, ten minutes?

What time is it?

Nova's playing with the black strands of hair framing her face, twisting them around her fingers in quick, restless movements like she can't keep still. That weird tattoo of a single cherry is barely visible under her collarbone, the stem cutting off where a second one usually is. Her nails are chipped and painted an obnoxious neon green. On anyone else, it would look like a mess. On her, it works.

I look around; I see how Nina is gathering her things to leave.

It has always baffled me how she can look so different from her own twin.

"Are you going to eat first, or should I go?" Eric's voice slices through the fog in my brain, snapping me back to the present.

Is it eleven thirty already? My stomach cries, screams. It begs that I should pay attention to it at least once in my life.

It's just now that I'm aware of the terrible urge to vomit I have.

"I'll go."

It's the first time all day that I look Eric in the eye since I had him in my throat. My legs tremble, but I force myself to stand.

"Do you want me to get you something from Fasty Food?" I ask him, almost pleading, and I hate how pathetic I sound.

6 Authorized Personnel Only

"insteadOfHimBeingYourBoy-toy, YouSeemLikeHisBitch."

W, as always, telling the hard truth. Even if it makes me want to cry.

I'm drowning, but no one's looking at me. His words rumble against the walls of my brain, and I know, with absolute certainty, that tonight, he'll remind me how much he hates when I play with fire.

I feel the fury in his tone, HAMMERING AT MY EARDRUMS.

And I know he does it because he cares about me and tries to keep me from getting into more terrible situations that I will have no idea how to get out of later.

Like before.

Many times before.

But what's wrong with offering food to my coworkers?

"A combo, one of those three-for-three, or something like that," Eric's white teeth, definitely fake, gleam with satisfaction.

I turn to look at Nova, but she shakes her head and goes to fix her uniform for the hundredth time.

I go to the back room, knowing that Eric won't be accompanying me this time because once a day is enough for him, and I grab my wallet and phone before I leave.

Just as I'm turning around the counter to go to the main entrance, a hand closes on my wrist.

It's slender and strong. I turn to ask Eric if he wants me to get him anything else, but I'm met with someone I've never seen before.

But I recognize them immediately.

"Do you have a light?" They ask in a soft voice, I immediately forget how to speak.

GLOWROT

7
Danger Keep Out

Their pupils were dilated, so wide they could swallow me whole.

That means they're happy, right?

I spent twenty of the thirty minutes I had to eat my burger thinking about it instead.

Why?

The bite of stale fries sticks to the roof of my mouth. I choke on it and force it down, but the taste never lands. Not even Fasty Food can distract me from thinking I've been here before. That I've seen those eyes before.

Déjà vu.

There's nothing special about Them, and yet, they're everything.

I feel stupid that I don't have a <u>white</u> lighter and didn't react in time.

They just walked away without uttering a single word.

"You'veGotTheBloodRushingToYourHead," W hums, his voice crackling like static.

It's easy to ignore W when I don't understand what he's saying

I like their moles; they're pretty and look like they were made with a Sharpie.

Like tiny constellations scattered across their skin.

My right eye squints, and I shudder with a shiver I don't recognize.

I hate how they walked away, silent. How they left me hanging, desperate for a word, a glance, anything.

The time!

GLOWROT

MY WATCH TUGS AT MY FEET. The timer on the phone screams at me that I have three minutes left, which is barely enough time to cross the street.

I grab the food I promised Eric, the phone, the headphones, and both sodas and finish grabbing what's left of the burger between my teeth.

Then I get out and cross the street without looking anywhere, and the certainty that this time I almost died makes me wonder if the man who was driving had a lighter.

"Burgers!" Eric shouts the second I go through the door, even though he has a guest at the moment.

A lady who doesn't even flinch, her dark circles are darker than my regrets, and she looks like she's running on automatic.

I smile and feel a warmth that I hate in my body, which can only be brought on by his proximity and the terrible thoughts that flood me every time he bites his lip like that.

Despite trying to shake them off as I circle the reception desk, my skin crawls every second I get closer to him.

We already did something this morning; no one has that much luck in a single day.

"Do you have a <u>white</u> lighter?" I ask Nova, watching as Eric tears into his food like a wild animal, not even bothering to clock out. Nova rolls her eyes, shooting him a disgusted look.

"Wtf, no," she says, flipping her ponytail over her shoulder. "If I could smoke joints at work, I would. But…" She pauses, narrowing her eyes at me like she's caught me in a lie. "Wait a minute, do *you* have any?" Her face lights up at the possibility, like a kid being offered candy.

"No, no. I was thinking maybe it's a good idea to have lighters, in case any guests need them. Just like about an hour ago." I grit my teeth in an attempt at a smile that goes horribly wrong.

Nova tilts her head, giving me a look that says she's not buying a word of it.

"Like when?" Eric asks with a french fry hanging from his mouth, smirking like he knows something I don't. He shrugs into his jacket, the one that reeks of his cologne, the one I wish I had wrapped around me right now. His eyes gleam with amusement. "And why the hell does it have to be white?"

"Oh, shut the fuck up, little brat," Nova lets out a laugh that sounds more like a bark and shakes out her perfect black ponytail that reaches her waist, 'This is an adult conversation."

7 Danger Keep Out

"Suck it, dicksucker," he grumbles, but when the other one turns around to ignore his words, he walks over to me and pinches my butt cheek before leaving on his break.

I freeze. My entire body tenses, but he's already gone, whistling some stupid tune as if nothing happened.

Mondays are not days when a lot of people usually arrive, and I start scribbling on a piece of paper leaning against the counter while Nova is in the bathroom. It seems as if time has stopped, I can hear my heart beating like a clock that is getting progressively worse.

"youNeedABandAid."

W's words, though meaningless, make me react.

I see the reddish smear I have left on the paper and the one covering my finger. I bring the sharpened tip of the pencil to my tongue and lick it, recognizing the taste of my own blood.

When did I go from drawing on paper to sticking the pencil into my skin until I bleed?

The dots I've left, full of graphite, look like moles.

Pretty moles.

Beautiful moles.

Neon moles lost in a spider web, and other drawings I can't remember. Dancing to music I don't know, lyrics I can't say out loud.

It doesn't matter that the anti-bacterial gel burns so much that it brings tears to my eyes, in fact, I decide to pour it on a second time just to be sure. And I smile, the pain feels good. It brings me back to my senses.

The family before me smiles, not even noticing that I'm hiding my right hand. The drawing on the sheet smiles, my memory smiles.

And then Nova smiles.

She's just returning from the bathroom, drying her hands on the hem of her jacket. She looks at my finger and the bloody paper but says nothing about it.

"You alive over there?" she asks, tilting her head exaggeratedly, making her ponytail swing like a pendulum.

"Surviving," I mutter, shaking my hand to dry it.

"Nina texted me while I was in the bathroom." Nova isn't even looking at me when she says it. Her voice is light and breezy like she's commenting on the weather. "She said you were acting weird this morning."

My head snaps toward her, but she's already opening a drawer, pulling out her phone as casually as if it belongs there.

GLOWROT

"Wait, if you didn't have your—"

"Twin telepathy, duh," she cuts me off with a grin, tucking her phone back into her pocket. Her teeth flash white, just a little too wide, a little too sharp.

She taps her nails against the counter in a slow, steady rhythm. Tick-tick-tick. Like a clock winding down.

"Don't worry, I told her you're always weird," she adds, her grin widening.

I want to ask what else she told Nina, but the question dissolves when the afternoon mailman bursts in through the back door, shouting loud enough to make the security guard on duty glance our way. Thank goodness this guard is at least a random dude and not my ex. Again.

I can't see her today.

I should stop having all my social life revolve around this hotel.

His enthusiasm delights me only because it means I can go now.

What was his name again?

When did Eric come back, if he just left?

At what point did three o'clock in the afternoon hit?

My body reacts for me, doing the basic things it usually does for survival.

Sometimes, I prefer to walk away from it all, to be a spectator to what's happening to me, to take the weight of responsibility for my actions off my shoulders for a second.

None of the three of them notice that I am not quite myself as I gather my things or say goodbye, no one asks about the blood-stained napkins in the clear garbage can.

No one cares.

W watches me intently, perhaps trying to guess what I'm thinking even though my brain is empty. I hear my heels click against the floor; they echo.

Or are they other footsteps?

I walk through the reception area door, and the white lights threaten to blind me. A van is about to run me over as I cross the valet parking lot, but I can't help but hear the echo. The funniest thing is that even if I stop, it keeps ringing. Faster and faster.

I feel a terrible urge to LOOK AROUND ME, but I stop it and start walking again.

7 Danger Keep Out

I don't turn to return the valet's greeting, but I wave to him to ensure I have him on my side in case I need another favor. And I keep walking, one foot after another, my mind blank and something in the back of my brain trying to tell me riddles.

I can't hear the sound the few thoughts I have left are trying to make, the footsteps behind me are too loud.

I don't want to run. I don't want to start running.

Running will mean giving in to the paranoia.

Again.

Just now when I feel I need help and I'm about to start gasping for breath, I look for W with my eyes and find that there is no sign of his presence.

Very convenient

I reach for the key as I move and slide it in front of the glass door to enter the elevators, hating every second I have to stand still and listen as they get closer and closer.

And closer.

Closer.

It's even worse when I slide through it and reach out for the button, barely able to graze it when I feel two firm hands closing around my waist and pulling me to the side.

The only thing that comes to my mind now is the conversation I overheard one of these days between the security guards, saying that they still hadn't repaired the security camera in the west wing elevator lobby.

I think about this as the scream I want to fire never leaves my throat, my chest tight and burning, every breath strangled before it can escape.

By the time I realize what's happening, I'm already being dragged to the emergency stairs, my feet stumbling over themselves. I'm too dazed to struggle.

Too numb to care.

Wasn't this exactly what I wanted?

I feel imminent death, or maybe my scalp being ripped off by some psycho tourist who wanted to take advantage of being in one of the most fucked up cities in the country.

But it's not a stranger.

The teeth sinking into my neck feel familiar, and I should be pleased. The bites stun me more than what the edge of a diamond razor would have done sliding across the crown of my head.

"I wanted to thank you for the burger," he murmurs against my skin.

My legs give out, and if it weren't for his grip, I would have collapsed on the spot.

Eric's voice sounds hoarse and tired, and his hands search the skin under my uniform shirt more awkwardly than usual. I feel like a rag doll and am unsure how to react.

Didn't we do something like this today?

The deja vu hits hard enough to make me dizzy. I can't focus on the tip of his tongue sliding along my jaw, can't process the way my body reacts on autopilot. I just tilt my head, panting against his neck, pressing my teeth to his skin like I need to leave a mark.

I see bursts of color as I close my eyes, and for a second, it's not his lips I'm kissing.

It's a wonderful memory of a place far away from here, in my dream. *A place that I've never been in.*

Because it doesn't exist.

I drop my wallet. I drop my dignity. I drop my thoughts entirely.

I'm about to drop my belt again when Eric jerks away, his curls tickling my cheekbones as he pulls back.

But he's not looking at me.

He's looking at his phone.

"Shit," he mutters, swiping at the screen with a swipe too casual for what just happened. "Sorry, doll. She's already asking where I am."

I blink. I don't know how I force my face into a smile, but I do. It stretches across my lips, tight and painful, like my skin is cracking.

"Are we going together in the elevator?" I ask, hating how hopeful I sound.

Eric doesn't even look up.

He shrugs, saliva still beaming at the corner of his mouth, his curls falling into his eyes. His sideways grin makes my stomach twist painfully, my mouth watering in a way that disgusts me.

Why is he provoking me if he knows he won't finish what he started?

"I'm leaving from upstairs," he says, slipping earbuds into his ears and adjusting his jacket. "You know how people are." He gives me one last wink, already turning away. "Figure you'll wait five minutes before heading out? Just in case."

I stay frozen against the wall, watching him climb the stairs two at a time. His footsteps echo until I hear the heavy thunk of the top door closing behind him.

And then the silence presses in.

The gray walls full of vertical lines around me generate the illusion that they are closing in on me. I feel less and less room to breathe.

I gasp, choking on stale air, my heartbeat pounding in my ears like a ticking clock winding down.

Five minutes.

I'll wait five minutes.

I cough, and tiny reddish drops fall to the floor like ink splashes. Suddenly, I feel cold and want to cry. I want to go to my room and disappear under the hot bath water, but it hasn't been five minutes yet.

Why does it matter? It's been long enough.

I push the door open, stepping into the hall just in time to see the elevator across from me closing.

There's only one person inside.

Despite the "No Smoking" sign glowing red above the buttons, they're smoking. Smoke curls lazily around their fingers, wrapping around them like a second skin.

They look straight ahead, gaze fixed on some invisible point in the distance. But for a fraction of a second, just long enough to knock the air out of my lungs, I feel their eyes on me.

Black, dilated pupils, wide enough to drown in.

Their face is a constellation of tiny moles scattered across their skin like stars, with a spider web tattoo spiraling from under their right eye.

Are they smiling at me?

The elevator dings. The doors slide shut.

And I'm left standing there, the bitter tang of smoke clinging to my senses as if they left it behind just for me.

GLOWROT

8

Push to Open

I don't know if I'm dizzy because I'm hyperventilating or hyperventilating because I'm dizzy.

I don't know if I feel this way because I didn't sleep well last night or because the work day sucked, and I hate the shifts where I get off at six.

I don't know if the images invading my head mean something or if they're playing a game to see which can drive me crazy first.

I also don't know if it hurts more that Eric didn't text me back this morning after our great time yesterday or that I stooped so low as to send it to him in the first place.

I'm not hungry and don't want to return to the apartment. I also refuse to linger at the front desk. I'm in no condition to fake conversations.

I sigh and press the button that leads up to the rooftop pool just because I have nowhere else to go.

"stopDeceivingYourself," says W, who conveniently doesn't want to leave me alone just now, especially when he disappeared for a good part of the afternoon yesterday.

But I guess that's how nightmares work, like a relentless plague that always comes back when you least expect it.

"I'm not deceiving anyone; I want to get some air," I whisper out loud as the elevator goes up, just because I know there are no people around me, and this metal box is not bugged.

"you'reTired,GoGetSomeSleep."

His suggestion sounds like a command or like one of those hypnotism acts from years ago.

I know what he means, but I try not to think about it too much.

GLOWROT

It's better this way.

He can't be always right.

Right?

It's not so much that I'm tired but knowing that I'm looking for something and don't want to accept it.

That THE SKIN ON MY RIBS IS PRICKLING for reasons I can't put a name to and won't let me breathe.

Looking for a dream I had last night that I can't remember no matter how hard I try. For the taste of something I know never happened but can still feel it perfectly curled in my teeth.

I walk out to the hallway that leads down to the pool, and for the first time I've lived here, I notice how many doors there are in it.

Have there always been so many?

One of the lights flickers, and it beeps.

"you'reChasingGhosts."

W's voice crawls under my skin, but I push it aside, my steps echoing louder than they should in the empty corridor.

I've never seen anyone enter or leave these rooms all the time I've lived here. Maybe it could be because I don't hang around here as much as the rest. The cold creeps in, sliding down my spine like a shiver I can't shake.

They're not deserted; you can always hear sounds inside most of them, even in the dead of night.

How do I know that?

But even that can't keep my mind off the most important thing.

There are cobwebs in the corners.

Like the one in my dreams.

The one under their eye.

Cameo is not the most luxurious hotel in Zampano, but its reputation makes it one of the most visited. Being able to rent every month also helps.

So, it's common to see housekeeping staff prowling the halls with vacant eyes and partially open jaws to ensure everything is spotless.

So why am I suddenly starting to notice cobwebs all around me?

The pool is nothing out of the ordinary despite being on one of the hotel's low roofs. It's actually pretty dull. I stand by the door after walking through it, almost like the floor is made of burning coals.

8 Push to Open

I scan the area with my eyes, and my ribs constrict when I don't find what I'm looking for.

Who I'm looking for.

There's something I'm missing.

I walk over to the empty tables and look for which ashtrays have been used, trying to find any lighters lying on the floor. It's a magnetic pull somewhere in my brain that I can't understand and don't question either.

Why did it have to be white?

Maybe I've seen it before.

"YouThinkYouKnowWhatYouWant?"

W's voice creeps through the air like smoke, curling around my thoughts.

"YouDon't."

I clench my jaw, ignoring him.

"there'sNothingHereForYou.

YouHatePeople.

Remember?"

He sounds amused; like this is a game, only he knows the rules to. His voice bounces around, but no one notices but me, coming from nowhere and everywhere at once.

But he's wrong.

I feel the pull.

Somewhere around here.

"FunnyThingAboutPulls:

TheyAlwaysDragYouDown."

His laugh flickers in my ears like static.

I shake my head and turn to the bar to quiet him down. The bartender looks cornered, forced into a smile while a group of guests press too close, their voices cutting through the air like knives.

My eyes jump from one ashtray to the other, go over the small crowd, and try to find a single bald head sticking out of the rest.

I don't try to understand why my brain is so sure I had to come. I never know why I do anything anyway.

So, I walk across the pool area from one end to the other, absolutely nothing. My hands start shaking in frustration, and I'm about to turn around to leave when a jerk of my wrist almost causes me to fall into the pool.

GLOWROT

"Another IPA," a voice drawls.

I look at the asshole on duty, shielded by ridiculous mirrored sunglasses.

I stare in shock and restrain my urge to bark at or kick him. I pull my wrist back, but he doesn't let go. His grip isn't hard enough to hurt, just enough to remind me he can.

"Hello? Are you deaf?" he says, waving an empty can like a demand, not a request.

I grimace at him, and he slides his glasses down the bridge of his nose. It takes me a few seconds to realize that he's not looking at my boobs but at what's written above them.

Because I'm the stupidest person on the planet and didn't bother to remove my uniform before coming out here.

His lips curl into a smirk. That smirk. The one I've seen too many times. The one that says, 'I own you.'

I bite my tongue until I taste metal, fists clenching at my sides. I can feel the blood rushing to my cheeks, burning with anger and shame. I force a smile. The one they teach you to give when you've got no other choice.

"No, no," I say, trying to keep my composure. "The pool has no waiter service."

I try to walk away, but he raises an eyebrow. Behind him, the people at his table chuckle.

"But you still work here, don't you?" He leans forward, voice dripping with mockery. "What does it cost you to bring it to me? It's not like you're busy."

He reaches for my wrist again.

This time, I slap his hand away. Hard. And turn around to leave.

The sound cracks through the air, silencing the laughter for a second.

His face twists, not with shock or pain, but with amusement.

"She plays the bitch just because she's pretty," he mutters, loud enough for everyone to hear.

And I can't help it. I smile.

Because, of course, that's what sticks with me. Not the insult. Not the entitlement.

The compliment.

I walk to the pool exit. My heart is pounding, and my knees are shaking, but I lift my chin, sway my hips, and play the role they expect. I know the act will hold until I'm swallowed by the icy hallway again.

8 Push to Open

The thoughts of self-sufficiency and, more so, the sound of disgust that W has just uttered are overshadowed by the sight of the back of a shaved head crossing the threshold that separates the pool area from the hallway with the doors.

My heart skips a beat, and although I want to run, I force myself to walk fast because I can't afford to make a fool of myself in front of the stranger who has just admitted that he thinks I'm pretty.

But I walk fast and try not to lose sight for a second of the rabbit tattoo on the back of their neck, almost glowing in the fading sunlight.

They round the corner.

I pick up my pace. My shoes click louder against the floor, each step hammering into my skull. By the time I reach the hallway, the figure is gone.

The door to the emergency stairs swings shut.

"Hello?" I call out, my voice bouncing off the walls, swallowed by the silence. "Hello!"

There's something familiar about them, almost like I met them in a dream.

But I already know that.

Of course.

My phone vibrates in my pocket, but I ignore it; my fingers tremble as I push open the stairwell door.

The clacking of the heels hammers my eardrums, and the material of the shoes digs into the wounds I already have around my ankles.

The walls have moles adorning them, and I feel them looking at me and judging me.

They don't understand, no one else does.

After three floors with no sign of the figure, the sound of my footsteps becomes unbearable. The clacking, the echoes, the shadows stretching along the walls. It all presses in on me, suffocating.

And then—

I slip.

My ankle twists, and I crash face-first onto the landing. For a second, I see stars, bursts of color dancing behind my eyes, blinding me.

I'm breathing so fast I'M SEEING DOUBLE.

I push myself up slowly, dazed, and that's when I see it.

The thing that almost sent me tumbling down the stairs.

A lighter.

GLOWROT

<u>White.</u>

It's just sitting there, innocent and out of place like it's been waiting for me.

It's a lighter.

A <u>white</u> lighter..

"don'tPickItUp,

ThoseAreBadLuck."

W whispers, his voice curling around me like smoke.

But I can't look away despite his obvious command.

The lighter gleams faintly in the dim light. I reach out with trembling fingers, start playing with it in my hands, and try to light it to no avail.

It's heavier than it should be. Cold. But when I shake it, I hear the soft slosh of fuel inside.

I shake it harder, my fingers aching.

"stopPlayingWithFire."

W is not screaming despite his discomfort. It's almost like he can't right now.

"it'sGoingToBurnYou."

But I keep inspecting it, almost in a trance. There's something written on it, only visible at a certain angle. The light makes it look iridescent.

"Flick me," it says, teasing me to try harder.

Just as I'm about to give up, the door on the floor below slams shut.

My head snaps up, I think I forgot how to breathe again. I feel W's claws digging into my back, sliding under my shirt, scraping down my spine.

"Please don't," I whisper. "Not right now."

But his grip tightens.

I crawl to the stairs and clutch the lighter with one hand like it's the holy grail. Every muscle in my body is screaming, my knees are raw, and my pulse is pounding in my ears.

When I reach the door, I push it open slowly, holding my breath.

The hallway is empty.

No one is there.

No shadow crouched in the corner. No figure waiting by the elevators.

For a moment, it feels like the hotel is breathing.

I look up.

Floor six.

8 Push to Open

My floor.

This time I let myself be dragged by W to the door of my room, dazed and disillusioned.

I smile at the woman who is always cleaning the same place over and over again, but she doesn't look up; she never does.

I stop at the door across from mine. It's open. It has been empty for months, but now the door seems like it's waiting for someone.

I turn away, pushing into my room. The door clicks shut behind me.

I don't open my mouth until I've laid on the bed and closed my eyes without even taking off my shoes.

"I'm going to sleep," I say out loud, the words muffled against the sheets. A lie.

W doesn't answer.

His claws press into my back, heavier now, pinning me down. I try to breathe through the pressure, but it feels like he's crushing my ribs.

I try to clear my mind and think clearly, but the images that come to my brain are a cascade of disjointed things that I can barely write down. I want to lose myself in my thoughts, but the weight is too overbearing.

The words attached to what I suppose are memories are lost in my mind. I can barely conjure up a melody that has been invading my head since last Sunday.

As hard as I try to concentrate, all my attempts are sabotaged.

I squeeze the lighter now in my pocket, and my nails dig into the cracked surface.

W has lost the will to talk to me and decided that crushing me is a more effective way to communicate with me today. I try to breathe as I think of neon lights trying to tell me something and force myself to be very still, not moving a muscle.

"YouAlreadyKnowHowThisEnds.

AreYouSureYouWantToKeepGoing?"

GLOWROT

9

Use Other Door

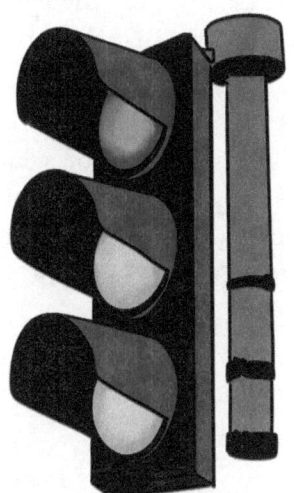

Waking up with scratches all over me is not the worst part of the situation Neither is not being able to move in the first few minutes I am conscious or in the last few minutes before falling asleep.

It's my brain, the thoughts screaming unintelligible things at me, the inability to remember what I dreamed, and being at the mercy of whatever psychological virus is lurking in the astral space near me, waiting to attack.

W usually takes it upon himself to defend me, to keep me safe from any outside influence that threatens to weaken my senses or burn them out completely.

He does this, of course, when he doesn't hate me.

Like now.

I knew it would be better to have listened and not picked up the lighter. But it was calling to me. It's important, I can feel it. Nothing feels important anymore, so I have to cling to this as much as possible.

I'd have thought that, by this point in my life, nightmares would have become second nature. After all, they are the norm.

My tongue itches, and I can't scratch it with my teeth because I'm choking.

I'm still on my stomach, pinned down by something that isn't there. W.

I don't feel his weight pressing on me, but I know he'll try to stop me if I get up without following his rules.

"StayDown,Bo." His voice slithers around my mind, creeping into the cracks, filling the spaces where I should feel control.

So, what did I do now?

GLOWROT

I feel pinpricks under my fingernails, and it triggers a flood of memories of the dream I had five minutes ago or an hour ago.

What's the difference anyway?

It runs through the crown of my head and spills over onto the wall next to the bathroom. Scratching off the paint in a way only I can see.

A place where the lights don't behave.

Faceless, shapeless bodies bouncing against each other, taking me with them.

Déjà vu.

The salty taste of what my mind swears is sweat revives in my taste buds. My fingers drift down my thighs, brushing against the sticky remnants of something I don't want to name.

"SeeWhatISeeYet?"

His voice is everywhere.

Above me, inside me, under my skin.

I shudder. I want him to shut up.

I feel TICKLES ON THE INSIDE OF MY THROAT, and now I have a different reason why I can't breathe.

Eyes glowing in the dark.

Fluorescent liquid dripping over our limbs.

Heat emanating from the ground, threatening to scorch my feet if I don't move them.

"YouCanKeepChasingGhosts.

ButI'llAlwaysBeTheOneWhoNeverLeaves."

I know that's a lie.

But I smile anyway.

Because it's easier to forget all the times he left me. When he vanished without a word because I ignored him. Or because I dared to question him.

Sometimes, he doesn't even need a reason. He just goes.

Maybe he'll leave me again.

The thought tightens my chest, like a hand pressing down on my ribs, squeezing.

I don't want him to leave.

I can't handle it if he does.

I don't want to argue, not now.

So, I try to fall back asleep and sink into slumber again.

9 Use Other Door

I'm transported to the blur of dreams one more time. There are signs on the ceiling trying to tell me something, but I can't make out the words. They flicker, silently screaming at me not to forget them. I can't find the entrance or the exit, but a hand grabs me, and I let myself be pulled out of the crowd.

"I was late again," I hear a voice whisper for a split second before everything vanishes.

I jump to my feet, ripped from my memory by W's monstrous strength, nearly tearing the fabric of my shirt.

Sitting up, dazed, I stare at the wall, pretending everything is okay.

I must've been out for hours.

But the sunlight hasn't shifted.

The room feels stuck in the moment I left it in, like time hasn't moved.

It's been probably ten minutes? Twenty? No more than that.

But my body feels like it's been days.

The dizziness and the urge to vomit remind me I haven't eaten anything but a banana and ten chicken nuggets all day.

"whyAreYouLookingForNightmares?"

Despite his words, his tone sounds kind and comforting. Maybe he just doesn't understand, maybe I can reason with him.

"They're not nightmares. I'm sure I've been there before," I try to raise my voice, but it comes out in a whisper.

"you'reLosingIt,YouShouldTakeABath."

He strokes my neck as though his claws wouldn't be able to pierce through my ribs in a matter of seconds if he wanted to.

I unintentionally smile and stand up; he guides me step by step to the bathroom without turning on the light. The hot water is running already, I stretch my hand, it burns.

It's good.

Everything is fine.

"You have better memory than I do," I keep whispering, unable to speak correctly, almost pleading for his help, "What is that place? Who is that person?"

My words bounce back at me like whips. Instead of answering me, he pushes me into the hot water. I shiver like I'm freezing. Can't move my lips, can't think straight. I feel W sneak up behind me and take my hands, moving them like I'm a doll.

Again.

It makes me want to throw up, but I smile and close my eyes.

Nothing is happening.

And then I remember.

Their face, but not just their face; the way it defies definition, soft angles meeting sharp lines, as if they're constantly shifting, always becoming.

Their silhouette dances between the lines of masculinity and femininity, becomes something entirely different. An angel maybe, a deity.

Their neat eyebrows are a perfect contrast to the tattoos that mark them, claiming their skin like constellations.

They shine under the lights, blinding me with a brightness I crave but can't touch.

That smile.

Their pupils dilated the same way as when I saw them at the reception.

The moles, of course, trying to draw the map to that place in my mind. The taste of smokey lavender and the feel of their skin that feels close without quite knowing why. Like I already know them, even though I've never known anyone like them.

I fall backward and gasp.

"I'm going out," I say aloud, even though I know I don't owe him any explanations.

"youNeedToKeepBathing," his voice tries to be calm, but it's starting to distort.

"I think I know where they are."

A second later, I'm out of the bathtub, like a hurricane taking over my bedroom with the lights still off. So fast even W has to take a second to figure out what's going on.

He's trying to pull me back to the back while I'm frying my hair with the blow dryer and flat iron. I plug the phone into the charger, and all the wires get tangled in the sink.

One drop, and I'm history.

"There'sNothingAnywhere," He insists, trying to grab my hands now and burning me with the iron in the process. **"AndYouKnowIt."**

"No, for real. I think I remember this time!" I'm smiling and don't know if it's from terror or anticipation anymore.

"STOPTHIS

YOUARENOT

GOINGANYWHERE!"

9 Use Other Door

His scream is so loud that I have to let go of everything in my hands. I shriek and start crying, staying on the floor while hugging my knees for five minutes that seem like an eternity.

Until he disappears.

And I stand up like nothing happened.

A while later I stuff myself with food out of obligation, standing in front of the kitchen sink. Can't remember the last time I cooked myself something, or why there are so many leftovers in my fridge. I guess I'm lucky.

I leave almost running, without looking at the time, ripping my cell phone from the outlet, and feeling what I hope wasn't a rush of electricity.

In seconds, I'm in the elevator, almost expecting Eric to be on the other side and ask me to go to my apartment so I have an excuse to send this stupid crusade to hell. But no.

I'm unsure where I'm going.

Even though I told W I was sure.

I had to leave. That was the first step.

The same pull I felt before, the one that led me to the lighter, is dragging me forward again.

It feels alive, like a voice trying to speak through static.

Again.

Almost like someone is trying to communicate but can't.

Them.

The elevator doors open, but before I step out, I see it.

A cigarette butt, crushed in the corner, coated in lipstick.

I freeze.

My heartbeat hammers in my ears, drowning out everything else.

They were here.

I almost throw myself to the floor.

It's a sign. It has to be.

They're real. They were here. They're leaving clues. They want me to find them. And I don't know why, and I can't possibly understand it. But I don't give a fuck. I've never felt so alive in my entire life. They're real, I didn't imagine them. They're not a dream and definitely not a nightmare. I have to find them.

I have to.

I have to.

I have to.

GLOWROT

I have to.

I grab it with trembling fingers, almost dropping it before stuffing it into my pocket next to the lighter.

I'm not thinking anymore. I'm running.

The parking lot feels too quiet, too still. My shoes slap against the pavement, and my breath comes out in shallow gasps.

I get in the car.

And I drive.

There's nothing I want more right now than to be able to focus or at least think clearly.

Wasn't that Eric's mom's car? Wasn't she working today? Why am I thinking so much about Eric?

I need to focus.

Lights, there were lights on the street. And something else. W was there, he has to know. Maybe that's why he's not here. He doesn't want to help me.

Maybe he can't, maybe that's the whole point. Me, doing all of this by myself. Some sort of test. A lesson.

What else?

A long street.

Lips. Fat, thick, juicy. I inhale more than I should, not knowing why, almost like it's an involuntary reaction. My phone vibrates in my hand, but I focus on the GPS. Trying to find the log of the places I went on Sunday, and the fucking screen won't finish loading.

"*Apúrate, coño!*" I scream at my phone, as if it would only understand me in Spanish.

And then.

Lights. Sounds. Inhaling. Lips.

Motels.

Of course, sex.

That's why I was thinking about Eric.

I step on the gas and ignore the red light only because I have it burned into my subconscious that this specific traffic light doesn't have cameras.

But something is missing. Something to make me remember. Something to stimulate my brain.

The last time I had an energy drink, I got such tachycardia that I felt like my heart would skip a beat. It has to be something else.

STOP sign.

I slam on the brakes, and the glove compartment opens as if it has a life of its own. The small glass bottle clinks against the other things hidden in there. As soon as I reach out to grab it, W's claws reappear, and he tears bits of skin off my fingers, trying to stop me.

He is furious.

What's wrong with wanting to go back to that place?

I ignore the red threads decorating my skin, open the vial, and place it under one of my nostrils.

A thousandth of a second after inhaling, I feel the pain flee, my body relaxes, and my mouth begins to salivate. I turn on the radio in automatic mode and start moving from side to side, even with the car stopped in the middle of a housing development I have never seen before.

It's getting dark.

"turnAround."

I press down on the accelerator. He can't control me, not right now. I can't stop looking back; for reasons I can't explain, I feel like someone is following me.

Allowing muscle memory to guide me, the car pulls up to the same sex-shop where I remember buying the popper. This time, I stay in the parking lot, with a sense of panic invading me that forces me not to open the door.

"nearHereThere'sAFoodPlaceYouSaidYou'dLikeToTry."

"No!" I scream at the top of my lungs and feel a tear in my throat. The glowing eyes through the rearview mirror are fixated on it. "You're not going to buy me off with food!" I wouldn't mind if someone came out of the store at this moment and saw me screaming.

Maybe they'd stop me. Maybe someone would finally see.

But there's no one.

Just me and him.

"Why won't you help me?! I know you know what I'm talking about!"

"you'reSleepDeprivedAndHallucinatingAgain," W says, his voice crackling in my ears.

I shake my head, refusing to listen. I can't listen.

"You were there!"

My hand tightens around the bottle, the little plastic lid cold and sticky against my fingers. Without thinking, I inhale again.

The burn hits harder this time, sharp and overwhelming. It crawls up my nostrils into my brain, like a thousand needles piercing through my skull.

It doesn't feel good.

Why?

It's supposed to feel good.

It's supposed to calm me down.

"You're supposed to help me!"

There's a pause. A beat.

Then W speaks again, his voice low and sharp.

"thisIsNoTimeForYou

ToBeHarmingYourselfLikeThat,

Bo."

And that's when it happens.

The air around me warps. The lights outside the car blur, twisting into neon shapes that stretch and ripple like oil on water.

The world tilts.

The bottle slips from my fingers.

I try to move, but my body won't respond.

My arms go numb first. Then my legs. Pins and needles crawling under my skin.

I blink, but the reflection in the rearview mirror doesn't blink back.

The eyes in the mirror glow brighter, and now there are too many of them.

Four. Six. Eight.

They blink in and out of sync, watching me from every angle.

I want to scream again, but I can't move my lips.

And then a hand wraps around my throat.

Not W's.

Something else.

Something cold. Sticky.

It presses against my skin, squeezing just enough to keep me conscious.

I gasp for air, the pressure loosening for a second, then tightening again.

Like it's playing with me.

The bottle lies on the floor. I can't reach it.

9 Use Other Door

The hand pulls away.

The lights outside the car stop warping, returning to normal. My body jolts forward, suddenly mine again.

I grab the steering wheel, shaking. The tingling in my arms lingers, like a cruel reminder.

"toldYouSo," W says, his voice quieter now. More serious. For once, he doesn't sound mocking. He sounds… angry.

"goHome,Bo.

BeforeYouDoSomethingStupidAgain."

But I can't.

The cigarette, the lighter, the pull.

It has to be here, somewhere.

So, I pretend nothing happened. I grab the fallen bottle and throw it out of the window; maybe that wasn't the way to go.

That doesn't mean I'm going to give up.

I look around as the lights try to help me.

I'm close. I can feel it.

Taste it.

Hot blood slips from my nose to my lips, and I lick, look at the red teeth in the mirror, and my smile widens.

So wide, I look like W for a split second.

I don't recognize my reflection, but I don't care.

I slow down as I look at each of the establishments around me. The letters on the signs overlap, so I don't even try to understand what they say.

In my brain, the place I'm looking for slowly begins to draw itself. W is again relegated to the back seat, trying to hurt me without succeeding.

I close my eyes, not caring that the car is still moving, trying to remember exactly what I did that night. I keep going straight until I can't go any further. And at the end of it all, of the street, of the motels, of my despair.

There is nothing.

I stare at the empty lot for what feels like hours while W laughs in the background. I don't feel chased anymore; in my memories, this parking lot is drawn to perfection. With a car next to mine and a neon sign above me.

Nothing.

Absolutely nothing.

GLOWROT

"ItWasAllADream.

I'mAlwaysRight."

But the moles, the pineapple-flavored air, the sweat of strangers clinging to my body, the feeling of familiarity.

It has to exist, and it has to be here.

I open the door and the frosty air, even though it's summer, hits me almost as hard as the certainty that there's nothing in front of me.

I search the nearby buildings, hugging myself.

I know what I'm looking for; if I see it, I'll recognize it.

There is no one else on the street. It's almost like the entire world has disintegrated.

I go back to the car.

Fuck it all.

My head hurts, and my nose is still bleeding. The emptiness in my stomach tells me that what I had for dinner wasn't enough and MY FINGERNAILS ARE SO ITCHY that I have to make a massive effort not to tear them out again.

So, I start to drive.

I leave behind the motels, the GPS and the little sense of direction I was trying to guide myself by.

Passing in between houses, onto a freeway, and turning left twice.

I refuse to go back without finding it, and if I have to stay on the street for the rest of my life, I will.

There's something about that place that draws me to it.

I think of the moles and the map that I sense guiding me, the caresses of the one I'm almost sure I recognized because they were there with me.

More than once.

It's a constant deja vu that my mind is still not assimilating.

They want me.

I inhale again and drive without opening my eyes.

It's a sign.

W screams, I scream and become completely detached from reality.

I didn't get my head stuck in a pole by a miracle.

And if it weren't for W maneuvering my hands at the last second, I would have gone on to some other life in the stupidest way possible.

At least my eyeliner is good enough today.

I would be a corpse worth going to see.

9 Use Other Door

Minutes, hours, millennia have passed.

Time doesn't exist anymore. I've forgotten what it feels like to belong to it.

I open the door and fall to the ground only to feel it's not hard.

The sand clings to my nails with as much desperation as I feel.

The smell of the sea floods my nostrils, as a burning reminder I should stop playing with stuff I know I can't handle. It takes me a few seconds to realize where I am.

The other side of the city.

How?

How did I get here?

How?

Everything around me seems surrounded by a trail of light and magenta-colored smoke.

I look up.

And there it is.

The sign that hasn't left my brain.

The sign I've been chasing, dreaming about, seeing in the backs of my eyelids.

N I U.

It flickers once. Twice.

I scream to the sky, raw and guttural.

Because I've finally found it.

And I don't know if I'm relieved or terrified.

10
HandleWithCarE

I found it.

It's real.

The glowing sign hasn't stopped burning into my brain since I saw it.

N I U

I should be scared. I should turn back. W told me this place didn't exist. He kept pulling me away; he didn't believe me.

Maybe he was trying to protect me.

But he doesn't understand.

And I found it anyway.

I can feel the same pull that hasn't left me. It's taking me inside, beating like the blood on my neck. Like something's reaching into my head, digging into my memories.

I pinch my thigh hard enough to leave a bruise. I can't forget. I won't forget.

If I go too far or stay too long, I'll lose something. My brain will get scrambled again.

I know it. I've always known it.

But I can't stop now.

I walk through the entrance, trying to count my steps. Trying to hold onto something.

One. Two. Three.

The bar is to the left. I know that.

I know what the drinks are called. I know which ones taste like nothing and which ones will burn all the way down.

I know how many steps it takes to reach the bathroom.

And I know I'll forget it all the second I let my guard down.

"YouWin," W says, his voice curling around my head. **"YouProvedMeWrong,NowLeave."**

But there's no urgency in his tone.

It's almost like he's also curious.

Like he feels the pull, too.

The pull hasn't disappeared, and I hold my breath, almost like I'm going to go underwater. They're here, somewhere, I know it. I smell the fair scent of lavender and smoke mixed with cotton candy and the rest of the intoxicating gases permeating my surroundings.

Here. Somewhere.

Looking for me?

Waiting for me.

I pinch myself one more time and exhale, walking with my smile widening each time. Somehow, this place feels like home.

So, I start dancing, grinding, following the river of people and letting the music guide me. I close my eyes in an attempt to heighten my sense of smell.

I have no idea how much time has passed when I open them again.

A guy is staring at me, my skin crawls as if his eyes were throwing daggers. They're white, and every time I move, they follow me like a predator.

He has my name tattooed on his arms in neon ink that changes color depending on how the light hits him.

I try not to drink anything. I know better.

But a hand grabs my jaw when I least expect it, and its fingers dig into my cheeks, forcing my mouth open.

I gasp, and suddenly, the air is burning my throat.

The drink spills over my mouth, my chin, my cheeks. It tastes cool, like dry ice. And somehow, it feels comforting.

That's the worst part. I can't even taste it but *feel* it.

And it feels good.

As much as I want to pull away, the hand is firm, and without realizing it, the liquid is now running down my throat. It stings. The hand is not letting go, and my vision is too blurry to attach it to a face.

So, I give in.

It's not like I had a choice.

As quickly as it appears, I feel the pressure on my cheeks dissipating, and I can move again. The place is spinning around me, and for no particular reason, I can't stop giggling like a child caught doing something terrible.

No!

I hold my breath and pinch myself. Hard.

I have to focus.

I can't forget why I'm here.

Maybe concentrating on the faces of everyone around me would help. Trying to tie myself to the real things within the dream, the nightmare, the limbo I'm in right now. But every time I try to focus on one, it starts blending with the next.

Keep going.

Between pushes and pulls, the sea of people leads me to the other side.

The place's walls loom around us, and it feels like the whole venue is shrinking and will eventually crush us. I lick my lips, and the salty taste around them feels like someone else's.

Keep going.

I'm sitting on the sticky steps with someone about to fall over me. Her electric red hair tickles my neck, I pull her to me, and she greets me with her mouth open. My thigh hurts, and I can't remember why.

The tip of my tongue is about to brush against hers when some fucking asshole puts his full weight on my free hand. I let out a howl of pain that is overshadowed by the euphoric screams of the others.

But at least it helps me remember.

The redhead's hands slide down my thighs, and I have to make a massive effort to stand up and push her away.

"TrustNoOne," W says with a tone too calm to be his usual one.

If anything, he sounds curious, amused. Almost like he's watching something unfold and doesn't want to miss the show.

"Careful,Bo.

StepsAreSlippery."

He helps me finish climbing the steps up to the VIP area, so I guess we're even. He no longer digs his claws into my skin, now he uses them to caress me.

Thankfully, this space is higher than the rest, so I take advantage of it and search among all the heads, one that shines among the crowd.

Here, on top of everything, I can see the amalgamation of bodies grinding against each other. Like corpses being puppeteered from way above. I look up, but I'm not sure what I'm expecting to find. The ceiling is so dark it just disappears into a void covered by a thin layer of smoke.

When I look back down, something is different, something I can't fully put into words at first.

A tall silhouette is moving against the crowd with fluidity, almost liquid. He's taller than the rest, and his orange hair shines under the neon lights. There's something around him, an aura, an almost imperceptible force that pushes the bodies around him.

Where did he come from?

I try to follow backward the route he is going through with my eyes, and something different pops into my vision. That one guy, the one with my name tattooed on his skin.

Staring at me.

Coming closer and closer.

I gasp and look away, my hands pressing on the railing. When I look back, he's still staring, smiling, closer.

Something's not right. I step back and trip over someone's foot. Somehow, I feel his presence cutting closer to me.

This is how prey must feel, small critters way too used to running for their lives, knowing they'll be devoured at any moment.

Of course I would know something like that.

I try to get away as quick as I can, on all fours, until I hit the leg of a table and use it to prop myself back up.

A tray with drinks waits for me on top of it. Pink, glowing in the dark. A shiny label is before them, and I can almost hear its calling. The pull.

"Drink me," it says.

And I can feel that man coming closer and closer.

A hand touches my shoulder.

I throw myself to the front and empty one of the bottles down my throat.

"nO!"

Too late.

In three gulps, I finish it, and I don't feel that hand on my shoulder any longer. The presence disappeared, and looking around, I find that the guy I was running away from has also vanished.

Something inside of me starts to shift.

I immediately bare my teeth in a gesture that can't be called a smile and remind myself of the transparent railing so I don't fall over the others. I move my hips against something that I don't know if it's a piece of furniture or a person. Now I feel not one gaze but several, and I'm about to try to make a mess of the glowing tube spinning next to me when I find completely black pupils staring back at me.

Moles.

And a spider web tattooed under one eye.

My entire world spins, and before I can recover my balance, I go face-first into the ground. Metallic blood soaks my lips, but it doesn't hurt. I can't feel my limbs or the rest of my body.

Someone or something whispers for me to stand up, and I listen and throw myself in the direction where I feel I have finally found my angel.

It seems as if all the hands pulling me are coming out of the walls, like they are part of the place itself, trying to pull me away from what I crave most at this moment, just as the rest of existence seems to be doing.

First at Cameo, now here.

I just want to be able to look into their eyes and tell them I found a lighter.

Their lighter, maybe?

To ask them why they refuse to leave my head and beg them to kiss me.

MY EYELID TWITCHES, and I gag but don't stop walking blindly.

It's like they're the center of gravity pulling me like my life depends on it, and for a second, I think maybe it does.

All eyes are on me, just in the way I like it. Somehow, my skirt is shorter than before, and I can't remember if I walked in with one shoe or both.

An unfamiliar arm wraps around my waist, and before I can say anything, I choke on two dirty fingers that appear out of nowhere.

I instinctively wrap my tongue around them and start to....

No.

No!

This is not the time.

I kick and flee, shaking my head and trying to run away from the thoughts that this place seems to be trying to implant in my brain.

Every time I remember more and more, it's always the same.

10 HandleWithCarE

What's the next step?

The tangle of people turns this microscopic space into a labyrinth; it takes me longer to navigate it than it should. It seems purposeful, like everything in this chaotic space.

Intentional.

How could chaos be deliberate?

I adjust my skirt, the line for the restroom looms in front of me, almost going around the bar.

Why is it always the restrooms?

How do I know that?

A rabbit bounces in the distance, hopping to the rhythm of music, trapped between layers of skin. Within a silhouette, I recognize immediately.

Finally.

I reach out my hand and move closer, carefully, like it's going to burn.

Because a part of me knows it will.

Then they turn around and I can see the sky hidden in their white eyeliner. Their moles dot their skin like a secret constellation.

"Yes?"

Their voice exists on a separate plane from everything around us. It cuts through the noise, trapped in its own quiet bubble, like a whisper meant only for me.

I open my mouth to speak, but no words come out.

I feel useless. Helpless.

The only thing I can do is smile and point to some random spot behind me.

Against everything I thought possible, they react.

They close their hand around my arm and pull me to themselves, closer, like someone who is saving another person from being run over would do.

It feels like they're rescuing me from the monsters attacking me a second ago. And yet, there's something in how their fingers twitch against my skin that makes it feel like an apology.

They glance around us, their gaze flickering between the bodies pressing in, the neon haze and the man with my name tattooed on his arm.

Then back to me.

GLOWROT

"They're a nuisance," they whisper in my ear, their tongue brushing against my skin.

Their finger, black nail polished to perfection, points to the man who's been following me all night.

The same one that choked me with his fingers.

How long ago was that?

"Stay away from him," they say. Their voice is steady, but there's a small crack at the edge of their words.

Like someone who's warning themselves, just as much as me.

Their movements try to convey confidence, but their hand hasn't stopped trembling.

But I can't think about that right now, because the only thing I can think about right now is how much I wish I could count their eyelashes and watch their eyes turn upward as their body twists on top of mine.

"We already know each other," is the only thing I can think to say to them, still in the mystical halo that envelops their presence.

They nod.

And I smile.

I feel like I'm on the moon.

"I'm pretty sure," they whisper. "This place is… It plays with your mind."

Someone walks past us, holding a plate of alcohol-soaked gummies that glisten under the lights. I grab one without thinking and offer it to them.

They freeze for a second, staring at it like it's something vile.

"No thanks." Their voice is flat, almost mechanical, as they glance away. Their hand twitches, curling tighter into a fist.

They're right; we don't have time for food right now.

The music fades, the stares don't matter anymore. None of it does.

All I need is two seconds alone with them. To ask questions. Or to hide in their teeth.

Because I'm sure this has happened before, again and again. We're stuck in a loop from which I never want to escape.

"The bathroom? The hallway?" I ask, and I know they know what I mean.

I can see in their eyes, a flicker of familiarity. It seems like something is buried in them, slowly crowling its way back out.

They remember, but it's hazy, like it is in my brain.

10 HandleWithCarE

Maybe we need a reminder.

To do it again.

They know exactly what I'm thinking right now.

I LET MYSELF BE CARRIED AWAY.

With fingers interlaced, we negotiate the obstacles of bodies sprawled on the floor and climb the walls. We arrive at the same hallway with thousands of doors, the one I saw the last time I passed this way. This time, I open one of them.

The room is dimly lit by a lamp that changes colors every three seconds, so small it looks like a closet with barely enough room for a mattress.

I search for their lips wildly, and they close the door behind them. With the music muffled by the walls around us, I can concentrate on their breathing.

"What was your name again?" The words escape my lips before I can contain them.

"Shut up," they whisper, pushing me down to the mattress, biting my jaw and my back arches.

I see pain in their eyes.

Maybe I can fix it.

Fix them.

Their hands roam my body with the expertise of someone who has done this more than three times and mine, with surprise, do the same. The skin of their chest brushes mine, and I exhale, closing my eyes, letting the tickle in my nipples spread through the rest of my body.

Every time I try to speak, they place their fingers around my throat, and I feel the wetness inside me begin to escape.

I try to keep my eyes open just to admire the perfection of their figure silhouetted against the changing lights. I can see the outline of their ribs almost perfectly. I lunge for their throat, unable to contain myself, and end up completely shedding their clothes, their fingernails leaving red trails on my legs as they return the favor.

Maybe I can take their pain away.

The air around us is humid and sticks to the bristling hairs on my neck as we grapple, trying to figure out who is in charge.

I end up surrendering, lying on my back as their lips slide across my belly.

An almost electric current overcomes me, announcing that the wait is over.

The next second, their tongue begins to move in slow circles that torture me. I want to beg them to stop teasing me, to leave the gentleness behind. But they keep torturing me, caressing the inside of my thighs with a single finger so shallowly that I can only stir uneasily.

They finally move their hands to my knees and spread them open.

Yes!

I let myself be manipulated like a rag doll, and the echo of that voice tickles me in a way that I'm sure is forbidden.

Then I arch my back, offering myself up completely, but their movements feel slow, careful, almost like they're holding back.

They press my skin against their lips, and their tongue begins to disappear inside me. As it grazes me, I moan loud enough to fill the space between us.

The soft, delicate touch makes every nerve in my body tingle.

The echo of their gasps makes me even more aroused, even though they feel shallow, muffled like they're afraid to be heard.

I caress their back with the soles of my feet; their skin feels like porcelain.

So cold.

Spreading my legs wider, they remind me that they are in control.

Please, take control.

They slip one of their fingers inside me and brush my mons venus with the tip of their tongue. As they stroke me from the inside, the second I allow myself to open my eyes, I notice they are pleasuring themselves with their remaining hand.

A vacant stare.

They start to play with the rhythm. Slow at first, fast, and slow again. They alternate discreet kisses with deadly caresses. With another finger, more moans intertwine above our heads, and I can't stop moving my hips. *Everything outside has ceased to matter.*

I squeeze my legs together, and for a second, I'm afraid to snap their neck, but I can't anymore.

Heat rises from my crotch to my jaw and I sit up with desperation and saliva sliding down my jaw. I stroke their head and then press them against me. They quickly withdraw their fingers and focus on torturing me instead by inserting their tongue again. They dig their nails into my legs, almost with fury.

I'm about to explode.

Everything stops in an instant and I hear my own voice pleading with them to finish what they have started.

"Please," I beg.

A little more.

Just a little more.

The involuntary trembling of what I can only describe as a happy ending accompanies my legs and I slump against the mattress, watching the magnificent work of art that is their expression as they focus on making themselves finish.

They smile, perhaps because they like that I'm watching the scene.

I'm about to sit up to help when the moans make my stomach churn with pleasure and a self-satisfied smile lights up that beautiful face.

They fall down next to me, their body folds onto itself like it's trying to evaporate.

Their skin looks fragile, almost translucent, like it'll crack under pressure. I turn to stroke it. My fingers slowly start outlining the border of their hips and going up to their ribs again.

And then I see their face.

The terror in their eyes.

They stare at their hands, their fingers trembling like they've turned into snakes. Their chest rises and falls too quickly. Frantic breathing, gasping for air.

Their gaze lands on me, sharp and accusing but also so full of pain it makes my stomach twist.

"I'm leaving," they whisper.

The words land like a knife and cut through the fog around us. Their voice is low, cracking, but it's not anger.

Something heavier.

Regret?

"What? How? Why?" I stutter. Their expression doesn't change.

They shift, their movements quick and desperate, like they need to escape. I turn around, trying to find where the threat is coming from, but I'm still dizzy and can't even focus my sight.

What's happening?

What's happening?

GLOWROT

Who is it? What is it? Is the door open? Did the man with white eyes find us? I try to open my mouth again, but I can't speak. Like someone stole my voice.

I lunge, pulling their body under mine in a desperate attempt to keep them here, to protect them, to reassure them we can make this moment last forever.

But they slip through my grasp, their skin feeling slick, almost like oil.

Like someone is pulling them away from me.

They sit up, running a hand over their shaved head, their moles catching the faint light like constellations I'll never understand.

"I shouldn't have come here," they say, their voice soft but distant, like they're talking to themselves more than me. "But I remembered I owed you this one."

They smile, but it's all wrong; sharp at the edges, breaking apart in the middle.

"What are you talking about? Owe me what?" I scream, my voice high and desperate.

They don't answer right away. They glance down at their hands as if looking for something, then back at me.

"We're even now, Bo."

Their tears are glowing in the dark.

The flashes of light get faster, and I can see their presence flicker. They're there, and in a second they're gone.

I cry out in desperation and try to search for their clothes, or any trace that might confirm their existence. I can feel my hands tingling and my brain screaming at me to do something.

I can't afford to forget again.

I look around me, there's nothing but the four walls and the miserable mattress.

La puta madre.

I look down at my arm and bite my tongue. My body still feels numb, and I feel dizzy.

It's not the first time I've done this.

I've done worse.

Way worse.

10 HandleWithCarE

I slide my half-broken fingernail down my right forearm with all my might; the scream is overshadowed by the urge to pass out.

After tracing another line, I see the first blood dots appearing on my skin's surface.

When was the last time I hurt myself like this?

I draw the rest of the letters one after the other until a bleeding "NIU" adorns my skin.

And I fall back to the mattress.

Knowing that this time I can't let myself forget.

GLOWROT

11
Out of Reach

A million needles stick into my skin, all at the same time. I can no longer be sure if the pain is coming from my brain or my body, or somewhere in between.

A limbo.

It's hard to move my limbs, harder than usual.

At least I'm a good actress and pretend everything is fine. At least no one cares.

The smile plastered on my face like every other day. It's still early enough, so I can pretend I'm tired.

But it's not like it'll matter anyway.

It's particularly slow today. I don't know if it's worse that way. Usually, whenever we're packed, I can go an entire morning without having to make small talk with the rest of them.

The guests are so much easier; just repeat the same script over and over like a robot, ignore their despicable comments, and call it a day.

But with the others, I have to try to be human or at least come up with excuses that make sense.

At least I'm a good actress.

At least no one cares.

"I got you coffee," Nina's voice brings me back from the void inside my mind.

I don't have time to deal with her, so I smile and grab it. And then wait.

Wait.

Wait.

Nothing.

By this time, W would have found something to comment on, even the tiniest excuse to diss Nina, accusing her of being fake and overly friendly. Or would have reminded me not to get involved, that she's too nice to be with someone like me.

Or something like that.

But his silence is palpable, and I never know how to handle myself whenever he decides to abandon me in this way.

Is he upset at me? Why?

Did I do something yesterday?

Last night?

Why the fuck can't I remember?

"Thanks," I respond because I have no idea what else I'm supposed to do. "I could use the caffeine right now."

Her eyes are sparkling, it's even more notable because of how red and swollen they are. Why is she acting like I've never spoken to her in my life?

"Yeah, I can see that," she says, immediately catching herself. "I mean, you look tired. You know, without makeup and all."

"I've never seen you wear a hoodie before. I thought you were going to rob us this morning when you came in," Nova adds, coming from the back room.

Makeup? Hoodie?

I barely recall my whole getting ready process from this morning; the nausea is what I remember the most.

Looking around, I find a small mirror and immediately regret it. They're right.

I look exactly how I feel.

Where's the perfect persona I've crafted so carefully since moving to this hotel?

Fuck it. To this country?

Right now, I just look like myself.

Disgusting.

Holy shit, what happened to me?

"So… rough night?"

Nova's way closer than before, and Nina hasn't left my side. I look around, trying to see if I can glimpse the familiar shadow that would have gotten me out of this mess already, or at least a family of fifteen to save me.

Deserted.

11 Out of Reach

THE HAIR ON MY ARMS IS SCREAMING.

The air in my lungs starts to become solid, blocking my breathing, suffocating me.

"*No tengo idea.*" The whisper that comes out of my mouth feels alien, like hearing from a dying radio. They look at me, confused; I shake my head. "I don't know."

It sounds like a whimper, like a cry for help.

I hate it.

"Drank too much? Been there," Nova insists, but I see something in her eyes. Fuck.

"Are you… okay?" Nina asks and puts her hand on top of mine.

I can't do this.

I hate when they gang up on me like this, and I know if W were here, he would have helped me, but he left me alone because he's a piece of shit that is clearly trying to teach me a lesson I can't learn because I have no clue what I did to bother him this much.

"I'm fine," I try to sound intimidating but can't muster the strength. "I'm used to this; I just had too much fun last night." I let out a laugh, but the expression on their faces becomes worse.

A scream pierces through the thick, uncomfortable fog that had started to surround us.

We all jolt, and Nina's hand finds its way away from mine; for a split second, I miss its warmth.

Another scream, then a chain of thunderous laughter. Guttural, startling, it bounces from the walls to the floor until it reaches the reception desk.

It's coming from a group of men just coming in from the street; from how they look, they had an insane night.

Like me?

We are the only ones in the huge lobby. I turn to look at the twins, and Nova is clenching her fists; there's something about this that tells me this is not the first time they have to deal with a group of drunks like this. Did something happen in the past? They're the ones that have been here the longest, so it makes sense they would have dealt with all types of shit.

But she's tense, almost afraid.

The men are dressed in suits, but their ties are loose, their shirts wrinkled.

And they're walking right towards us.

Dragging their feet with vacant stares.

Nina immediately forces a smile so big I feel her head will split in two, and it's about to talk when Nova slaps her hand.

"No!" her stare seems to say. One of her fingers twitches, the only part of her body she doesn't seem to be in control of right now.

There's definitely something I'm missing.

The closer they get, the stronger their pungent smell becomes, smoke with something metallic interlaced in between. It's clawing at the walls of my nostrils like they want to make them bleed.

"She said she'd follow me anywhere," one man mutters, staring blankly at the ceiling while another drags him by the arm. "But I don't think she can anymore."

Their limbs look limp, heavier. They move slowly as if trapped in molasses.

"Itrieed tofind it, yaknow?" another one says, loud enough so we can hear it too. His eyes are devoid of light like the rest; his speech is so slurred I can barely understand. *"Duuing theday, Itooka taaaaxi and walkandwalk. Itook notesbut Ijust cooouuldn't. Untilwe-"*

"Shut up! All of you!" This time, the one speaking is the only one that appears somehow sane. "You're drawing attention. We- We can't stay here. For God's sake, Emil, get up!"

He's dragging the other three like a frustrating group of children, trying to scream in whispers.

What could have been a pretty decently looking suit the night before now is no more than a wrinkly amalgamation of black fabric. He looks at us from time to time, his hands shaking.

They're getting closer.

"Ute, please, you know how to get there," the last one cries out and looks at the one dragging them all.

He wipes a drop of sweat from his forehead, and I see how it falls to the floor in slow motion.

"Can I help you with something?" Nina says it in a saccharine tone, but trembling slightly, Nova shivers. Now, she has two fingers out of control.

The man releases his grip on the second one, who immediately slumps to the ground like a puppet with its strings suddenly cut. He walks towards us, dragging his feet at an unnatural slowness, his shoes squeaking against the ceramic flooring.

He's clearly the one with the most success at existing in the group, but there's something still off about him.

Something wrong.

Something familiar.

"I'm sorry, ladies," he says while putting a hand to his chest in a dramatic gesture.

His voice is thick and feels like an intruder in my ears, like it's trying to leave his throat desperately and cling to absolutely anything else. Then tumbles to the desk like an avalanche of meat, sweat, and mustache.

"It seems like my coworkers over here can't hold their drinks pretty well."

He trips on his own feet, and something falls from his pocket. Nova's eyes flicker with a spark I haven't seen in her before, and she lunges forward to grab it.

Her side hits the outside corner of the desk when she runs toward the small object, but she doesn't seem to react. She grabs it, holding it in her hand, completely stiff.

She's close enough so I can see it's his wallet, engraved with an oyster symbol and the words "Open me" on it.

Almost shining under the lights.

Shiny.

Like what?

She stands there, staring at the thing like it's the holy grail. That something I hadn't realized she could feel still permeates her eyes. A hunger so potent her throat moves with a gulp. A second later, her eyes drift towards Nina, who's still trying to customer service her way into forcing these people to go and shakes her head.

It looked like she was in a trance for a second, but something in her sister made her snap out of it.

"Please take some water," Nina is now offering a bottle to the man with a strained smile. Her lips haven't stopped trembling.

He's impossibly tall, towering over us and uncomfortably close to the counter. The skin on his face seems too tight around his features, like a mask just a bit too small to fit correctly.

"Thank you, sweetheart," he whispers with a smile almost entirely obscured by his long mustache. The girl visibly forces a retch to stop and stiffens, but nothing indicates he noticed.

"You dropped this," Nova pats his shoulder and hands him the wallet, staring sadly but somehow forcing an angry tone out.

The man's head snaps to the wallet, and for a moment, his mask slips. His hand twitches, and his mouth contorts into a horrified expression.

"Ah, yes," he says after a beat, his voice trying to be soft again. He snatches the wallet like he's afraid someone else might touch it, clutching it to his chest.

The movement sends the water bottle tumbling from his other hand, and the liquid splashes across the counter and onto me.

Nina squeals and jumps back. I curse under my breath while shaking water from my hands.

The man who looks more like a walrus half apologizes. He tries to reach behind the desk to the napkins lying next to Nina, and she flicks his hand off with a force I had never seen before on her, even Nova gets startled. She smiles again and steps back, bringing the napkins with her.

And then it hits me.

That disgusting feeling, the wetness soaking the fabric.

The dampness spreads across my hoodie and tears at my skin. It feels like it's become more solid, heavier; it wants to bring me down with it.

Gravity is more intense now, it's constricting my lungs, the fabric strands trying to rip the little hairs of my arms hairs off.

It's alive.

It's going to eat me.

I tug at the soaked fabric —now turned into a monster—, peel it away, and throw it to the floor.

It lays in a puddle of its own revolting sweat, looking at me with sorry eyes.

Even once it's off, the phantom sensation lingers on my arms like a clammy ghost that refuses to leave.

He smiles, and it seems like he's prepared to speak when his eyes fix on a point in my forearm.

"It seems like we've already caused quite some situation," he whispers and slowly backs up. "We'll send a tip down to the lobby for the trouble."

"It doesn't even work like that—" Nova starts to say, but he's already far, dragging the other the same way as before.

We stand silently, watching them leave, like after some weird alien abduction. The air still feels tense after they go, suffocating.

I look to my left, Nova is lost somewhere inside her head. Then turn to my right, Nina dabs the same point of her shirt over and over again with the same napkin.

What just happened?

Everything is silent again, empty. Everything is back to how it was before, yet nothing feels the same. I can't know what to do about it because I have a way out whenever there's an uncomfortable situation.

A way that bailed on me today.

"I didn't know you- had a- a cat," Nina drags her words when she talks to me, I turn around and look at her confused. She points her finger at my forearm. "Do you need disinfectant?"

I have to stare at the scratches for a few seconds to realize they are even real, the hoodie comes back to my brain. Was that why I chose it today? How did these even get here?

"Bo, do you *have* a cat?" Nova says, coming closer with the tone of someone who thinks they know what's happening.

I turn to see her, suffocated once again, being pressed against both of them like in an interrogation scene.

"You can tell us, we can help you," Nina's whispers are soft and curl up in my neck while her fingers start running through my wrist.

"I've been there, I understand," Nova points at my arm and then the hoodie.

No.

No!

They have no idea what they're talking about.

I don't...

Not like that.

A flood of colors invades my brain. I close my eyes and see all of it.

The lights, the colors, the eyes of strangers looking at me.

I feel everything.

The mattress under my body, soft skin that isn't mine. The pain, so much pain.

And then my arm, the lines my own nails made. It burns, it has its own heartbeat.

My eyes open against my will, and I can see my forearm, red and swollen; it's hard to focus my eyes on it.

Maybe I imagined it all, maybe last night I drifted from reality and ended up going into a spiral of self-destruction.

That may be the reason W is gone, he may be irritated to know that I fell into the same thing from years ago.

But this time, it feels different.

"Bo, do you need to take the rest of the day? I can cover you."

I vaguely nod and start to walk away, unable to stop staring at my arm. I keep walking without caring about my hoodie on the floor or even stopping to check if I even have my phone with me.

It's different, this time it's different.

The lines on my arms.

They look like letters.

They're trying to tell me something.

Something I promised I wouldn't forget.

12

Danger High Voltage

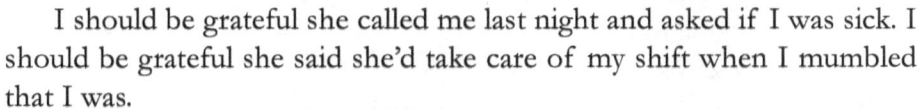

I should be grateful.

I scold myself while still lying in bed, staring at the ceiling. The smell of the air-conditioning presses against the walls of my lungs.

I should be grateful Nina is so nice to me.

But I didn't ask her to cover for me.

Now, I probably look like a needy idiot.

I should be grateful she called me last night and asked if I was sick. I should be grateful she said she'd take care of my shift when I mumbled that I was.

But the guilt sits too heavy in my chest, it's competing with the air-conditioning to see which one is going to RIP ME APART first.

When she spoke so gently, so softly, saying she'd take my shift, the part of me that was ready to protest just... stopped.

Back home, people talked about The States as a perfect promise, a place where you could be someone if you worked hard enough. But when I got here, I learned that you are only worth what you can produce. Resting is weakness. Wasting time is a sin. If you're not grinding yourself into the ground, you don't deserve to be here.

So now everyone probably thinks the worst of me.

I worked until my feet bled since then, until my hands ached, and I could barely think beyond scripted smiles until I passed out from exhaustion. Being here feels wrong, like I'm betraying myself from the past, the one that fought so hard for a seat at this pathetic table.

I should get up and go anyway, prove I deserve my place, that I don't want to go back to the hellhole I escaped from.

But I can't.

My body just refuses to move.

GLOWROT

The throbbing pain in my arm keeps getting worse, and a worm inside my brain is trying to convince me it's getting infected. I would be throwing up if I had something other than bile in my stomach. Getting up seems impossible.

So, I should be grateful.

Instead, I feel like I'm disappearing.

Maybe today will be the day when the weight of my worries finally crushes me.

And I die.

Once and for all.

I close my eyes and try to force the bedsheets to swallow me, but the minutes pass, and I'm still here.

I open them back, and the plastic container with a piece of the microwavable lasagna I ate at noon stares at me from across the bed. For a second, I had forgotten what time it was. I reach over and take it in my hands, not looking at it, chewing like an automaton.

Something else is pinching the nerves in my brain.

Is Eric working today?

Why do I care so much?

I jump on my phone and check the schedule picture, searching through our names until I get to his.

Perfect.

I hope he misses me.

What now?

I choke on a piece of meat that slid down the wrong side of my throat, and every time I cough, the scratches on my arm throb with more intensity.

I stare at them like some alien virus.

The guilt I felt for having missed work is gradually starting to be relegated to a dark corner of my brain.

Some things are more important than exploiting myself.

I need to find a way to go, to remember how to get back. I've gone over what happened so many times in my head that I feel like I can even taste the salty smoke floating around.

And the moles, those moles.

This time, I don't go over the feel of their hands on my body, the sense of their tongue exploring inappropriate nooks and crannies inside my core. Their lips, or even more so, the sound that came from them.

12 Danger High Voltage

The certainty with which they uttered those words.

"We're even now, Bo."

As if they knew what they were talking about.

As if they remembered.

The food I just tried to down knots in my stomach, and I feel it coming back up. I can't sit with this. I can't stay immobile anymore. I push it down along the self-deprecating thoughts and force myself to sit upright. All the bones in my body ache in unison, screaming my name in languages I keep forgetting to learn.

The room feels too small, too heavy, staying here is going to render me useless. So, I jump to my feet and throw a dress over my head. This is the first time I've worn clothes since I dragged myself out of the shower in the early morning.

The seconds start blending into routine and slowly bring me some control over myself again. Makeup, hair; and once again, the mask to make sure I appear to be the epitome of perfection.

But then I just end up grabbing the baggiest sweater in my entire closet.

Hiding myself.

Again.

No more crying, no more time to mourn. I need to act, and this time, I need to act smarter.

It's as if the crisis has opened my eyes, and despite W's glaring absence, I can think more clearly than I have in a long time. It's exactly what I imagine the high of some drugs would be like, maybe one handcrafted with moles and a hint of lavender.

One that needs a lighter and neon lights to be taken.

I need my phone and the room card, but no more than that. I close the door behind me and try not to let the woman still cleaning the hallway see me.

I fail to avoid the mirror as the elevator doors close, but I try to at least ignore the dark circles under my eyes. With a deep breath, I stand for a moment, not pressing any buttons.

It's a ridiculous plan, but it's the only thing that makes sense now.

One, two, three.

Nothing happens, and I start to shiver; the metal box starts asphyxiating me, and I wonder if it's going to squash me alive. It's static, like time has stopped, like nothing else exists outside these walls.

GLOWROT

Up. Up. Up.

Finally, moving.

I hold my breath as the doors slide open.

A couple with a luggage cart. They don't even glance at me. Disappointment coils in my stomach, tight but expected.

We go down, a man enters. I don't greet him.

Up again, two kids in damp bathing suits, tracking water all over the floor. The laugh is too loud, and the echoes scratch at my face while bouncing off the walls.

Down again. The doors open, everyone gets off.

Up, in. Up, out. In, out, down. Up. Up.

Up. Down. In.

Down.

Out.

I don't check my phone. I don't check the time. I don't need to, because time isn't moving, not really.

Out.

Down

In. Down. Up.

Up. Up. Down, out, in. Out, up. In, up.

It's just doors opening and closing, an endless rotation of strangers stepping in, brushing past me, leaving. I wait. I watch. I breathe the same elevator air over and over again.

I scan them, dissect them, catalog them. Too much hair. No tattoos. Wrong eyes. Wrong faces.

They have to show up, right?

Eventually.

I close my eyes to remember better; this has to be the same elevator I saw their face in. I could bet my ribs on that.

If I stand here the whole day, they have to show up.

Are they looking for me, just as I am for them?

Could that be the reason they asked me for a light?

Time hasn't moved, and even then, it's way too much. My chest starts to sting, and the air slowly becomes denser; it's getting harder and harder to fill my lungs. Maintaining balance is hard, standing upright absolutely impossible. Slowly, I turn into a small ball on the floor, relegated to a far corner.

No matter how many times the door is opened, I feel that so many people coming in and out are robbing me of oxygen.

I try to avoid it, but I start hyperventilating.

And I know what that means.

So, I give up, obviously.

As soon as the door opens the next time, I bolt out in a panic like someone threw up inside.

I'm shaking and hug myself as I stagger down a hallway with flickering lights.

I need air, air.

Just a little, two seconds, then I'll go back to the elevator to keep waiting patiently. I swear.

Weird.

Why's the pool door here?

Was this just the floor I got off on?

I open it and breathe in as if I've never done it before in my life.

It's sticky hot outside, and I regret it immediately. The condensation is clinging to my arms like termites. Before I can even think about turning around, I feel a prick on one thigh.

"Do you want to lick it?"

I jump in place and stifle a gasp. I turn to find a thing with tousled hair poking out of a bandana and an open button-down shirt looking at me expectantly. The thing has a candy ring on its middle finger, it reaches out toward me and moves it close to my face. The tension I feel slips through my body, and I shrug, licking the ring without taking my eyes off him.

Him.

The one interesting thing that has happened in weeks besides my dreams.

Even with the sun shining, the gesture feels obscene.

I love it.

"Bo, right? With a B, as in Britney?" He asks and plops down on the chair closest to the door. I smile and sit next to him, the termites in my arms start disintegrating. "The one who turned down my stripper money!

"That one," I answer with a giggle that surprises me. "Nick, right?"

His strange way of treating me, like we've known each other forever, makes me feel something.

I'm not sure what.

Before I give up completely, I look around, searching for the white rabbit tattoo that tells me it wasn't a total failure to leave the apartment.

GLOWROT

My neck itches, and I'm starting to sweat, droplets sliding down the crown of my head.

"Did you lose your condoms?"

The shock of his sentence brings me back to the conversation. The droplets evaporate.

Maybe they weren't even there to begin with.

He laughs, the sound rattles in his chest and makes all his ribs move.

"*Es que*, you're looking for something," he continues with teeth that shine just a little too much by how bright it already is outside. "And the only thing I'd be looking for with such dedication would be condoms."

"Why would I be looking for condoms in the pool?" The absurdity of the situation hugs me and forces my muscles to relax.

Nick shrugs, his expression flickering between playfulness and something unreadable. He rolls the ring between his teeth, biting it like a nervous tick, or a habit too ingrained to break.

"Look, I don't know where you put them, but I always have them stashed everywhere, just in case."

And as if proving a point, he pushes himself up in one fluid motion.

His legs are too pale and almost incandescent under the sun, and his movements are too loose to be real. His entire existence seems like a fever dream.

Pure chaos.

A couple of people stare at him, at the heart-shaped glasses he takes out of his party pocket, but Nick's living in a different reality. He kneels down and looks for something in the dirt until he pulls out a square gold-colored package and shows it to me triumphantly like a magician revealing a card.

It. Can't. Be.

"Magnum! Like ice cream." He places the package on the table and looks at me, raising his eyebrows.

My laugh bubbles up before I can stop it, but it feels unfamiliar, like something has changed.

"I thought they were named after the gun?"

Nick's grin widens, but his eyes stay exactly the same.

"Who the fuck cares about putting a gun in your mouth?" He taps the wrapping and licks his lips. "Besides, this one has a bit of flavor."

Maybe this level of absurdity was what I needed, so I could breathe and count to three.

12 Danger High Voltage

Pure nonsense.

It feels good to have a ridiculous conversation occasionally, something that doesn't make me force myself to sleep or throw myself out the window for a change.

Slowly I drift off, listening as Nick tells me that he finally did find some famous people to ensure a good time during his stay in Zampano.

It feels good to turn my brain off even when W is not around, to sit and listen to rambles so illogical it doesn't matter if I pay attention to them.

I put my feet on one of the empty chairs and lean back. I feel sleepy, relaxed, comfortable.

No need to pretend to smile or say polite things. His stupid chatter is comforting and just observing how his mouth moves or the flicker in his eyes under the glasses brings me back to myself.

Wild.

<u>Mad.</u>

He breathes in more times than necessary.

And can't stop showing his teeth.

"Are you a stripper?" He suddenly blurts out.

Addressing me directly breaks the spell, I'm no longer free to be a spectator of his existence.

"You know I work downstairs at the front desk..." I start, somewhere between confused and flattered. He cuts me off.

"And do you have a stripper girlfriend or something?" Seeing my confused face, he rolls his eyes, "Then why do you have a strip club tattooed on your arm?"

I follow the line drawn by his finger up my right arm, as if in slow motion. The wound looks nasty, and it's obvious it's not a tattoo, but he makes sure not to point that out.

Did I really leave the apartment without a sweater?

Shit.

But...

Why did he just say it's a strip club?

"NIU?" I ask, lowering my voice as if it were something top secret. It is almost like speaking too loud will make it slowly unravel until it disappears forever from my arm and brain.

"Uh-huh, that. I'm always pretty stoned when I go there, so I have no idea where it is." He licks the ring again, a trickle of saliva flies from his tongue. "Hell, I don't even know how I end up leaving."

"But NIU is not a strip club, it's a nightclub."

The sentence comes out too casually for comfort, like it's the most natural thing in the world, but my chest tightens when the words hit the air.

He doesn't seem to notice how much that realization is freaking me out right now.

"Well, I don't know. There are tables and poles," he's speaking like he's recalling his favorite childhood memory. "The girls are hot, but I don't remember their faces. Not that it matters much either, obviously." He laughs and licks his front teeth like he's savoring something. "It's got posters on the ceiling and neon lights, the air smells fruity. It's cool, we should go."

"Yes!"

I shout without realizing it.

Several people around us turn to look at us. I clear my throat and pretend I don't look completely deranged.

"Do you know where it is?"

This is it.

I'm not crazy.

My arm screams, my skin tightens.

I already know this is real, but the confirmation feels like ice on sunburned skin.

Coincidences don't exist.

If he knows how to get there, I could arrive before the object of my desire does, maybe I can wait for them there.

Perhaps we can meet halfway.

Would Nick know them?

"I just told you I don't know where it is, Bo."

His eyes take a severe tone, so suddenly, the world dims for a few seconds. His stare fixates on the candy briefly, and he closes his teeth over it.

Crack.

My whole body locks up.

He meets my stare. Doesn't blink. Bites down.

And slowly, casually, he rips the candy from the ring with his teeth.

Like he's testing something.

Like he's testing me.

12 Danger High Voltage

"Look, I don't know about you," he says, tucking the candy between his cheek and molars. His words reach me, thick with sugar. His smile curls in a way that isn't entirely friendly anymore. "But I haven't slept in, like, thirty hours, and I'm about to go into a coma." He gestures vaguely toward the hotel behind him. "If you help me to my room and make sure I don't pass out, I'll give you an empanada I bought from a nice Caribbean lady this morning."

The normality of the sentence doesn't land. It warps and curls at the edges, like something painted over a wall to make it seem solid.

I should say no.

I should say no.

But.

"Moles!" I try to scream but choke. He chuckles, and a red droplet slides from the corner of his lip. "Have you seen someone there?"

"I see lots of people," he starts, rolling the candy in his mouth, but I interrupt before I can stop myself.

"No, no! They're really tall, skinny, bald. Their skin is almost translucent, it glistens." My pulse pounds so hard I can hear it in my teeth. "They have a rabbit tattoo, spiderweb, and these beautiful moles."

My mouth waters.

"Mami, todo bien?" He asks sing-songly, but there's a flicker of something else underneath it.

Not pity.

Not concern.

Something else.

"You look like you're the one in the middle of a trip."

He's playing with me.

He doesn't believe me.

It doesn't matter.

"Listen, I'll help you if you tell me everything you know about that place."

I push myself up to my feet and reach out my hand.

For a moment, he doesn't move.

Then, he takes it with a flourish and way more force than necessary. His bony fingers curl around mine, too firm, too warm, too sharp.

He leans in, his face so close I could count his pores. Looking into his eyes through the rose-colored lenses, I realize I can't see myself reflected back.

He's smiling differently now.

A kind of smile that knows something I don't.

A kind of smile that terrifies me.

But his voice is soft. Sweet. Almost affectionate.

"Oh, Bo."

He pronounces my name like dessert and wraps his tongue around it like he doesn't want to let it go. And suddenly I'm hungry too.

His breath brushes my cheek, and my lips part involuntarily. He's still holding my hand.

I forgot how to move.

"Didn't anyone ever tell you not to make a deal with the devil?"

13
Use at Your Own Risk

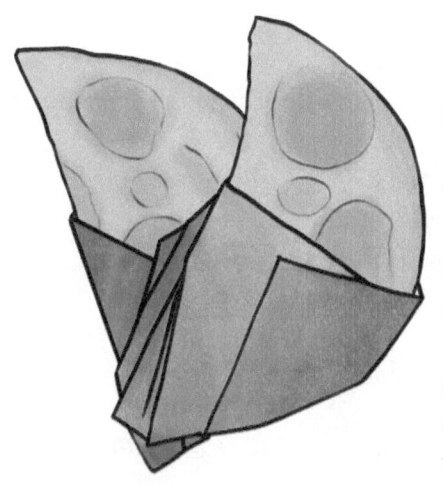

He acts like nothing has happened.

Like he didn't say something that made my skin crawl.

Like he didn't look at me with eyes that threatened to steal my soul.

We walk across the hallway in silence. He's slumped over my shoulder, and I have to hold him with one arm to keep him from falling. Dead weight. I have to keep an arm around his waist to stop him from collapsing entirely.

He's much shorter than me and so thin that I can practically drag him across the carpet with no problem.

It's too early for anyone to see us. Too early for anyone to question what we're doing, where we're going, what kind of illicit things we might be about to commit.

To be honest, even I don't know.

But his words still claw at me.

They feel more than a joke, almost an omen.

"Hey," I start, keeping my voice low. "Why did you say that? About the demon?"

Even saying it out loud makes my stomach twist.

It's not superstition, but the certainty that there are things beyond, so strange that they're often impossible to describe. And if a stranger more eccentric than ordinary, even by Zampano standards, acts like he knows something I don't, I think it's worth listening to.

Nick doesn't answer.

He just hums and keeps sucking on that fucking candy with a terrifying fascination.

"Hmm," he rolls the candy against his cheek, the sound almost obscene. "Tastes like apple."

"Nick. Nicholas." I press the elevator button harder than necessary.

I don't know why I'm shivering.

The air gets heavier and thicker, like the candy still rolling inside his mouth. The instincts I've barely developed while living here keep screaming that something is wrong.

The elevator isn't coming fast enough.

He exhales sharply like I've just broken a delightful silence, and then his fingers are in my hair.

Not gentle. Not quite violent either. Just... sudden.

Possessive.

He pulls me toward him without effort, and for a moment, I don't resist. I don't know how to.

I freeze.

Because when I see myself reflected in his pink, heart-shaped glasses, I see someone I don't recognize.

His breath curls against my lips. Heavy, uneven. I don't know if he's out of breath or savoring something.

His voice drops low, thick with amusement.

"I was playing."

His grin is sharp, full of teeth.

"You're naïve," he spits the words with a snake-like grin, like they taste bad.

And then he lets go.

But we're still close to each other, too close for comfort. Nick is smiling, enjoying it, like he now owns the tiny space between us.

Ding.

The elevator doors glide open.

A sharp cough.

Coño de la madre.

"Bo?" Eric's voice makes me almost faint.

His uniform is rumpled, his hair disheveled, like he's been through a shift that drained the life out of him, as usual. His jaw tightens slightly as his stare flickers between me and Nick, scanning too much, too fast.

"Weren't you sick?"

The way he says it isn't an accusation, but it isn't nothing, either. And I like it.

13 Use at Your Own Risk

His fingers play absently with his earbuds case, turning it over and slipping it between his knuckles.

But his eyes are sharp.

They flick from me to Nick.

Then back to me.

I swallow.

"I was dying in the morning, not so much anymore," I say in a small voice.

I can't move, and Nick is pulling me this time. He does it so naturally, like we've been doing this dance forever, like it's second nature for him to close the space between us. His grin twitches, barely contained like he's watching something hilarious unfold.

I want to die.

"How are you today?" I ask because I don't know what else to do.

Eric just shrugs, barely looking up.

"Did you see what I sent you?" I try again.

He pulls out his phone, scrolling distractedly but too forcefully, like he wants to break the screen.

"Yes, but I have no idea who you mean. What bald person from the other day?"

I open my mouth to respond, and Nick, who has been perfectly silent until now, lets out a loud, exaggerated gasp.

"The other one at the front desk!" he squeaks, like he's been holding back all this time. "Are you guys, like, dating or what?"

I wish the elevator cables would snap, and we would just plummet to our deaths right now.

Eric winces. His shoulders stiffen, his grip on the phone tightens, his eyes harden.

Neither of us answers.

But I want him to answer.

Even if it's a lie, I want to hear it.
I want him to pretend to like me as much as I pretend to like him.

We don't get the chance.

The elevator dings again.

Eric's floor. He steps out without looking back. No hesitation, no parting glance. He's just gone.

The doors slide shut. And I collapse to the floor, hugging my knees.

GLOWROT

Stupid. Stupid. Stupid. Stupid. Stupid. Stupid. Stupid. Stupid. Stupid. Stupid. Idiot. Stupid. Stupid. Stupid. Stupid. Stupid. Stupid. Stupid. Stupid. Stupid. Stupid. Stupid. Stupid. Idiot. Stupid. Stupid. Stupid. Stupid. Stupid. Stupid. Stupid. Stupid. Stupid. Stupid. Stupid. Stupid. Stupid. Stupid. Stupid. Stupid. Idiot. Stupid. Stupid. Stupid. Stupid. Stupid. Stupid. Stupid. Stupid. Stupid. Stupid. Stupid. Stupid. Idiot. Stupid. Idiot.

The world keeps moving, the elevator keeps going up. The weight of the stranger beside me makes me open my eyes, which I didn't realize were closed in the first place.

"Can you pick me up?" He whispers in my ear, so close to it that I can feel his spit make its way down my ear duct like a bug.

> *It's so easy to not have to think,*
>
> > *to let myself be ordered around like this.*

He strokes the back of my neck with his fingers and wraps his hands around me.

I could get used to it.

"Aren't you embarrassed to reveal that you have mommy issues to a stranger?" I ask and stand up without thinking about it.

He's clinging to my back like a monkey, and I walk out of the elevator, dragging my feet.

"We're not strangers, *nena*, we're Nick and Bo!" He announces, trying to strike a victorious pose with his hands up as we walk past the mirror, but cuts it off with a yawn.

We're on the hotel's top floor, and I can't help but look to the side as I follow the hallway he pointed out. He won't tell me the room number.

"More, more. A little more. That's right, keep going."

He babbles and sometimes shuffles his feet, his eyes completely closed, still half wrapped around me.

> *So close, so warm.*

"Hell yeah!" He screams when we come to a halt. "Put it in there!" he says, handing me the keycard and pointing to the enormous penthouse door.

I look at him, expecting him to laugh any second and turn around, but he does nothing.

He throws himself to the floor, waiting for me to do something or react. It has to be a joke. How could someone like him land the most expensive room in the entire hotel?

"*Bo, tengo sueño!*" He complains, shaking the keycard in front of my face. Like a spoiled child. "*Por favooooor?*"

"Well, since you said please…"

I don't know why I'm playing his game, but I grab the keycard from his hand and slide it on the door. It opens silently, like another omen.

Way too many for today.

I take one step forward, then another; he crawls over to collapse again, this time on the foyer floor, and stares at me as if I hold all the truths in the universe.

Something in the way he looks at me makes me feel less invisible. Or it may be the fake dependence game he's forced me to be part of.

He looks cute, with his hair completely messed up and his eyes lost somewhere between my nose bridge and my forehead.

Almost harmless.

Almost.

I can't bear to look at him any longer, not sure what I would do if we stayed like this.

This place is so different from my apartment that it's almost hard to believe they exist inside the same hotel.

It's not as big as I imagined, but the strangeness compensates for that. One giant room.

One uninterrupted wall of windows stretches from floor to ceiling. The glass is too clear, too clean. The outside world feels impossibly distant, like it isn't even real. Every time I glance in that direction, a frightening sense of VERTIGO grips me, like I might tip forward and fall through it, straight into nothing.

If Alexia was here, she'd call me an idiot for walking into a hotel room with a man I barely know.

She'd be right.

I turn away from the windows.

The coffee tables don't make sense either.

They're low, too smooth, the same color as the floor, and almost look like they're merging into it. I nearly expect them to sink into the carpet entirely if I blink too long.

They're covered in a pink powder I don't want to name.

Jars of liquids of unnatural colors clutter the countertops, sealed but somehow still fizzing, still alive.

The fridge hums louder than it should, and its door is fully open. Inside, half-eaten candy sits exposed, forgotten. The air is thick with the scent of sugar and something sharper beneath it.

Like everything around him.

The bed is a mountain of pillows and cushions, stacked so chaotically that I can't even see the mattress beneath them.

The wall is decorated with clocks. They tick too fast, then too slow. In unison, yet not one of them is telling the right time.

Has the penthouse always looked like this, or did he decorate it in the few days he's stayed here?

Nick's voice drags me back to the moment.

"Ah, you like it, don't you?"

I freeze.

He's right behind me.

When did he stand up?

Why is it that every guy I meet has a habit of coming at me from behind without warning?

Before I can step away, he grabs the hem of my dress and tugs me toward the bed.

He collapses onto it, wrapping himself around one of the oversized cushions, sinking into the ridiculous mass of pillows like he's been here forever.

The candy has almost disintegrated in his tongue, entirely red now.

His gaze flicks up.

"How much do you want?" He looks at me expectantly, and I stand there confused, having no idea what I've gotten myself into.

Is he offering me money?

"What? No!" I step back and bump one ankle with another. He laughs and rubs his eyes.

"I can't believe how much you bark but how little you bite."

He's having fun making me squirm.

And for a second, I can't even remember why I'm here in the first place.

Ah. Right.

La empanada.

And NIU.

13 Use at Your Own Risk

I exhale through my nose and throw myself on the bed next to him. Nick doesn't stop me.

I pull his heart-shaped glasses off his face and slide them onto mine without asking, ignoring his half-hearted protests.

I glare at him through the pink-tinted lenses.

"Tell me everything you know," I whisper, moving closer than I should.

Trying to beat him at his own game.

The thud of my shoes hitting the floor after I kick them feels like an exclamation mark. Or maybe a period. Nick purrs and fiddles with my white locks. We look at each other for a few seconds, and then, without warning me, he takes what's left of the candy from his mouth and shoves it into mine.

I swallow it whole.

"I think you realize I have money." His fingers trace along the collar of my dress.

"People ask me for favors. I don't ask questions."

"I don't care about your money, Nick," I lie. "I'm talking about NIU."

It's obvious this is a ridiculous decision, even by my standards. I'm in the room of someone I barely know who could throw me out of the window in a millisecond, and he keeps looking at me with those eyes.

The entire scene feels different looking at it through these glasses, like it's not real, not entirely.

And if it's not real, it can't hurt me. Right?

I know it's not right, but my blood bubbles with the adrenaline of the unexpected; the mere thought that I might have made a mistake that cost me my life makes me feel pricks of electricity all over my body.

I smile.

"Ok, but it's your fault. Talking about strippers turns me on," he whispers, with the expression of a scolded child. He looks at me, evaluating my reactions, perhaps wanting to know whether to take another step, or a leap.

"Let's play a game."

I can't take it back now.

Nick perks up immediately.

A second ago, he was half-asleep, practically sinking into the bed. But now? He snaps upright and leans in, teeth flashing as he bites the air near my face, like a wolf snapping at prey that's just out of reach.

His smile is unreadable.

GLOWROT

I think about what he told me, but what he has no idea about is how far I'm capable of going to find answers.

"Like what?"

Even with his black curls obscuring parts of his face, his eyes glitter with sharp, undeniable curiosity.

I don't let myself hesitate.

"Twenty questions. I start."

Nick doesn't answer.

Instead, he barks.

It's abrupt, a sound that shouldn't belong here. The absurdity makes me laugh before I can stop myself.

I reach out absentmindedly, toying with the collar of his open shirt. He still hasn't buttoned it since we left the pool, his skin warm under my fingertips. I'm shivering, freezing, but Nick seems untouched by the cold like his body runs at an entirely different temperature.

"What do you remember about NIU?" I ask, and he yawns as if he's been expecting something else. It's theatrical. Drawn out.

"Not much, what I told you. I've only been there a couple of times." He rolls his eyes, then coughs and grabs my thigh. "Their asses, those I remember."

His fingers graze the scratches on my arm. I jerk away on instinct, but he tries again.

This time, I sigh and let him touch them.

His fingers trace the letters slowly, deliberately, far gentler than I ever would have expected from him. He stares at them like he's reading something private, something only meant for me.

Then he looks at me.

"Why?" He asks in a whisper.

"I've been going for a few days, and I didn't know if I'd imagined it." I'd rather stare at the ceiling than admit the absurdity of my situation by looking into his eyes. "I did this hoping to remind myself. What do you do for work?"

Maybe that's why he knows about NIU.

"The whole thing about parties I said when we met wasn't a joke; sometimes people hire me because they need someone to keep things moving."

He rolls his hips, a lazy, exaggerated movement, dancing to an invisible melody. I snort despite myself. I should be uncomfortable, but I'm not.

13 Use at Your Own Risk

"Other times, I cry at funerals. Weird shit from rich people who want to throw their money away, and I'm happy to receive it, obviously."

He yawns again, and I can't take my eyes off him. He's beautiful, with his delicate features and snake-like smile. I look at him for a second, and he looks at me.

"I thought you were selling drugs," My voice drops lower, conspiratorial. For a second, there's silence. Then, we both burst into laughter at the same time.

"Beyoncé or Rihanna?" His random-ass question slams into me like a brick. It takes me a second too long to process it.

"Beyoncé?" I answer with some hesitation as if he's testing me.

Before I can react, he throws his arms around me, dragging me down.

I fall forward, landing on top of him. His body is solid beneath mine, warm and comfortable.

Too comfortable.

I shift, knees pressing into the bed on either side of him.

His eyes gleam.

"Have you ever seen anyone you know in NIU?" I drop my voice lower, careful not to lose his interest again. "Or anyone you've seen there, outside that place too?"

"I think you." He's staring blankly and stammering, he's falling asleep. "Hey, can you pet my hair a little?"

"Me?!"

"Pets, please!!" He grabs my hands and pulls me to him, placing them on his head but making me lose my balance in the process.

I fall on top of him and end up with my nose in his neck, he smells of some citrus perfume I can't make out.

I settle in, still having him trapped between my legs, and without really knowing why, I start nibbling on his jaw. I stroke his hair as he asked me to, and he relaxes like a tamed animal, but still squeezing my thighs.

"I don't know, because your hair is so white, sometimes it shines in the dark." I have to put my ear close to his lips to hear what he says, his voice is barely audible, "You were with a guy with tattoos, I think. Or several, several guys." He yawns in my ear and officially drops onto the bed.

Completely.

Like a puppet whose strings just got cut.

I shake him, but he doesn't respond. Instead, he wraps his arms around me, trapping me like a stuffed animal.

GLOWROT

His breath ghosts over my skin. I freeze. It takes me several minutes to untangle myself from him. I'm dazed, confused, and strangely excited when I finally pull away.

It's all real.

I'm not crazy.

Letting myself be dragged into this was worth it. It doesn't matter how insane the whole situation was.

And now that he's asleep, it's like his spell over me has been broken, and I can think again.

Think about what's important.

About them.

I have to find them.

When I manage to stand up, I walk barefoot to the refrigerator. It's not my house, but I don't mind too much rummaging through other people's stuff. Besides, I highly doubt he cares.

Among all the candy and things of dubious origin, I find a brown paper bag with two radioactive-looking, spicy empanadas.

Perfect.

I heat them up in the microwave and hesitate, because I don't know if it's a good idea to serve me some of the colored sodas I see.

What if they're something else?

I opt to fill a glass of water from the tap.

And just as I go to take the first bite, my blood freezes.

"you'veBeen

PrettyBad,Bo."

I don't see him, but I hear his voice inside my head. For a few seconds of my life, I had forgotten his existence.

Nick looks peaceful, melted into the bed, not even realizing there's a shadow crouched over him. W's long claws hover over the man's eyes for a split second, I freeze and look away.

I don't want to answer him, preferring to keep pretending he doesn't exist, but he jumps towards me.

Invading my space.

My lungs.

My brain.

13 Use at Your Own Risk

"youShouldn't
PlayWithStrangers."

He scolds me, and I suddenly feel like throwing up.

I bite down on the empanada to spite him, knowing I will most likely regret it in a few hours.

But I got what I wanted.

Neither W nor anyone else can convince me that it's not real, that I'm crazy, that they're all dreams.

And if I'm not the only one, and if at some point Nick saw me, it means that maybe I have hope of finding who I'm looking for.

My angel.

GLOWROT

14
Under New Management

It's impossible to focus.
Everything is so loud.
They don't make sense.
The sounds.
They're not mine. He put them there.
Static. Needles. Hammer, cut.
Whispers roaring.
He's doing this.
He wants to hurt me.
He's never this loud unless he wants me
to suffer.

I don't ask where he goes when he disappears. I never ask. But he always comes back angrier than when he left.

And now, he won't come near me. Won't talk to me directly. Just stands there, pressing against my mind, pushing, pushing, whispering in the walls, hissing between my ribs.

And I hate myself again.

I hate that I missed him.

I hate how comforting this feels.

Dizzy.
I stagger toward my apartment.
Room.
Whatever.
I had to stumble out of the penthouse. Had to tear myself away.

All because an impulse beyond what I can explain led me to plant myself in front of the giant window longer than I should.

And now I can't stop thinking about what would have happened if I had jumped.

My arm throbs.

I read the name over and over, trying to decipher any hidden meaning it might come to have.

I spell it out, try to taste it.

My mouth is dry. Smudged with the spice from the food I shouldn't have stolen from Nick.

It's not stealing.

He gave it to me.

Right?

I saved one for him, so it's fine; put it next to him on the bed. I'm a good person.

I'm a good person.

I'm a good person.

I'm a good person.

I'm a good person.

I'm a good person.

I'm a good person.

"playingHouseWithAStranger."

I hate how right he is.

It's the attention that does it, how Nick asks me questions and wants to hear the answers. How he treats me like we're already friends.

He acts like I'm interesting. Fun. Worth it. Alive.

When I get to my door, I close it at full speed, just as if I could shut W out.

But he's waiting for me already.

On the bed.

Staring.

The room is so much colder than it should be.

The tiles prick the soles of my feet.

My bare feet.

How long have I been walking like this?

I'm a fucking idiot.

Something hard is pressing against my palm, something I hadn't noticed I was squishing.

I let out a little squeak, my fingers tighten.

Smooth, light plastic. I bring it to my face like it's some kind of alien artifact.

Nick's heart-shaped glasses.

What?

I don't remember grabbing them, much less holding onto them this whole time. They feel warm, like they've been in my palm for hours.

Why?

But if I've been holding these, where's my—

MIERDA.

I throw them on the floor and start patting my pockets, pulling them inside out.

A receipt.

Lipstick.

Three coins.

The lighter.

Candy wrapper.

My phone.

I start breathing again.

At least I didn't lose it, ten points for me. I clutch it like it will vanish and open the notes app. Read and reread, again and again. Every single one of the notes I wrote in the morning. Pieces of a puzzle that I don't know what it's supposed to look like in the first place.

Then I open a new one and start typing everything I can about my interaction with Nick. Everything from his bandana to the way his teeth glisten.

Some words end up repeating more than once, but I prefer it that way.

They must be important.

Everything must mean something.

There must be some reason for having met him right when I'm going through this.

There has to be a reason for seeing moles everywhere, for the cobwebs, for the <u>white</u> lighter.

Flick me.

Why doesn't it work?

What is it even supposed to do?

Everything is connected, it has to be. There is no other logical explanation. It's real, perhaps the most real thing I have ever known in my life.

For the first time, I feel awake.

Fuck, for the first time, I *feel* something.

It's intoxicating, but I love it. Some sort of purpose after years of living like a zombie. After that horrible breakup, after having to drop out because I had to run away, after learning the American Dream is bullshit, after exchanging my soul from one type of misery to another one.

Finally, something else, something magnificent.

Dangerous.

Exciting.

<u>Wonderful.</u>

Do I have paper? Pencil?

I rummage through the things I have lying around as W's glowing gaze judges me. I know he knows something has changed but, as amazing as it seems to me, I don't feel him poking around inside my mind.

I pick up one of the many pens I stole from the front desk and a piece of the receipt I threw on the floor.

The notes on the phone are not good enough, not tangible enough.

Real, it needs to be as real as it feels.

I need to touch them. The words. Feel them with my fingers.

Maybe the words have other words inside, hidden, waiting for someone to come along and set them free.

I try to rearrange the letters of each thing that comes to my mind, and I'm unsure if I'm still breathing.

Shaking, thrilled.

Intoxicated still.

I can't fix my eyes on a particular point because they are too focused on the only important thing in my life right now.

And W quiet, so quiet.

Maybe he's realizing I'm not crazy. Maybe he can see now that I'm not making it up because the words are real, on the paper, on my fingers.

He can finally see what I see. He can't try to convince me that NIU is nothing more than a dream because now I remember. I remember it all. Now I know I'm not the only one, Nick saw me there.

And if NIU is real, it means everything in there is, and even more so, everything that has come out.

Them.

I reach for another piece of paper, this time the back of a book I never read and use it to jot down everything I remember that might serve as a feature to stand out from the rest.

Them.

Their moles, of course.

The spider web tattoo under their eye and the rabbit on their back.

14 Under New Management

Black, empty eyes.

Their bald scalp.

Pale skin and slanted eyes.

Slim, tall silhouette.

Skeletal.

Soft, delicate hands.

Thin lips, quiet smile.

Sad smile.

I read the pathetic description in list form. Is that it? How the fuck am I supposed to ask around with just this?

I can picture them so perfectly in my mind's eye, but the second I try to put words to them, they slip away.

They're too perfect to be described by someone like me, it has to be that.

And holy shit, I don't even know their name.

Why didn't I ever think to ask for their name?

I get to my feet and run out into the room.

The second I pass in front of W, he holds out his foot and tries to knock me off my feet. I stumble, but the nightstand saves me from a worse fate.

He's pissed.

Furious.

He grabs my wrist, and I feel his claws close around it. In every single one of my nerve endings.

The pain is electric, it spreads like wildfire under my flesh.

I feel him inside me.

Twisting.

It's a sensation I'm used to, but it doesn't make the pain go away, no matter how frequently I've experienced it. I turn to look at him even though I don't want to and lose myself in the two balls of light in his eyes and the absence of features in his shadowy face.

Trying to break free is idiotic.

He has full control now.

And I can't look away.

Something's different.

He changed.

His claws wrap around my other wrist.

Tighter.

Tighter.

Tighter.

Now I'm a puppet, his puppet.

Like when I was little, when I still fought, when I still thought ignoring him would make him disappear.

But he's here to stay.

He owns me.

And I can't look away.

"What?" I finally ask. My voice breaks and I taste tears running down my cheeks.

I need him to let go; I don't have time for this. I don't want to argue, I have to write down everything before I forget.

I can't forget again.

Not again.

I can't.

"it'sNotWorthIt," he tells me, and I don't know if I'm relieved that he finally spoke to me, or if I hate him for it.

The feeling of uneasiness increases, but at least his claws are no longer digging into my wrists.

Now, he grazes my skin as softly as possible and pulls me to him. I fall silent and try to hold my breath, his eyes are getting brighter and brighter. *Beautiful.*

So comforting.

"youKnowYouCan'tBelieve
AnyoneButMe."

A part of my brain knows it's right, and I smile. It's the docile, almost trained part that has helped me survive all this time. I know, after all, that the things W says and does are because that's how he feels it's right. To help me.

To protect me.

"I know you don't trust Nick… Or Eric… Or anyone else," I whisper, afraid of the sound of my own voice. "But you know it exists, you've been there with me before."

He stands up without saying anything and pulls me to the bathroom.

But I don't want to take a bath.

I'm too busy, I have to write down the stuff.

14 Under New Management

I just told you.

Not now.

No, please don't.

No!

Before I think about it, the boiling water is running down my skin, and I feel the drops make the wounds on my arm burn.

No, I have to go.

My nails hurt when I dig them on the floor, trying to get out of the bathtub.

My tears burn when I try to scream, but he muffles it with his hand.

He shushes me, wraps me on his arms. It should feel consoling, but it's suffocating.

Tighter and tighter.

Until I feel him in my bones.

Until I can't move.

Maybe I can go somewhere else with my brain. Maybe I don't need my body to move after all.

So, I let the water carry me; I use its murmur to try and transport myself back to the music and the colors, to find the missing piece of my puzzle.

"NoENOUGH!!!"

The scratches bring me back to reality, to the pain. I'm not sure if it's his claws or my nails doing it. I open my eyes and look at my feet, and the water starts to turn pink. I can only smile.

"It's important to me," I try to explain, unable to stop my cheeks from contracting.

"I'mTheOnlyOneThatKnowsWhat'sRightForYou"

I feel his breath, hot, on my neck.

"You'veMadeTooManyMistakesAlready"

He's right.

He would never hurt me.

The pain, I'm doing it to myself.

His smile stretches, feline, feral. He knows all the world's secrets and will never share them with me. But it's okay, I know I don't deserve them.

He knows better.

Some parts of my brain feel disconnected from each other, and a large percentage of my being moves to the back seat of my consciousness.

I'm not myself, finally.

And isn't that what I always wanted?

What I'm the best at.

To stop fighting it.

To stop questioning.

To just let go and let someone else tell me what's right.

I can sit back, in a corner, and watch.

It is already starting; my mind clouds and I remember over and over again the words that always come into my head before they happen.

This corner is my corner.

I have been here before, not just with W.

I was here when I first realized that what I wanted was different from what I was told I should want.

I was here when I tried to tell myself that maybe I didn't. That maybe if I just let go, let myself be carried along, it would all go away. That it would be a phase.

I hate that word.

But I've always known, and now I don't have to think.

My body is immobile, unable to tell if the falling water is hot or cold.

Every so many minutes, a spasm runs through it, and my neck twitches in ways that would make no sense in any other circumstance.

The smile is still there, an echo of his. The reflection in the bathtub faucet makes sure I remember.

Inhale, exhale.

Everything looks better from this corner.

"I know you're taking care of me, but—"

"allOutsidersAreDangerous."

"If NIU is dangerous, I still have to—"

Reasoning with him is futile. Maybe I am the one that's not being reasonable.

Something hammers through my brain, I try to push it away, but it's stronger than my will to disappear. A memory, a reflection of what doesn't exist anymore.

Did it ever?

Alexia.

Here we go again.

14 Under New Management

A hotel night like this one. My brain scrambled like the eggs we ate that morning.

Not again, not again. No more.

Exhausted, but back then, someone else was holding me.

She held me.

She let me fall apart on her chest, told me it was okay. She let me break down and swore it was going to be fine.

She whispered things.

Lies.

Told me she wasn't going anywhere.

But when I woke up, she wasn't there.

She left.

They always do.

"You're just too much, Bo. I just can't."

They always do.

But W always comes back.

Maybe if I smile more, he'll want to hear what I have to say. If I submerge more, I make the water hotter.

Maybe. Maybe.

The sensation of NEEDLES UNDER MY FINGERNAILS brings me back.

I try to scratch them with the water, but it's no use, never has been.

When was the last time that I did this?

Stop thinking about her.

There's someone new now.

I stay still and let my brain wander as my body moves on its own.

W's words hit me like a distant echo in a foreign language, they slowly draw shapes in front of me. Reality is slowly unraveling.

Perhaps because it is not real.

I am not real.

GLOWROT

None of this is.

Maybe I got it all wrong. Maybe nothing else but NIU is real. Maybe the only thing that matters is <u>the rabbit,</u> the moles.

Them.

Them.

Them.

Them.

Maybe I'm finally opening my eyes.

A purpose, a reason to live.

The puzzle pieces fit together so perfectly that I feel tears running down the cheeks of the body that, at this moment, doesn't quite belong to me.

I think I understand.

I think he does, too.

The claws loosen, but they don't let go. They never really do.

He's protecting me, holding me.

"You'veBeenDoingItWrong," he murmurs in my ear. Something has shifted inside him, inside me. **"You'llGetBurnedAgain."**

"Please," I can barely open my lips; the water starts sneaking in. "That place. Them. Please."

Maybe if I ask nicely.

Maybe I just need permission.

The water carries my breath away, taking it somewhere I can't follow.

W's eyes glow brighter inside my eyelids.

"YouWantTheFire?"

"Please."

"ThenBurn."

14 Under New Management

ForDisplayOnlY

The streets are already dissipating in my mind.

I'm not sure if I was driving or walking. How far away was I from home before finding it again?

It doesn't matter.

But what if it does?

The neon haze rumbles through my arm; the scratches have transformed into a neon tattoo that glows as my hair does with the changing of the lights.

Darkness invites me to the corners, it reminds me that I belong.

My skull reverberates with the music taking control of everyone and everything around me. It's inside me, it has been all along.

How long?

For how long have I been here?

I'm here now, nothing else matters, my senses let go.

I gulp down the almost toxic concoction served to me by one of the fuzzy-faced waitresses that swarm the place, the requirement to get into the VIP section.

Every time I come, I find them. Somewhere, somehow, they have to be here. We're connected, I feel it in the pull that has led me here before. The one pulsating through my veins.

I didn't need Nick or W to help or tell me what to do. I just need to follow it.

It's destiny.

My fingers curl around the white lighter in my pocket, my reminder of what's truly important. Fear consumed me the last time I was here, back when I didn't understand. It's useless to fight this place, it's where I belong.

I navigate the maze of bodies, limbs tugging at my clothes and lips, trying to get close to my skin.

Nothing has changed, but nothing is the same.

"IsThisWhatYouWanted?"

He's testing me, but I don't have time to prove him wrong. They're here, I know it. If only people weren't moving that much.

"WhatIfTheyNeverWere?" he says in a mocking tone.

I know he's upset. He has stopped tugging at my clothes and has resorted to making me feel guilty.

Like I'm hurting him.

But he knows me. He knows —better than anyone— that once I put my mind to something, I get it, no matter the cost.

I'm full of sweat, and I doubt it's mine.

Tasty.

Every time I try to take a step, the ground sinks, or I stub my toe on the toe of some wretch like me. But I keep going, grasping at the invisible thread connecting me to my goal as if my life depends on it.

Because it does.

I breathe normally again when I finally manage to escape the tangle of flesh and blood. There's residue on my skin, the stickiness of their touch; it makes its way through my body and clings from under my clothes.

I keep moving. I don't know where I'm going, but my body does. I'm nothing more than a passenger for my subconscious. And that's fine.

Better.

I reach the hallway with endless doors and take special care not to step on the syringes on the floor, or the dying bodies that fill it.

I know better.

I grab at hands, yank at arms, rip at collars, desperate to catch a glimpse of the rabbit on their back, but every time I think I have them, I don't. Every time, it's the wrong face. The wrong body. The wrong touch.

I taste copper. I don't know if it's mine.

The walls shift. The air warps.

I feel the pull again, dragging me forward, deeper, closer.

They're here, somewhere. They have to.

Somewhere, somehow, they have to be here.

We're connected.

I replay in my head over and over again the mental image Nick put in my head.

NIU is bigger than it seems. NIU is endless. Now I know that.

The lights flicker.

Then the world goes black.

Inhale, exhale.

Quiet, even though the music hasn't stopped.

The floor is trying to suck me in, the walls pull me back. W's eyes glow in the darkness, but his hands stand on his side. The wallpaper scratches me and he doesn't react, he doesn't carry me away, he doesn't clean the red dots decorating my skin.

I'll prove him wrong.

I'll show him this was the right choice.

With my hand shaking, I hold the <u>white</u> lighter before my eyes. The click echoes. The flame stutters.

It shouldn't work.

But it does.

The wall in front of me shines white, empty, like canvas.

Like invitation.

I begin, slowly at first, then faster.

CAMEO. 669. BO.

The wall tries to swallow the ink. I press harder.

CAMEO. 669. BO.

Again.

Again.

Again.

Someone passes behind me and pushes me against the wall. I continue, I can't stop now. Not when I already started, not when I'm so close.

I keep writing, illuminated by the faint, trembling flame.

My breath shudders, my fingers cramp, my vision blurs.

The hotel, so they know they saw me too.

My room, so they can find me.

My name, so they recognize me.

Because they're looking for me too.

Right?

That's why they've been trying to reach me. Their eyes the last time we met confessed it to me. I feel their desperation in mine, and I want to let them know I won't rest until we help each other, until we find each other again.

Again.

Again.

Again.

15 ForDisplayOnlY

The marker smears, my fingertips bleeding ink. It's worth it, everything is worth it if it means I'll find them.

When I reach the end of the corridor, all the lights come on.

I have left a thick line of words and numbers, like a trail of crumbs that can help them keep up with me.

"andNowWhat?"

His voice scratches my eyes.

"sometimesYou'reTooDumb."

I could swear he's almost having fun with the whole thing. Just another way of punishing me for not doing what he wants me to. But I can't get distracted, they need me. They need me, and I need to find them.

He comes closer, his eyes shine so brightly that I lose myself in them for a second.

He's smiling.

My lips part when he tilts my chin up with one claw.

"howDoYouKnow

TheOneYou'reLookingFor

WillFollowYou,

AndNotSomeoneElse?"

My stomach drops.

He's doing it on purpose.

He's worried.

He's jealous.

I freeze and clear my throat.

It's not possible. They know me. Their hands are used to my body, their lips feel at home with mine. I know they're looking.

They're *looking for me*, somewhere. They have to.

Somewhere, somehow, they have to be *looking for me*.

My knees lock, but I have to keep moving.

CAMEO. 669. BO. CAMEO. 669. BO. CAMEO. 669. BO. CAMEO. 669. BO. CAMEO. 669. BO. CAMEO. 669. BO. CAMEO. 669. BO. CAMEO. 669. CAMEO. 669. BO.CAMEO. 669. BO. CAMEO. 669. BO. CAMEO. 669. BO. CAMEO. 669. BO.CAMEO. 669. BO.CAMEO. 669. BO. CAMEO. 669. BO.CAMEO. 669. BO. CAMEO. 669. BO. CAMEO. 669. BO.CAMEO. 669. BO.CAMEO. 669. BO. CAMEO. 669. BO.CAMEO. 669. BO. CAMEO. 669. BO. CAMEO. 669. BO.

I keep writing like I can erase what he said.

GLOWROT

And here it is, on the other side, just as I guessed.

The seats are similar to those in the club but arranged differently. They surround the tubes and cages scattered around the place.

The ones trapped inside are different than the others, the ones I've grown used to.

I see the vacant eyes of the patrons and the sharp smiles of the strippers Nick mentioned.

I avert my gaze, pretending not to notice, and follow the line I've left on the wall.

CAMEO. 669. BO. CAMEO. 669. BO. CAMEO. 669. BO. CAMEO. 669. BO. CAMEO. 669. BO. CAMEO. 669. BO. CAMEO. 669. BO. CAMEO. 669. BO. CAMEO. 669. BO.

CAMEO. 669. CAMEO. 669. BO.CAMEO. 669. BO. CAMEO. 669. BO. CAMEO. 669. BO. CAMEO. 669. BO.CAMEO. 669. B

GLOWROT

The more I write, the more parts of me I leave behind, the easier it will be for them to find me.

I don't dare turn around, even though the back of my neck is itching to do so.

There's an unfamiliar presence behind me, then another, then another, then another.

W does nothing, says nothing.

My eyes are fixed on the tiles on the wall, changing color as I move away from the hallway exit.

The music plays here too, but it's a different tempo and is drowned out by laughter that doesn't seem entirely human.

My fingers cramp, but I continue to hold the lighter and the marker tightly, like two charms, not sure yet if it will be bad or good luck.

I repeat the words until they become letters.

Letters until they become lines.

Scribbles.

Until they become a part of me.

Until the ink comes from my fingers and the marker disappears, swallowed by its reflection on the floor.

The words are now figures without meaning or form, no longer static but dancing around me like shooting stars.

Blinding.

Beautiful.

The knowledge that my love will read it helps me keep going, despite feeling the edge of my shoes cutting into the skin around my ankles. It's the certainty that each time, the wait will be shorter.

How long has it been?

One hundred and ninety-two hours since the first moment I remember, that is not a gap in my memory. They are etched in the front of my brain, even if I have no logical explanation.

The lights flicker in unison and make the floor move with them.

I try to hold on to the wall, but the dizziness is followed by a countless urge to vomit. Instead of going forward, I go backward, and two arms greet me.

Reality is spinning.

Spin.

Spin.

Spin.

15 ForDisplayOnlY

Thousands of pairs of glowing eyes looking at me expectantly.

The floor spins, but it's not floor. Something, a platform, a circle. Goes on and on and on. Spins.

Voices rising in crescendo. Echoes of themselves, of the lights. They spin. Spin.

The music has stopped.

I don't want to look back at them, but my head turns regardless. My arms move along my legs. I can only sit here and watch.

From a corner.

The lights beat almost as fast as my heart, and I slip and fall flat on my face every time I try to stand up.

The platform spins round and round. I can't figure out how to get off. I hold onto the tube next to me, and I can hear cheering.

Like I've done something good.

For a few seconds, I hold on to the tube, and just when I feel like I'm going to fall again, I hug it tighter.

They cheer. They laugh. They pant.

The pole is slick beneath my hands. My grip tightens. I slide up, down, up again.

Applause.

I fall, now on my knees and hit my forehead on the metal. A white goo spills down my brow, and I can't help but taste it when it hits my lips.

Expectant silence.

It tastes like piña colada.

Then, the screams increase.

They love me.

They love me.

They love me.

My skin tingles, but I can't tell if it's from the hands, the movement, or the way the room won't stop turning.

The platform begins to spin harder and harder, and I squeeze the tube tightly. I hug it with my legs, so I don't fall off.

Their cheers taste so good.

And I am thirsty.

I should get up. I should stop.

I don't.

My brain is shut down. Something is happening, I know it. Something beyond being trapped in a spinning circle on the ground.

But it doesn't matter, not now.

It's not until they start trying to brush against my knees or the tips of my toes that I open my eyes again.

Shiny pieces of paper are all around me, and thirsty eyes adorn salivating faces. And they come closer, closer and closer.

The graze is fleeting, but it's there. It multiplies exponentially with each passing second.

I look for a familiar silhouette among the crowd, but they're too close. It's getting harder and harder to breathe.

No rabbit.

No moles.

No cobwebs.

And even though the fingers touching me and not theirs, the contact feels good.

They feel like caresses telling me everything will be okay.

They confess that nothing exists but this moment, going round and round.

A white object falls next to me, but I have forgotten its name.

The almost extinguished flame brushes my knee but doesn't burn.

"The race is over!"

"Everybody has won, and all must have prizes!"

I don't know who says it first, but the words echo from every mouth.

"Everybody has won, and all must have prizes."

"Everybody has won, and you are the prize."

Their hands are too close now. They move with the platform, in perfect sync, in perfect unison.

Their mouths part, and I can hear their breath quicken.

I don't need to look, I know W's there. I can feel his presence close, quiet. I can feel his stare.

"You are the prize."

"You are the prize."

"You are the prize."

"You are the prize."

"You are the prize."

"You are the prize."

"You are the prize."

"You are the prize."

"You are the prize."

"You are the prize."

"You are the prize."
"You are the prize."
"You are the prize."
"You are the prize."
"You are the prize."
"You are the prize."
"You are the prize."
"You are the prize."
"You are the prize."
"You are the prize."
"You are the prize."
"You are the prize."
"You are the prize."
"You are the prize."
"You are the prize."
"You are the prize."
"You are the prize."

The echoes continue, fusing together.

And W watches.

He doesn't stop me.

The lights flicker one last time, and I don't know if I'm falling or floating.

Teeth glisten.

Did I win?

GLOWROT

16
No Vacancy

I think I just swallowed a mosquito.

I'm still spinning.

Fuck me.

I can't stop coughing, so much that tears are shooting out of my eyes. They burn neon colors in my skull.

What time is it?

I hope she's in pain, that the fucking bug is being crushed by the walls of my scratchy throat.

Had she been drinking too much blood?

Am I a vampire now?

I shouldn't be here; I have more important things to do than just be here. Now I know.

I was supposed to stay. To spin. I had won.

The eyes, the hands, the voices. They wanted me, I let them take me. But now I'm—

I press my fingers against my temples.

The lights are too bright.

My shoulders feel itchy, and I duck under the reception counter to avoid eye contact with a guest. I can't waste my time with people anymore, irrelevant.

Not real.

My hands shake, and my chest burns. I rub at it, where my heartbeat still pounds too fast, too wild, like I never actually left.

Why am I here?

An intense burning starts in my armpits, taking over my whole body like in every coughing fit.

I smile.

"At least cover your mouth. What the fuck," Nova says with a laugh but looks at me wearily. Like I have some parasite sticking out of my forehead. "Do you need a mask or something?"

"It's... a mosquito," I can barely say.

W stares at me from the back wall, refusing to give me a hand.

"A what?!" She sounds amused, but her eyes betray her.

Nova's eyes flicker toward her phone.

Texting.

Watching.

Telling someone.

Who?

What is she saying about me?

She thinks I don't notice.

I snatch my makeup bag, still filled with everything except makeup, and sprint to the bathroom, nearly colliding with the swarm of idiots pouring in for whatever stupid, meaningless long weekend they've decided to waste here.

My eyelids can't open all the way, it feels like saliva will escape my lips at any moment, and as I walk, my body rocks back and forth almost imperceptibly.

I make sure no one is in the reception restroom and look in the mirror, but I don't recognize the person on the other side.

Maybe if I come closer, I can go through it.

I press my face against it, but it just laughs back. I try again, and again. Nothing.

I turn on the faucet and let the hot water run over my hands until I stop feeling cold. The warm sensation runs along my nerves, from my knees to my forehead.

A faint neon line bleeds from my nose, but the second I blink, it's gone.

The lights flicker and buzz.

Everything, too familiar.

Everything, too different.

A sudden noise rips through the silence, and I have to muffle a scream. The sound of a toilet flushing behind me makes my breath skip. I'm not

16 No Vacancy

as alone as I thought.

The stall door creaks open.

The woman steps out. Too slowly.

She's tall, wrapped in expensive clothes that I have only seen in the windows of shopping malls where I don't dare to set foot in a single store.

She looks like a mannequin, her skin too smooth to be real. Her face doesn't move right.

She doesn't even notice me, and I don't blame her.

I'm just part of the furniture for them when I'm in uniform. And when I don't, I become an orphaned street dog.

Her hands move automatically, too practiced, washing under the stream of tap water. She rubs the soap between her fingers, again and again and again, like she's trying to scrub something invisible off her skin.

Her fingers pull her skin too far back when she stretches her face to fix her lipstick, like doing it enough times will make it permanent.

Then, she leans down to the faucet and drinks directly from the tap.

I freeze.

The water dribbles down her chin, over the red smudges of her lipstick. She doesn't blink. Her short heels click against the tile as she turns on and glides toward the exit.

She never looks at me.

Not even once.

When the door swings shut behind her, I start breathing again.

Shaking, I scan the bathroom through the mirror as if its reflection was accurate. Checking every single stall, making sure no feet are sticking out or shadows that shouldn't be there.

The coughing fit again.

Am I allergic to mosquitoes?

Without even thinking about it, I open the case and take out the bottle of pills. My throat still hurts, and I force myself to sneeze. Once, then again and again.

The two turquoise blue anti-allergy pills look like candy in the center of my hand. I swallow them dry, then help myself to the hot water that hasn't stopped running since I opened it.

"RegrettingItAlready?" says the voice that has been with me since I came into existence.

But I'm not upset; two can play this game. At least he's not actively stopping me from doing anything. He's just watching, expecting me to fail, waiting for me to beg him for help.

He'll see.

I'll show him.

At least he's not antagonizing me about NIU.

The smile the mirror reflects back seems different. I grit my teeth and open my eyelids wider than usual, softening my expression and pretending I'm talking to anyone.

It doesn't look that bad. I almost seem normal.

It's not like anyone would care anyway.

It's not like it matters.

As I leave the bathroom, I see that Nova has finished carefully sorting the envelopes of the guests who arrived a couple of hours ago. She looks at her work satisfactorily, like someone else, but she cares.

"Did you see a woman walk by?"

"Bo, we literally work at a hotel. I've seen people walk by the whole day."

She's texting again.

Is she talking to Nina? What are they saying?

"Excuse me," a vaguely familiar voice says as I walk back behind the counter.

Nova shrieks and continues with the envelopes.

I turn around. It's him, the tall man with the belly and the long mustache. His eyes are piercing through my brain.

"Hello again," he says, but the way he lingers on the words makes it sound like he's not happy to see me.

He hesitates before stepping closer to the counter. I don't think he wants to.

"You—" His gaze flickers over to my arm, covered by a sleeve this time. His jaw tenses. "You work here often, yes?"

Nova shifts uneasily beside me.

"Unfortunately," I mutter. I don't have time for this.

He exhales through his nose, and the mustache twitches slightly.

"I am looking for someone."

A thrill shoots through my chest.

Them.

"Who?" I lean over the counter, my tone too loud to be considered normal, acceptable.

He steps back and flinches.

16 No Vacancy

"My coworkers." His words are drowned out, slow, painful. "Everyone else missed a lunch meeting; they were here last night, but——" He swallows and turns to look at Nova, even if she's trying to ignore him. "Their things are still in their rooms, so they didn't leave. Does this happen... often?"

"What does that even mean?" Nova whispers to herself, and when she realizes she has said it out loud, she turns around and pretends to be doing something else.

It's the same weird attitude she had when we saw him for the first time. The first time I have truly seen her uncomfortable.

And this man, the way the rest of them were behaving. Something, a piece of the puzzle, so close I can taste it.

Everything is connected.

Nothing is a coincidence.

"Where were you?" I ask before I can catch myself. W's eyes flicker, but he stays quiet.

"In my room," he responds, but his face tells me he knows exactly what I mean.

"No. The other day. Yesterday? When you came back through the door. With them. Your wallet."

It's so hard to put long sentences together.

"We went drinking——"

"Where?!" My throat scratches, and I cough again.

Nova texts behind my back. I can hear the clack of her nails against the screen.

"Somewhere I wouldn't go back again." He inhales sharply. "I wouldn't recommend that place to anyone."

"If your friends disappeared, you should call 911; we're not the police," Nova says, exasperated, but she still has fear in her voice.

Like she understands.

Like she knows.

He watches me, waiting for a reaction. I stare back, refusing to blink first.

For a moment, it's silent.

"A rabbit," I try but my brain is scrambled. He furrows his brow, and I try again: "someone with a rabbit tattooed on their back. Bald, tall, skinny. Have you seen them?"

"Bo, you can't ask the guests about other guests!" Nova grabs my wrist and pulls me back. I feel her fingers start to twitch, like a tic that's coming back to her.

A pause.

A long, awful pause.

"I don't know what you're talking about," the man responds with an exhalation.

Liar.

My nails dig into the counter.

"Think." My voice comes out cracked, a whisper barely held together. "A spiderweb under their eye, moles all over their face. Black eyes. Pale skin. No hair. Did-you-see-them?"

His mustache twitches.

W laughs.

"No," he says, his upper lip trembling under the mustache.

I nearly scream.

"I KNOW YOU'VE BEEN TO THAT PLACE. I KNOW YOU SAW THEM!"

"Holy shit Bo what the fuck?!"

Nova thinks I didn't notice, but I do. She knows, too. Her twitching gives it again.

She knows exactly what I'm talking about.

I grab at the counter like I'm going to climb over it.

"WHERE ARE THEY?!"

He takes a step back.

Not irritated.

Not confused.

Afraid.

Like something clicked into place in his head, and he suddenly sees something in me that he shouldn't.

Like I'm the thing he should be running from.

"If you find out where my coworkers are, let me know." He's ignoring me, talking only to Nova now. "Room 711."

"Give me some gum."

The man has disappeared in the blink of an eye, and in his place, I see an arm outstretched towards Nova.

The fingers at one end of the hand wiggle expectantly, nails half-painted black. And on the other side, Eric's dark curls beckon to me.

She's no longer holding my wrist; it's like the world has skipped forward in time.

16 No Vacancy

I can still hear the man.

Room 711

What does it mean?

What does it mean?

What does it mean?

What does it mean?

What does it mean?

What does it mean?

What does it mean?

"What, did you get out of school early?"

She scoffs, bursting into laughter, everything is back to normal. It can't be.

"You know I graduated two months ago, idiot," he says as he gestures to spit in her direction, "Besides, it would be vacation time anyways."

I thought it was just a long weekend.

He looks nice today, I wish I cared. I bite my bottom lip and give him a smile, but it doesn't feel the same as before. He winks at me as Nova snorts and turns away to find what he asked for in her purse.

"Vacations don't exist when you grow up," she replies under her breath.

Her phone chimes.

She's hiding something.

"What were you doing outside, Mr. Graduate?"

He looks at me like I'm an alien. The words sound weird even to me. But I have to know. I see him open his lips, trying to answer.

"Oh, they let you go out alone?" The girl adds fuel to the fire as she hands him the gum. Interrupting me. Like she doesn't want me to know.

He puts it in his mouth, and his cheeks turn red.

"No! I mean, yes! I've always been able to go out alone. Bitch." he spits, his eyebrows twitching anxiously, not knowing what to say. "I was with my mom buying some stuff." He mumbles this last, lowering his gaze.

"My feet hurt," she announces, now it's her turn to go to the bathroom. Her hand wrapped around her phone, holding it close to her chest.

There's no one coming through any of the doors, and instead of leaving, Eric just leans against the counter, watching me.

When he's sure he has my absolute concentration, he turns his head to an angle he knows the cameras can't see and runs his tongue across his lips, leaving them glossy, wet, juicy.

"Do you still have no idea?" I ask in a very low tone like it's a secret.

He narrows his eyes.

"The only idea I have right now is about everything I'm thinking of doing to you." His words come out in a whisper that trails through the air, from his lips to mine and down my neck.

"The message, *estúpido*," I reply with a shudder.

"No one has come asking for <u>white</u> lighters, and I have no clue who you're talking about. I told you already." He inhales and exhales, leaning more on the counter. "But I can help you find some in the back."

If the cameras could see the perverted look with which he is caressing my collarbones, they would lock us both up.

"Did you go out drinking?"

"Bo, it's the middle of the day," he's just confused at this point. "Also, I don't have that ID with me. And I was with my mom, and I—" He stops and smirks. "Is this you being jealous?"

"There's a rabbit on their back, that's the important part." I don't have time to deal with his games.

"Why are you being so weird?"

His face shrivels.

A phone chimes behind him, but it's not the sound Nova uses.

"Your mom's calling you," a voice says and Eric walks away grumbling.

I want to scream.

The phone chimes again.

"That kid is so annoying. Does he still have that stupid crush on you?"

The voice.

The voice I ran away from.

The voice that's attached to the lips I've forced myself to forget.

The voice coming from the body I've been avoiding for months. Switching shifts when I know she'll be doing rounds.

Alexia.

Nova walks out of the bathroom, her nails clacking on the phone screen. The second she puts it away, my ex's phone chimes one more time.

Nova called her.

She set this up.

I finally look at Alexia; she's staring at me. Confused, worried.

Like something's wrong with me.

Like she was waiting for it to happen.

17
Help Wanted

"**Y**ou look upset. Is everything okay?." Her voice is collected.

Undisturbed.

It's the kind of calm of someone used to controlling every room she enters. Commanding but mellow. *Unshakable.*

Royal.

She knows I'm not stupid. This is clearly a setup.

Nova slips behind the counter like she's trying to disappear. She doesn't look at me. She doesn't need to.

Ashamed?

"I'm fine," I say, but it's hollow. A performance like hers.

"I hear a guest mumbling about someone from the reception screaming at them." She says, straight to the point.

No hesitation, no softening the blow.

Her posture is the same as when she's breaking up fights around the pool.

Like she's here to contain me.

Like she's expecting me to snap.

And I don't believe her for a second.

"Nova texted you."

It's not a question or an accusation, just a plain fact.

She doesn't deny it. She just watches me with that stare ready to cut me in half. The weight of her attention is suffocating.

Why is she here?

Does she still care?

"Are you doing okay, Bo?"

GLOWROT

My name on her lips sounds weird and bitter. The last time we really talked, she was holding me. Whispering promises into my hair. Saying she wouldn't leave.

Right before walking away while I was still passed out.

The rest has been just polite nods in the hallway.

Now, she stands there smiling like nothing happened, like she didn't break me, like she never once cared enough to lose sleep over me.

Like seeing me now doesn't shake her at all.

"I'm great, actually," I say slowly, trying to imitate her speaking style. "Very busy lately. But, like, busy good. I've been doing so many things I've barely had time to breathe. Are you doing good? Did you finally start therapy?"

Nova winces. I can feel the way she shrinks back, her fingers still stacking and restacking envelopes that don't need organizing. I see her turning her head towards the door with the corner of my eye.

But Alexia doesn't flinch.

Of course she doesn't.

Instead, she smiles, slow and practiced, too perfect. Not a single crack in the surface of her mask.

"Yes," she says. "I've been going for a while."

Her voice feels like velvet, and I want to be enveloped in it just one more time. I catch W's smile with a quick glance and force myself to be stronger; I won't let him win, and I won't ask for help.

Alexia hasn't stopped smiling, but her head twitches almost imperceptibly.

Like I hit a nerve.

Good.

She glances quickly at Nova and then back at me.

Nova's nails click against the counter, and she slides away from us. I hear her phone before she mutes it, the game she plays when bored. Or when she wants to tune everything out.

Nova doesn't get uncomfortable easily, but something about today has her fidgeting. Something tells me that it's not only my conversation with Alexia that has her like this.

It's that man.

Something about him, about what he said.

"Hey, have you seen any disappearing people?" I ask. Alexia looks at me, puzzled and caught off guard.

17 Help Wanted

"Any what?!" Her brow furrows.

"The guy you supposedly hear mumbling about me screaming—"

"I did hear him, Bo."

"Whatever," I say, waving it off. "That man. He came asking if we knew anything about his coworkers. They disappeared, he thinks. Isn't that something you're supposed to take care of?"

Alexia crosses her arms, shifting her weight to one side.

She's taller than me, stronger than me.

More feminine, more graceful in every way.

Like an obsidian sculpture. Polished and unbreakable.

Classy.

Elegant.

Strong.

"I'm Security, Bo," Her voice brings me back, low and smooth but also commanding. "Not the police."

The tension is pressing against my ribs.

Did I forget how to breathe?

Nova shuffles back toward us. She hesitates, glancing at Alexia, then at me.

"You can go home early," she blurts. Fast, sharp, but firm. She clears her throat and tries again. "It's clearly dead, and you've been sick, so yeah, go and rest, or something."

But I know by her face she regrets it the second it's out of her mouth. Even if she's trying to hide it.

She doesn't want to be the one pushing me out. But she doesn't want to be stuck here, watching this, either.

They planned this.

Alexia smiles and starts walking, slow enough so I can catch up with her but fast enough to rush me.

I protest, but Nova is already clocking me out and handing me my stuff. She doesn't look angry, but her stare is clearly a warning.

I drag my feet until I match Alexia's pace.

"I'm going home," I say, even though I know I don't owe her any explanation. The habit is too strong.

Maybe she cares.

Maybe she realized she missed me.

"I have to take the elevator, too," she responds with a smirk. And then, silence.

Her signature move. The kind of silence that stretches, tightening tension like a rope, waiting for the other person to crack. She's perfected it.

"ItAlwaysWorks," W mutters. He never liked her, but now he seems content. He wants me to break.

I.

Won't.

Ask.

Him.

For.

Help.

But I break, not with him but with her. Of course I do.

"I don't know what Nova told you, but I really am okay." The words come out slurred, like a child who has been caught doing something they shouldn't do.

"Her and Nina are worried—"

"Nina too?"

"They are worried about you," she interrupts my interruption. "And I *did* hear that man mumbling. You know you can't treat guests like that, it's literally my job to prevent that from happening. You'll get in trouble if you don't control yourself."

We cross the parking lot. She's all smiles, all warmth. The kind of effortless authority that should be intimidating, but instead, people lean into it.

They love her.

How couldn't they?

Everyone just feels immediately comfortable in her presence, like a benevolent queen.

"He was too much, was saying crazy stuff. I felt... attacked!" I lie; if she notices, she doesn't show. "He said his coworkers went to this crazy nightclub and never returned. He said the name is NIU. Have you ever heard of it?"

I try to hold myself still. Not too eager, not too desperate.

But I am.

She knows everyone. She sees everything. Maybe she knows NIU.

Like Nick.

Like that man.

17 Help Wanted

She doesn't answer right away. She takes her time, looking around and smiling at everyone she recognizes. They smile back.

Again, the silence.

But this time, it's different.

She knows something.

She has to know something.

I knew it.

She tilts her head slightly when we reach the elevators, like trying to brush off dust from a memory.

"I've heard it before," she says finally, like it's barely worth mentioning. "A couple drunks have talked about it in passing." She shrugs, so casual, so dismissive, like it's not the most important thing I've ever heard. "Nothing out of the ordinary."

Nothing out of the ordinary.

I want to scream at her. Shake her. Tell her she doesn't understand.

But I don't. Because I need more.

I soften my voice. Try to make it sound like I don't care as much as I do, distracting myself with the elevator button to avoid looking at her in the eyes.

"How did they look?"

"Like random people. I think. Why are you asking me all of this?"

"Did they have any tattoos?" I turn around for a second and immediately regret it.

Alexia turns around and looks at me like she sees something she doesn't like.

Like that night.

"Bo."

That's all she says.

Like a warning.

Like she knows.

Like she's watching me crumble apart again.

The elevator door opens, the older woman I saw in the bathroom steps out. Again, she doesn't notice me, but she smiles at her. We get in.

She pushes only the button that leads to my floor.

"You don't look very much in control, <u>Heart</u>."

The air drops out of my lungs.

That last word coming out of her lips, like she still cares.

I hate that it makes me want to forget what happened. I hate that I want to tell her everything.

But I won't.

"Maybe I don't need you watching over me anymore," I say, but my voice betrays me and cracks. "It's not like you care anyway."

But I want her to care.

She exhales, not quite frustrated, but with a sad tint on her voice I wasn't expecting.

And that's worse.

"I just want to make sure you're okay," she says, too soft. "I do care."

She doesn't.

I hate her.

The elevator door opens, and I storm off before she can see the way my hands won't stop shaking.

"YouDon'tSeem

VeryMuchInControl

RightNow."

His voice wraps around my spine.

He doesn't understand; she doesn't either.

No one does.

I run past the hallway mirror where I refuse to see myself, past the cleaning lady. And then slam my door so hard my shoulder pulses.

W sits on the kitchen counter, curled up like a cat.

I throw my stuff to the floor. The clatter is loud, but not loud enough. Nothing ever is.

I need proof.

I need to prove them all wrong.

Nick.

That man.

Alexia.

And I'm pretty sure Nova too, judging by how weird she was acting today.

They have heard of it, at least. Something is going on with that place. I grab my laptop, barely remembering how to breathe as I type.

strange club rumors Zampano

I type and forget to blink. The search page takes forever to load. I open another tab.

Zampano people disappearing after clubbing.

The same thing, like something is trying to restrict me from finding the truth.

But I'm smarter.

Another tab.

<u>Hallucinations after partying without drugs</u>

Urban legends from other places, creepypastas that look like they were written by a twelve-year-old. People trying to push some sort of game too hard. It's too obviously not real.

Nothing. Nothing.

A forum post, a few years old.

It's like it's been waiting for me.

ECHOES FROM ELSEWHERE

Trapped in Club?

Posted by: The5andAHalf || 2 years ago.

My friends dragged me and left me alone. Tried to breathe, lungs wouldn't work. Hands shaking so bad I thought my nails would fall off. Lights wouldn't stay still. Kept hiding. Kept fucking with me. Tried talking, but the words weren't real. Just noise. Couldn't tell if I was awake or if this was the dream and everything else was fake. Someone did this. They did this. Why? Couldn't remember what route we took. Couldn't find the door. Pink light. It was part of the wall, bleeding into it. Melting. Something next to me. A shape, glitching, breaking. Hands on me. Didn't scream. Didn't even fucking think to. Now I'm in the back. Can't feel my body anymore. Try to scratch my head but what if my hand goes through it? Time is not real. It never existed. I never said bye. Knocking on the door. Fuck. Low battery. Help. I think they're here.

I read through it without breathing.

It's too real. So real I can almost touch it. Like I'm back there.

But I have been there.

Nothing is a coincidence.

The user's account is gone, deactivated.

I keep scrolling. Keep searching. Most of it is noise. Conspiracy theories, delusions, people desperate to believe their lives are more interesting than they are.

But some of them feel different. Just a few.

They aren't pretending.

They're onto something.

And I think I am, too.

ECHOES FROM ELSEWHERE

Weird Club Experiences

Posted by: DancingLobster || 4 years ago.

I wasn't going to post this, but I need to know if anyone else has seen it and this seems like the right place to ask.

There's this place I remember finding a few months ago, it wasn't normal. I remember walking in, but I don't remember leaving. I woke up miles away. My clothes were wet, and my hands smelled like something burnt.

I thought it was a dream but it happened again last night. Since then I feel like someone's watching me.

It had a short name, but I can't remember it exactly.

Has this happened to anyone else?

Absolute silence. I can hear my heart beating in my ears. W is now sitting next to me, his claws on my shoulder.

He doesn't squeeze, not yet.

This thread is not empty like the other one.

It's mostly noise, people making jokes, or insane alien abduction theories.

They don't understand how important it is.

They can't.

But then something.

Hidden under all the trash.

ECHOES FROM ELSEWHERE

Re: Weird Club Experiences

Posted by: d0nni3 | | 4 years ago.

It's not a club. It's a door.

It's not a door. It's a mouth.

It swallows.

It swallows you whole, and you don't even notice.

Not until you look in the mirror and see something else staring back.

Stop searching. If it sees you looking, it will never stop watching.

The screen flickers, then goes dark. My stomach twists. I click everywhere, but the cursor is gone.

I press every key, over and over, until something finally happens.

The screen twitches back to life, lagging. But it's moving on its own.

The thread closes. The forum scrolls backward faster than I can process, skipping years in seconds.

I try to stop it. Try to exit. Try to do anything. But the more I fight it, the worse it gets.

Tabs open. More and more.

Threads buried in time.

This isn't a virus.

It's intentional.

Like it's talking to me. Like something is behind the screen.

And then, it stops.

One thread. One post.

17 Help Wanted

The first post ever made.

The text flickers, disappears, and comes back.

The username, illegible, broken symbols.

What?

Edited 2 minutes ago.

The screen glitches again, distorting.

Like it's breathing.

I rub my eyes.

> He doesn't interfere.
>
> He only watches.
>
> But once he sees you, he never looks away.

GLOWROT

18

Broken Glass Ahead

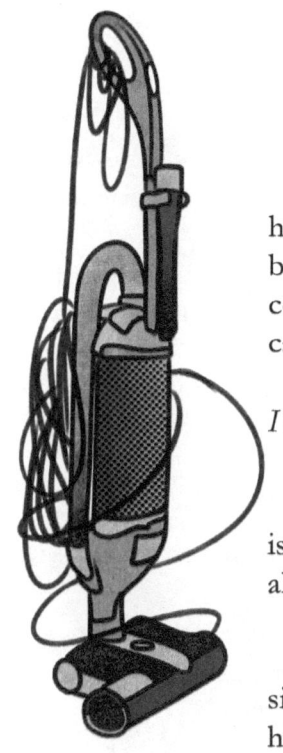

I'm not tired, not anymore.

I don't have time to be tired.

The buzzing in my skull has settled into a hum that tickles my scalp. My brain shouldn't be functioning after forty-eight hours of coffee, sleeplessness, and chasing something I can't even name. But it is. It's sharper than ever.

It's not even the first time. So, it's fine.

I'm fine.

Perfectly fine.

I take a breath, but it feels wrong. The air is too thick, too still. Like something else has already been breathing it before me.

My fingers twitch at my sides.

It's too quiet; not even the dishes in the sink make noise, not anymore. The AC stopped humming; a piece is missing inside it.

A piece of the puzzle?

The silence is swollen, like the room is holding its breath.

The wall is focused on me, white and wide like the rest. It sees me, like it can understand what I'm thinking. I don't doubt it.

It's been watching me the whole time.

Who else is watching now?

There! On the table.

The napkin I nearly forgot about, next to the dirty plate.

I pick it up and try to find the spot where it fits best.

Right there, next to the first receipt I put on the wall and the packaging of the empanadas, now covered in scribbles.

Perfect.

The words come together and intertwine like they've always belonged to each other.

They all do.

Little by little, I've been filling in the blanks with everything I come across.

Pieces of the puzzle, clues that They surely left for me to find.

They want me to find them.

They need my help.

They need me.

Names. Fragments of the songs I remember. Sketches of people. Eyes. Faces. A map that assures me that I will never again take my brain for granted, never again forget anything.

Whenever something remotely related to NIU appears in my head, I run to the nearest surface to write it down before it slips through my fingers.

There are pens and pencils in every pocket of my clothes, even the ones in my closet, just in case.

I can't forget.

Not when I am so close.

My masterpiece is staring back from the wall, but something is missing.

I can feel it.

I feel the memories crouching deep in my consciousness, crawling like a <u>caterpillar</u> and tickling me, bleeding in the process.

Like my finger.

Have I been bleeding for long?

I blink hard. The room flickers, like it's lagging behind reality.

Have I been sitting here too long?

The clock on my laptop blinks at me, useless. The time doesn't make sense. Nothing does.

When was the last time I drank water?

When was the last time I ate?

Irrelevant.

I crawl across the floor to find my phone and put on any song that sounds remotely similar to what usually exists inside NIU. The beat fills the silence, wrapping around me like a cocoon. I close my eyes, swaying, letting go, because that always brings the memories back.

A foreign sound.

My body reacts before I can think; the pen in my hand leaves my

18 Broken Glass Ahead

fingers, flying toward the noise. The sharp sound of plastic against wood barely registers before my pulse skyrockets.

The door is half-open.

Mocking me.

I choke back a scream before getting to my feet and running to it.

Are they here?

The hallway is desolate. The carpet yawns as I desperately search for any vestige, any trace of any living thing that has passed through in the last few seconds.

There's only the same cleaning woman —the one who never leaves— scrubbing the corners that join the wall to the ceiling.

I stare across the hall, squinting, my heartbeat trying to crack through my ribs. I have to fight the urge to open my mouth. Call out to someone who isn't there yet.

My arm itches. I scratch hard. Too hard.

A mosquito?

I probably deserve it. After all, I swallowed its friend. He's probably looking for revenge.

I leave the door ajar like before, making sure it's at an angle where no one can see in, but indicate I'm here.

"aStrangerIsGoingTo

ComeInAndHurtYou."

I shake my head and look at him with a smile, kinda thanking him for addressing me again. He doesn't believe I can do this alone, but I'm closer than before.

"Not a stranger, you know who I leave it open for." Every time I think of their gaze, my smile widens. "Besides, I closed it last night when I went to bed, didn't I."

Taking advantage of the fact that I'm standing, I stumble toward the fridge. My body is on autopilot, but my brain is dry.

There's a glass half full of some drink I don't recognize right now; I try to take it, but it slips through my fingers and falls to the floor.

Crashes.

The sound is too loud, too blunt.

I have to close my eyes to keep my balance and my heartbeat out of my throat.

My ears are ringing.

I wait.

GLOWROT

Nothing happens.

No one is coming.

I inhale, shuddering. Then, I kneel.

Big shards first, hands moving on their own. Into the trash. Small ones dig into my skin, sharp little kisses. My feet tingle as I stand, like something is tickling me.

The blood that comes out isn't enough to stain the floor. So, it's not a problem.

The music is still playing, but my brain has gone dry.

The wall is calling me.

I read and reread the notes already plastered across it, frantic lines cutting across pages of receipts, napkins, scraps of notebook paper. Anything I could find.

The things I know I can't forget.

Lines in every possible direction, drawings with trembling lines, an attempt at the artwork that decorates my senses every time I think of the last time we saw each other.

NIU.

Pink Light.

Watching.

Nova?

Where are They?

Nick?? Knows something??

The man at reception.

Coworkers.

Disappearances.

Alexia?

Motel street.

ECHOES FROM ELSEWHERE.

What else?

What else?

What else? What else? What else?

What else? What else?

What else? What else? What else? What else? What else? What else? What else?
What else? What else? What else? What else? What else? What else? What else?
What else? What else? What else? What else?

Tiene que haber algo más.

My neck twitches, and my vision blurs for a second. One of the glass
shards has somehow traveled under my toenail. I try to control my breath,
but it is controlling me instead. Quick, sharp, like the silence around me.
What else?

There is something I'm not seeing, something I've forgotten and
cannot dig out, no matter how hard I try.

Neon. Pink. Pink neon lights. N I U . Neon-NIU.

Neon-NIU lights are pink.

Like w h a t ?

lights. Signs. Neon signs.

Exist?

n o.

NOEXIT.

w h y ?

something'swrongIhavetofindthemsoon.
Con-nec-ted. Everythingis c o n n e c t e d.

to what?

the music   *the lights*   *the touch*

Missing.

GLOWROT

Missing.

missed.

Shh

SILENCE.

S o m e o n e   i s   w a t c h i n g

I peek back into the hallway; the woman is closer now, vacuuming the carpet.

There is a cobweb on the door in front of me, where no one lives, the one that is usually open. It's been closed for days now.

Or has it been weeks?

How come I never see anyone get in or out, no matter the time of day?

I'm sure the dark dots on the wood were not there last night. They look like moles.

I want to run inside the empty room, but the cleaning lady would see me.

Maybe it's not empty anymore.

I leave the door ajar once more and return to my project, to what's truly important.

I know the words I wrote on Niu's walls will help because everyone always sees them, no matter how crowded the place is.

I'll make sure they're still there when I go back, and if they cleaned them up, I'll write them again and again. Until

every single surface contains the name of the hotel, my room, and my own name.

I have no idea why They didn't tell me their name, but something inside my gut assures me that they know who I am, what my name is; and that they recognized me at the front desk.

So they'll find me.

They have to.

That's why leaving the door open is so important.

"someoneIsGoingToHurtYou."

I have a feeling that, if that were to happen, this time he wouldn't move a finger.

Maybe it happened already.

But that's not important.

Not now.

18 Broken Glass Ahead

Back to Them.

The most logical thing is that they're staying here, that they haven't come looking for me yet because they don't know how to.

Or maybe they can't.

Maybe they're forgetting, just like I did.

Maybe something is making them forget.

I grab a marker and scratch the word MEMORY onto the wall, over and over, until the letters become a smudge.

I step back, breath heavy, staring at it.

MEMORY.

Missing.

FIND THEM. FIND THEM. FIND THEM. FIND THEM.

Help

h e l p THEM.

where?

where? where?

where?

where? where? where?

where? where?

help them.

GLOWROT

My body trembles, my fingertips stained in red ink.
Or is it blood?

What if it's too late already?

No, that's impossible.

The thought freezes my veins, I'm so close, it can't be too late.

I just want to hold their body in my arms and kiss their scalp. To drag them out of whatever darkness is trapping them.

Because they have to be trapped.

That's why I have to save them.

I need to ask them to tell me about the times before, the ones I know happened, but my consciousness refuses to acknowledge them yet.

The music shifts.

I sway. I let go.

Side to side, back and forth. It's glorious.

It tastes like pineapple.

My bare feet crunch against the glass slivers.

I don't stop moving.

I'm floating.

The music isn't playing anymore, but I can still hear it.

The hairs on the back of my neck rise.

Someone is watching.

Someone is listening.

The music is back, like it never left.

But the screen of my phone is dark, and the battery sign flashes one more time before it dies.

The red marker rolls from my hand, tapping against the floor, once, twice.

A shadow moves under the door, but I don't dare look away from the wall.

19

Surveillance On

A week.

The wall smiles at me every time I leave the apartment and every time I come back.

Proud of me, of my progress.

I add to it in passing. Scribbled notes, torn receipts, whatever I have on hand. The connections are forming, stronger every day.

I keep my door open. Sometimes I forget to close it when I sleep. But that's fine. That's how They will find me.

Work still exists, I guess.

The clock still ticks, and my uniform sticks to my skin after hours under those awful lights. But everything outside the wall is garbage.

Static on a broken TV.

I know they've noticed.

But I don't care.

The way Nova looks at me when she thinks I won't catch it, all the drinks and little gifts Nina keeps bringing me. Pitying me. The mumbled words cut off when I enter the room.

I don't care.

They don't understand.

None of them do.

I tried to reach out to any of the people I felt were worth it from that weird forum, but it doesn't have a messaging system and my account is too new to even respond to threads.

Whatever, I don't need them.

I'll just have to rely on myself as usual.

Now I scurry through the corridors as if the very cobwebs I'm looking

GLOWROT

for so hard are trying to bind me to the walls so I can't go on. But I know I'm getting closer.

And I just fucking saw Them.

Them!

For some cursed reason, whenever I'm about to finally brush against their skin, the doors close, something falls, or someone walks by.

Something always happens, but I won't let it beat me.

Maybe fate is trying to play with me and trying its hardest to stop me, but I'm the most stubborn person I know and sometimes that has its advantages.

I've learned to smell their scent in the air, those smokey lavender tones.

That's why when I push through the emergency stairwell, I'm not surprised to see the edge of their fingers disappearing behind a corner.

My heart is about to rip my skin off.

This time.

This time, I'll reach them.

I pick up my pace.

They want this too. I know they do. We've been circling each other, spiraling more and more into this game with no beginning but hopefully an end soon. This trap that we're both creating around each other.

As I turn the corner, I see them moving through the parking lot, almost hovering. The rabbit on their back peeking from under their jacket.

This time, I'll do it.

I cross without thinking, without looking at my sides. It doesn't matter; nothing else matters other than them and how close I've gotten. How this time I'll be able to touch them.

My steps follow theirs without being too fast, making sure I'm not scaring them away.

They move through the parking lot with the grace of a praying mantis: tall, deliberate, distant.

No one watches them. No one stops them. The world doesn't know what to do with someone like them. It's like they don't fit the roles people expect, so they just disappear between the cracks. But I see them. I always see them.

Their whole existence is effortless and deliberate at the same time. Not soft, not sharp, not anything so simple. Just *them.*

The kind of beauty that can't be pinned down. That shouldn't exist, but it does anyway.

And they're getting away.

They slip past the valets without a glance, and I try to do the same. But before I can follow, an arm blocks my path.

"Damn girl, don't you say hello anymore?" The usual guy says, looking at the others.

"Sorry, I'm in a hurry," I answer with a smile as I watch the transparent doors close as they go through.

I can't stop.

They are leaving; I can't let them get lost again.

They need my help.

They're slipping away again.

I follow their footsteps until the door closes behind me. The entrance is almost deserted, and they don't stop for a second to look around.

They go in a straight line to the doors outside, and my heart skips a beat, startled.

Then they stop.

For a millisecond, I pick up my pace, ignoring that whoever is working today is looking at me strangely.

Meanwhile, I watch as their tattooed hand pulls the phone out of the back pocket of their pants. I lose myself in the curves hiding behind the leather that hugs their skin like there's no tomorrow.

They start walking again after staring at the screen for less time than they should have, so I could get closer without having to run.

Maybe They know someone is watching us.

They're trying to be cautious.

But now it's the doors leading out that close behind them.

I slip and skid to the handle, grabbing it before it's too late. The metal is cold and stubborn; I have to yank it open with both hands.

I almost shout a name I don't even know.

A black car with white lights is waiting.

They hesitate.

Not for long, not for enough time, but just enough for me to see how their shoulders stiffen before they move.

And a miracle happens.

They look at me again, really look at me. Like at that time in the elevator.

Their expression is unreadable, a mix between recognition and something else. Like a memory just out of reach.

Their eyes flicker over me, scanning, searching, but for what?

I open my mouth, the words stuck in my throat, but I swear—I swear on everything—that for a second, just before the door closes, they do the same.

"Bo!" the golden dream I'm living splinters as I hear a voice I know all too well yelling at me from a point of reality I wish didn't exist.

And after that, a horn threatens to drive me deaf.

"you'rePuttingYourselfInDangerAgain,"

W says. He's trying to contain himself; I know how easy it would be for him to step in. How easy it'll be for me, too, if he did.

"AtLeastLookBeforeThrowingYourselfToTheCarsLikeThat."

But he doesn't stop me.

As a hand yanks me back like a rag doll, I get out of the way. A car's horn screams past me before I can process what's happening.

Now I'm far again, away from the only reason I wake up every morning.

"Heart, you're going to get yourself killed!"

Alexia's voice cuts through the noise. Her braids snap against her shoulders as she shakes her head, exhaling like she can't believe she has to deal with this again.

With me.

Her grip on my arm lingers a second too long before she releases me. Then she steps back, scanning my face with those perpetually alert eyes by which I have come to recognize her all too well.

"I almost had it!" I scream without being able to contain myself.

She stiffens and looks around, not at me but for who else might be watching.

"Had what?"

"I needed to tell them something important," I try to speak normally, but my throat starts to close, and my voice wavers. "Why did you have to yank me away?"

Alexia stares at me like I have worms coming out of my nose.

"Bo, you were about to get run over. What the fuck?"

"But now they're gone," I whisper.

My hand trembles as I point down the road where the black car disappeared. Like I can still pull it back, as if it's not already too late. She tries to follow my gaze and frowns.

"Who's gone?"

"There, right now. Didn't you see?" I look at her without blinking.

"That guy?" She tilts her head toward a man getting into his car. "There's a gun in his glove box. These people come in here and think we're in a fucking videogame."

Her words come to my ears like a foreign language. I can't respond, can't focus. Not when their lingering smell is still flooding my senses, not when they were looking at me like that.

Again.

Pleading for help.

"This place brings in the worst kinds of people," she mutters and clicks her tongue, unaware I'm miles away from the point where we're both standing.

"You've seen them before?" I whisper, still looking in the direction the car disappeared on.

"The guy with the gun?"

"No, Them." My voice is almost begging now. "My—my friend. The bald one. With a rabbit on the back of their neck and a spider web under their right eye."

She takes a slow breath, tipping her head back like she's trying to keep her patience intact. Sweat glistens on her dark skin; she's probably been standing in the sun for too long. But she doesn't snap at me, doesn't mock me.

"Bo," she says carefully. "Do you know how many bald people pass through this hotel? It's like a fucking trend."

She laughs, placing her hands on the belt where I know she also carries a gun.

Her eyes are puffy and tired, but her white smile contrasts so beautifully with her lips that I forget to listen to what she's telling me for a second. I remember how they feel against mine and it almost makes me forget.

But no.

I can't forget.

"If you see them again," I whisper, "could you—could you let them know they left something at the front desk? That I have it?"

I'm pretty sure she doesn't sleep.

Not just because she's always at the entrance, by the pool, leaning against the front desk like she owns the place. Not just because she's the only security guard I've ever seen pull twenty-four-hour shifts, days in a row.

But because I remember the nights.

I remember waking up before sunrise and finding her still awake, still watching over me.

I remember how she ran her fingers over my arm and back like she was trying to remember every inch of my being.

Like she already knew she wouldn't stay.

Alexia could never rest. Not when she was with me.

And that's why she left.

Nova teases that she's a vampire, but I doubt it less and less.

If anyone can help me, it's her.

She looks at me with a gentleness I'm not used to anymore. She then tilts her head slightly, and I can see how her braids form a perfect <u>heart</u> above her ear.

I freeze.

She did that on purpose.

What kind of game is she playing now?

She was the one who walked away, the one who said that everything was too much.

Too much drama, too much crying, too much impulsivity, too much. Too much. Too much!

That's unimportant now.

She strokes one of her braids between her fingers, smirking before she winks at me.

"Only if you tell me why," she whispers almost inaudibly.

If it weren't for the uniform, the gun at her hip, and the command she carries in every movement, the question would have sounded innocent.

But Alexia doesn't ask innocent questions.

Is she jealous?

"Oh, it's just that they lost something a few days ago and I just found it and wanted to give it to them. That's all," I throw up the words without realizing it.

"nowYou'veJustGiven
TheOpportunityForOthers
ToTalkTrashAboutYou."

Alexia just smiles, that knowing smile that makes my stomach sink.

19 Surveillance On

She winks again, slow this time. Calculated.

She's smart. Of course she is. She wouldn't be here otherwise.

"But you have it, not anyone else at the front desk, right?" She arches her brow with a smile, but I sense discomfort in her voice.

Her fingertip traces a slow circle against my arm.

Is she flirting?

She has to be flirting.

But she was always good at this, wasn't she? Letting things sit between us, hanging in the air.

"No worries, I got you."

She laughs, lips parting just enough for a flash of white teeth.

And yet, there's something there, under the surface.

I don't have time for this.

Before I have time to react, she walks away, and I have to force myself to do the same before I completely forget what's important right now.

Because there's one thing left for me to do, and I have to take advantage of it now that I know They have left the hotel.

I've been thinking about it for days, but I was terrified that They would plant themselves in front of my door when I wasn't there.

"WhatNow,Bo?"

I don't want to answer them because, even though he hasn't stepped in lately, he would probably lose his shit if he knew what I'm planning to do.

I circle the parking lot so I don't have to deal with the valets again and go around the bushes.

It's now or never.

W suspects nothing as I enter the elevator and let the others push the buttons for their floors.

He just watches.

Like he's waiting.

For what?

I lean against the mirrored wall, forcing my mind to be blank because if I think too much, he'll see it. He'll know.

I have to be smart. Have to play the game.

I don't know for how much longer he'll decide to behave.

When the last one gets off the elevator, I pluck up my courage and touch the button that will take me straight to the top floor.

He stiffens, and his eyes become brighter.

I have to. If not now, I never will.

He doesn't follow when I step out. He stays in the elevator.

A test.

The doors slide shut behind me.

I know the way perfectly.

Something in my mind feels like it's going to snap.

I know the way perfectly; it's as if I've been secretly going over it in some corner of my mind daily. Like this is just another part of the obsession that allows me to continue with the will to live.

They key, this has to be the key.

I turn the corner of the hallway and start walking. I want to run, but I know I'll get lost in a spiral of madness that I won't get rid of if I lose control of it.

When I reach the end, I gather my courage and knock.

Softly at first, almost hesitantly.

Then harder, my knuckles trembling.

Nothing.

I sway, my weight tips against the wall. A sudden vertigo consumes me.

I knock again. Harder. Then I kick, first gently, then with force.

The hallway swallows the sound.

I lower myself to the ground, pressing my ear to the door, listening.

But there's no sound.

Nothing.

Like he was never here at all.

A pit opens in my stomach.

"heDoesn'tWantToSeeYou," he says, kneeling beside me and wrapping his arms around my waist.

I knew it.

I knew he wouldn't let me go far with this.

"How do you know that? You don't know anything." It's at this instant, when I hear my voice crack, that I notice I'm crying. I clear my throat. "Nick, Nick?" I move my lips near the bottom of the door, trying to be heard on the other side.

**"he'sNotGoingToHelpYou,
NoOneIs."**

There they are. W's sharp claws feel soft against my skin, even though they are scratching it. **"onlyICanDoThat,**

AndI'mTellingYou

YourLittleGameIsOver.

It'sTimeToGoHome."

"Nick?"

No answer.

"Nick, are you there?"

The silence grows. The air tightens.

W exhales, almost amused.

Then he moves.

His arms grab my waist and start dragging me away from the door, I try to clear the tears from my eyes by shaking my head, but it doesn't take long for more to appear.

I try to call out to him again, but the words no longer leave my lips.

I'm drowning.

I let myself be pulled.

The elevator doors slide open.

W presses me against the wall, his claws tracing my cheek, and I forget to be angry for a moment.

Because I know he doesn't mean to hurt me.

He just wants to help.

He's the only one who understands me.

The moment snaps. His hand moves toward the button.

Sixth floor.

I lurch forward, dragging his hand to the *first* floor instead.

And I smile, empty.

He says nothing.

I don't want to sleep anymore.

The doors open, and before he can stop me, I run.

Out of the lobby. Past the valet. Past the reception.

I don't stop.

I don't look.

I sprint down the driveway, across the street.

Everything is so bright.

A car horn is trying to split my skull in half. The tires screech against the asphalt.

My body locks up as the car swerves and misses me by inches.

The driver yells, something furious, something distant. But I don't hear it.

All I hear is the pounding in my ears, the echo of my own breath, the realization that I almost—

Almost.

I turn.

The car's taillights vanish into the dark.

Maybe the next pair of lights might finally run me over.

And if I'm lucky, the same lights might lead me to NIU again.

Back to Them.

To the moles I can't stop dreaming about.

Again.

And again.

20
Slippery When Wet

"Are you listening to me?"

Actually, I'm not.

I don't want to think about last night, about how Eric's mom almost ran me over. About how he was in the car and didn't do anything.

Not that I blame him.

I'm sure he knows I secretly want to die.

"You think everything happens for a reason?" I say it absently, more to the air than to him, and he chokes on his gum.

"What are you talking about? That's exactly what I'm saying! You've been acting weird as hell." He rolls his eyes and pulls his cheeks down with his fingers.

I glance at him with the corner of my eye, but my brain doesn't really process the details.

He looks tired; the dark circles below his eyes are bigger than the last time I saw him. Maybe it's his brother again, maybe his dad this time. Maybe it's nothing.

It doesn't really matter.

Instead of answering him I stare at a curl falling across his forehead and force a smile.

"Look, I've been busy lately, " I whisper, barely moving my lips, more out of habit than anything else.

"It's not like you owe me anything." He shrugs and pretends not to care, but I know him, and I know he's dying inside.

I know he's used to having me whenever he wants.

But that's a problem for him, not for me.

GLOWROT

He clears his throat and straightens up. I do the same, shifting into autopilot. The smile that got me this job slips onto my face before I even register the movement.

A male voice with a tone too tired to be this early in the morning greets us; Nina's voice greets him as I turn around.

The mailman is carrying a suitcase with packages and envelopes so heavy he has to separate them into three groups to put them on the counter. Nina's ponytail whips as if in slow motion, he turns to look at Eric and me and his pupils shrink.

"Not it."

"Not it."

They say in unison, placing their palms on their foreheads. It takes me a minute or two to understand what they mean.

What's written there?

One of the envelopes is a different color than the rest, black with gold lettering.

It stands out.

Is it a piece of the puzzle?

One of them grabs my elbow.

"Bo, we already said we are not it. It's your turn."

"My what?" My brain is lost three galaxies beyond this reality.

"Did you drink the coffee I got you? You look like you fell asleep." Nina bumps my shoulder playfully, her smile melts when I don't react. "Bo? Come one Bo, let's go." She sighs and pulls me by the wrist to where the new mail is.

I don't mind sorting the packages in the back. I don't mind it being light because the lamp still lacks a bulb.

At least cooped up there, I don't have to deal with annoying customers, and I can think.

Think about what's important.

It takes me three trips to load the boxes, and I balance the envelopes held together with rubber bands that are about to tear.

I clutch them like they'll disappear if I let go.

The paper looks so white, so empty.

Then it hits me.

MY FINGERNAILS ITCH.

Every name. Every guest. Every piece of information the hotel holds, right here in my hands.

20 Slippery When Wet

Them.

My angel.

I swallow hard and kick the door shut behind me, fumbling for my phone.

My eyes burn when I turn the flashlight on, but if that's the price I must pay to get answers, so be it.

"writeThemDown."

W's voice cuts through the silence like a knife. I do a double-take when I hear him. He's crouched in a corner, his smile illuminating it.

He's helping?

"doItOrYouWillForget."

Maybe he just hates Nick. Maybe he thinks this will drive me further from him. Or maybe, finally, he understands.

I choke a manic laugh, and my chest tightens; my smile widens so much that it makes my cheeks ache. My breath hitches. My skin feels electric.

I can't open any envelopes because I know they will notice, and there are no garbage cans here.

No loose papers or anything to lean on either.

So I pull the marker from my pocket, yank up my skirt, and start writing on my thigh.

Fast. Tight. Small. No wasted space.

I can't stop.

I only discard the ones I already know.

Every name is a key.

This is what I had to do, it's fate.

That has to be why I wore a skirt today.

"Oops, did I catch you at a bad time?" Eric's thick, musical voice makes me flinch.

How didn't I hear him come in?

My fingers tighten around the envelopes. The itch creeps under my skin, the letters blurring together. I have to keep writing. I have to keep going.

I adjust my skirt. How long has it been?

When I turn around, he sighs tiredly. He scrunches his eyes, he definitely didn't sleep last night. Maybe I should care.

But it doesn't matter.

The names are all that matter.

GLOWROT

The envelopes I've sorted sit in their respective lockers, but there are still too many left. I don't have time for this.

Not now.

Not with him.

Not again.

"What's wrong? Are you going to take a nap?" I ask quietly, without really looking at him.

I keep my eyes down.

He chuckles and takes the stool, leaning it against the door. Then, he sits on it and throws his head back. Curls fall down his forehead.

His smile is smug, like he knows exactly how this will go.

Of course he does.

BERNICE VUKOVIC

I repeat in my mind, hoping not to forget. My fingers itch, begging me to grab the marker again, to keep writing.

But he's watching me.

And I know what that means.

I know what's coming.

I know what it takes to make him leave.

The urge to kick him out, to scream, to throw something at his head is suffocating. But letting him do what he wants is faster than fighting.

It always is.

I exhale and grab a handful of envelopes, walking towards him. His eyes are closed, and his lips tense. Like something is hurting him.

Because something is hurting him.

And he wants me to take care of it.

I don't want to.

But this is how it works. We both know it.

NOE FINLEY

I read on, trying to burn all the names into my head. It's better to keep my hands moving and my mind somewhere else. Somewhere far away.

My muscles are stiff when I finally step between his legs.

He starts breathing more rapidly.

I don't look at him. I don't need to.

It's better if I don't.

I sit on his lap, and his fingers grasp my waist immediately, possessive. His breathing is already different. Hungrier.

"I was falling asleep," he mutters. Lying.

"My legs hurt, I have to sit down, and this is the only chair," I reply, my voice completely flat. Another lie.

VICTOR COLEMAN

I move to another envelope; I know he's getting comfortable by how he stirs under me.

I keep reading. Flipping envelopes, committing them to memory. *Not thinking about him.*

I move slightly. His body reacts.

I feel his hand on my thigh.

I want to throw up.

The marker is still clutched in my fist, pressed so tight against my palm it might snap in half.

I don't move. I don't pull away. I can't.

For a second I close my eyes and can see neon lights, but they get snatched away the second his hands travel up the tops of my thighs, until they reach my hips.

CODY SCOLA

He slowly raises the hem of my skirt, and I spread my legs because that's the easiest thing to do.

I keep clutching the envelopes, trying to memorize the names.

BERNICE VUKOVIC NOE FINLEY VICTOR COLEMAN CODY SCOLA

They have to be here, somewhere.

If I can just go back to it, if this finishes fast enough, maybe I can find their name hidden in the pile of all the other ones.

He straightens up, and I feel how his breath makes the skin on the back of my neck bristle.

But it doesn't feel good, not this time.

Not many of the other ones, either.

It's better if I don't think about that right now.

His fingers travel up my inner thighs and up under my skirt. He pinches them, not playfully but hard, just enough to make sure I feel it.

A sense of relief invades me because at least I sat down giving my back to him, so I don't really have to kiss him.

The touch of his hands awkwardly caresses the fabric of my underwear. I steal a glance at the next envelope. Try to focus on it. Try to stop feeling.

GLOWROT

JULIANA KAPONO

Think about the name.

Spell it out in my head.

J U L I A N A K A P O N O

His fingertips drag higher. My legs stay open because it's easier that way.

Don't tense up.

Don't resist.

With my feet firmly on the ground, I stand up just enough for Eric to slide his hands down and wrap them around me.

He finishes pulling up the back of my skirt, and I hear like he's undoing his belt frantically, like the world is going to end. Like he's going to explode himself.

BERNICE VUKOVIC NOE FINLEY VICTOR COLEMAN CODY SCOLA JULIANA KAPONO

My breathing doesn't change. My pulse doesn't spike. I don't move.

His knee knocks mine apart, forcing me to shift. It hurts.

I bite the inside of my cheek and swallow the sound.

Don't think about the bruise.

UTE RENAUD

Yes.

The names.

Think about the names.

I lean forward to try to get a good read of what the envelope says, but he pulls my underwear down and grabs my hips hard, making me sit back down.

I hold my breath.

BERNICE VUKOVIC NOE FINLEY VICTOR COLEMAN CODY SCOLA JULIANA KAPONO UTE RENAUD

Even if I had wanted this, I would never have been ready for his abruptness.

The eyes in the corner are watching. I can feel his gaze, his stillness.

He's not angry, jealous, or even entertained.

He's horrified.

He isn't speaking, he isn't trying to do anything. It's as if he's as frozen as I am.

And somehow, that is worse.

20 Slippery When Wet

Why aren't you stopping it?

I don't know if I mean him or myself.

But I can't. There's nothing I can do now but help it end faster.

I lift myself just enough to let Eric pull me back down, shifting against him because it has to end faster if I help. His fingernails draw lines on my hips, and end up leaving my skirt like a belt.

My legs are burning, but the muffled moans from his lips tell me I'm almost done with it.

I'm exhausted.

Spasms make me bend over, and my abdomen contracts.

It's not pleasure, I know it.

Deep down, I think he knows it too.

But he doesn't care.

His skin burns against mine, scalding hot, suffocating. My body wants to flinch, to shake him off, but I don't.

I won't.

I stare at nothing.

If I close my eyes, it'll be worse.

If I let myself think, it'll be worse.

I keep my hands flat on his legs, grounded, steady.

Just let it happen.

Just let it happen.

Just let it happen.

Just let it happen.

Just let it happen.

Just let it happen.

Just let it happen.

Just let it happen.

GLOWROT

Just let it happen.

                                                          Just let it happen.

                         Just let it happen.

          Just let it happen.

                                   Just let it happen.

                         Just let it happen.

          Just let it happen.

                                                          Just let it happen.

Just let it happen.

                                   Just let it happen.

                                        Just let it happen.

Just let it happen.

                                                          Just let it happen.

                                   Just let it happen.

                                   Just let it happen.

               Just let it happen.

                                                          Just let it happen.

20 Slippery When Wet

Just let it happen.

GLOWROT

W steps forward, I can't even look him in the eyes.

"Bo," he whispers in a tone I'm not used to hearing from him. Worried. Sad.

I shrug.

"I'm used to it, you know that," I mouth without making a sound.

I feel something sticky on my thigh. I don't react.

It'll be over soon.

I focus my eyes on the envelopes now lying sprawled on the floor. *The only thing that matters.*

REI NULL

Eric's arms wrap around me and break my concentration.

It hurts.

I start to shake, he chuckles.

BERNICE VUKOVIC NOE FINLEY COLEMAN SCOLA VICTOR CODY JULIANA KAPONO UTE RENAUD REI NULL

I inhale, inhale, but I forget how to exhale. I feel my blood bubbling, and it's not long before it reaches boiling point.

He lets out a guttural grunt and wraps his hands around my hips.

He stands up without warning, and the next second, I'm on my knees, my face almost glued to the floor and his abdomen bouncing against me with each thrust.

My hips ache from the impact.

Eric's movements turn frantic. Erratic. Mindless.

Like he isn't even thinking.

Like he doesn't even realize I'm here.

W recoils and takes a step back.

That's never happened before.

I clench my jaw. Bite the inside of my cheek.

LOUISE BROCK

"Fuck, fuck. Shit" I hear him whisper as he comes out of me faster than normal.

Something hot and wet drips down my spine.

I stay there for a few seconds, trying to breathe normally again.

BERNICE FINLEY NOE COLEMAN SCOLA VICTOR VUKOVIC CODY JULIANA UTE KAPONO RENAUD REI NULL LOUISE BROCK

The world spins around me, and I can't control the contractions in my limbs.

I'm not smiling, it's not necessary. He's not even looking at me.

I sit on my knees and look for another envelope with my eyes. Desperately.

TERRY MAKARIOS

One of those names has to be the one I'm looking for.

Behind me, Eric moves.

I hear the crinkle of napkins.

He holds out a handful, shifting from foot to foot.

I take them and wipe my back.

It's still warm.

"It wasn't what I was planning, okay? I just came prepared, just in case."

We both know that's a lie.

He smiles, I look away.

"What happened?" His voice is too casual, too normal. Like this is just another conversation. "Too tired?"

BERNICE FINLEY NOE COLEMAN SCOLA VICTOR VUKOVIC CODY JULIANA UTE KAPONO RENAUD REI NULL LOUISE BROCK TERRY MAKARIOS

"Do you need help getting up?"

"Uh?"

Why is he still here if he's done with me?

He shifts, uncomfortable. Like he knows what he's done.

Of course he does.

He exhales through his nose, rocking back on his heels.

"Damn," he mutters, rubbing a hand over his face. "I thought this was at least gonna help with your mood."

He laughs at his own joke. I fix the skirt so he can't see the names on my thighs.

Fuck.

The ink.

Did it smudge?

"I'm gonna take a nap," I say in a low tone.

It's a simple lie, all of us have taken naps in this room at some point.

And he got what he wanted. He'll leave me alone now. Right?

GLOWROT

I stand in the middle of the room until he finishes fixing his clothes and hair, wraps the dirty napkins in some more, puts them in his pocket, and leaves like nothing happened.

Now, finally.

I drop to the floor where the marker fell and pick up the phone, making sure to point the flashlight at the part of my thigh where I wrote the names before Eric interrupted me.

At least not all of them were erased.

21

Do Not Cross

I'm still missing names, a lot of them. The wall stretches out in front of me, it's almost alive. Breathing, shifting constantly.

It's not just paper anymore, I should have known better when I started. There are clues everywhere, little details that someone else wouldn't have noticed.

But I did.

I'm different than the rest.

Better.

Napkins, keycards abandoned in hallways, all those receipts. I ripped fabric from all the clothing I remember wearing at NIU and put them there as well; maybe there's a message in the threads that I haven't figured out yet.

Everything is stitched to the wonderful chaos that can finally translate what's happening inside my brain.

The puzzle is getting bigger.

Back to the names.

I've already finished transferring all the ones I wrote on my legs to the wall. Some are crossed out so violently the pen tore through. Some are rewritten so many times the ink looks like it's bleeding into the wall like a wound.

The ones that make my brain itch, I circle again and again. Until my fingers cramp. Until my hands ache. Until they mean something.

They have to mean something. The phone is burning in my hands because of how much I'm forcing it to work. I've searched more than half of it in every social network I can think of, in every possible combination.

GLOWROT

Absolutely nothing.

I recheck my messages. Nova still hasn't answered my last text.

I know she doesn't like how I've been lately, but maybe this will make her believe I'm back to my old self.

A normal person would check in on missing guests, right?

> **Bo**
> Hey you remember that massive guy
> with the missing friends?
> You know, the one I… screamed at?

Nova
Yeah
That was kinda fucked up Bo

> **Bo**
> Well I feel bad

> **Bo**
> I swear
> Do you know if he found them?

Nova
No clue

> **Bo**
> I'd like to check in

Nova
With the dude?

> **Bo**
> No no, the friends
> Like
> I want to see if they're back
> You know?

> **Bo**
> Did he leave their names or
> something?

21 Do Not Cross

A normal person. Just showing concern.

She'll believe it. Or at least she'll want to believe it.

I exhale and rub my temples, my legs falter for a second and I have to hold the chair to not fall to the floor.

The blurred reflection on my phone screen shows the smudges of ink my fingers left on my face. My hands are stained, my cuticles raw, my arms filled with scribbles.

I try to examine my appearance better in the mirror I brought from the bedroom, but something is wrong.

The words I put up earlier should be there, but they're not.

What were they again?

It's muddy now, like it's been wiped away.

By whom?

I turn away before I have to think too hard about it.

Something's missing. The envelopes weren't enough, and I'll be out of ideas if Nova doesn't respond.

"Where should I go next, then?" I ask myself out loud.

"thatDependsAGoodDeal

OnWhereYouWantToGetTo.

Remember?"

Of course, W doesn't miss the opportunity to tease me with that again.

Still, it's nice to have him like this now, after our truce. He promised to help me as long as I promised to not let myself be helped by anyone else. Simple enough.

He's lying on the bed with his head tilted and eyes half-closed in something like amusement. But there's something else there, too. Something heavier.

Something I can't describe.

"To NIU, obviously, but I don't know where—"

"thenItDoesn'tMatterWhichWayYouGo," he responds with a chuckle, his <u>smile</u> growing bigger by the second.

Why would I have expected anything different?

He's not helping, but at least he's not digging his claws on my neck either.

My phone vibrates in my hand, and I yelp.

Nova
I'm not at the desk right now
but one was Terry something I think?
Top floor? Somewhere near the
penthouse?
946?

Bo
Terry Makarios?

Nova
I guess…
How did you know that?

Bo
Idk, I guess I remember him
mentioning it or something

Nova
Bo

Bo
Yeah?

Nova
Are you sure you're okay?

Bo
I'm fine I just feel bad
I know I've been acting weird
I'm sorry
I want to fix things
Tell Nina I said hi

Nova
She's literally blushing rn

Bo
Aww

21 Do Not Cross

My fingers hover over the screen, but I don't type anything else.

Terry Makarios. I see the name on the wall, circled with a hot pink highlighter one million times.

One of the names that itched.

This has to be it.

I move before I even think about it.

I run to my closet, and my fingers slip against all the hangers when I start picking clothes. My whole body is vibrating. W's stare is weighing on me, but I'm trying not to give it too much attention.

Clean up.

Get dressed.

Bathroom.

Makeup.

It feels good to be back.

"ifYou'reJustGoingToCheck
IfTheGuyIsStillMissing,
WhatAreYouGettingAllDressedUpFor?"

He always exposes me.

I look at him through the mirror and sigh, trying not to ruin my eyeliner. I don't even want to answer him. He may not care about other people's opinions, but I do.

What if I see Them in the hallway? I need to make sure I look good because my luck is finally turning around.

I need an outfit that says I don't care what I look like but that I can wear with a belt that won't let me breathe so I can show that, despite what people may think, I do have a waist.

I look at my reflection and try to control my breathing, mascara fluttering from the trembling in my hands. My mouth is watering for no reason.

Of course I have a reason.

I haven't seen that perfect face since a couple of days ago, in that black car, but maybe I'll be lucky enough today.

Maybe Alexia will have told them something about me by this time, as I asked her. I need to know when they come in, when they go out, and why they haven't come looking for me.

Why are they trying to get me to follow in their footsteps instead of talking to me directly?

GLOWROT

Are they in danger?

They have to be.

They need my help.

Maybe someone is forcing us to be apart, the same one watching me, stopping outside my door when they think I'm not paying attention.

What if They have been looking for me all this time but haven't been able to mention it?

"getTheKeyFromTheCleaningLady.

GetIn.

GetOut.

AndStraightBackHome."

I put on those heels that are high but not annoying and keep my phone in a cross-body bag, like I have a social life and do what normal people do on Friday nights.

That way, if someone sees me, I'll look like a guest.

That should work.

"youLookBeautiful,

YouLookGorgeous."

I look beautiful, I look gorgeous.

Maybe if I repeat it enough, I can come to believe it.

I lock the door and look down the hallway. There she is. The woman who's always there, standing in the same spot, vacuum in hand, eyes fixed on something invisible.

Come to think of it, I've never seen her in a different section of the hotel. She just stands there, humming.

Or maybe she isn't humming.

Perhaps the sound comes from the vacuum itself.

But the cable is not even plugged in.

I force my feet forward and grip my bag tighter, I had no idea this would feel so wrong.

It's fine.

It's not like she actually watches people.

She never even looks up.

Still, I slow down when I pass her. MY SKIN PRICKLES, waiting for something, anything.

Nothing.

21 Do Not Cross

I hear W behind me, whispering sharply like he doesn't want her to hear.

"quick.Quick.QUICK."

I move my hand slowly until my fingers brush against the edge of the keycard, hidden between two towels. My heart is racing, I'm about to throw up and pass out at the same time.

Just take it.

Get in.

Get out.

Go straight back home.

The cleaning lady shifts the tiniest bit, my heart jumps. Did she see me?

Her head tilts, but her eyes don't meet mine. They don't meet anything. I move. Fast. I yank it and keep walking like nothing happened.

Don't look back.

Don't.

Her humming stops, and I immediately feel dizzy again.

Then, it starts one more time.

I don't breathe until I turn the corner.

We ride the elevator in silence to the top floor, and my nerves start to come down.

Once out, I walk with my head high, like I belong here. There are no cobwebs in the corners, no moles on the walls, but the warmth in the air tells me I'm close to something.

946.

The room I'm looking for. I mouth the numbers under my breath while doing my best impression of a bespeckled foreigner on vacation.

The same expression I had when I arrived in the US years ago.

When I find the room, I don't even think about it.

The entire floor is deserted, and even though the silence would have freaked me out in the past, now I feel relief.

The master keycard works perfectly.

I go inside.

The room is bigger than mine, but it feels stuck in time. The air is thick, like it's been held in for too long. I take a step forward and hold my breath. This place isn't just abandoned; it's like the guy just vanished one day.

GLOWROT

The room is much bigger than mine. I look around me, doubtful, almost expecting him to jump out at me from around a corner.

A plate sits in the sink, the food now an unrecognizable mess. Stiff, black.

When I open the fridge door, I have to make an inhuman effort not to vomit.

The bin is overflowing with bottles. Beer. Whiskey. Vodka. So many shot bottles. So much more than one person should drink alone.

I step into the dining room. There are newspapers on the table, scribbled over and over. I try to read them, but the words shift every time my eyes focus. They change. Twist on each other.

They spiral.

What the fuck was he trying to figure out?

There's an envelope almost hidden under all the mess, I slide it over to see it better. It's addressed to him. Thick.

Why didn't he open it?

I rip it with trembling hands.

Inside, I expect a letter, some kind of clue. Instead, I find a black card with gold lettering.

YOU WERE NOT SELECTED.

I have seen something like this before, I'm sure of it. I just can't picture it right now.

"YouHaveToFocus."

Yes, I have to focus. I take a deep breath and move forward, then I see it.

The bathroom mirror, ripped from the wall and lying flat in front of the bed.

A sheet has been thrown over it, covering half.

Dread crawls up my throat, but I force myself to step closer. I crouch and slowly peel the sheet back.

Another clue.

Scratches. So many scratches. Thin, frantic, all gouged into the glass.

Words.

But backward.

I inhale sharply and tilt my head. The only way to read them is through the reflection.

21 Do Not Cross

<u>HE WATCHES.</u>
<u>HE SEES YOU.</u>
<u>HE DOESN'T BLINK.</u>

Right when I'm about to scream, something moves in the mirror. My reflection, a second too late.

I throw the sheet over it and jump back. My spine hits the wall, and I hear a small crack. My pulse is threatening to explode in my ears.

When I turn around, the napkin on the nightstand catches my eye. *It's calling to me.*

It's from a casino, but the name has been cut out. Underneath it, there's a printed forum post.

Ay no.

I stop breathing.

He doesn't interfere.

He only watches.

But once he sees you, he never looks away.

That man, Terry. He was looking for something. Just like me.
Something or someone?

I reach for something small next to the napkin. A casino chip.

Neon pink.

It feels weird against my fingers, too heavy and slippery. The image shifts when I tilt it in the light like there's a secret underneath its surface.

Behind me, a door creaks.
Suddenly.

Soft.

Nervous.

Like someone was watching.

Waiting for the right moment to step inside.

I freeze.

Did I close it?

I think back, trying to remember the moment I came in. I swiped the keycard, pushed the handle down, walked inside.

But did I turn around?

Did I hear the lock click into place?

The floorboards whine.

I clutch the chip and shove it into my pocket like I found the answer to all the prayers I don't even make.

A pause.

A heartbeat.

And then—

"*Oye nena*, where are you going all dolled up like that?" His voice inundates the apartment, loud and decorated with a giggle.

22
Expect Delays

I choke on my own saliva and turn around. My heart rises to my throat and then drops.

What the fuck is he doing here?

"Nick?!"

He leans against the doorframe and crosses his arms with a smug face.

"This is not your room," he whispers, but his tone is not accusing. "What happened? Does he owe you money, too?"

"You know the guy that stays here?"

"I know a lot of guys. I stay here, you stay here, everyone's always staying somewhere, aren't they?" He walks forward and looks around, almost as if looking for something.

I rub my eyes with my hands; for a moment, I can't believe my eyes, but then it makes sense. Of course Nick would know about him, it seems like he knows about everything and everyone.

When I open my eyes, I find W hissing in a corner.

"He does owe *me* money," he says and shrugs. "I don't remember what I sold him, but he said something about losing all he had in the slots."

The casino chip in my pocket burns so hot it might make a hole.

"Do you know where he is?" My mouth is dry, my heart is racing.

"rememberOurDeal."

W's voice is starting to form cracks in my skull. But I can't deal with him right now.

"Playing blackjack? I don't care really. It wasn't a lot of money anyway," he responds, shrugging.

"Nick, this man disappeared. You're telling me you're not even a bit curious?!"

But he *is* curious because he starts snooping even more the second I stop looking.

Yes, he's clearly looking for something.

But what?

Why on earth would he be here?

Wait a minute.

"Nick?" I ask, and my voice trembles against my will.

"Yeah?"

"What are you doing here?"

He stiffens for a second, and his smile stretches just too wide for comfort. He then cocks his head and stares at me with vacant eyes.

"The same thing you are?" he responds slowly and cocks his head, squinting like he's trying to read my mind.

"I'm looking for information about NIU." The second I speak, he clicks his tongue and rolls his eyes.

"*Ay no, Bo.* Not this bullshit again," he mutters and rolls his eyes. "Same thing with him; he always talked about this weird casino he found."

"I thought you barely knew him…"

"I'm staying two doors down; I saw him all the time walking back and forth in the hallway," he's barely moving his lips when he speaks. "Why do you look so hot and ask such boring questions? You're going to break my brain."

I stop and smile.

Hot?

I look hot?

But I do. I'm beautiful. I'm gorgeous. Am I not?

I glance at W, and Nick follows my gaze.

His pupils shrink, and he squints like something's not right.

"STOP**NOW**"

The sound of W's voice makes my stomach twist.

Then, he lunges at me, but I don't move.

His grip is tight, cold, and way more tangible than usual. His claws lock around my wrist. My skin feels like it's being crushed.

Nick shifts. He stopped looking at me for a split second.

I shake my head and turn around.

I need to calm down.

Inhale, exhale.

"Let's go out. You can ask me whatever you want over drinks." Nick's voice is coming from my left ear now. Too close, but not uncomfortable. His breath, warm on my neck, eases me.

When did he get so close?

W's grip flickers.

Flickers?

Like static, like a broken radio.

"THECLUESTHEMYSTERY YOUHAVETOFOCUS."

His voice distorts. The sound of it is wrong, doubled over itself.

Nick blinks hard, and I can see his jaw tightening. His smile is still there, but something in his eyes changes.

And then it's gone.

He's back to his absolutely charming and nonsensical self.

"You know you want to!"

Maybe it's not a bad idea after all.

Why would I be trying to figure out clues when I have my biggest informant right in front of me?

"Look, I'm dolled up too," Nick says while pouting.

He turns around, holding his jacket open to show me how his crop top reveals more skin than necessary, and begs me for approval with his eyes.

"Wow, so hot," I reply sarcastically and pull the edge of his bucket hat, but we both know I mean it.

He offers me his arm in a gallant and exaggerated way, and I take it, leaning a little. The height difference is even more noticeable now that I'm wearing heels.

A low but relaxing hum begins to take over my brain; it tickles me, and I smile. The hum gets louder the closer I get to Nick.

He'll tell me everything.

He's the key.

That has to be why he's here.

"Where are we going?" I ask without trying to mask my newfound excitement.

This feels nice.

"Wherever," he looks at me with an arched eyebrow and starts walking towards the open door, "I was thinking Pantheon because that's where everything is."

GLOWROT

"*Ajá,* but do you have money?" That's the only question that matters.

I've seen his room and the kind of clothing he wears, I know his tastes are expensive, and I don't plan on getting back home with a leaky wallet.

"I've got it all covered baby, you just worry about keeping up with me."

I clutch his arm and follow his steps, the hum buzzing still inside my ears. Like the white noise on the TV I used to listen to fall asleep.

We go down the elevator and I guide him to my car because, even though I like him, I would never trust someone like Nick to drive. Even less so knowing that we'll have to return in a highly questionable state of mind.

And if, worst case scenario, the night ends up being a fiasco or he dumps me somewhere, at least I'll be able to get home.

He takes over the radio the second I start the car, but I don't bother. It's better to keep him happy. It's easier to get him to talk that way.

"TURN AROUND NOW!!!!"

A screech inside my skull, the broken radio signal again, but this time cranked to full volume. My hands slip on the wheel, and everything starts melting at the edges of my vision.

W is in the rearview mirror. Not just his eyes. His whole face.

His mouth is stretched open <u>too wide</u>. His silhouette is flickering, glitching.

Wrong.

Breaking.

The lights outside turn into long and distorted streaks. I try to cover one of my ears with my hand, but the sound goes through it. It's not a scream anymore.

I know I should stop the car.

I know I should listen to him.

He never behaves like this.

Never this bad.

Never this weird.

I can't deal with this right now; everything is too much.

So I turn the music up even louder and start singing along with Nick. Maybe if I scream loud enough, I'll deafen W's screams.

"This is my playlist *para perrear hasta el subsuelo,*" he explains very proudly, putting the phone in front of me and making me almost skip a red light.

"Do you want to crash?!" I squeal, forgetting how to breathe.

As much as I try to keep my gaze fixed straight ahead, I end up joining him in chorus and moving side to side.

I missed this music, it brings me back home, ages away from here. His cheeks are red from screaming so much and he's massaging them, they probably hurt from smiling all the time too.

I can't even remember the last time I had this much fun without having a few drinks in me.

"Hey, can I ask you something?" I say when the situation has calmed down a bit.

"Yeah, but if you let me tell you something first." He turns to look at me and swallows saliva. I almost stop the car out of surprise at his suddenly serious expression, but we're on the highway.

"Everything okay?"

"Yeah, but it's just that… it's very important." He looks at his hands for a few seconds, suddenly doubtful.

"No worries. What happened?" My body tenses, and the inside of my mouth goes dry.

Chills run all over my body.

Did I do something?

Did I say something?

Is he kidnapping me?

"I've been practicing it for days…"

"*Coño* Nick, just say it!"

He sighs and turns to look at me in slow motion, says something between his teeth like he's practicing the words that have supposedly been bouncing around in his head for days. Then he clears his throat.

"*Des-*" He starts but catches himself. Takes a deep breath and tries again, belting the chorus to *Despacito* at full volume.

His smile gradually widens until he lets out a hysterical laugh.

I throw the phone at him, but he just keeps laughing. He turns up the volume, and his tone grows louder and louder until it envelops both of us.

When he finishes, he applauds himself and looks at me, wanting to kill me until I do the same.

He's incredible.

GLOWROT

"*Ok, dime,*" Nick says once he has recovered from his emotional rendition.

"Have you been going to NIU again?" The question sounds about as casual as I can ask it, but he deflates.

La cagué.

I fucked it up.

"Yeah, I guess, I don't know. All those places are the same." He sighs and looks out the window like a scolded child. "Are you going to ask a thousand questions again? Party pooper."

"No, no. It's not like that. "I reach out and instinctively caress his knee; he stretches like a cat and turns to look at me. The red contact lenses he's wearing match his outfit. "It's just really important to me."

The GPS interrupts me, announcing that we've arrived at the area.

I look for a free spot on the street and park. Nick looks sideways excitedly, like a kid about to get off at an amusement park. He pats his pockets like he's looking for something and curses.

"Did you lose something?"

"Nothing, it's fine. I'll just shop around here, I guess," he whispers tiredly, then turns to look at me, strokes my cheek, and grabs my chin with the delicacy of a saint. "Let's get fucked up and commit questionable acts, okay?"

His thumb traces my lower lip like he's shaping something.

I don't move.

I don't even breathe.

He presses down, gently at first and then harder, until my lips part on their own.

A test.

A trick.

His smirk sharpens when my body betrays me and I stare at him with my mouth wide open. Then he winks and releases me like it never happened.

I swallow down the heat rising to my face.

He's already out of the car.

My head is spinning.

I shake my head to play it cool, but I know it won't work. He saw me.

He knows.

I check my purse to make sure I have everything. And to have an excuse not to look him in the eyes until my face stops being red.

The keys, the phone, and the ID they probably won't even ask for.

Nick grabs my wrist like he owns it and starts guiding me as if he knows exactly where we are and has a mental map of the situation.

He knows the bouncers at the door by name. They don't just greet him; they open the doors for him. He acts like he owns the place, every place.

Electronic music reverberates against the walls, and he places a glow-in-the-dark bracelet on my arm.

He's focused, looking in every direction, like this is his comfort zone.

I let him guide me until we're pressed against a crowded bar, and he starts commenting about the hot bartender with the beard.

The playful, boyish attitude he had when he got in the car is behind him; now, a seductive and dangerous air surrounds him, and I can't help but wonder if it's the angle at which the lights hit him.

"Drink this, everyone else has a head start on us."

He places a shot glass in front of me and one in front of himself.

He blinks quickly when I don't act right away. I panic, grab the glass, and down it in one go.

"Another one, come on."

I choke again on the second one he hands me, this time in my hand. It burns more than the first.

My chest feels hot, and my brain begins to decompress. The sounds around me become THICK, and I can't help but smile.

From this angle, he reminds me of—

I look at him and run my tongue over my teeth.

"Are you trying to get me drunk?" I say, leaning down so I can speak in his ear.

"Last one," he replies, this time placing the glass to my lips and tilting it for me to drink.

The instant I swallow, he hands his card to the bartender, and as soon as it's returned, he takes me by the hand and leads me through the people who are moving in strange ways I couldn't call dancing.

"Hardly anyone here has any seasoning," he explains loudly so I can hear him, pointing his finger at several people dancing near us. "But the drinks are the best to start with."

"How many times have you come here?" My throat is scratchy, and I can't remember when I had dinner or if I even did.

"More than I can remember."

He pulls me to the back door, and the wave of heat and humidity slaps me in the face. I try to fan myself with my hands and then to tie my hair, but I have nothing to do it with.

Nick just stares at me like he's looking for something again.

"I want to see how well you know how to have fun," he says out of nowhere and starts walking.

I follow in his footsteps closely as he starts reading the signs outside all the places. There are too many of them, and many blend into each other. He avoids like the plague the ones with a line to get in; it's the most focused I've seen him.

In a moment, he comes up to me and wraps his hands around my waist, and to my surprise, the act doesn't displease me.

IT BAR

He leads me to the next place on his mental list, and this time, I have to show my ID to the man at the entrance.

Out of the corner of my eye I watch as Nick exchanges more than just words with the guy's partner and puts something in his pocket, then looks at me and smiles.

In the split second that he turns around to go inside and gives me time to put the ID away, I look around, hoping that the miracle I need will happen and one of the signs on the street can show me the way I need.

"Are you coming?" he asks exasperated.

I turn around and look at him smiling, he wraps his arms around my waist again and kisses my neck without warning.

Maybe having fun just for one night is not such a bad idea.

23
Lost & Found

It's someone's birthday, I know because she has a crown and is singing loudly.

Every time they play a song she knows, she takes a different person's hand and starts using it as a microphone. Right now, it's mine, and she looks at me with a smile that says the world has ceased to exist.

It's only us now.

I see her blurry face after rubbing my eyes because someone spilled beer on me again.

She looks so happy, I want to be like that.

I get on the couch she's jumping on and opt to sing nonsense because I have no idea what the lyrics are. She turns and smiles, and I do too. She grabs my hips, swaying hers against them to the changing music.

I see her eyes with a frown and the twinkling lights make it take longer than necessary for me to notice.

It's not a random girl celebrating her birthday.

It's just Nick, in a silver wig.

At this point, noticing the amount of stares at me brings back memories I don't know if I want to uncover.

And it's not the same anyway; it's far from enough.

I may be just as dizzy as I was those times, and people may be trying to drown their sorrows as much as they would in NIU, but here, everyone has a face; they are alive.

Unfortunately.

Now my body is moving only because my mind is elsewhere; I don't remember how many clubs there have been before this one since we arrived, and I have no idea how many will be.

GLOWROT

My stomach is an awful mix of drinks.

I want to get lost in the crowd, get so carried away that I forget my name and where the exit is.

But it's so different.

I touch Nick's face, and he playfully bites my finger. His teeth are sharper than I expected.

"You taste like déjà vu," he says, grinning against my hand.

I laugh with my teeth but not my eyes.

I keep dancing out of inertia and try to imagine I'm there, but it all feels too tangible.

Too real.

After a while, he takes my hand and leads me back to the same spot we came in, saying goodbye to a couple of girls I don't even know where they came from.

Sweat sticks to his skin like glitter, his nose is red and his lips dried. He looks at me between the black locks that adorn his forehead, coming out of his hat like short tentacles.

He tilts his head with a smile that also doesn't reach his eyes, like he's waiting for me to say something.

Like he's testing me again.

I just smile back, not even thinking about the present.

"You got drunk that fast? We're not even halfway through!"

He shakes my shoulders, and I shake my head, laughing. A loud gasp comes out of his mouth.

"Time must be running faster for you! Or slower for me. Or maybe…" He starts, his eyes darting left to right, like he's counting something in the air. "Maybe it stopped altogether. Are we stuck?"

"You're so fucked up already," I say, but the words come out more slurred than I anticipated.

The ground shifts beneath me, though not so much that I end up wobbling inelegantly on the sidewalk.

Unfortunately.

We're on our way to another club, bar, or mortuary. I don't think the difference matters anymore.

I can tell by how he looks around like there's a path with glowing arrows that only he can see.

"How could I be drunk?" I start teasing him, pulling his jacket collar toward me. "It's not like you've been buying me a lot of drinks."

I want to stroke his hair, but a bead of sweat falls on my finger, and I remove my entire hand. I gag.

The heels don't bother me, but they tremble with every step I take, and for a few seconds, I wonder if this will be the day they give way completely.

My breath becomes heavier as I walk, the heat increasingly unbearable, and I'm tempted to take off my dress just to walk in the street. Maybe I would have if I had a bra on.

"We've come full circle!" Nick laughs, rounding a lamp post and using it like a makeshift stripper pole. "Your turn, where to next?"

"We obviously haven't, it's just that all the streets look alike," I answer, pushing him and laughing.

He's definitely fucked up.

"But they don't." He grabs my hand and twirls me like a dance partner, the neon lights streaking past in blurs. He lets go, stepping back to admire me. "Maybe you're just walking in circles. Omg, or spirals!"

But something catches my eye.

The nausea is worse now. Even with all the heat, my body freezes.

Right there, one of the neon signs.

IT BAR.

No.
No. No. No. No.
No. No. No. No. No. No. No.
No. No. No. No. No. No. No. No. No. No. No.
No. No. No. No. No. No. No.
No. No. No. No.
No.
No.
No. No. No. No.
No. No. No. No. No. No. No.
No. No. No. No. No. No. No. No. No. No. No.
No. No. No. No. No. No. No.
No. No. No. No.
No.

It's impossible.

I whip my head around, scan the street, and grip my bag like it has all the answers inside.

"Nick, tell me we didn't get to the same place." The few dizzy spells I felt from my drinks are gone now.

"Are hoes deaf or what?" he shouts. "Yeah, we went full circle and it's your turn. Come on!"

Here they are.

I've got them.

I take the keys between my trembling fingers and press the button.

Absolute silence.

Again.

I press it harder.

Mierda. Mierda.

I look around and start walking.

I place the clicker under my jaw and try to make out something from my surroundings, but at night all the fucking cars are black, including mine.

"Bo."

It's got to be around here somewhere.

There's the door to the first bar over there, and on this side the graffiti I saw and thought was pretty.

"Bo."

When we arrived, I noticed these lines on the sidewalk and wondered if it was the pipes because they were going to do some work on the street.

And this light pole, this—

"Bo!"

I nap my head toward him and feel my brain bouncing against the walls of my skull.

"What?!"

His smirk is gone. He looks smaller, even in his ridiculous platform shoes.

"Please tell me you paid for the parking."

I open my mouth, but his expression shrinks the words in my throat. It's like he's shrunken and pale at the same time.

"Of course, I paid for the parking."

"Because I didn't see you paying for parking, Bo. I swear I didn't see you, and I thought you did. But I didn't see you actually doing it."

His voice is distant. My mind is louder.

But did I pay for it, or did I just think I did?

I plop down in the middle of the sidewalk. Fuck, I didn't do it.

My fingers start to tremble, crying feels so stupid right now but I can't stop myself.

Nick stares at me from afar for a minute, then picks up a metal stick from I don't know where and starts poking me with it, afraid to come closer.

I keep pushing the button on the key with desperation that tells me that maybe, if I do it hard enough, the car will appear to roll towards me like some magic trick.

Suddenly, I just want to go home.

I rummage through my purse again, and this time, I pick up the phone and stand on my tiptoes to read the sign on the pole, where it says in giant letters that you must pay to park in the same spot where I'm standing.

I breathe once, twice. The call goes to an answering machine that puts me on hold from the first second. I look at him, and he seems concerned, but after he sees that I'm trying to talk to someone, he shrugs and starts doodling on the ground with the stick.

It's like I'm watching myself from outside of my body.

The guy on the other end eventually answers me with the correct license plate number and confirms they have my car.

I just want to lie in the gravel and wait for a biker to run me over.

The tears running down my cheeks make it all even worse.

They're burning.

Like acid.

It's frustration, with myself for being so careless and with a shitty system for taking what's mine and ruining my night in the process.

GLOWROT

When I turn to see Nick he's checking something on his phone. I walk towards him, and an unnatural breeze blows past me; the heat makes me dizzy, but at least my face isn't sticky anymore.

"I'm checking to see if we can get a ride on one of these apps," he says, focused on the screen, "But there are no drivers nearby. I figure that I have to wait because we're in rush hour or something."

I hate everything.

I try to do the same, but he's right. There is no charitable soul out there right now who wants to give us a hand, or make us at least not die of boredom or dehydration.

Maybe if we ask a random stranger, they'd at least take us to the place— The car dump.

The place for the cars.

The car trash can.

Fuck.

"Nick!"

"What?" He jerks his head and stares at me like I'm about to cast a spell.

"What's the name of the place?" I ask without looking him in the eye. "*El depósito.* Where they take the cars… Like, when they take them from the street?"

"The car pound?"

I nod, and he shakes his head like he's just gotten out of the spell.

Maybe if we ask a random stranger, they'd at least take us to the car pound.

But we're in Pantheon, and I'm not that crazy.

I'd rather be run over by someone than have my organs sold on the black market.

We start walking. Again.

Nick tries to make jokes to lighten the mood, but I can't with him right now.

It's too much.

Everything is too much.

My shirt sticks to my skin, and the GPS says it'll take forty fucking minutes to get to the place.

The car pound.

I should be furious at myself, and I am, but mostly I'm just exhausted. We pass a gas station, and Nick disappears inside. When he comes back, he's grinning, holding up two cans.

"Lime-rita," he sings, shaking a green can. "Or Straw-rita?" He tilts his head, eyebrows raised.

"I don't want to drink Nick, I fucked up."

He doesn't listen. He steps closer, tilts my chin up, and presses the cold rim of the can against my lips.

"Say aaaaah."

I hesitate; he doesn't care and presses slightly on my throat with his fingertips. My mouth opens, and he tilts the can, letting the cheap lime sugar bomb pour in.

It burns like poison but awakens me with a jolt of electricity. My heart kicks. The overwhelming sweetness almost makes me gag.

"You don't have to come with me." My voice is raw, and I feel like I have swallowed broken glass.

"Yeah, sure." He rolls his eyes. "You're gonna walk through Pantheon alone at night? Great idea."

I don't answer. I just keep drinking.

And then shouting.

Nick stands up like a wind-up toy and bolts toward a group standing under a streetlamp with a scream that yanks me up. He high-fives them, grinning ear to ear.

"It's The Unbirthday Crew!" He shouts from the other side of the street, waving at me.

I don't want this. I want to get my car and go home, maybe cry a little bit first.

But Nick is calling my name.

And they're closing in.

Dressed in too much black, with extravagant colored details. Faces sunken in; under the elongated shadows of the street lights, they almost look like demons.

"I love your hair!"

"Nikky, aren't you melting?"

"Oh, don't you have any more of that left?"

"Do you have any cigarettes?"

They talk all at once, their voices overlap and blend in together.

They surround me like I'm a zoo animal and my senses sharpen.

I should run as fast as I can. But I don't.

I can't.

GLOWROT

"I'm Bo," is all I manage to say, and I put on my customer service smile for some meaningless reason. Apparently, it works.

They introduce themselves one by one, but their names shuffle and blend together. At some point we start walking again, this time with all of them.

Are we going the right way?

Another gas station, I pull my phone out to call the place—

"This'll look good on you." A <u>sleepy</u>-looking girl puts her jacket around my shoulders and caresses my hair.

Why is my phone in my hand?

I put it back, I don't want to lose it.

We keep walking, they keep talking.

Laughing.

But we're not on the street anymore.

It's not a club either.

There is music warbling in the background, but the place is empty. Just an enormous circular table with cushions instead of chairs.

A thin layer of smoke rolls over the table, rising from glass tea kettles. The scent is sweet but chemical, like fermented fruit.

Cloying.

Reminds me of something.

Of what?

"No room here!"

The guy next to me moves forward, almost hissing, waving his arms as if I've committed some great offense.

I blink. There's clearly space.

I try again. Same reaction.

And again. And again.

Until I can finally sit.

"Do you like wine?" The <u>sleepy</u> girl is drinking out of a tiny teacup; for a second, it looks like the liquid glows in the dark.

My tongue itches, and I think I have something in my mouth. Heavy, like honey.

How much time has it passed?

"What is an Unbirthday?" I hear the words coming from my mouth, but I don't remember thinking them.

"A day when it's not your birthday, silly," she responds with a giggle.

"But that's 364 days out of the year," I say, squinting; they clap.

23 Lost & Found

"Exactly! Isn't that amazing? We celebrate all of those!"

Their laughs erupt, all at the same time, like a dormant volcano about to drown me, perfectly in sync.

"We were more before, of course, but the rest vanished."

There's a pause in the laughter, a second of silence. Then it starts again.

"They what?" That word reminds me of something, something important. Something I should be thinking about right now.

"You know, disappeared." One of the guys shrugs. "Like people usually do."

But that's not normal.

Is it?

Nick slams his hand on the table.

"Let's play a game!" His voice thunders around us, and everyone swallows their laughter. He smirks, and there's a mischievous glint in his pupils.

He starts counting with his fingers.

"One, two, three."

The rest are just looking at him without even breathing.

"Four, five."

I look around, I don't understand, but suddenly I'm too afraid to move. Too scared to break whatever tension has just overcome us.

"Six. Fuck"

My saliva feels thick inside my mouth, and I try to focus on breathing. I might pass out.

"It'd be great if we had one more." His eyes bounce from one to the other until they reach me. "What about that guy friend of yours? From the hotel? He seems cool enough to be my number two."

Something's wrong.

Nick claps his hands together, and the rest seem to return to their usual, cheery selves.

"Oh, me, me, me!" Another girl raises her hand.

"No, no, no, I go first," Nick grins, twirling a tiny spoon between his fingers before tossing it over his shoulder. "First rule! If you lose, you drink."

"Lose at what?" I ask before I can contain the words. One of the guys looks at me, visibly containing laughter.

"Exactly," Nick responds and points at one of the teapots. "And you're the first loser. Come on, drink."

"Drink! Drink! Drink!"

I look around to see if I'm missing something, but their voices grow louder.

"Drink! Drink! Drink!"

And louder.

"Drink! Drink! Drink!"

I grab the first cup I see and down it, they immediately quiet.
All at the same time.

"Second rule!" He starts, but I'm not listening anymore.

The entire world tilts, like it's melting in the corners of my eyes.

Nick is still laughing, but his mouth moves too slowly. Like there's a delay between what I see and the sounds he's making.

Someone else drinks, someone else laughs.

Did I lose again?

Did I drink again?

"I'm going to the bathroom," I whisper to the air and stand up.
I can't throw up.

Not here.

Not in front of them.

What will they think?

The smoke feels intoxicating, and it's becoming harder and harder to breathe. It's like it's slowly taking control of my brain.

I walk away from the table and instead of a door, I find stairs going up.

Were we in a basement?

My hair covers my eyes so I can barely see; when I start going up, a hand wraps around mine.

It's Nick, smiling innocently.

"I need some air too," he says in a complicit tone, like we're both in on a secret.

What secret?

The hallway we reach at the top has no doors except the one at the end, and for a second, I think I'll fall into the void when we open it.

But no, it leads to a blind street.

"Look," He pulls me towards him and grabs my face with both hands. His pupils are dilated and he's slurring his vowels. "Maybe there's a bathroom there."

He's close, so close.

He points randomly to one of the many rundown places surrounding the presumed exit of the place we were in, and I nod and let myself be led to it.

A pink neon light bathes us as soon as we enter.

Pink.

Neon.

Light.

We arrive at a counter made of mirrors; the receptionist has so many ornaments in their hair and face that I can barely make out that there is a person underneath all the stickers. Her smile is fixated on her face by safety pins.

One of the stickers catches my attention. I rub my eyes and focus on it a bit more. They smile and move their head forward like pigeons do.

"Two people?" They ask.

But I can't look away from her collarbone, from what I thought was just one of those stickers.

But no, it's a tattoo.

A cherry cut off of a larger stem.

Too familiar.

Why?

I swear I've seen the other half somewhere else.

"Bathroom," Nick says, breaking my concentration.

I look around at the place and then cough.

And drool.

And thump my chest.

Behind the receptionist is a giant, pink sign in all capital letters.

And I know it all too well by now.

24

RestrictedAreA

We follow the receptionist to a door that leads to an endless hallway. I try to ask them about their tattoo, but every time I go to say something, my words get stuck in my throat.

My feet follow them as if they were being piloted by someone else.

I smile when they open it

I smile when they close it.

I even smile when I hear them turn the lock.

What's better than being locked inside the place I've been longing for so long?

The air feels the same as the other times I came; when it was a nightclub, when it became a strip club. And yet, something is different.

It's as if I were standing on the opposite side of a mirror, and everything was almost the same, but not completely.

Uncanny.

I rub the wood with my fingertips.

Nick laughs next to me.

We're alone, no sound comes from any of the doors.

"Are you making a wish?" he slurs.

"What?"

He traces a line from my fingertip all the way to my shoulder.

"When you touch the wood, that's what's supposed to do. Or is that mirrors?" He tilts his head back and lets out a sigh. I chuckle.

The walls seem made of velvet, but they itch. I swallow and brush my cheek against one of them. He imitates me, and for a second, he stares into my eyes.

The fabric squirms under me, like something breathing.

The red contacts Nick is wearing have lost their rim, almost as if they were absorbed by his globes.

From there, he jumps to my lips.

Slow breaths, I have all the time in the world.

It has stopped now.

Maybe it even did at the beginning of the night.

I return his gaze, and my smile mimics his.

Sharp.

I push aside a lock tangled with his eyelashes, and he snorts like his nose is itching.

My mind turns into a spiral.

All the images liquefy and slowly merge, forming molasses that seems to be going down a drain to the back of my mind.

Sticky ribbons.

Memories running away.

And something else.

But that's not relevant.

Nothing is.

Because, finally, I'm here.

He doesn't move, so I intertwine my fingers with his and hold the glowing key in my free hand.

When did I get this?

I start walking again.

The light flickers and becomes brighter the closer we get to the room. *It knows.*

Nick grabs my hand, presses his middle finger against my palm, and moves it in circles. He traces symbols I don't understand but feel correct.

My whole body tingles.

"What's that?" I ask in a daze, with eyes half closed.

"What do you mean?" He whispers in my ear; his breath is moist. "You asked me to do that?"

I close my eyes and let the light streaming through my eyelids guide me the rest of the way.

The doorknob is warm, and I shiver; Nick steps forward and places his hand over mine.

It opens easily, like it already knew we were coming.

There are no windows, but the walls are covered with curtains that give off light behind them. I caress them, soft like they've never been touched. They smell blue, bright, intoxicating.

Electric.

Like the buzz from the lightbulbs.

GLOWROT

The sound of something falling to the floor makes me turn, and his belt kisses the carpet next to his jacket.

He winks at me, and I smile. A lazy, stretched smile. Like someone else is pulling from the corners of my mouth.

I walk to the bathroom, dragging my feet, and he relaxes on the cushions of the bed.

I look down at my hands as I sit; for some reason I'VE GROWN EYES IN MY KNUCKLES, but by the time I flush they're gone.

"Maybe they were always there, and you hadn't noticed before," my reflection whispers with eyes so bright they almost blind me.

I smile.

Just smile.

The water in the sink is electric blue, like the air.

Warm, like everything else around me.

Just the perfect temperature.

Without thinking, I lick my fingers. It tastes like the light too.

It snakes under my skin, and for a second, my veins give off that familiar glow that I have been chasing for so long.

"Tasty."

Nick's now standing under the doorframe, his eyes almost glowing in the dark.

Like the light.

Like the water.

Like my veins.

I look at him in the mirror's reflection.

His eyes flick from mine to my mouth, still tasting the drops on my skin.

Then he moves towards me, his reflection approaching, sliding like it's going to escape the glass prison from which it's contained.

It reaches me before he does.

He delicately grabs my hips and moves me aside so he can taste too.

I stare at him for an unimportant amount of time.

He swallows the liquid like it's the only thing that keeps him alive.

He moves around this place like an expert.

I fucking knew it.

I feel more oxygen every inhale than I should get into my brain.

I kick off my shoes, and the shower faucet bursts open as soon as I step in. A bright, electric blue curtain drenching me.

The droplets prickle my cheeks, my neck, my chest.

They cling to me, seep into my pores.

"It's good, isn't it?" Nick's voice fogging my ear makes me shiver. It runs through me.

His hands find my waist; his heat is behind me, his hardness pressing.

He's sinking into me.

My body's reacting in ways I can't recognize, but I let them be.

All of it.

Breath.

                          Shiver.

Pain.

                                                Desperation.

                          Surprise.

                          Misery.

Excitement.

                                                Nostalgia.

                                                Sweat.

Lust.

Instead of battling the liquid that threatens to make me stop breathing, I open my mouth and let it fill up. I bring my hand back and wrap it around his neck, applying pressure with my fingernails.

He howls.

"You should have seen this coming from the beginning," he whispers, pulling up the fabric of my shirt.

I hear my own laugh before I even think to do so.

I turn.

My hands find his face, but it's like he's already waiting. Smiling.

Like he is already inside my mouth before I part my lips.

The water slips between us. We drink it. We breathe it. We drown in it together.

My dress spills to the floor, liquid, intangible, running down the drain.

I run my hands over him, feeling every curve of his spine like tracing a map to somewhere it would be good to get lost in.

"I'm not an idiot, Nikky," I mock the way his friends call him, barely moving my lips.

He closes his eyes and chuckles, then lunges at me like a starving beast.

His red eyes.

We are nothing more than a tangle of the same inexplicable sensations, those that I still don't know whether they are attacking me or enveloping me.

His soft touch leaves a shiny path from my jaw to my chest. His lips follow it, savoring me.

Like dessert.

Like food.

I hear music dulled by a million walls. Somewhere, in this same place, hundreds of desperate souls are letting themselves be driven to the point of extinction on a dance floor that has no way out.

Just disappear.

Must be nice.

I squirm, he growls.

"What, you don't like it?" he asks playfully, trapping me between his teeth.

My legs wrap around him like my entire body is trying to consume his very essence of life. The walls ripple like we're underwater.

"Ah, you really like it, don't you?" He continues the path his mouth was following. I gasp.

My foot slips, and he holds me down. He has one hand on my back, and he holds on to the water faucet with the other so I don't fall to the floor.

He then starts sucking again.

I tangle my fingers in his hair and pull him. He lets out a satisfied squeal, and then I pull harder.

His soaked skin is scalding hot but doesn't burn me.

Again.

It's a hot, gratifying sensation that makes my insides hum with desperation.

Again.

This one hard enough for him to pull away from me and rest his gaze on mine curiously.

He narrows his eyes and raises an eyebrow when I smile.

The liquid is warmer than before, and I feel thirstier as it slides down my throat.

And I know exactly what I'm thirsty for.

I walk out of the bathroom, and he follows me excitedly.

The steam from the shower has permeated the room as well, it hangs over the bed like it's waiting for us.

I know it does.

I reach over to Nick and guide him to the bed. He follows obediently, but with a smile I can't quite figure out.

Like he thinks he's in control now.

But he's wrong.

I'm the one who wanted this.

I'm the one guiding him and telling him what to do.

I'm in control.

A trickle of saliva slides down his chin, he breathes rapidly and begins to lick his lips. His red eyes look at me.

I'm on top.

I'm making all the decisions.

I'm in control.

I'm in control.

I'm in control.

His jaw quivers, he nods his head with narrowed eyes.

I'm the one that made him crave me.

I'm the one staring into his eyes while the lace of my lingerie suffocates him slowly.

I'm in control.

I'm in control.

I'm in control.

I'm in control.

GLOWROT

I'm in control.

"What, you don't like it?" I repeat in a playful tone as he inhales and catches the fabric between his teeth. I try to pull away to test his patience, but he responds by drawing lines on my legs with his nails. "Ah, you really like it, don't you?" I tease.

He's begging for more.

He's clinging to my body.

He's thirsty.

He's hungry.

He's looking at me, smiling.

He's not in control.

He's not in control.

He's not in control.

He's not in control.

He's not in control.

He's not in control.

He's not in control.

He's not in control.

My breathing becomes heavier and heavier as he plays, sucking and nibbling; he moves in circles and then side to side.

But I'm in control, so I start moving too.

His hands squeeze my skin desperately. I hold onto his hair.

I lower my face and look into his eyes, they are lost somewhere. His pupils are dilated, but he's not really there. Then he smiles and starts to slide his finger down my spine, but doesn't stop.

Because I don't want him to.

Because he's not in control.

His touch finds places on my body that even I had forgotten about. His smile joins mine, and I let myself be carried away wherever he goes when his eyes lose focus on reality.

On purpose.

I want this.

I need this. He looks at me for a moment, and I slowly nod. His smile widens so much that, for a moment, I think the edges of his lips are going to tear.

His fingers remind me of the pleasure I've been missing out on in real life.

Again.

And again.

And again.

And again.

And again.

And again.

GLOWROT

And again.

   And again.

      And again.

     And again.

       And again.

        And again.

     And again.

      And again.

     And again.

    And again.

And again.

   And again.

    And again.

     And again.

    And again.

   Again.

I feel my leg muscles spasm, and I fall forward in a scream I didn't expect myself. My whole lower body throbs, and suddenly, the whole world turns red.

Like his eyes.

Nick moves one of my legs carefully and then drags me backward, leaving me lying face down. His fingers trace my back and drag slowly up until they reach my neck.

"Your hair wants cutting," he whispers with the softness of a sorcerer.

"What?" I try to turn around, but he places his palm firmly on my back.

Soft but firm.

Gentle but sharp.

"It's too long." His nail traces a horizontal line along my neck. "Do you ever wonder why ravens and desks are so alike?"

His voice echoes, bounces around the walls of the room. It repeats, loops in itself. I shift under his palm, and for a second, I'm not sure if I moved or thought about moving.

I decide to stay still.

Not him, me.

Because I'm in control.

"You're so drunk," I laugh.

But he's not laughing.

I can finally turn around and see him. He's smiling ceremoniously. Studying me like I'm made of glass, like he's trying to figure out which part of me will break first.

For a moment the lights help me remember that thing I swore I'd never forget, but his eyes drag me back to the moment.

His red eyes.

His sharp smile.

He leaves for a moment and comes back. The walls melt in his absence, and I sink in the bed, now turned into quicksand.

I watch as he tears a square foil with his teeth, it glistens under the glow of the water sprinkling around us.

Water?

A condom slides out, curling in his palm like it's alive.

It glows.

And then he puts it on, the glow starts spreading on his skin. His wrist's tendons shine neon, and his arms' veins are lined with light.

He stares at it, relaxing his head like a puppet with strings cut off.

Like he's trying to remember something important.

A second passes.

Another one.

Something's wrong, something has to be wrong.

The glow grows all the way to his shoulder and starts spreading up through his neck.

"Look," he whispers, gesturing with his arm. "I'm radioactive!"

He bursts out in laughter, doubling over like he just told the funniest joke in the world.

The tension shatters like broken glass.

I shove his chest.

"You're an idiot."

"A glowing, gorgeous idiot," he corrects, tossing his hair. Then his eyes lock onto mine, pupils blown out.

He then lies down next to me, his warmth reminds me how much I want this.

Like the flip of a switch.

Too sudden.

How much time has passed?

Time is unimportant.

How long have we been lying here?

It has stopped, maybe it never existed.

His gasps against my skin render me mute; when I feel him inside me, I just smile.

Finally.

I don't have to be in control anymore.

Like he's been reading my brain this whole time, he starts making his own decisions.

Gentle, making sure I'm still responding to his every touch. He checks and smiles when I do. He nods, I mimic him.

Chuckle.

Slow.

Hard.

Intense.

Calculated.

Something else.

He rests his hands on my back, and the rubbing of the sheets feels almost like several pairs of hands begin to caress my sides, writhing over my body.

Slow.

Soft.

Airy.

Impulsive.

He picks up the pace.
Sudden lips on my ribs.
His?

It doesn't matter.

I don't have to be in control anymore.

I can let go.

The colors dance in front of my closed eyelids, and the droplets falling from his hair tickle my hips.

Sheets.

A scream.

Don't stop.

Again.

And again.

And again.

GLOWROT

Everything inside me feels effervescent and is about to explode.

And then, nothing.

Full stop.

The room exhales around us.

He pulls back slowly, I haven't stopped smiling.

My whole body trembles, my nerves are on edge and my senses throb with envy.

Nick's eyes dart across me like he's trying to memorize me. He licks his lips.

"Do you think I'd serve a cake and not let you lick the icing?" Both of his hands wrap around my ankles, and he flips me over with his hands. I muffle a surprised scream. "I don't believe in unfinished business."

His fingers move with the expertise of someone who's spent a lifetime perfecting this act.

Smile.

Slow.

Fast.

Narrowed eyes.

Focus.

Muscle spasms.

Up.

Down.

I bite into the pillow to keep myself from shattering.

This time it's stronger, the sensation makes my toes stiffen and spreads through my body like a burning wave that makes my skin raw.

A burning star explodes in my chest.

It's glowing.

Somewhere in the distance, I hear a laugh.

Nick's fingers leave me.

He sucks them clean, like he's tasting the answer to a riddle only he understands.

"See? That's better."

I can't speak. The world is blurry, I see shadows in corners that weren't there before.

None of them looks familiar.

The room starts breathing again.

He plants a kiss on my forehead and walks back to the bathroom. I hear the shower turn on.

And then, a moment of clarity, like the wave that already overcame me twice.

So I follow him.

Because I want to.

Because I need to talk to him.

Because I'm in control.

I hear the colors on the walls.

I see how now they're trying to hold me down.

"Hey, Nick." I poke my head inside the bathroom and see him taking a shower; steam has already filled the space.

Hazy.

His skin still glows.

Blurred.

Like looking at a mirage.

"Are you coming?" he asks, pulling the curtain back further.

I nod and step forward.

I don't feel my feet touch the ground.

"Yes," I say. "But after that, I need to ask you for a favor."

Nick shrugs, winks.

Stares at me.

"I know, Bo."

His smile stretches, it glows too.

"I'm not an idiot."

25

TrespassersWillBeProsecuteD

It was convenient to have clothes in the closet after ours melted through the floor.

Nick rummages through them like a kid in a candy store, pulling out a kaleidoscopic suit without a shirt and a top hat on. He spins in front of the mirror and tosses his hair back.

"I'm really pulling this off, huh?"

I barely hear him.

The dress feels cold in my hands, glossy like it's made of the same plastic as an old doll's eyes.

Pink.

Like the lights.

I step into it and it wraps around my skin, as if it was always meant to be there. Nick watches me as I tie the velvet ribbon around my neck, his red eyes flickering.

"I've never seen you wear light colors before," he murmurs, his eyes running through the sheer fabric while I zip it up.

"You've seen me like, three times." I don't look at him, rolling my gloves up to my elbows.

"And yet," he says slowly. "And I've seen a lot more than most."

He doesn't understand the urgency, how important this is to me.

That finding Them is a matter of life or death.

Them.

My beloved.

I inhale in an attempt to keep calm. Composed.

I'm dressing for the moment of re-encounter. The moment where I find them.

I want to look perfect for Them.

"Let's go, let's go, let's go!"

Nick's movements are light, like a paper doll swaying on the breeze.

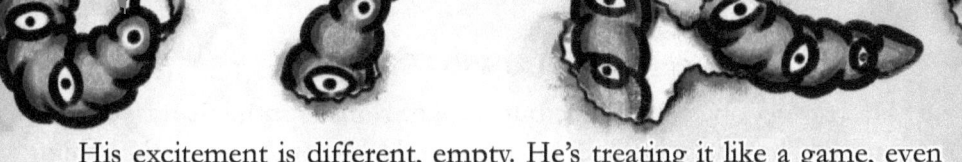

His excitement is different, empty. He's treating it like a game, even after I explained to him how important it is.

It's everything.

We walk around holding each other's waists like we have magnets attached to our bodies.

He can't stop laughing, even as the light bulbs flicker above us. The sound hovers over us like static.

A bulb goes out.

BEEP.

The sound pops into my brain.

BEEP.

The bulb is back to normal.

It feels like a bug crawling inside my skull.

Which one?

It tickles.

I rub my eyes.

Did I bring my key?

Did I lock the room?

I have my bag hanging, I know that much. But what about the rest?

I look at him, pupils dilated and teeth gleaming; he's stroking the walls like I was when we first arrived.

I try to pull him to go our way, but he pulls me back. He brushes against a door frame and brings his face close like he's going to kiss it, smell it, lick it.

"See," he whispers without looking at me.

"Yes, they're velvet," I answer patiently, and he clears his throat.

"No, you idiot. They're scratches, look!" He reaches back until he finds my hand and pulls it to be where his was just seconds ago.

And he's right.

Little nicks in the frame and walls surround the door. Sometimes four, sometimes three. Together. I put my nails on them, they're the perfect distance apart.

They're almost throbbing, screaming.

The echo of someone else's bewilderment lost in the same universe but in entirely different galaxies.

He tries to open the door, but the knob melts in his hands, and he screams like he's been burned. He turns and looks at the one right behind us, also with scratches imploring us not to pass by.

This time the knob splinters, and thousands of tiny pieces fall to the ground.

Two more.

Same thing.

Again.

And again.

And again.

He gives up, and he's not even upset about it. His curiosity had been piqued for an instant and now he's hollow again, empty.

Like me.

Like me without them.

I keep walking, it's better this way.

A part of me wants to go to the front desk just to steal a marker so I can write on the walls again.

No.

It's different this time.

I can't wait for them to find me, they're probably trapped. They need my help. If they didn't they would have come to me already.

"What's their name?"

I jump when I hear him.

How much time has passed? I had already gotten used to the silence and the flickering beeps.

"I don't know their name," I sigh, searching the corners for spider webs.

Will they let me know if they're around?

Nick gasps dramatically.

"Idono Therneim! Idono Therneim!" He starts to scream, wrapping his hands around his lips.

He pauses, tilts his head, and lowers his hands.

"Well, no, no answer." His expression is dead serious now.

In another life, I would have laughed. But my throat is dry, and I have stopped wanting to play games. My lungs feel crushed under the weight of every second that passes.

I need to find them.

I need to help them.

So dizzy.

So thirsty.

Didn't I drink liters of that blue water already?

Keep walking.

"I think they can't tell me," I answer after the silence. "Something is wrong with them. That's why they're looking for me but can't talk to me directly."

"At the hotel?" I nod, and he chuckles. "And all this because you fucked? *Nena*, you'd better not fall in love with me then, I'm not into that kind of stuff."

"No, no! That's not why," I regret having told him. I regret making it real by saying it out loud. "It's different from anything I've ever known in my life, I feel like there's a connection... I don't know."

"And the other guy too? Terry?" He doesn't look at me when he asks these things; his gaze is fixated on something else, something right above my head.

"I don't care about him. It's this place, I think he came here and I wanted him to tell me how to come too."

"That dude was crazy; he said he had worms inside his ears." Nick makes a face of disgust and laughs. "Caterpillars. That's the word."

Caterpillars.

Why does that sound familiar?

I scratch my ear absentmindedly while we walk.

We reach the stairs, almost so narrow that I feel like someone with a slightly wider back would be unable to climb them.

The steps light up one by one as we move.

Nick watches them in fascination, then laughs.

He jumps two at a time and points at them, looking back at me.

"Look, look!" he calls and nearly misses a step. "If we move fast enough, they look like different people!"

His shadow warps. For a split second, it's not his.

I blink.

He's just Nick again.

I shake it off and keep climbing.

A lone drinking fountain in the middle of the corridor greets us; it's not attached to anything.

Is it even touching the floor?

GLOWROT

I rush out and close my eyes as I let the ice water fill my mouth and slide down the corner of my lips.

It tastes different, not blue anymore but purple.

Brighter.

I open my eyes and watch the glowing liquid running down the drain.

I drink more.

And more.

And more.

Until I feel like my stomach is going to burst.

I pull away, and Nick lunges as desperately as I did.

Above us, the bulbs keep flickering, and I keep hearing their screams.

BEEP.

BEEP.

BEEP.

"This one opens!"

I turn and my breath disappears.

When did Nick go from standing next to me to that door?

He holds it like a game show host about to reveal a prize, bathed in the incandescent light coming from inside.

I run to him without thinking.

At least having him next to me reminds me that I am not imagining everything.

He is real.

He exists.

This place exists.

I do too.

Limbs are sticking out of the walls inside the room, unmoving.

Covered in eyes.

Eyes that are also still until I look away.

I can seee them.

I can see them.

See them.

In the borders of my eyes.

That pupil just moved.

That other one just—

Nick steps inside.

Lo voy a matar.

25 TrespassersWillBeProsecuteD

The floor starts to sink in like quicksand.

And then, they move.

The limbs.

The eyess.

   Eyes.

They go fast, stand still, and then move forward a few more inches. They peel off the walls and leave a slimy trail behind them. The lights crash against them and project onto the walls.

"*La puta madre!*" Nick shouts as I drag him back; his ankle pulls free with a wet noise.

I can't talk, I can't scream.

The second we're out, the door slams shut behind us.

The rattle of its hinges echoes down the corridor like a pinball ball.

MY SKIN FEELS WRONG.

I keep going like my life depends on it.

He's laughing.

Not just laughing, but cackling.

What the fuck?!

"Again! Again!" he says and even starts to jump.

He knocks on all the doors around us, and I crawl across the floor to stop him.

"*Qué carajo te pasa, Nick?!*" I scream, my bran—

my bre—

my brain can't even process English for a second.

His eyes are lost again. Like he's high.

High on the fear, on the thrill.

On whatever this place is doing to him.

He runs to the nearest drinking fountain and drinks more.

More.

More.

More.

"That was amazing!"

He starts running again, his fingers twitching simultaneously as his ankles.

For every door that breaks or disappears, he tries to open more.

And more.

More.

GLOWROT

More.

   More.

The floor tilts to one side when I try to follow him.
I'm walking on the walls now.

   Ithink

      I'mgoingto

            throwup.

He jumps to run again in a burst of adrenaline.
Hunger.
Madness.
But this time I manage to tackle him.
Too late.
The door swings open, the light floods the hallway. All the bulbs go
out for a moment.
BEEP. BEEP. BEEP. BEEP. BEEP. BEEP. BEEP. BEEP. BEEP.
BEEP. BEEP. BEEP. BEEP. BEEP. BEEP. BEEP. BEEP. BEEP. BEEP.
BEEP. BEEP. BEEP. BEEP. BEEP. BEEP. BEEP. BEEP. BEEP. BEEP.
BEEP. BEEP. BEEP. BEEP. BEEP. BEEP. BEEP. BEEP. BEEP. BEEP.
BEEP. BEEP. BEEP. BEEP. BEEP. BEEP. BEEP. BEEP. BEEP. BEEP.
BEEP. BEEP. BEEP. BEEP. BEEP. BEEP. BEEP. BEEP. BEEP. BEEP.
BEEP. BEEP. BEEP. BEEP. BEEP. BEEP. BEEP. BEEP. BEEP. BEEP.
BEEP. BEEP. BEEP. BEEP. BEEP. BEEP. BEEP. BEEP. BEEP. BEEP.
BEEP. BEEP. BEEP. BEEP. BEEP. BEEP. BEEP. BEEP. BEEP. BEEP.
BEEP. BEEP. BEEP. BEEP. BEEP. BEEP. BEEP. BEEP. BEEP. BEEP.
BEEP. BEEP. BEEP. BEEP. BEEP. BEEP. BEEP. BEEP. BEEP. BEEP.
BEEP. BEEP. BEEP. BEEP. BEEP. BEEP. BEEP. BEEP. BEEP. BEEP.
BEEP. BEEP. BEEP. BEEP. BEEP. BEEP. BEEP. BEEP. BEEP. BEEP.
BEEP. BEEP. BEEP. BEEP. BEEP. BEEP. BEEP. BEEP. BEEP. BEEP.
BEEP. BEEP. BEEP. BEEP. BEEP. BEEP. BEEP. BEEP. BEEP. BEEP.
BEEP. BEEP. BEEP. BEEP. BEEP. BEEP. BEEP. BEEP. BEEP. BEEP.
BEEP. BEEP. BEEP. BEEP. BEEP. BEEP. BEEP. BEEP. BEEP. BEEP.
BEEP. BEEP. BEEP. BEEP. BEEP. BEEP. BEEP. BEEP. BEEP. BEEP.
BEEP. BEEP. BEEP. BEEP. BEEP. BEEP. BEEP. BEEP. BEEP. BEEP.
i TRY—

25 TrespassersWillBeProsecuteD

I try to scratch the sounds out, but too many of them burrow into my ears.

Like what?

Like an insect.

Without really wanting to, my gaze goes up.

Are those people?

No.

It's food.

An infinite table stretches into a dark abyss. The dishes look obscenely decadent. But something's not right.

Bleeding fruit, raw meat with flies erupting from it, chandeliers sweating something that looks like grease, cakes exuding something that isn't frosting.

The smell.

Rotten sugar.

Nick steps forward and nothing jumps to attack him. He takes another step, and another one.

"Holy shit," he whispers. His pupils dilate.

There are figures seated at the table, but only some of them look human. They eat without looking down, with their eyes fully locked on us. I can't focus on their faces for too long; they morph whenever my eyes fixate on them.

I look back at Nick; his fingers are still twitching, and he's dragging his feet to the table.

I grab his wrist with all the strength I don't have.

"They're going to fuck you up. Let's go," I whisper in his ear.

He doesn't move.

"Good," he replies without looking at me. He seems to be hypnotized.

His voice sounds too far away, as if it were coming from somewhere other than his lips. Like an echo of something that no longer exists.

The figures at the table smile, and their teeth glow.

The blood in the fruit does too.

Everything glows in this place.

None of them move when I drag him away with me; they just keep smiling. He doesn't even protest, just stares back dumbfounded.

Those people, those things.

What if They are trapped in this place?

I have to save them, I have to make sure they're okay.

GLOWROT

I can't be late.

I can't be late.

I can't be late.

I can't be late.

I can't be late. I can't be late.

We stumble down the twisting hallway; with every breath I take, I feel my lungs filling with something other than oxygen. Instead of my heels hurting, my wrists ache. And my throat is still dry.

Don't look back. Don't look back.

Where did Nick go?

I had him next to me a moment ago.

I turn around, and a door is closing slower than normal. He's inside, looking at me; the walls around him look like missing posters.

I scream his name but the sound doesn't come out. He moves his mouth, but the sound escapes him as well.

I run towards it but it's too late.

It clicks.

The lights flicker.

BEEP. BEEP. BEEP. BEEP. BEEP. BEEP. BEEP. BEEP. BEEP.
BEEP. BEEP. BEEP. BEEP. BEEP. BEEP. BEEP. BEEP. BEEP. BEEP.
BEEP. BEEP. BEEP. BEEP. BEEP. BEEP. BEEP. BEEP. BEEP. BEEP.
BEEP. BEEP. BEEP. BEEP. BEEP. BEEP. BEEP. BEEP. BEEP. BEEP.
BEEP. BEEP. BEEP. BEEP. BEEP. BEEP. BEEP. BEEP. BEEP. BEEP.
BEEP. BEEP. BEEP. BEEP. BEEP. BEEP. BEEP. BEEP. BEEP. BEEP.
BEEP. BEEP. BEEP. BEEP. BEEP. BEEP. BEEP. BEEP. BEEP. BEEP.
BEEP. BEEP. BEEP. BEEP. BEEP. BEEP. BEEP. BEEP. BEEP. BEEP.
BEEP. BEEP. BEEP. BEEP. BEEP. BEEP. BEEP. BEEP. BEEP. BEEP.
BEEP. BEEP. BEEP. BEEP. BEEP. BEEP. BEEP. BEEP. BEEP. BEEP.
BEEP. BEEP. BEEP. BEEP. BEEP. BEEP. BEEP. BEEP. BEEP. BEEP.
BEEP. BEEP. BEEP. BEEP. BEEP. BEEP. BEEP. BEEP. BEEP. BEEP.

I'm alone.

One step after the other.

Dry mouth.

There's blood on my knees, I must have fallen. It's okay, it doesn't hurt.

Breathing is hard, the tears are absorbing all the oxygen.

The time, what is it?

Has it passed?

Of course it hasn't.

Something, there has to be something at the end of this hallway.

It can't end here.

There's no point in coming this far if I can't finish what I started. Fate brought me here, so close.

Another water fountain, this one glows red now. I drink.

A sound, a different one from the lights.

CLACK. CLACK. CLACK.

It echoes down the hallway and swallows my breathing. Ahead.

Maybe it's a clue.

I have to keep going, just a little bit further. When I turn the corner, I see a typewriter illuminated by a single desk lamp. But I'm no longer in a hallway, the place looks like an old, rotten cubicle.

Stale.

Blood ink on pages that look like they're going to crumble like pastry.

GLOWROT

Worms are crawling around on the keys.

No, not worms. <u>Caterpillars.</u>

Why do I feel like they're watching me?

    They wriggle between the metal and the ink, some ending up squashed by the keys.

    The next word smears.

Ding.

    The paper flies violently until it reaches my feet.

What does it say?

Bea.

Ba.

Bo.

Bo?!

Bo

Bo. Bo. Bo. Bo. Bo. Bo. Bo. Bo. Bo. Bo. Bo. Bo. Bo. Bo. Bo. Bo. Bo. Bo. Bo. Bo. Bo. Bo. Bo. Bo. Bo. Bo. Bo. Bo. Bo. Bo. Bo. Bo. Bo. Bo. Bo. Bo. Bo. Bo. Bo. Bo. Bo. Bo. Bo. Bo. Bo. Bo. Bo. Bo. Bo. Bo. Bo. Bo. Bo. Bo. Bo. Bo. Bo. Bo. Bo. Bo. Bo. Bo. Bo. Bo. Bo. Bo. Bo. Bo. Bo. Bo.

25 TrespassersWillBeProsecuteD

With my heart in my throat, I start to run, terrified. My entire body is shaking compulsively. The lights are still ringing, but it doesn't matter anymore.

I have to keep going, to reach the end of the corridor that doesn't exist anymore or wherever I can find my angel.

They have to be here, I can feel it in my skin.

I don't care how much effort the universe makes to separate us; our love is stronger.

I miss their moles, their face, their tattoos, and the way they touch me with their delicate fingers.

Another water fountain.

Pink, this time.

I miss the spider web under their eyes and the tone of their voice. I have a pain in my chest matched only by how light my head feels.

I scream over and over until my voice is gone. My knees still ache, but that doesn't stop me from continuing to crawl on the floor.

How can I miss something so much if I don't even remember it well?

Something I don't even know exists?

But it's real!

I'm here right now!

In the hallway, again. This time, it starts to change slowly.

26
No Refunds

The floor is not carpeted anymore.

I stand up and walk through the grey tiles illuminated by the faint pinkish light. It takes a second for my eyes to adjust.

It feels like a dream I don't remember but still lingers somewhere hidden in my mind.

There are cubicles all around me, separated by half walls that look too flimsy, and a sneeze would probably disintegrate them. They're also grey, but with the light's pink tint, they look almost like flesh.

There are cracks in the floor, and I could swear that they are contracting and expanding, that they are breathing.

At least the lights no longer scream every time they flicker.

The silence is deathly, not even the hum of the air conditioning you would expect in a deserted office.

And the place is almost deserted.

Almost.

I try to focus on the walls, although they increasingly give the impression of being alive. At least they're not moving; they don't have arms coming out of them, with eyes wanting to tear my soul out.

Eyes.

Red

eyes.

The memory of Nick hits me like a bucket of cold water and I stop for a few seconds.

Nick.

Did I abandon him?

No.

He abandoned me.

Something starts twisting around my ankle and I scream, jump, and shake it off. It's the hand of one of the people lying on the ground, the same people I was trying to ignore.

The reason I have to keep focusing on the walls.

On the lights that are getting brighter at that distant point. That has to be my target.

It has to mean something.

A piece of the puzzle.

I try not to look at them, but I feel them under me, trying to get under my skin.

Like a bug.

The echo of my footsteps accompanies me almost as much as the urge I have to vomit. Nausea spreads through my body like poisson.
Poison.

But I keep going.

The lights, they're trying to tell me something.

They have to—

They have to be there.

I'm getting closer.

I have to find Them.

I try to focus on the walls, although now I'm sure they are alive.
I have to find Them.

I can't be late.

A security camera I hadn't noticed before blinks at me.

Blinks.

A red light.

Someone's watching.

But I blink back and it's gone.

The wires hang from the ceiling and writhe and squirm.
Like what?

I have to keep going.

There are desks with papers spread on them, covered with scribbles I can't understand. Frantic lines that loop on themselves and spiral, as if someone was trying to draw letters by memory but forgot how they're supposed to look.

A message.

A clue.

I try to grab one of them, and a hand wraps around my ankle. I scream, jump, and shake it off. It's the hand of one of the—

Déjà vu

A radio plays somewhere distant, with a conversation I can almost understand.

Almost.

It sounds familiar.

Keep walking.

Keep walking.

That's it.

The door is open.

Finally.

I step through

Everything is white, antiseptic. The walls, the desk, the shelves, and the books on them. The carpet is decorated with golden details that seem to move.

Like worms.

No, like <u>caterpillars</u>.

The corners give off white noise, like a broken TV. My lungs are begging for oxygen, but it's heavier here than anywhere else in NIU, almost solid as soon as I breathe it in.

A clap in front of me rumbles in my ears and makes everything go black.

But how?

There was no one there.

The darkness is so intense that it doesn't feel like the absence of light but like a void.

I don't know if my lungs or ears will give out first, but when I feel like I can't take any more, the clap rings out again.

Pink, neon lights.

Of course.

They bathe everything around me and give the place the tint I'm so familiar with at this point.

And then someone.

But not Them.

A thin, tall man with orange hair. His skin glows white despite the lights. He finishes buttoning his shirt collar, smiling. Something underneath it squirms. Something in his skin.

I turn around to leave, but the door is gone.

A screen embedded in the desk before him gives off a similar glow. He looks at it for a few seconds, then slides his hand over it and covers it with papers that weren't there a second ago.

It's too cold in here.

Almost unbearable.

Deathly.

He just looks past me to his golden fingernails and then back to me again.

There's something wrong with his eyes.

He hasn't blinked, and his smile is not reaching them either. They reflect the light too well, like glass.

Something flickers under his shirt collar again, in the space between buttons. Another flicker under his sleeve.

But with all that confidence, he doesn't look like another wretch.

No, he can't be one of us.

He has to be in charge.

Something has been watching me.

A red blink, similar to the one I saw before, mocks me from a point in the ceiling. When I look directly it's gone, the cables again writhing.

I snap back to him, but he was already looking at me.

"Yes, Bo. One second, please," he says, holding up his index finger as he moves the papers. They are white, like his fingers, and the ink is golden, like his joints. Vibrating.

I want to scream.

Throw something at him.

Run away.

Ask for help.

My body is not responding correctly.

I can't—

I can't think.

GLOWROT

I can't   think   straight.

Too weak.

Like with every second this place is stealing my energy.

It's different from other times, because before it made me feel alive.

He gestures with his opposite hand for me to sit down, and I do so without being able to stop shaking.

Without wanting to.

I don't think I'm in control anymore.

Breathe.

Breathe.

I have to breathe.

But I can't.

It hurts.

My chest.

My head shakes, I look around, looking for something, somthing i know too well, but I can't remember, a shadow that can't form in my head right now, something, something that's been with me for so long.

Where?

Where?

Where?

Breathe.

I have to breathe.

The man stares at me with those unmoving eyes.

A flicker again, under the fabric.

Something, there's something on his skin.

He's hiding it, I know so.

Something is still watching.

I feel it from all angles.

Everywhere but his eyes.

"I'm looking for someone," my voice comes out way too calm, like it was domesticated. I wish I had tears left. "A rabbit. A rabbit on their neck, the back. They're bald. Tall. Skinny. More tattoos. Moles. Please. Please I need them. I have to. They need me."

"You have a fascinating case of obsession, Bo." He says, his voice sounds like smoke and curls around my throat. "It's like watching a beetle try to climb out of a jar."

"Please! It's an emergency," I lean over to take his hand, my skin sticks to it because it's so cold. It feels like dry ice.

"Of course, it's an emergency. If it wasn't, you wouldn't be here."

His words reach my ears backward, but somehow, my brain can translate them correctly.

His voice is sweet, soft, cloying.

He's pointing those lifeless eyes at me.

"Bo." He savors the word like it's longer. "How are you?"

"Stressed, I don't understand what's going on, and I need to know they're okay."

It itches.

My arm itches so much.

Why am I scratching?

Scratching.

It's my skin.

There's something under it.

"Anxious? Tense?" his words layer on top of each other. "Aren't you worrying too much about someone you don't know?"

"Yes, I am!" I try to sound intimidating, but my voice comes out shaky. "Clearly, if you know my name, you know theirs. Where are they?!"

He tilts his head.

Slowly.

Too slowly.

Everything he does seems to be with some sort of delay.

Half a second.

Like a video out of sync.

"Why does the bird long for the cage?" He asks but his lips barely move. "Strange little moth, fluttering toward the flame and calling it love." *I can't.*

I need to.

I have to.

Get out of here.

What does hE KNOW ABOUT LOVE?!

I grab a paperweight off the desk and throw it on the floor.

He doesn't even flinch. Calm, collected, Calculated.

"I know your name because you wrote it seven hundred and eleven times on my walls."

GLOWROT

It itches. There's something, something in my skin.

Is it the numbers?

Seven.

One.

One.

There's someth—

"Most people come to get lost, Bo. Not to find things."

How long has it been?

Probably over twelve hours.

Maybe more.

It has to be the next day.

But I'm still here.

It's the longest time I've been here.

The longest without fading.

But I'm stuck.

I have to get out.

Get out.

Get out. Get out.

Get out. Get out.

Get out. Get out. Get out.

Get out. Get out.

Get out.

Get out. Get out. Get out. Get out.

Get out.

He looks at me, I don't respond. He moves his hand closer to mine, and I pull it away.

He clears his throat, I don't care.

I don't want to talk; I need to get out.

Get out. Get out.

Get out. Get out. Get out.

Get out. Get out. Get out.

Get out. Get out. Get out. Get out.

Get out. Get out. Get out.

Get out. Get out.

Get out.

Get out. Get out.

He presses a button on the desk, and—

♥ 264 ♣

26 NoRefundS

BEEEEEEEEEEEEEEEEEEEEEEEEEEEEEEEEEEEEEEEEEEEEE
EEEEEEEEEEEEEEEEEEEEEEEEEEEEEEEEEEEEEEEEEEEEEE
EEEEEEEEEEEEEEEEEEEEEEEEEEEEEEEEEEEEEEEEEEEEEE
EEEEEEEEEEEEEEEEEEEEEEEEEEEEEEEEEEEEEEEEEEEEEE
EEEEEEEEEEEEEEEEEEEEEEEEEEEEEEEEEEEEEEEEEEEEEE
EEEEEEEEEEEEEEEEEEEEEEEEEEEEEEEEEEEEEEEEEEEEEE
EEEEEEEEEEEEEEEEEEEEEEEEEEEEEEEEEEEEEEEEEEEEEE
EEEEEEEEEEEEEEEEEEEEEEEEEEEEEEEEEEEEEEEEEEEEEE
EEEEEEEEEEEEEEEEEEEEEEEEEEEEEEEEEEEEEEEEEEEEEE
EEEEEEEEEEEEEEEEEEEEEEEEEEEEEEEEEEEEEEEEEEEEEE
EEEEEEEEEEEEEEEEEEEEEEEEEEEEEEEEEEEEEEEEEEEEEE
EEEEEEEEEEEEEEEEEEEEEEEEEEEEEEEEEEEEEEEEEEEEEE
EEEEEEEEEEEEEEEEEEEEEEEEEEEEEEEEEEEEEEEEEEEEEE
EEEEEEEEEEEEEEEEEEEEEEEEEEEEEEEEEEEEEEEEEEEEEE
EEEEEEEEEEEEEEEEEEEEEEEEEEEEEEEEEEEEEEEEEEEEEE
EEEEEEEEEEEEEEEEEEEEEEEEEEEEEEEEEEEEEEEEEEEEEE
EEEEEEEEEEEEEEEEEEEEEEEEEEEEEEEEEEEEEEEEEEEEEE
EEEEEEEEEEEEEEEEEEEEEEEEEEEEEEEEEEEEEEEEEEEEEE
EEEEEEEEEEEEEEEEEEEEEEEEEEEEEEEEEEEEEEEEEEEEEE
EEEEEEEEEEEEEEEEEEEEEEEEEEEEEEEEEEEEEEEEEEEEEE
EEEEEEEEEEEEEEEEEEEEEEEEEEEEEEEEEEEEEEEEEEEEEE
EEEEEEEEEEEEEEEEEEEEEEEEEEEEEEEEEEEEEEEEEEEEEE
EEEEEEEEEEEEEEEEEEEEEEEEEEEEEEEEEEEEEEEEEEEEEE
EEEEEEEEEEEEEEEEEEEEEEEEEEEEEEEEEEEEEEEEEEEEEE
EEEEEEEEEEEEEEEEEEEEEEEEEEEEEEEEEEEEEEEEEEEEEE
EEEEEEEEEEEEEEEEEEEEEEEEEEEEEEEEEEEEEEEEEEEEEE
EEEEEEEEEEEEEEEEEEEEEEEEEEEEEEEEEEEEEEEEEEEEEE
EEEEEEEEEEEEEEEEEEEEEEEEEEEEEEEEEEEEEEEEEEEEEE
EEEEEEEEEEEEEEEEEEEEEEEEEEEEEEEEEEEEEEEEEEEEEE
EEEEEEEEEEEEEEEEEEEEEEEEEEEEEEEEEEEEEEEEEEEEEE
EEEEEEEEEEEEEEEEEEEEEEEEEEEEEEEEEEEEEEEEEEEEEE
EEEEEEEEEEEEEEEEEEEEEEEEEEEEEEEEEEEEEEEEEEEEEE
EEEEEEEEEEEEEEEEEEEEEEEEEEEEEEEEEEEEEEEEEEEEEE
EEEEEEEEEEEEEEEEEEEEEEEEEEEEEEEEEEEEEEEEEEEEEE
EEEEEEEEEEEEEEEEEEEEEEEEEEEEEEEEEEEEEEEEEEEEEE
EEEEEEEEEEEEEEEEEEEEEEEEEEEEEEEEEEEEEEEEEEEEEE
EEEEEEEEEEEEEEEEEEEEEEEEEEEEEEEEEEEEEEEEEEEEEP

GLOWROT

"I don't know! I don't know how I can explain it!" I scream, covering my ears with my hands, but it doesn't help.

The second I speak, the beeping stops.

"It's like... I had no reason to wake up before, and now I do."

"Because of someone you met here?"

He writes something down, but his fingers aren't in sync with the pen either.

Again, that flicker.

There, under a sleeve.

A blink.

"Why are you so fixated on this... <u>White Rabbit</u>?"

"I don't know, but it makes me feel good. I feel like when they look at me, they really look at me. At Bo, not at *the idea of Bo* others have." My voice shakes again, I feel weak but start to smile. "I keep remembering. Every day, more and more. The things we lived, the moments. I know them now. They're not dreams, they happened. And they need to know. They need me. They're not okay, I can feel it in my skin. They've been calling but someone... Someone..."

I can't finish speaking, my throat freezes.

He sits still.

Silent.

Waiting.

Then, a smile.

"Someone...?" he echoes my words with his tongue.

A bifid tongue.

"You've been keeping them away from me!" The scream burns my throat.

My body moves before I can process it. I lunge forward, desperately searching for the collar of his shirt with my hands.

Something, whatever is moving under the fabric, flutters against my fingers.

The lights attack me.

They convulse, turning on and off again and again.

On.

Off.

On.

Off.

I sink into the desk, which starts to twist against my side. I search for his throat with my nails.

The lights are stronger, pulling at my wrists.

On.

Off.

On.

Off.

Like the fading beat of a heart.

On. Off. On.

I lunge again, if only I could scratch out those fake eyes with my nails.

And I try.

But no.

Lights.

Convulsion.

The lights are pounding on the walls of my skull. They are buzzing inside my teeth.

Pulsing.

The scream doesn't come from my mouth anymore, it comes from my pores.

He doesn't move, doesn't need to.

Another burst.

On. Off. On. Off. On. Off. On Off. On. Off. On. Off. On. Off. On.
Off. On. Off. On. Off. On. Off. On. Off. On. Off. On. Off. On. Off. On.
Off. On. Off. On. Off. On. Off. On. Off. On. Off. On. Off. On. Off. On.
Off. On. Off. On. Off. On. Off. On. Off. On. Off. On. Off. Off. On.
Off. On. Off. On Off. On. Off. On. Off. On. Off. On. Off. On. Off. On.
Off. On. Off. On. Off. On. Off. On. Off. On. Off. On. Off. On. Off. On.
Off. On. Off. On. Off. On. Off. On. Off. On. Off. On. Off. On. Off. On.
Off. On. Off. On. Off. On. Off. On. Off. On. Off. On. Off. On. Off. On.
Off. On. Off. On. Off On. Off. On. Off. On. Off. On. Off. On. Off. On.
Off. On. Off. On. Off. On. Off. On. Off. On. Off. On. Off. On. Off. On.
Off. On. Off. On. Off. On. Off. On. Off. On. Off. On. Off. On. Off. On.
Off. On. Off. On. Off. On. Off. On. Off. On. Off. On. Off. On. Off. On.
Off. On. Off. On. Off. On. Off. On. Off On. On. Off. On. Off. On. Off.
On. Off. On. Off. On. Off. On. Off. On. Off. On. Off. On. Off. On. Off.
On. Off. On. Off. On. Off. On. Off. On. Off. On. Off. On. Off. On. Off.
On. Off. On. Off. On. Off. On. Off. On. Off. On. Off. On. Off. On. Off.
On. Off. On. Off. On. Off. On. Off. On. Off. On. Off. On. Off. On. Off.
On. Off. On. Off. On. Off. On. Off. On. Off. On. Off. On. Off. On. Off.
On. Off. On. Off. On. Off. On. Off On Off. On. Off. On. Off. On. Off.
On. Off. On. Off. On. Off. On. Off. On. Off. On. Off. On. Off. On. Off.
On. Off. On. Off. On. Off. On. Off. On. Off. On. Off. On. Off. On. Off.
On. Off. On. Off. On. Off. On. Off. On. Off. On. Off. On. Off. On. Off.
On. Off. On. Off. On. Off. On. Off. On. Off. On. Off. On. Off. On. Off.
On. Off. On. On. Off. On. Off. On. Off. On. Off. On. Off. On. Off. On.
Off. On. Off. On. Off. On. Off. On. Off. On. Off. On. Off. On. Off
On. Off. On. Off On. Off. On. Off. On. Off. On. Off. On. Off. On. Off.
On. Off. On. Off. On. Off. On. Off. On. Off. On. Off. On. Off. On. Off.
On. Off. On. Off. On. Off. On. Off. On. Off. On. Off. On. Off. On. Off
On. Off. On. Off. On. Off. On. Off. On. Off. On. Off. On. Off. On. Off.
On. Off. On. Off. On. Off. On. Off. On. Off. On. Off. On. Off. On. Off.
On. Off. On. Off. On. Off. On. Off. On. Off. On. Off. On. Off. On. Off.
On. Off. On. Off. On. Off. On. Off. On. Off. On. Off. On. Off. On. Off.
On. Off. On. Off. On. Off. On. Off. On. Off. On. Off. On. Off. On. Off.
On. Off. On. Off. On. Off. On. Off. On. Off. On. Off. On. Off. On. Off.
On. Off. On. Off. On. Off. On. Off. On. Off. On. Off. On. Off. On. Off
On. Off. On. Off. On. Off. On. Off. On. Off. On. Off. On. Off. On. Off.
On. Off. On. Off. On. Off. On. Off. On. Off On Off. On. Off. On. Off.
On. Off. On. Off. On. Off. On. Off. On. Off. On. Off. On. Off. On. Off

26 NoRefundS

My body is vibrating, and I'm back in the chair.

"Are you done?" His tone is not mocking, just matter of fact.

I go to lounge again, but the second the lights start flickering, I sit back.

He goes back to the papers with the twisting ink.

"Better or worse?" His smile widens. "Which one do you prefer?"

The glow is coming from inside his shirt.

A dozen little dots shine under the thin white fabric.

"Better! What? I have— I have a purpose now. With them!" I try to put into words what I feel, but I don't even know precisely what it is.

If he's the one keeping them away, he can help me find them.

Why is he hiding them from me?

Is this a test?

"And what will you do when you get this… important person? Keep them in a jar? Throw away the key?"

I've been thinking about the search for so long, I haven't gotten that far. Reassure them that everything's okay? Try to get them to remember if they don't already? Ask them why they're playing this cat-and-mouse game with me? Cry? Laugh?

"Why? Why are you doing this?"

The energy that I didn't even have before vanished. All that remains is the echo of despair, of tears that dried up even before reaching this horrible clinical cubicle.

I'm finally, slowly, slowly fading away.

"Who are you?!"

"Oberon," he shrugs and finally breaks eye contact.

But those aren't his real eyes.

He opens one of the desk drawers and takes out what looks like an orange ice cream, he starts eating it with all the calmness in the world.

Crunch.

I flinch.

Ice cream isn't supposed to crunch.

"You're not very bright, are you?" He bites into the ice cream, unbothered. What kind of beast bites into ice cream? "I sit here, and I observe whatever I find *interesting*." I'm melting through the chair. "And I've got my eye on you."

GLOWROT

He points his index finger at me and reaches out to almost touch me.
The tiny pupil right in the center of his fingertip contracts.
It's happening.
My insides feel like wet glass.
I open my mouth to scream.
His voice doesn't come from his mouth.
It's inside my head.
"See you soon, Bo."
The office rips a p a   r   t.

27

Wet Paint

The sun is shining. The waves are gentle.

The air is no longer heavy; my lungs are working again. My heart is beating at a normal rate.

I want to die.

I was so close, if only I'd held on a little longer. NIU is gone.

And I don't feel safe.

The walk from the beach to the car lot is quiet, but the world is still spinning around me.

People are coming and going; the GPS in my phone is working perfectly; it even has a battery left!

Everything is too normal, like I wasn't consumed and spit out by a sentient, wonderful and awful nightmare. Like this city is not constantly chewing up people left and right.

How can it all just keep existing?

By the time I sign the papers and pay, I see double.

Maybe I even paid double.

I finally get into my car and drop my forehead on the steering wheel. The silence around me is usual, and the absence of voices filled with noises is too commonplace to be pleasant.

Cars, birds, people walking.

It's so painful.

Frustrating.

Pathetic.

How am I supposed to go on existing as if nothing had happened?

But the silence disappears before I can get used to it.

W's voice attacks me from every possible angle, escaping through the holes in the air conditioning, the slits in the windows, from the rear-view mirror.

Screams.

Unintelligible screams that stun me and leave me transfixed.

Sounds whose sole function is to tear at the skin of my senses until I am incapable of existing.

Relief washes over me.

I don't ask him why he left, where he was or why he has come now. None of that matters anymore.

Instead, I tell him everything.

"soTheIncompetentJack-of-all-trades DecidedToAbandonYou."

He sneers when he decides to start spouting complete sentences.

"howMuchDidItHurt WhenYouGotBurned?"

I don't complain, I just handle and answer his questions, I put up with his taunts, his scolding.

Deep down, I know I deserve it.

Going straight to work is probably one of the worst things that could have happened to me.

The lobby lights are threatening to blind me. They're humming softly but not in the way I wish they would.

BEEP?

Nothing.

Nina is leaning against the reception desk, bored. When I walk through the front door, she runs up to me.

"Bo! I thought you weren't coming!" she says, looking at the time on her phone. "What happened to you?"

I'm still wearing the clothes I found at NIU, the semi-transparent pink plastic dress. Definitely not something I could wear at work.

My hair is a mess, and I probably have shit breath.

"I went out... for a drink... I don't know," I reply without much conviction.

Her expression becomes serious.

"Come on, I can give you my sweater, and we'll grab some work shirts from the back or something."

She takes my hand and drags me with her without waiting for me to accept.

27 Wet Paint

Warm.

Human.

Sweet.

"haven'tYouLearned
AnythingAbout
TrustingStrangers?"
W asks me, irritated and fascinated at the same time.

But she's not a stranger; she's Nina, and she's always buying me coffee, and offering help, and asking me if I'm okay.

"youThoughtAlexiaWasn'tAStrangerEither,
AndSheAbandonedYou."
A shock runs down my spine.

"Thank you," I reply dryly when Nina finds a change of clothes. "I can dress myself, you know?"

I go to the back and, with pain, I take off the dress I brought from NIU. I need to protect it, get home and, examine every detail, find the hidden smells and messages.

When I put the crossbody bag back on, something tinkles inside. Against all logic, I still have the casino chip I took from Terry's room. The <u>white</u> lighter is there too.

Did I pick it up when I left the house?

There's something else.

A compact mirror, like for make-up. I open it, and the LED edge glistens with a glow that is too familiar. Embedded in the lid, a message that says, *'look at me'.*

Flick me.

I take the casino chip and, as I thought, it also has something written on it.

Use me.

Something clicks in my brain. Didn't that man's wallet also have a message?

Open me.

"Do you know what day is today?" Nina asks me as soon as I come out of the back.

"What?"

"You disappeared the whole day yesterday," she continues with a soft voice. "Nova and I went to check in on you, and your door was open, but you weren't there."

"WhoTheFuckDoesSheThinkSheIs?"

Who the fuck does she think she is to talk to me like that?

"she'sNoOne."

W is right, his voice makes my teeth vibrate.

And yet.

She's not even giving me shit for it; her eyes look teary and

She's been crying.

She's been crying over me.

Her nostrils flare up.

Why?

"It makes sense," I whisper to myself, but she hears me. I had a feeling I was gone for longer than I thought, but time stopped working properly a while ago.

"Look, you know that we all know you're going through something," she's talking slowly as if she's putting a lot of care into choosing the correct words. "And it's hard, but you're not alone."

"Nina, I'm fine, I got blackout drunk, and now I have a migraine, that's all."

But she can see right through me.

Her fingers twitch like she wants to reach out, like she wants to touch my arm.

Maybe I can tell her, I'm sure she would understand.

"wouldShe?"

W's voice smears over everything like thick oil.

"sillyGirl.

Silly,

Foolish,

EasilyDistractedGirl."

I blink.

Nina's still looking at me.

"Look, don't tell Nova I told you this, but a couple of years ago, she started acting weird too." She stretches her arm a bit more.

27 Wet Paint

"sheKnows,

She'sTryingToDragYouBack."

I don't answer.

"aHandOutstretchedIsn'tAGift,Darling.

It'sALeash."

I step forward, he screams. But something in what she said.
Something rings a bell.

"What do you mean?" I ask, my voice trembling.

I need to know.

> *I need to know.*

> > *I need to know.*

> > > *I need to know.*

> > *I need to know.*

"It was a hot mess; she said she found a place where she was happier, but she looked way worse. Like something was sucking the life out of her." I let her hold my hand. It's warm and clammy, but for a moment, I don't mind it. "She said she met someone and came home with this weird tattoo that itched at night."

The tattoo.

The receptionist.

"TrustNoOne

TrustNoOne

TrustNoOneButMe."

His claws start clinging to my shoulders.

> *But I need to know.*

"A place? What place? How did she find it?" My hand's shaking, my breath is short, and I can't help but stutter. She squeezes my hand.

She's close, so close.

And the reception is empty.

"It's the same, isn't it?" Nina's voice warps when it reaches my ears. "Bo, you're not alone. We can help you. I can help you."

"lookAtHer.

LookAtHowSheTreatsYou

LikeAWoundedDog."

"Do you think she can help me find it?"

Her smile stiffens.

"rememberWhatAlexiaSaid.

You'reTooMuch,

TooBroken,

TooRottenForThem."

No.

No, that's not—

"you'dLetHerIntoYourRibs,

YourBones,YourTeeth.

YouWouldGiveHerAllYourSecrets.

AndWhenSheSeesWhat'sInsideYou,

She'llLeave,Too."

No.

"BecauseEveryoneDoes."

I gasp.

Nina takes a step toward me.

"Bo…" She tries to touch my cheek with her fingertips but retrieves them.

"She started remembering, didn't she?" I ask with a shaky breath. My pulse is hammering through my ears.

I knew she knew something.

Her twitching fingers.

I knew it.

"Nina," I insist. "If you want to help me, you have to tell me everything you know."

She moves her face close to mine, pulls back, squeezes my hand and then lets go.

I can almost see the million thoughts running through her head.

Silence, everything gets too quiet.

"Yesterday," she finally says. "There was a cop here, asking about missing guests."

I go still.

Just when I was gone.

It can't be a coincidence.

"And?"

I start shaking.

"He wanted to check the records," she continues. "Said someone reported them missing, but we checked and they just checked out early."

27 Wet Paint

My nails dig into my palm.

"And Nova started twitching like she couldn't breathe. She got like... well, like how you've been getting recently." A shameful blush bathes her cheeks.

"That guy, Ute. Did Nova tell you about him?"

Nina asks.

Why am I so dizzy?

"useHerAndLeaveHer,

BeforeSheUsesYouAndLeavesYouFirst."

"She doesn't like him. He's still here. Bo, listen. I care about you," she grabs both of my hands and moves closer in a desperate attempt at distracting me.

"ButYouKnowBetter"

But I know better.

Him.

Nova.

The puzzle pieces.

Flick me.

Open me.

Use me.

Look at me.

It's all the same.

It's all connected.

I blink and realize that everything is blurry.

I do it some more and start to be able to focus on her with my eyes.

She's crying again.

I open my mouth, but I'm not sure if I remember how to speak. She keeps talking, something about me, I think. Her breathing is labored, and the words don't make sense anymore.

I can't make a scene, not here, not now.

It's going to get worse. I won't be able to keep looking, and for sure, any hospital bill will be more even than I had to pay for the car.

"Oh my FUCKING GOD BO, are you having a seizure?! Oh shit, shit."

She's about to scream, running around. She's not holding me anymore but buzzing back and forth.

"it'sOkay,It'sOver."

"It's okay. It's over," I hear myself say, and I slowly start to breathe normally.

I look at my hands, I can move them again.

My head no longer feels stiff. I remember the words.

She looks at me and exhales like I've lifted a weight off her shoulders.

She then hugs me, so tight it opens up my lungs.

I wrap my arms around her too, out of politeness. Her hair smells good, I have always liked it. What would her tears taste like?

"it'sOver.NoMoreGames."

But she has perfect skin, and her voice is sweet.

And when I go into the back room, she always covers for me.

Maybe I could give her a reason to stop crying; maybe she could teach me how to braid my hair like she does.

Maybe we can cry together.

"STOPGETTINGATTACHEDTO EVERYSINGLEPERSONWHO PAYSATTENTIONTOYOU."

I let go.

"I'm okay, I need to rest, that's all," I whisper and kiss her cheek.

"I could come by you know?" Her tone is slow and shy. "To make sure you're okay…"

Cute.

"NO!"

"I'll text you," I lie.

W is right, she's trying to distract me.

She doesn't understand.

No one does.

"noOneButMe."

But does he?

"iDoNow."

Flick me.

Open me.

Use me.

Look at me.

27 Wet Paint

Something, I need to find something to tell me what the next step to take is.

I could ask Nova.

"youCan'tTrustAnyone."

Writing on the walls didn't work, trying to look for Their name didn't either.

How did Oberon call them?

My White Rabbit.

Oberon.

His name tastes like a worm in my brain.

A worm with feet.

W is right, I can't trust Nova. If she stopped looking for NIU maybe she'd try to get me to stop too.

What's left?

Not Nick.

Not Nova.

Not Nina.

The silhouette of the massive man with the mustache towering over the desk hits me like a train.

Seven.

One.

One.

That number.
His room.
I have to find him.

GLOWROT

28

Objects in mirror are closer than they appear

Time still doesn't work properly.

Right now, that this is urgent; it's as if the whole universe has conspired to make my life miserable and force me to be late. To force everything to happen with ceremonial slowness.

Dreadful.

The elevator has taken seven centuries to arrive.

Seven.

And when it finally does, one person gets out.

One.

And one person stays inside.

One.

I go in quickly and press the seventh floor without thinking, without even realizing who is left inside the metal box.

Seven.

The hardest part is the waiting, the slowness, and the fact that everything is still too normal, like whoever is standing next to me. I wish I could take them by the shoulders and give them one single shake, shout at them that they're blind and cannot see that the world around us is falling apart.

One.

At least time hasn't completely stopped, and my anonymous companion stops on the sixth floor.

When she comes out, she says goodbye to me, and I feel chills; I'm not used to hotel guests noticing my presence.

GLOWROT

I notice her for a second before the doors close: a woman with dark circles under her eyes and a vacant expression. She is wearing a necklace with a silver hammer.

I don't have time for irrelevant details.

There's only one floor left.

One.

We go up, this time just W and I.

I turn to look at him, and a glowing line appears where his mouth usually is, slowly transforming into a smile with pointed, sharp teeth.

"Please, please don't leave me this time," I beg him.

I'm close. I can feel it.

I can smell it.

"asLongAsYouListenToMeAndDoWhatISay," he replies, his voice almost tangible.

"ifYouHadListenedToMeFromTheBeginning,
YouWouldSurelyHaveFound
YourWhiteRabbitByNow."

I am left speechless.

Has the elevator stopped moving?

"You hate NIU."

"ofCourseNot,
I'mSureYouJustImaginedIt."

His voice comes from the intercom under the buttons, which for a moment all glow at once.

"iOnlyHateStrangers
WhoTryToTakeAdvantageOfYou,
That'sDifferent."

We should have arrived by now. It was only one floor.

One floor.

Why is this thing not moving?

I step backward, but my back touches the cold metal wall.

The two glowing orbs appear on top of his smile, he cocks his head in a gesture that's too familiar to be comforting.

"You left me alone; every time I've tried to reach NIU, you—"

"youHaveItAllWrong."

I freeze, he comes closer. The elevator is still not fucking moving, and

28 Objects in mirror are closer than they appear

I can't stop shaking.

"you'veBeenOnTheVerge

OfGettingCloseToYourGoal,

ButSomethingAlwaysHappens.

What'sTheThingThatAlwaysHappens,Bo?

It'sNotMe,YouKnowThat."

"Something distracts me," I answer without thinking, and he nods.

"inTheElevator,

AtTheFrontDesk,

AtTheEntrance.EvenInsideNIU,

There'sAlwaysSomeoneWhoShouldn'tBeThere."

And he's not wrong. I've been close, so close I can smell their perfume. But then someone grabs me, calls me. Something always happens.

They distract me.

Something.

Always.

Happens.

Why?

"I thought you didn't want me to find them," I whisper almost inaudibly, but I know he can still hear me. He has ears everywhere.

"iJustWantWhat'sBestForYou."

The elevator doors open, and he gets out of the way; I bolt out.

I run down the corridor. I don't care if anyone sees me.

Déjà vu.

Seven.

One.

One.

From the first moment that man and his friends set foot in the lobby, I knew something was strange. Something was different.

It may be too late for the others, but Nina said that according to the hotel records, he is still here.

Out of inertia, I reach into my bag and take out the compact I found.

I read the inscription on the lid and smile without stopping.

Look at me.

I open it, and the lights around the part with the mirror illuminate my face.

GLOWROT

And they flicker.

They flicker?

I stop; they stop flickering.

I start walking again, and they start flickering again.

I turn to look at W, but he just watches. I could swear he's as curious as I am.

I take the lighter in my hands; it's still not working, but it's warm.

Flick me.

The casino chip feels heavier and I accidentally drop it. It falls on the side with the inscription.

Use me.

I frown and let it fall again. And again. And again. Every time, it falls on the same side.

The pieces of the puzzle are talking to me. They are trying to show me the way.

They tell me that I am on the right path.

I put them away and finish making my way to the room that has been etched on my mind almost as much as the white rabbit with the spots.

711

The door is ajar, almost as if it were an invitation.

I put my hand on the doorknob and it's warm, almost as warm as in the motel.

No, not just any motel.

The details don't matter.

I inhale and close my eyes, trying to hear if anyone is inside, but the silence is deathly.

It doesn't feel like the absence of sound but like a void.

I go in.

The room is clean, immaculate, as if it hadn't been touched by anyone. I'm about to scream in frustration, but I notice a suitcase by the door, and a wave of relief washes over me.

A suitcase?

It's not one of the bigger rooms like Terry's. This one is almost a perfect reflection of my apartment.

But that's normal; this is a hotel, and all the rooms are identical.

And at the same time…

Nothing is a coincidence.

28 Objects in mirror are closer than they appear

The threshold is illuminated by a single lamp; the shadows it casts are longer than they should be, and somehow, that causes me relief.

Because at least everything feels less normal here.

A draft suddenly chills me, and I realize all the windows are open.

They're huge.

What would happen if I jumped?

I need to concentrate.

I scan the rest of the room and there he is.

The colossal silhouette, sitting at the dining room table, with the table set and an empty plate. The shadows make it look for a second like he has enormous fangs protruding from his lips.

Like a fat, slippery <u>walrus</u>.

He doesn't look surprised by my presence; he just sighs sadly and then smiles.

I step forward, and the breeze causes the door to close behind me.

"Your friends," I begin. "Your missing friends. You always knew where they were."

He doesn't reply; he continues to look at me with those huge, sad eyes and his half-smile hidden by his mustache. His fingers are caressing the cutlery in front of him.

"You went to reception to ask about them, but you knew where they were. Didn't you? Because you went to that place too. To NIU."

He exhales calmly, and the sound somehow feels heavy. Almost acted.

"How kind of you to come," he says in a deep voice. "And you're very nice for caring."

Tears slide down his eyes, but he doesn't wipe them away. He continues touching the cutlery but does not attempt to pick it up.

"Why? Were you jealous because they got to go again, and you didn't?" My voice is trembling. I don't want to get closer but I do it anyway. "Is that why you went to talk to us? To try to get information out of me?"

"I miss them, you know? I really do. I tried to warn you."

"Warn me about what?' He just shakes his head.

W stiffens and moves closer to the man like he's studying him.

Like he can see something I don't.

"The first time we found that place," he says, his voice thick with nostalgia. "It felt like the sun was shining over the sea in the middle of the night."

And I understand exactly what he means.

GLOWROT

A wave of envy runs over my body.

Why does he get to remember his first time there so vividly?
Why can't I?

And then he shivers.

"It was terrifying." Ute's voice is humid; it clings to every surface it touches. "I wanted to get away since the first minute, but we were too far gone."

There's something under the plate.

The corner of a paper is poking from underneath.

A black, folded paper.

An envelope.

"Get... away?"

How?

Why would someone, anyone, want to get away from a place so wonderful?
A wonderful place with hands in the walls.

With eyes in the corners.

Wonderful, because I met Them there.

Because I belong.

He remains silent. Silence surrounds us.

W continues to look at him and gets closer and closer. His eyes begin to shine and illuminate the man's face. The shadows that look like fangs are even more pronounced.

Then, he slowly picks up the plate and sets it aside.

Underneath, I can see the black envelope with gold lettering.
Like Terry's.

Something—

Something doesn't add up.

He's crying, yes. But he's too calm.

"It's hard to get rid of that place, you know? Even if you think you have," he explains matter-of-factly and takes the envelope. "Like the other girl, the one with black hair. She convinced herself she wouldn't go anymore, but the second something reminds her of it, she starts to doubt it, doesn't she?"
A chill.

There's something in his voice.

Something in the way he talks about Nova makes me shiver.

28 Objects in mirror are closer than they appear

I take another step forward without realizing it and open my mouth to speak, but I can't find the right words.

"She's not the only one who has tried to escape, but I guess you know that." After saying this, he points to my hand.

He points to the <u>white</u> lighter in my hand.

When did I pick it up?

Wait—

What does he know about—

"Where are They?!"

"calmDown,

You'veComeThisFar.

Don'tLetHimBeatYou."

He just smiles and opens the envelope, takes out a black paper with gold lettering, and eyes it for a second. It's not a black card, like the one I saw in Terry's room.

He looks at it like he's proud of whatever that says.

Then, he sighs and leans forward.

"The time has come then, to talk of many things."

"letHimTalk."

"Then talk." I try to sound angry, intimidating.

I can't stop shaking.

It's too cold here.

Why are all the windows open?

He just offers me a seat at the table, next to him. I sit down reluctantly.

"The person you're looking for, I've seen them," he explains cautiously. I immediately perch up, and I'm about to lunge at him, but W holds me down. "They come and go, they've tried to quit it but it's that godforsaken place. It finds you."

"Quit what? Smoking?" I ask. Maybe that's why they gave me their lighter.

But no.

I know the answer.

But why?

He doesn't clarify.

"Some go willingly. Some just need a little nudge," he continues. "Your bald friend didn't need one; you didn't either. But some…"

His eyes move to some point in the room, a wave of nostalgia again and then a wave of tears.

He lets them run down his cheeks.

I want to scream.

"I had to do it, I needed a way out. He came to see me, you know? Here, to this room." I look around, almost expecting to find something otherwordly, out of the ordinary. "It seems a shame, to play them such a trick…"

"Who came? The tall man with the eyes? Oberon?"

He nods and inhales.

Exhales.

Then inspects the envelope again and looks at me.

"He promised me the way out, an infallible way to ensure that place would never find me again." He points at the envelope, now with the letter carefully folder inside. "I just needed to push people over the edge, just enough to have It find them."

"What did you do to Them?!" Despite W's grip reminding me to stay calm, I'm starting to lose my composure. He doesn't say a word. "Answer me, now!" Now my voice sounds guttural, inhuman.

"Your friend is already lost; I didn't have to nudge them. "He's fully crying now; his voice comes up and down. "But my coworkers, my *friends!* It ate everyone."

In between sobs, he clasps the envelope and hugs it. Then, he puts it in his jacket pocket and stands up with such abruptness I almost fall down the chair.

I want to scream again, but there's something in what he said.

Your friend is already lost.

Push people over the edge.

It all makes sense.

Nick has only gone to NIU when he's in such a questionable state that most of the time, he can't clearly remember anything that happened before he arrived.

Nova was acting strange, when it happened to her, she was probably way too fucked up, but Nina didn't want to tell me that.

Oberon said most go to get away from everything, not to look for something.

Every time I go, I get there when I'm lost.

Empty.

"whenYouHaveNowhereToGo."

28 Objects in mirror are closer than they appear

And if everyone who goes to NIU is going through the same situation…

La puta madre.

I was right.

My <u>White Rabbit</u> does need help.

My help.

And it might be more urgent than I thought.

He knows, he has to know.

Judging by what he said, he's been helping people get there.

Even if he didn't cause Them to go in the first place, he has to know how I can find them.

Maybe they're trapped.

They have to be.

I jump forward and close the distance between us, try to grab the envelope, and something inside of him also snaps.

The 6-foot tall, fat, bald man screams like I'm poking his eyes out, and a second afterward, my head bounces off the wall.

A second later, I'm on the floor.

"THIS IS MINE!"

My vision blurs, and I feel like throwing up, I want to jump at him again, but W holds me back. His claws are so deep in my skin I feel how soon blood will start to come out.

"don'tWasteYourEnergy,

He'sUselessNow."

And since I can't move, I just do the only thing I know how to do in times like this.

"I just want to understand, please!" I beg with such a pathetic tone I almost vomit for real this time.

"He called it Wonderland, Terry." He's back to his sad politeness. "Because his winnings there were wonderful. It would always come to him like a casino. For me, it was just a bar."

"I need to go back, I need to find them." I struggle with W, but he's stronger. Now I'm the one crying.

"That won't solve any of your problems, but if you really want to go, you already know how to."

He points at my bag, then at the lighter I'm still holding.

"Go, child. I have a plane to catch," he hugs the envelope one more time and lets out one last sigh.

GLOWROT

I stand up, mostly held by W.
He was right; he's useless now.
But I have the answers that I need.
I walk to the door and open it; it's not warm anymore.
I step out and look down.
The carpet is a different color.

It's not—

This is not the seven—

Seventh floor.

I look up, right in front of me.
My door.
I jump back, and Ute's smiling, way closer to me than I anticipated.
"How do you think I've been watching you this whole time?" He asks, holding the door. "You really shouldn't leave your door open at night."

29
Entrance Closed

The door is locked, isn't it?

Of course, it is.

It has to be.

I locked it.

But the lock feels wrong. Something inside of it is rattling.

No.

Everything is fine; I'm inside. Nobody is looking at me.

That's a lie.

I can still feel it.

But from where?

From where?!

And why doesn't it say anything to me?

I know it can't be Ute, the colossal walrus. This morning, I checked at reception; he checked out last night. Everything's fine.

It has to be the other one, Oberon.

I know he's watching me.

I run to the bedroom and slide on my knees along the floor, checking again under the mattress and behind the television.

There isn't a single <u>caterpillar.</u>

But why do I feel them crawling under my skin?

It's the third time I've turned on the hot water in the bath and the third time I've turned it off.

I need to think.

Why? What does he want to tell me?

And what the hell do I have to do to find my White Rabbit?

Lose myself.

I have to get lost.

GLOWROT

It's the only way to find Them.

"theOnlyWayToGetBackToNIU," W whispers in my ear.

"You knew all—?" my voice sounds sharper than intended, but I can't help it.

"yes,Bo?"

"All of this. Already. Did you... know?" It's harder to connect the words. But I try.

I still try.

"ofCourseNot,

IWouldHaveToldYou."

He replies with frustration, it's not often he shows such... human emotions.

"butIWasThereWithYou

WhenYouLearnedIt,

WhatDidYouLearn,Bo?"

There's something different in his voice.

"Lose." I start and try again. "Lose myself. I have to. That."

And I know exactly how to do that.

How to let myself go to the point of disappearing, of being a zombie.

It's not new, really. Sometimes, I wonder how I am even alive at this point.

I'm used to it.

It's the key; maybe that's why something happens every time I try to get close. I'm not lost enough.

But still, lost.

Empty.

Until I met Them.

If I found NIU, it had to be because I needed help. A purpose. And that's what I exist for.

To help them.

That's it, the divine reason why our bodies came together from the first moment, why they saw me, and I looked back at them.

Nuestro destino.

The reason they sought me out.

Destiny.

The reason why their lips felt different from the rest.

29 Entrance Closed

Fate.

Water. I have to drink water as much as I possibly can. I fill each of the glasses I have in my apartment.

That way, I don't even have to open the fridge.

Doing that, somehow, makes me feel more connected to Them.

Did they teach me that?

They're so smart.

Drinking one at a time is enough, at least for a while. The less I think about food, the better.

Because eating fills me up,

and I have to be empty.

Ice, as much as I can, filling the entire bowl.

I put my whole face in it and feel the cold BURNING MY EYELASHES

But at least my eyes don't hurt anymore,

and I'm a little more awake.

With an ice cube in my hand, I start leaving little red marks on my skin.

Freezing.

Reminding me, I'm still here.

I have to keep going like this.

"you'veAlwaysBeenGoodAtThis," W praises me, and I feel the heat rising to my cheeks. He's never sounded this eager before.

For a second, I forget about his sharp teeth and gloWing eyes. For a second, his voice reminds me of a person's.

But the second passes.

And I have to focus.

The wall isn't screaming at me anymore; it's patiently explaining what I couldn't see before.

All the threads, the connections, the hidden messages.

I've been an idiot, but I know better now.

"notAnIdiot."

He reminds me.

"theOthersHaveBeenDistractingYou,

That'sAll."

But I won't be distracted anymore.

This time, I have all the pieces. I can't lose. I can't go back to the beginning.

GLOWROT

Because if it's true that they're nothing but a lost soul, how long before there's no going back?

But I am hungry.

    Being empty is harder than I remember.

        I'm in the bathroom now.

Better.

I open the hot water again.

        Fourth time?

    Fifth?

Maybe it's better to disassociate completely.

I could bathe, isolate myself from my surroundings, and lose myself for hours underwater.

W holds my hand and leads me inside. It's such a good idea.

I'm so smart.

"pinkWaterAlwaysHelpedYouThink," his whispers wrap around my thoughts like a spiral.

Like a tail.

    Like a snake.

But—

But what if—

What if I lose myself too much this time?

If it ends up being too late?

If the water turns red instead of pink?

How do I know I won't go too far?

"youDon'tHaveToWorryAboutAnything," his voice caresses my ears, and his claws slide over my skin without leaving a mark. **"rememberThatI'mHereToHelpYou."**

        Help me with what?

There are bubbles in the bathtub; the water is hot. Very hot.

As it should be.

    But the bubbles. Did W put them there?

When?

        How?

"howManyBubblesAreThere?" he asks me. I turn to look at him for a moment, confused. **"look,They'reDifferentColors."**

He's right.

29 Entrance Closed

"TouchOne,Bo."

A small mountain of bubbles, small, medium, and large. Right in front of me. One, two, ten, twenty-seven, sixty.

"watch,Watch," he buzzes.

"seeHowItPops?

seeHowItDisappears?"

Pink, blue. The glare of the light makes them change color depending on the angle.

Almost as if they were glowing.

Twinkling.

> *Twinkle, twinkle*
>
> > *little bat*
> >
> > > *How I*
> > >
> > > *wonder*
> > >
> > > *what you're at*
> > >
> > > *Twinkle*
> > >
> > > > *twinkle*
> > > >
> > > > *twinkle*
> > > >
> > > > > *twinkle*
> > > > >
> > > > > *twinkle*
> > > > >
> > > > > *twinkle*

The sudden blow of a breeze rouses me from my daze. The night is humid and dewy.

Am I wet or sweaty?

I shake my head; I am no longer surrounded by my bathroom but by the pool deck. Someone is holding my hand. It's W.

He is smiling widely.

GLOWROT

Am I… outside?

Dressed.

How?

When did it get dark?

That's not important as long as I lose myself.

I have always been so good at this.

My body is starting to complain; I can't let that happen.

I walk, looking everywhere, seeking to distract myself from any possible ideas that might remind me that I'm hungry, sleepy, or any other need that goes against my attempts to die while remaining alive.

The sacrifice will be worth it.

"they'llUnderstand," W murmurs next to my neck.

"they'llSee

HowFarYou'llGoForThem."

Yes. They'll see.

They'll know I'm serious.

They'll know I won't stop until I find them.

Breathing fresh air might help me keep my mind focused on my goal while I'm purposefully disintegrating.

Maybe that's why I'm here.

But how?

The air is sticky.

I lean out over the railing and look at the city below me. The lights call out to me and beckon me to jump.

But I can't, not right now.

Not anymore.

I have a purpose now; I can't forget that.

Now I have someone waiting for me.

I just have to get there.

I have to get back.

And this time, I need to make sure I don't leave.

I will stay there until I can find them.

"I didn't expect to see you here so late, alone," I turn to find Alexia also leaning over the railing.

It's the first time I've seen her out of uniform in months.

Or maybe not, but I didn't pay close attention.

She's wearing a red blouse, white slacks, and this time, two <u>hearts</u>

made of braids on either side of her head. Her braids have golden hoops tangled in them, that sparkle when the light hits them.

"I couldn't sleep," I lie without looking at her in the eye.

Because she'll know.

"Yeah, me neither," she says.

I'm weak, so I look at her.

Her gaze strays to a point between my nose and chin, I smile and she smiles back.

Her pretty smile, with her lovely teeth.

And her pretty skin.

Her pretty nose.

And her gorgeous lips.

What the fuck am I doing?

I push myself back and turn around, but she's not stupid.

She knows something's up.

So she holds my wrist, delicately but firmly, and pulls me to her.

There are a few guests around us, but they're probably drunk. No one who matters, it's like we're invisible right now.

"Are you high right now?" she asks with an accusing tone.

I gasp.

What the fuck is she doing?

"Oh my God, Alexia, of course I'm not; what the fuck?!"

"calmDown,

You'reActingGuilty."

W, who was so nice and gentle before, now is furious.

At least it's not at me.

"I saw you when you got here; your eyes were glazed. You didn't even see me." There is concern in his voice, as well as anger.

"I was thinking about the immortality of the crab," I reply sharply. A prick in the chest makes me tremble. "And what do you care?"

"I've been trying to talk to you for days, Bo." She tries to take my hand again, but I pull it away. "I need you to listen to me as a friend."

"What? Are Nina and Nova gossiping about me with you? Is that what they're doing now? Gossiping about what crazy Bo is up to?"

I recognize this moment perfectly. The anger that comes with hours of hunger and lack of sleep. The desperation to pick a fight with absolutely anyone who crosses my path.

"Gossiping? No. Bo. Listen to me for a moment!" Her every move seems coldly calculated.

"she'sLying," W hisses at her.

I swallow hard.

My pulse is too loud in my head.

I can barely hear her.

"Weird things have always happened here, but they're usually stupid, like rumors of the pool being haunted because some idiot forgot they can't breathe underwater." I can't help but laugh; she looks at me sternly. "But this is different. People are acting strange, more than ever, including you. And it scares me, <u>heart</u>. You know I worry about you."

People.

> *People are acting strange.*

> > > *Strange how?*

> *People like…*

> > *Could it be?*

They're people, after all.

My lips part, but I can't make any noise.

I forget how to breathe.

I try again.

"Who else have you seen lately? You know, doing… strange things, I mean."

My throat is swollen all of a sudden.

"I don't know. You, that man with all the fake missing coworkers panic, Nova, Rei—"

"Rei?"

"Yeah, your friend. The one who left the thing at the desk. You asked me to tell them—"

I cough, spit, cough again.

Rei.

Rei.

Rei.

Their name is Rei.

> > *Isn't that one of the names I had memorized?*

"Rei, yes. Rei." I love how their name sounds on my lips and tickles my tongue when I say it.

"It was them, right?" Alexia squints her eyes and moves a few inches away from me. "Because they, for real, left something behind, right?"

"Yeah, of course," I answer without thinking, taking the lighter out of my pocket. "Here, look."

"Ok, but." She moves further away and pulls her phone out of her pocket. "Why are you carrying it around?"

I think the surprise has made her forget that blinking is important.

Or breathing.

Or moving naturally.

She shifts her weight like she's preparing for something.

Like I'm dangerous.

"youHaveToThinkFast."

"To give it to them, of course." I grit my teeth to make my smile look more authentic, less desperate.

I'm dizzy and have no idea if I'm seeing colored dots from hunger or if there are fireflies around Alexia's face.

My lips stretch wide.

That should help, right?

Maybe I look good again.

Normal.

Alexia flinches.

Oh.

Maybe I don't.

"But you *do* know them. Right?" She moistens her lips and looks at my hands like she's waiting for me to do something. "Bo. Bo, please tell me you're not stalking the fucking guests."

She's texting.

Who is she texting?

I tilt my head to see what she has on the screen, but she suddenly moves the phone.

"Of course, I know them! Alexia, please don't be ridiculous. You know me!" I don't think before I speak.

Every time I open my mouth, throwing myself into the void it looks like a more tempting offer than being cornered by Alexia.

"It's exactly *because* I know you too well that I'm asking you this," she's choosing her words carefully. "Tell me why you didn't text them or go to their room or something."

Wait a second.

GLOWROT

"Do you know their room number?!"

Mierda.

Mierda.

Mierda. Mierda.

Mierda. Mierda. Mierda. Mierda. Mierda. Mierda. Mierda. Mierda. Mierda.
Mierda. Mierda. Mierda. Mierda. Mierda. Mierda. Mierda. Mierda. Mierda.
Mierda. Mierda. Mierda. Mierda. Mierda. Mierda. Mierda. Mierda. Mierda.
Mierda. Mierda. Mierda. Mierda. Mierda. Mierda. Mierda. Mierda. Mierda.
Mierda. Mierda. Mierda. Mierda. Mierda. Mierda. Mierda. Mierda. Mierda.
Mierda. Mierda. Mierda. Mierda. Mierda. Mierda. Mierda. Mierda. Mierda.
Mierda. Mierda. Mierda. Mierda. Mierda. Mierda. Mierda. Mierda. Mierda.
Mierda. Mierda. Mierda. Mierda.

Mierda. Mierda. Mierda. Mierda. Mierda. Mierda. Mierda. Mierda. Mierda.
Mierda. Mierda. Mierda. Mierda. Mierda. Mierda. Mierda. Mierda. Mierda.
Mierda. Mierda. Mierda. Mierda. Mierda. Mierda. Mierda. Mierda. Mierda.
Mierda. Mierda. Mierda. Mierda. Mierda. Mierda. Mierda. Mierda. Mierda.
Mierda. Mierda. Mierda. Mierda. Mierda. Mierda. Mierda. Mierda. Mierda.
Mierda. Mierda. Mierda. Mierda. Mierda. Mierda. Mierda. Mierda. Mierda.
Mierda. Mierda. Mierda. Mierda. Mierda.

Mierda. Mierda. Mierda. Mierda. Mierda. Mierda. Mierda. Mierda. Mierda.
Mierda. Mierda. Mierda. Mierda. Mierda. Mierda. Mierda. Mierda. Mierda.
Mierda. Mierda. Mierda. Mierda. Mierda. Mierda. Mierda. Mierda. Mierda.
Mierda. Mierda. Mierda. Mierda. Mierda. Mierda. Mierda. Mierda. Mierda.
Mierda. Mierda. Mierda. Mierda. Mierda. Mierda. Mierda. Mierda. Mierda.
Mierda. Mierda. Mierda. Mierda. Mierda. Mierda. Mierda. Mierda. Mierda.
Mierda. Mierda. Mierda. Mierda.

I shouldn't have yelled.

"youReallyFuckedUp."

She steps back with a calculating stare, like counting the exact steps she needs to take to do something.

What?

Maybe she's deciding if she needs to restrain me.

Like a wild animal.

Is that what she thinks about me?

That I'm a rabid beast?

She then collapses onto one of the sun loungers by the pool, holding her head in her hands and trembling.

29 Entrance Closed

Like she's trying to contain herself.

"Ok, look. I don't know them that well, but I want to. That's it. We've talked several times, but you have no idea, you can't imagine…" I'm trying to speak as calmly as possible, but I salivate every time I think about their moles.

"No, and I don't want to imagine! What the fuck, Bo?!"

Maybe she's jealous.

That's it.

Maybe the texts were just jealousy because she saw I moved on.

She saw how I talked about them.

About Rei.

She looks around, like a beast preparing to defend itself or attack. Her lips no longer curl into a perfect smile but are pressed together so tightly that they almost form a straight line.

"No, you don't understand. Look, the last time we saw each other ended very abruptly." Without any context, it sounds terrible, I know. "And they're always in a hurry, and we haven't been able to talk again."

"Nonsense." She doesn't move, doesn't do anything.

A tiny moth settles on her forehead, but she doesn't even flinch.

"You're fucking stalking a guest! Oh Lord, and I helped. I helped without knowing, but I did. I should cut off my head!" Her voice is trembling with fury. "But I should cut yours first!"

"I'm not stalking anyone!" I squeak, but then I make an effort to lower my voice. "Besides, I just asked for their room number, and that's it."

"Don't you think that if you don't have it, it's for a reason?" She's looking at me like I'm a creature that must be restrained.

"It's not like we don't know each other…"

"Did you even know their name before I told you? Because I remember perfectly well that you didn't tell me; you just gave me a very vague description, Bo. I'm not an idiot!"

"you'reGoingToTellMe
You'veNeverHadACrush
OnAnyone?"

"You're going to tell me you've never had a crush on anyone?" I sit in the pool chair next to her. W holds me and helps me not lose my balance.

"When I have crushes, I don't stalk them; I ask for their phone number and ask them out." This last, she says with a serious expression; I don't think she's blinked for several minutes. "Sounds familiar?"

"Alex, you know I'm not like that..." I lunge forward to hug her without thinking.

She tenses and pushes me away but being careful not to hurt me. For a second, I feel her warm breath on my neck.

I'm scared.

I want to cry.

"don'tFallForIt.

It'sTooLateForHerNow."

W has a more hateful tone than usual; he never liked her.

I swallow saliva and reach out my hand, brush her knee over her pants, and notice how she shudders.

"I knew I had a bad feeling about you for some reason," she whispers quietly, with spite. "I should have stayed the fuck away from you."
Cold.

Absolute.

Then she stands up and turns around, holding her phone to her ear.

I reach out my hand to try to stop her from leaving.

What is she doing?

Who is she calling?

W pulls me back.

"letHerGo,YouDon'tNeedHerAnymore," he says in my ear, and for some reason, his voice sounds raspy, attractive. **"butIt'sOkay. YouHaveMe."**

I lie back on the pool chair; the sky seems to sink against the few buildings around us.

Nothing else matters right now.

W is right.

He has always been right.

He will always be.

The air is thick, almost as thick as the tension was a minute ago.

Only one thing matters.

Rei.

I think about the names again, close my eyes, and try to visualize the ink staining my skin.

The letters pulsate.

Rei Null.

30

Lights Out

Rei.

I dreamt of their name and woke up thinking of their touch.

I'm getting closer and closer.

We'll be together soon.

"don'tLoseFocusNow."

That's right.

First things first.

It should be simpler now that I have their name.

My fingertips tremble over my phone screen. I type those seven letters that have been avoiding me for far too long.

Seven.

r e i n u l l

But there's not much, barely anything at all.

No recent updates, no posts from the past few months.

From the past few years.

No secret email connected to a random account in which they had left a single comment on something they liked that coincidentally led to a hidden identity they now used religiously.

But there was something, once.

I cross my legs and curl up to the wall while scrolling.

And scrolling.

And scrolling.

A picture-perfect life. Their skin stretched over the skeleton of someone they never were.

Someone only I know.

I have before me a frozen corpse embalmed in pixels. Button eyes, empty and begging for mercy at the same time. As if they could see me from the past, begging me to release them from the torture they once called life.

They don't have to say it for me to know.

Because I know them better than anyone.

I know their soul.

I see the corners of their lips and how they stretch, and stretch, and stretch until I can almost see them cracking. As if they were held to their skull with nails.

A couple of red drops appear on the screen for a few seconds, and I feel tingling on my tongue.

What would they taste like?

I blink.

They're not there anymore.

I bring my face closer to the phone anyway and lick the screen for a few seconds.

There they are, with that perfection that they pretended for others.

Beautiful.

Perfect.

Preserved in chloroform, in a display case.

Waiting to be unwrapped.

Discovered.

By whom?

They had long, straight hair, and their moles were covered by a thick layer of make-up. Softer, rounder cheeks.

It feels blasphemous to see them like this, so stripped of everything that makes them themselves.

Everything that makes them special.

No ink at all.

Not a single one of those tattoos that say too much about them without even speaking.

The self from the past is nothing compared to who they are now, and I fully understand the change.

I can't imagine the despair they must have felt being a generic mannequin like the ones in those photos.

The subtitles are so short and careful that no one in a million years could have believed they were authentic. As if they were trying not to say too much, but at the same time making sure they maintained the appearance expected by others.

30 Lights Out

A new beginning!

Grateful!

Everything is a learning experience.

I keep scrolling.

And scrolling.

And scrolling.

More photos, these with professional lighting and manufactured poses. Smiles surrounding them sometimes, just like theirs.

Devoid of anything.

They were different back then, they weren't themself.

I know I shouldn't be watching this; I know that all too well.

But it's **not** *wrong.*

Not **that** *wrong.*

I'm sure you'd understand, Rei.

That you'll know I'm doing whatever it takes to get to know you better, to find you, to save you.

It's as if I were pulling at their skin to finally see what lies beneath, the purest essence of themself.

For my eyes only.

Because I am the only one who can understand Them.

I can almost feel myself pulling at the staples holding this mask in place.

Does it hurt when I do it?

Even if they're not here with me?

An unpleasant taste fills my mouth.

A phantom sensation of dirt under my nails.

I dig as hard as I can, trying to unearth something that had been buried too long ago. Until now.

But I know they would understand.

That they will understand.

Deep down, a part of Rei **wants me to** do this, to know who they are not in order to understand who they really are.

Besides, I've come too far.

I can't stop now.

I have to keep going, I know they want me to.

All their clues, all their games. They need me as much as I need them.

They just can't tell me directly.

GLOWROT

But I know

I'm so close.

There's no trace of their long eyeliner, the leather jacket, the tattoos, their shaved head. Their eyes don't have the sparkle they get when they make a choice, when they laugh.

Did they even laugh back then?

I love the present version of them.
The one that feels genuine, authentic. That feels right.
The them I know.
This is them.

Not just Rei, **my** *Rei.*

The real one, the one they are with me.
For me.

Away from the mold someone else put them in. Away from everyone, but with me.

Soon enough.

We'll be together.
Forever.
They'll thank me for this.
I can almost see it so vividly in my head.
The sparkle in their eyes.

Their laugh.

These ghosts of the past bring back memories I had yet to find inside my brain.
I have seen them smile, laugh. Time and time again.
Moments that were lost until now flood my brain.
Suddenly, I'm dizzy.
"bo,AreYouHappyNow?"
Not yet, but I will be.
Now I'm letting the water run down my back, *it slides,*

30 Lights Out

it wraps around my ankles, like fingers.
I'm not sure when I got to the bathroom.
The phone isn't in my hand anymore.

When did I—

Where—

But that's not important.

I was thinking about them.

I have to keep remembering.

For their sake.

I think it was a good idea to take the razors out of here,
to avoid accidents.

"itWasABrilliantIdea.
You'reBrilliant,Bo."

I'm brilliant.

My mouth hasn't started bleeding. I guess that's a good sign.

Now what?

The water helps me think.

I can't wait until tomorrow, I need to know if it's too late.
Tell them they'll be okay, that I'm here.
I have to make sure they haven't broken completely.
I have to.

I have to—

"emptyYourself,
SoYouCanFillUpLater."

I have to empty myself.

It's now or never.

The smoke flutters around me and reminds me that there are still
things my mind doesn't want to finish understanding.

Memories s t r e t c h like they're made of rubber.

Time, the order of things. They escape from my fingers.

I try to put them in order but I can't.

I am not empty enough.

I need to get worse.

I close my eyes and wrap my hands around me, just enough for my
nails to brush against my back.

A hug that I have given myself so many times.

GLOWROT

I feel the skin on my back, sensitive from the hot water. Run my nails over it and inhale. I press down, just a little at first, to remember how it feels.

ore

And then press down a little more. Two nails first, then three.

And more.

And more.

And more

And more.

Little needles awaken on my skin. They dry my throat.

And more.

And more.

And more.

And more

And more

They remind me that I am alive.

And more.

d more

And more.

And more

And more.

Little by little, I fade away, my essence draining through the increasingly deep holes.

And more.

And more

And more.

And more

And more

And more.

They burn, but it is working.

And more.

And more

And more.

And mo

And more.

And more

I am emptying.

And more

And more

And I can see now.

I can see the first time playing back crisply, almost perfectly.

I feel it, smell it, as if I've been transported to it.

Rei was crying.

They had finished vomiting, and I was petting their head as they tried to stand up. From the way they were moving I know we hadn't met yet.

They had yet to long for me as much as they do now. As much as i do now.

But they smiled at me, thankful. Grateful.

The beginning of our love story.

We went out onto the dance floor and began to dance; slowly, their lips began to draw into a grin. Their slender body was swaying like a willow tree in the breeze.

30 Lights Out

And I remember imitating them because I wanted to be like that.

I wanted to be like them.

They looked happy.

With me.

But how could they really be when the tears had not yet dried?

At some point in the night one of the faceless girls who melt with the walls came over to where we were and offered us something. But it wasn't a drink.

Peanuts?

Chickenwings?

Rei threw the tray on the floor at her with one swipe and started screaming.

Screaming.

SSSSSSS

CCCCCCC

RRRRRRRRRR

HHHHHHH

AAAAAAAAA

MMMMMMMMMM

IIIIIIIIIIIII

NNNNNNNNNN

GGGGGGGGG

GLOWROT

I could see the pain in their eyes and I wanted to **kill** that girl, even if she didn't exist. If she wasn't entirely human.

How dare she?

I grabbed their shoulders and looked for any place where they could calm down.

I understood even then the pain they were in.

No one around us seemed to notice.

They were covering their face with their hands as if they didn't want anyone to notice what the source of the fuss was.

Even if no one cared.

But I did.

Then I saw the hallway, the one that always has people thrown on the floor and syringes and spikes coming out of the floor.

And I stepped on them, as I later did many more times, dodging the thorns coming out of the walls.

It was like the room had swallowed us, a hole just like the one that plagued my thoughts since we last saw each other.

I saw their tears dancing with the colored lights, and they looked at me as if no one had ever seen me before.

That's when we fell in love.

I could see it in their eyes.

They smiled, embarrassed. They had begun to breathe normally.

I stroked their hand, frightened, not knowing if I could break their bones from how delicate they seemed.

"I'm sorry. I hate those things." That voice, I remember their voice that day.

How could I have forgotten them?

"The chicken wings?" I said, trying to show I got them, still not sure what was happening.

But deep down I knew.

"The food," they responded in a murmur.

I smiled.

Or did Rei smile?

No, no.

I'm losing it.

I need to try harder.

I repeat the task.

Hug myself.

Nails, digging deep.

Different gashes, to empty myself more.

And more.

and more.

The water running
down
my neck.

And more

And more

And more

And more

And more

And more

Inhalo.

Exhalo.

Then I go back.

"goOn.

You'reDoingWell.

Perfect."

W's voice generates a new question mark in my brain.

Where the fuck was he that day?

We had argued, I'm sure of it. But he was there, at NIU, with me.

What was he saying to me?

"it'sDangerous."

The place was as new to him as it was to me.

He hates others and knowing that so many strangers were reaching out to touch me made him sick.

But I get it, he was trying to protect me.

"Food makes me sick," sighed the Rei in my memory, their voice barely above a whisper.

They spoke like it was something shameful. Like it was something they weren't supposed to say out loud.

"It's fine. You can drink water and smoothies!" I suggested shrugging my shoulders.

They looked up and down at my neck, at the scratches I had.

The lingering marks W's claws had made; luckily, he wasn't making more at that moment. Rei studied them like they could read them, like they could understand.

They looked at me for a few seconds, like they were waiting for me to say something else.

Like they thought I was joking, mocking them.

But no. And they realized that.

GLOWROT

I just blinked and tried not to stare at how W was curled up in a corner, weaker, as confused as I was.

BUT REI SMILED.

And I smiled back.

The memory of the first time we met feels warm in my chest.

Or is it the water still falling?

Then I remember the other times.

How could I have forgotten them if there were so many?

Sometimes, I was the one who cried, and Rei was in charge of comforting me.

Their skin has always been so soft.

Their lips so full.

Their taste so entrancing.

Their gasps so addictive.

How could someone so wonderful have ended up in a place like that?

Had they done the same things I did?

Are they going through a hard time?

Deep down I knew.

I know.

I've known.

I remember our conversations but nothing about them. Nothing about the person they are outside of that place. Of NIU.

Had they even told me their name back then?

They seemed to be hiding from the world.

And it's okay, because soon we'll hide together.

Just the two of us.

But how am I supposed to find them?

Why are they making it so hard?

I don't even know why they're at Cameo or how long they've been staying here.

But the memories seem to come from way back. Way before the first time I saw them here.

Since when?

Since Alexia?

Since before that?

What if…

30 Lights Out

What if they came here looking for me?

What if all this happening to me is just a reflection of what Rei had to live through first?

I have to write it down.

I have to put the pieces together on the wall.

The puzzle.

More, and more pieces.

The pieces they left.

For me.

Ute mentioned NIU does something similar to so many people.

People who sometimes need an extra nudge.

Maybe that's why Nick is so eccentric, maybe that's why he's always desperately looking to party and seems so out of reality.

And where is Nick?

I abandoned him.

"no.HeAbandonedYou.

YouToldMeSo."

He abandoned me.

Is he still there?

That's unimportant now.

Rei knew all of this; they have to have known.

That's why they approached me to ask for a light.

That's why they dropped the <u>white</u> lighter.

All the pieces of the puzzle.

And of course, of course, that has to be it.

I move my feet to get out of the tub, but I'm no longer in it.

It takes me a few seconds to realize that what is around me is no longer the bathroom, but the wall.

My wall.

The puzzle pieces I've been collecting.

THEY LOOK AT ME.

THEY JUDGE ME.

THEY KNOW MORET HAN I DO.

I don't remember it being this full, this suffocating.

The sheer volume of it slams into my chest.

The papers, the receipts, the scribbled-on napkins.

Held together by threads or lines drawn by markers, sticky tape, and

GLOWROT

scraps of memories and pain.

The torn-out notebook pages, the photos, the mirrors—

the mirrors?

I didn't put those there.

I didn't put those there.

I didn't put those there.

I didn't put those there.

I didn't put those there.

I didn't put those there.

I didn't put those there.

I didn't put those there.

I didn't put those there.

I didn't put those there.

I didn't put those there.

I didn't put those there.

I try to step aWay, but the web of scribbles pulls me in like a spider. Tighter and tighter.

It spread out.

Like a Web?

Like a disease.

30 Lights Out

But hoW?

The handWritting is my oWn.

But it's not.

"iHelpYouToBeHappy,
YouForgot?"

I turn to look at him in disbelief. W, who hated everything about NIU and anyone Who came out of there.

He is helping me.

Because **he has alWays helped me.**

So, what noW?

Crossing the hallWay.

The pieces are saying something to me.

He strokes my neck, this time without hurting me.

Soggy hair begins to leave a puddle on the floor, and I can only folloW the threads that are binding the puzzle together.

I am starving.

"butThereAreMoreImportantThingsThanThat."

Water and smoothies.

That's what I told Rei. Why?

"toEmptyThemselves."

"To empty themselves," I roar, and I'm startled to hear the sound of my own voice.

Distinct, almost inhuman.

I Walk closer to the Wall. To the little mirrors sticking in betWeen the pieces.

I need to see myself.

I need to knoW if I made it.

AM I EMPTY NOW?

The reflection on the other side returns a sunken gaze, With almost violet sockets.

I inhale and shake my head in aWe.

The eyes looking back at me are empty.

Perfect.

31
ElevatorBrokeN

Empty.

Empty eyes.

I touch them.
The surface of the small mirror.
The mirror.
The glass mirror.
I look at it.

The looking-glass.

I pretend the glass gets soft, like gauze, so I can poke my eye on the other side. Just for a second.
And it hurts.
I do it again and again until it gets red and teary.
My eye.

Not mine, the other Bo.

The one that's real.

I look at it more, and it starts to turn into a sort of mist. It raises and raises until it fills my reflection's nose.
My nose.

It's in my lungs.

My empty lungs.

In a blink, I'm outside my door. Maybe that's what I need. To walk, and walk, and keep walking. Walking until I get somewhere. Until I get there.
I turn left, then right, then left again. Right.
Left, right.
Like it's a game.
Like doing so can bring me to another reality.
Bring me to Rei. I can feel them, so close to me. My angel.
Mine.

What's that smell?

Is it coming from there?

I knock on the door but no one answers.

It's not them. They would answer.

The pieces finally fall into place, little by little, making space in my brain. I've cleared it enough to be able to make room for them, to make room for them all.

Por favor.

Because whenever I tried to go to NIU I was thinking about finding it. Obsessed. Poor me. Thank goodness I know how to do it now.

I have to stop thinking.

But if I think about not thinking, I end up thinking. Right?

That's why I have to keep myself busy.

Busy, seeing things.

Busy with something else that fills my brain, ridding me of all thought.

What's around me?

Broken glass on the floor, someone must have dropped some room service dishes. Why does it hurt so much to step on them?

I'd better go to the emergency stairs.

They're warmer, they feel better than the elevator. And right now, I just want to walk, and walk, and keep walking.

I could count the steps.

That would keep me busy.

I'm sure that if I walk long enough, I'll be able to get somewhere.

Get to—

No!

I have to stop thinking.

I drag my bare feet across the floor, and the little cuts on the soles make me uncomfortable, but they are not enough to stop.

Focus on them.

I'm downstairs, I think.

The rug is different, but the numbers on the doors don't make sense. The air here is not intoxicating, but a peculiar hum reigns on it.

This floor is not EMPTY.

People.

So many people.

GLOWROT

Walking back and forth, past me. Busy. Luggage wheels coming and going, filling my ears like thunder.

But they walk past me as if they do not see me, as if I am not important enough for them to pay attention to me.

Of course I'm not.

Fuckers.

I feel as if I were underwater, in some fishbowl or bubble.

Behind glass.

Separated from real reality, trying to reach a sea to which I have no access.

But no!

I have to stop thinking about it!

I look for details in the corners that join the walls to the ceiling, in the floor tiles.

I count each and every crack and hum.

Uno. Dos. Tres. Cuatro. Cinco. Se—

Uno. Dos. Tres. Cuatro. Ci—

Uno. Do—

What was I doing a second ago?

It doesn't matter, I have to keep going.

Anything to keep my head busy, and the dizziness increases.

The blood inside me is trying to sing with a melody I don't recognize, but I play along and hop downstairs.

Again.

The steps are moving.

Electric.

Down again, but where?

There are more lights and doors.

And people.

So many people.

Walking back and forth, past me. Busy. Luggage wheels coming and going, filling my ears like thunder.

But they walk past me.

As if they do not see me, as if I am not important enough for them to pay attention to me.

Of course I'm not.

Fuckers.

31 ElevatorBrokeN

Cough.

Blood?

It doesn't matter.

Keep going.

More stairs again. Narrower and narrower. They change color as I go. *Greyer.*

Lifeless.

Just like me.

There is water on the floor now.

It's not too much; it barely reaches my ankles, but it covers everything. It looks like a perfect mirror. An upside-down looking glass.

But I'm the reflection this time.

Everything on the other side is dark.

And broken.

I hear a phone ringing in the background, faint, getting louder and louder as I get closer.

Where to?

Someone is running and bumps into me.

I fall to the ground, but it's no longer wet.

The phone is still ringing and I start to run.

Someone is calling me.

It's important, it's for me.

I keep running.

And running.

And running.

And running.

And running.

And running.

And running.

And running.

It rings, it rings.

And I run.

Slip. Fall. Run again.

Run. Run. Run. Run. Run. Run. Run. Run. Run. Run. Run. Run. Run. Run. Run. Run. Run. Run. Run. Run.

Blood on my nose. On my lungs.

That smell. It's still ringing.

Run. Run. Run. Run. Run. Run. Run. Run. Run. Run. Run. Run. Run. Run. Run. Run. Run. Run. Run. Run. Run. Run. Run. Run. Run. Run. Run. Run. Run. Run. Run. Run. Run. Run. Run. Run. Run. Run. Run. Run. Run. Run. Run. Run. Run. Run. Run. Run. Run. Run. Run. Run. Run. Run. Run. Run. Run. Run. Run. Run. Run. Run. Run. Run. Run. Run. Run. Run. Run. Run. Run. Run. Run. Run. Run. Run. Run. Run.

Run. Run. Run. Run. Run. Run. Run. Run. Run. Run. Run. Run. Run. Run. Run. Run. Run. Run. Run. Run. Run. Run. Run. Run. Run. Run. Run. Run. Run. Run. Run. Run. Run. Run. Run. Run. Run. Run. Run. Run. Run. Run. Run. Run. Run. Run. Run. Run. Run. Run. Run. Run. Run. Run. Run. Run. Run. Run. Run. Run. Run. Run. Run. Run. Run. Run. Run. Run. Run. Run. Run. Run. Run. Run. Run. Run. Run. Run. Run. Run. Run. Run. Run. Run. Run. Run. Run. Run. Run. Run. Run. Run. Run. Run. Run. Run. Run. Run. Run.

GLOWROT

The elevator doors close behind me.

Up. Up. Up.

Back at the beginning.

The ringing comes closer and closer, and I run.

This is my floor. I know the rug. I know those cobwebs. I know that woman cleaning that corner.

I know that door.

My door.

And I know the one across it way too well.

It's open, just a smidge, just like Ute's forever ago.

Thinking about him reminds me of—

No!

I come in, but it's not his room, not the one I went to first.

The phone keeps ringing, buzzing. So close.

There it is, on a coffee table. But it's not a phone; it's the compact I found in my purse, the one that led me to him initially.

Did I leave it here?

Look at me.

I hold it, and it's warm, slowly swollen, like it's breathing. Soft, like skin.

Alive.

I open it, and the neon lights around the mirror flicker.

The mirror is fogged.

Breathing.

Breathing on the other side.

Something on the reflection is different, something behind me. Neon lights are on the walls, and I can't see them with my own eyes.

This piece of the puzzle, this tool.

That's it.

I follow the lines as I angle the mirror to get a better look at them, pulsing like veins pumping blood.

Wet, bulging.

Alive.

But where is the heart?

I follow them, follow them, follow them.

The veins pulse against the walls and stretch the paint, which slowly begins to turn into translucent skin.

31 ElevatorBrokeN

Sweating.

The smell of something rancid overpowers every other sensation, burning my nose until it reaches my skull. They're pulsating more and more.

Glowing.

Rotten.

Something in between raw meat, neon lights, and white noise.

They burrow into the floor and form what should be the bathroom door frame. The threshold looks dark, illuminated only by the shimmering blood that I can only see through the mirror.

A hum fills my ears and pulls me like a magnet.

I look around, trying to grab hold of something so as not to be pulled completely away. There is nothing to hold on to; there is no one.

Not even a shadow.

Not even bright eyes judging me.

Where is W?

Too late.

The veins detach from the wall like tentacles and wrap around my limbs. They coil around my neck and squeeze. Harder and harder. Tighter. A crack from my bones. A splinter somewhere.

The pressure is unbearable, and my wrist is about to break. I can't let them make me let go of the compact.

I inhale, inhale, inhale. But I forgot how to exhale.

And the world becomes blurred.

Darker and darker.

Empty.

Quiet.

At least for a while.

For a moment, I become truly empty.

Devoid of anything.

Of life.

I don't know how long I'm out, but I come to on the bathroom floor, inside that abandoned room.

My head is pounding, and I can't feel my legs.

GLOWROT

But I can't stay here. The lights in the compact kept flickering and I know I'm close.

I start to crawl.

My eyes

bounce

against the

walls

And then I stand up.
Outside of the door.
I am alone.
Alone.

I can't find the stairs or the elevator. The lights consume me like fire trying to extinguish my skin. The hallway goes on and on. It forks into two, three, seven. More.

More.

A maze of neon-hued pathways smiles at me and taunts me.
And my smile widens.
There have to be clues, something. More pieces of the puzzle.
I have the space for them now.
In my brain.

S   e
o   m
*   p*
*   t*
*   y*

My feet keep moving, or is it the floor below me?
The walls groan and close in on me, compressing my ribs until I have to push my way forward with my hands.

31 ElevatorBrokeN

The hallway is shrinking.

No, not shrinking, swallowing me.

The colors floating in the air bleed into each other, twist, and intertwine in viscous strands. They come out of open wounds in the walls.

Pulsing.

They smell of smoke, fruit, and the lies I constantly tell myself.
Rotting sugar, saccharine.
They stretch, stretch, and stretch.
Until they touch me back.
Slithering against my skin, like a million sticky and minuscule groping hands making their way under the fabric.
Not hands. Not all of them.

Nails.

Hair.

Tongues.

Asphyxiating.

I keep pushing myself forward; I have to.
"Rei!" I scream as I break free from the blue and violet grip.
Their name bursts from my lips in yellow flashes that dissipate as soon as they touch the air. Far away from me, music begins to increase in volume.
When was the last time I heard it?

It goes

on

and

on

But I'm not alone.

When did I stop being alone?

The people around me are trying to shut me up, they talk to me. But what are they saying?
The words blur in the air, and I try not to see them; I can't distract myself. It's getting harder and harder to stay focused on finding them as hands pull me backwards. And sideways.
And down.

Through the floor.

Like quicksand.

GLOWROT

My ears are ringing, and I cover them with my hands. The warm liquid that begins to slide down my fingers smells of rust, of BLOOD.

When I stop to look at my fingers, something grabs me.

Its hand isn't just a hand; its fingers feel longer and softer like they don't have any bone inside. And it's sinking into my scalp.

I jerk back, but it pulls my hair with such force that I think my skin will peel off.

I can't make out his face because it's melting, his features sag like wax too close to a flame. Thick, bubbling, dripping.

But I know that smell.

The cheap cologne.

I know the way it's grabbing me.

The way he's grabbing me.

I can see the tattoos shining in the dark, dancing beside me.

My name.

He opens his mouth; his voice doesn't reach me through my ears but through my skull.

And even though the creature has no eyes, I know it's looking at me.

I scream.

Beg.

Scratch.

Bite.

He laughs, and the sound is all wrong, coming out of the floor, reverberating and bouncing from one faceless figure into the other.

Then, he lets go.

Like he's bored.

And somehow, that's what hits me the hardest.

I collapse and slam into the sides of the corridor, trying to dodge the rest of the unhappy souls who scream for me to succumb to them even for a millisecond.

"Rei! Rei!" I can't stop calling, but the desperate moans drown out my call.

I manage to break free of the melting, inhuman figures and keep running as much as I can. Until my knees give in and my feet start bleeding, until my teeth start feeling like jumping out of my mouth.

Until my—

My what?

31 ElevatorBrokeN

Mis pulmones.

Until my lungs empty and don't fill back in.

And when I stop, I hear something. For a split second.

Steps.

Stopping just a moment after me.

There's someone fucking following me.

There's only one explanation.

Someone doesn't want me to find my White Rabbit.

Rei is in danger.

Rei. **Rei.**

Finally, the corridors widen. Fast. Like a throat opening up to swallow me whole.

But I have to keep going.

The walls become translucent and start exposing what's behind them. Desks, chairs, cubicles. Papers that rustle even though there's no wind.

Radios blaring without moving.

Photographs that blink with dead eyes. Dozens of them. Forgotten.

I know exactly where I am.

Finally.

It is now or never.

I slam the door open, and the office swallows me whole.

The cold rushes though my veins and starts CRUSHING MY TEETH.

He's sitting there exactly where I left him. Just like time hasn't passed.

He has the same expression, immovable, chilling.

This time, he doesn't ask me to sit down; he stares at me and drums

GLOWROT

his fingernails on the pale table.

He is now surrounded by square screens, arranged around him like a disturbing throne, engulfed in smoke.

Like windows into dying worlds.

The screens are gloWing, and the images start to become sharper.

The corridors I just walked down.

The lights that tried to swallow me.

The inside of that room with the rotting buffet.

The scratches on the walls.

The motel room.

The faceless crowd gathered around a spinning pole.

His lids flicker too many times, too fast.

Then he exhales slowly, drawn out. His shoulders start twitching.

Like he's been waiting for me to catch up. Like I've already done this before. Like his patience is running out.

There's something else, another screen.

The place where it all began.

The club that I remember so well now that I could draw a map of all its nooks and crannies right then and there.

I see souls like mine, dancing between despair and hunger. Devouring each other as if it were all an illusion, as if they were going to wake up the next day from the nightmare and nothing they had done up to that instant would have any consequences.

What if it is true?

What if tomorrow I can wake up and forget everything?

Would I even want to wake up?

To go back to the pathetic thing I call life?

I stretch my hands out and place them on the last screen. It's vibrating, and all the faces turn to me.

"Come back," they say through the screen. Staring at my soul like a reflection in a mirror. "Wasn't it easier when you didn't have to remember? When you didn't care?"

They whisper in my ear to numb my senses until the worries fade away. To let go.

But the memory of Rei's moles begins to tear apart the signal trying to break in with my brain.

Their eyes implore me to understand them, their lips smiling as they realize that I do.

That I'm the only one who does.

And they are **mine.**

I turn to look at Oberon and lunge towards him.

He barely moves; his expression is distorted for a few seconds, and then he returns to normal.

A glitch, again.

The smoke surrounds him and is getting thicker, as if it were protecting him.

I start to remove the chains decorating his chest, one by one. He moves his hands with the slowness of someone who has all the time in the world and holds my shoulders with his hands as if he were throwing out the garbage.

"What did you do to them?! Where are they?!"

I tear off the buttons holding his silk shirt one by one, and the glow that had disturbed me so much before starts to appear through the fabric.

"*¿Por qué coño de la madre me estás siguiendo?!*" He smiles like he understands me. "Why the fuck are you following me?!"

The glow becomes stronger.

Little dots slowly coming out of hiding.

Blinking.

Eyes.

They glow, pulsating, as they stare at me.

Judging me.

They populate his chest all the way up to his neck. They all stare at me with an intensity that makes me suddenly break away from him. All of them except the ones on his face. Dead, empty, fake.

I let out a scream when I feel the room contorting around me, and a second later, I'm sitting on the chair in front of him.

My legs feel heavy like they're made of cement.

"Hello again, Bo." His words again sound backward, but somehow, I can understand them. "What is it you're looking for?"

"Rei, you son of a bitch! Where did you put them?!"

"Oh, Rei," He strokes the name with his tongue, tastes it. I grit my teeth, unable to move. I want to rip it out of his tongue. It's not **his** to savor. "Where did I...put them? Tell me, Bo. This Rei is... a person? Or an object?"

My stomach twists on itself, he starts scribbling on the papers in front of him, smiling as he takes a breath.

GLOWROT

Way too calm.

Way too slow.

Deliberate.

Stretching the moment.

Why?

"You've been watching me. You know who Rei is!"

Am I crying?

He hums, reaching for something. A tissue. He offers it to me gently. I slap his hand away. He catches it before it falls into the stack of black envelopes piled up on the corner of the desk.

"Oh, but I don't think you understand at all, Bo." He leans back, watching me through the eyes sticking out of his skin.

I open my mouth to speak, but no sound comes out.

"I study, I analyze. Do you understand now?" He brings the pen to his mouth, and when he pulls back, a column of smoke emerges from his lips and spirals toward the ceiling. "**I** haven't **put** anyone anywhere. If **they** hid, it wasn't **my** fault."

The tears scald my cheeks. Boil my skin.

The screens flicker like a dying heartbeat. They show the same hallway, over and over, distorting itself.

I can't control the crying.

The sound is making me dizzy.

The sound is unbearable, it swells around me until it reaches my throat.

The tears keep multiplying, and the salt burns. They flood my face until it's hard to breathe.

I open my mouth but can't speak.

They stream down my nose and down my mouth. I am blinded and intoxicated.

The room tilts.

I'm gagging.

I feel the flood come from my feet, and that's when I realize the drowning has stopped being a metaphor.

More and more saltwater surrounds me until it covers me entirely.

I wish I hadn't cried so much.

I'm going to drown in my own tears.

The current rips me from the chair and slams me against the floor and the walls. I try to open my eyes, but all I can see is the blurred brightness of the screens.

My lungs are deprived of oxygen, and I start to tremble.

I try to hold on to any surface I can find, but it's as if I'm floating in a void beyond existence.

Until finally.

Stillness.

Peace.

The flood gradually recedes until I can breathe again.

I feel the carpet under my feet again, and when I open my eyes, I can see that I'm lying in a corridor. Not a trace of the office or even Oberon.

In that corridor.

The one shown on the screens.

Inhale. Exhale.

At least I'm not crying anymore.

But if I stopped crying, why am I still listening to myself do it?

Unless it's not me.

I follow the cry that is not mine and ignore the eyes that sink into my body from the locks.

the

cry

doesn't

stop

I have to keep going.

I try to start running again, but the air feels rough, almost solid, blocking every attempt to continue.

But I try to look for an invisible thread that I feel is becoming more and more real, tangible. The thing that connects my nightmares and illusions.

The nexus that made it possible for Rei and I to meet.

I take it in my hands, even if doing so makes my palms bleed.

I pull on it, and slowly, my body finally decides to move.

I keep pulling until I feel it has pierced my skin, until it cuts through the muscles.

I keep going until my feet are swollen and bleeding.

Until I can see the door in front of me, and the crying gets louder and louder.

I try to twist the doorknob, but it's locked.

"I'm here!" I cry out as I rush to them.

The crying increases.

I pound the door with my shoulder until I feel the splinters digging in.

It gets louder.

I kick it once,

louder

twice,

louder

three times.

louder

Slowly, the door gives way.

The cries have become screams, wailing.

No. *No.* No. No. No. No. No.No. No. **No.** No. No. No. No. No. No. No. No. No. No. No. No. No. No. No. No. No. No. No. No. No. No. No. No. No. No. No. No. No. No. No. No. No. No. No. No. No.No. No. No. No. No. No. No. No. No. No. No. **No.** No. No. No. No. No. No. **No.** No. No. No. No. No. No. No. No. No. No. No. No. No. No. No. No. No. No. No. No. No. No. No. No. No. No. No. No. No.No. No. No. No. No. No. No. No. No. *No.* No. No. No. No. No. No. No. No. No. No. No. No. No. No. No. No. No. No. No. No. No. No. No. No. No. No. No. No. No. No. No.No. No. *No.* No. No. No. No. No. No. No. No. No. No. No. No. No. No. No. No. No. No. No. No. No. No. No. No. No. No. No. **No.** No.No. No. No. No. No. No. No. No. No. No. No. No. No. No. No. No. No. No. No. No. No. No. No. No. No. No. No. No. No. No. No. No. No. No. No. No.No. No. No. No. No. No. No. No. No. No. No. No. No. No. No. No. No. No. No. No. No. No. *No.* No. No. No. No. No. No. No. No. No. No. No. No. No. No. No.No.No. No. No. No. No. No. No. No. No. No. No. No. No. No. No. No. No. No. No. No. No. No. No. No. No. *No.* No. No. No. No. No. No. No. No. No. No. No. No. No.No.No. No.

31 ElevatorBrokeN

No. No. No. No. No. No. No. No. No. No. No. No. No. No. No. No. No.
No. No. No. No. No. No. No. No. No. No. No. No. No. No. No. No. No.
No. No. No. No. No. **No.** No. No. No. No. No.No. No. No. No. No. No.
No. No. No. No. No. No. No. No. No. No. No. No. No. No. No. No. No.
No. No. No. No. No. No. No. No. No. No. No. No. No. No. No. No. No.
No. No. No. No. No. No. No.No. No. No. No. No. No. No. No. No. No.
No. No. No. No. No. No. No. No. No. No. No. No. No. No. No. No. No.
No. *No.* No. No. No. No. No. No. No. No. No. No. No.

It can't be too late.

"I'm here, I'm here." I can't stop repeating it.

I need them to understand that everything is all right. That I've finally found them and that this time, I won't let anything separate us again.

That whatever is happening to them, they're safe with **me.**

32

CheckEnginE

The door finally opens with a groan.

On the other side is a room only slightly larger than my apartment. The light green walls make me feel like I'm in a hospital.

The floor is littered with fragments, broken mirrors reflecting incomplete snippets of our surroundings. The walls are still breathing, like outside, like when I was coming. Unpainted spaces mock us, the spaces where the mirrors used to be.

A sound fills the air. I look around but can't seem to find its source.

Tic. Tac. Tic. Tac.

"Rei?" I whisper, with some doubt.

Their name sounds like the hypnotic song of a siren. A magnet that has driven me for so long until I could finally arrive.

The crying gets worse for a few seconds, and their whole body starts to tremble. Their moans are distorted, like echoes of a past that has been repeated many more times than necessary.

Terror rises through my veins and reaches my throat.

It can't be; I can't have arrived too late.

No.

No.

No.

I breathe with difficulty and have to hold back my tears. I can't cry again. I can't let them see me like this. They've been calling out to me for so long, begging me to save them. I have to be stronger than ever, for them.

I approach carefully; now they are little more than a bundle curled up in a corner, hugging their knees.

They are tall, but right now they seem tiny.

Tears glisten on their cheeks, they have left a pool of them on the floor.

Will they have drowned in them too?

We are so alike.

We are perfect for each other.

Their hands tremble almost as much as their jaw.

With the slowness of someone who can only breathe with pain, they open their eyes.

Of course, it makes sense. They were still crying because they hadn't realized that I'm here. But I'm here and everything is fine now.

We are together.

I'm here.

And everything is fine now.

I smile.

I want them to know it.

To know that everything is fine because I'm here.

I came to save them.

Tic. Tac. Tic. Tac.

"I'm here." I hold my hands out to them; the mirrors dig into my feet like the broken glass once did.

Everything repeats itself.

Then they start crying louder.

But they shouldn't be crying.

"What's wrong?" I whisper carefully like I'm handling something fragile. "I'm so sorry it took me so long to find you. But I'm here now, you're okay."

They freeze.

Their breath starts faltering, and their shoulders draw inward, as if they're trying to fold in on themselves. The walls begin to tremble, to shake.

Like they're about to collapse.

An earthquake coming from within.

I stand there, patiently, with all the love I have.

I can't even begin to imagine the relief they must feel now, to let all of that go. All of their worries.

Because they're finally okay, they're with me now.

I'm here, and now they know it.

But they don't stop trembling.

They only get worse.

It's too much; it has to be that.

GLOWROT

I keep approaching slowly, patiently.

The sound keeps growing but my ears have become accustomed to it by now. It's muffled by the overwhelming burst of emotions I feel.

Tic. Tac. Tic. Tac.

Tic. Tac. Tic. Tac.

Tic. Tac. Tic. Tac.

I smile towards Rei.

I want to give them time to fully process their safety.

The room keeps shaking; what is this place anyway?

There are white ribbons with small lines and numbers strewn across the floor.

Measuring tape.

One of them is wrapped around what appears to be a headless mannequin lying on the floor away from us.

Empty diet soda cans are overflowing several garbage cans.

Was someone torturing them?

"It's all right," I insist, wiggling my fingers as I approach.

Finally, when I have got close enough, Rei reacts.

They slowly stop hugging their knees, tries to catch their breath. Their crying gradually begins to disappear.

They breathe in, processing the relief.

I smile and extend my arms, waiting for them to throw themselves on my chest, but wanting to give them time to do so only when they are ready.

Because I understand them, I'm the only one who can.

They stand up and lean their head against the wall behind them. With one hand they wipe away the tears that have left gashes on their skin.

Even so, they look beautiful, perfect.

Their eyes look for me, but they stray at the last second. They part their lips but stop themselves from doing that too.

They inhale deeply and clear their throat.

I keep my arms outstretched. I know they've been through a lot, I know I must be patient with them. And I hold back, because I know that even though what I want most is for them to fall into my arms, they need time.

Rei takes a deep breath and clears their throat.

I understand them.

32 CheckEnginE

Because I am theirs, and they are mine.

They look at the floor and drop their arms as if they were dead. I can see how their cheekbones, more pronounced than ever, give them a ghoulish appearance.

But they still look beautiful.

Perfect.

The air smells of concentrated cigarette smoke mixed with their intoxicating lavender perfume, as if the room has no ventilation.

I remember the lighter, pulling it out of my pocket and extending it toward them. Whatever has happened, they are obviously sensitive, and I want to make sure I treat them gently.

They look like an unfinished painting, a perfect sculpture that has been chipped with time.

If I could come closer, just a bit more, I could fix them.

"Rei, I'm here," I whisper, like a prayer. "I brought you this."

As I approach them like a wounded animal, Rei kneels and feels around on the ground for something.

They pick up a spoon lying nearby, look up, and gasp when they see the lighter in my hand.

They immediately throw the spoon and it lands right on my forehead.

It hits it with a dull, metallic clink.

I close my eyes from the pain, drop the lighter, and pick the spoon up while rubbing the wound.

The sting is sharp and starts spreading, blurring my vision. Everything turns reddish at the edges.

The spoon is strange. There's a huge hole in the middle.

Of course there is.

I tilt my head to one side, still trying to get the pain to go away. *They're confused, overwhelmed.*

That's all.

"What do I have to do to get you to leave me alone!"

The words catch me by surprise, rippling through the air around us. Distorted, far away.

Tic. Tac. Tic. Tac.
Tic. Tac. Tic. Tac.
Tic. Tac. Tic. Tac.

There's someone here.

GLOWROT

I turn to look for the intruder but couldn't find anyone.
It's just us.

Alone.

Like we're supposed to be.

"Are you listening to me?"

The same voice, this time coming from right behind me. Raspy, broken.

High-pitched.

Beautiful.

Their lips stop moving. Their chest rises and falls. Their fists tremble at their sides.

It's strange.

It almost seems like they're the one speaking.

But that's not right.

That's not right at all.

It doesn't make any sense.

They squat down again and reach for the lighter. Their fingers shake, their ribs are sharp and look like they're about to rip their skin. The shadows carved by the soft neon light make them look like open wounds.

Rei picks up the lighter and I smile. They understand; they finally can see I'm here.

That I came all the way to be with them.

To save them.

They were confused, that's all.

They hold the lighter in their hand,

and then—

what?

They... toss it?

They toss it... at me?

Why?

It strikes my chest, but I barely register the impact.

What's happening?

They're still confused.

It's okay, they just need time.

I need to—

"Are you deaf, you fucking psycho? Why are you following me?!"

Their words take on a life of their own. They run up to me and punch me in the face. The impact makes my nose start to bleed, and I see stars.

"What?" The sound I make is so low I'm not even sure I said it out loud.

"I've been trying to get better for so long. I've even made progress!" They're crying.

But they're moving now, their body trembling with something alive, something furious.

Rei starts to walk from one side to the other, staggering on the broken glass of the mirrors. They point out small indentations in the walls that I had initially overlooked.

Tic. Tac. Tic. Tac.

That sound.

Tic. Tac. Tic. Tac.

Tic. Tac. Tic. Tac.

There's something in the cracks. At first I think they're eyes, but the closer I get, the more I can hear them.

Tic. Tac. Tic. Tac.

Small clock hands, sticking out, flooding the walls.

"I was about to make it," they shout and throw more spoons, this time at the clocks embedded all around us. "Time was running out for you, finally!"

The bones in their knees and elbows are prominent, and a lot.

Too much.

Seeing that the only thing they are wearing is underwear the same color as their skin only reinforces how much they look like a corpse.

My Rei.

What happened to them?

They seem broken.

Brainwashed.

That's the only logical explanation.

"What are you talking about?" I also start to tremble.

They open their mouth in surprise and let out a roar of agony that makes my ears ring. Then, they extend their arms and point around us.

In pain.

They point at hollow teaspoons and empty sodas, at unopened cans of food and a broken scale near the bathroom entrance.

I kick the broken mirror pieces, and they start scratching their head.

GLOWROT

They squeeze their eyes shut, and the spider's web under their eye twitches.

The rabbit on their back looks like it wants to jump out, but it's trapped forever, suffocated within their skin.

Tic. Tac. Tic. Tac.

Their moles look sad and desperate.

They begin to cry again.

Then, turn off the light, and the tears glow in the darkness.

"Please, I can't believe you're so dumb." Each of their words becomes a razor, they begin to make cuts along my limbs. "I was in a bad moment, okay? That's why I came here. We all came for the same reason."

They're shaking uncontrollably, like a rabbit being caught in a trap and trying to gnaw at its own leg.

I want to hold them.

I take a step closer, and they recoil.

"Yeah. We're all broken. Empty. I understand." I can't string the thoughts together sanely.

I repeat the discovery that took me so long with concern because they say it like it's self-evident.

"Just because I was in such a dark place when I met you, doesn't mean I wanted to be there permanently."

Their voice breaks on that last word.

They start punching the walls, and I hear some bones starting to give way. Like they're trying to dig their way out.

They grab a vase and throw it. A chair. A book. More spoons. Glass. Mirror. Fabric. Anything that isn't nailed down.

All of them directed at me.

I don't dodge them.

I let them hit me.

I let them hit me.

I let them hit me.

I let them hit me.

I let them hit me.

I let them hit me.

32 CheckEnginE

"At first, I liked it, you know," they say with ragged breath.

Their hands shake as they reach for another object, then hesitate, then grab something else.

"Oh, but you don't have to eat."

A crash.

"Drink water and milkshakes."

Another crash.

"It's normal to feel like this."

The next object doesn't hit me. It shatters behind me, against the wall.

I remember every single word they mention, I nod without thinking about it.

Until slowly, it all makes more sense in my head.

Oh.

Fuck.

Fuck. Fuck. Fuck.

Maybe I didn't have all the pieces.

Maybe I—

But it's okay, right? Because we're together.

And it's fine.

We can fix this.

I was broken, and they fixed me.

Now I can fix them, too.

Right?

Right?

Right?

Right?

Right?

Right?

Right?

Right?

Right?

Right?

Right?

Right?

Right?

But why didn't they tell me before?

GLOWROT

I could have helped them bett—

"I had stopped smoking and started eating. Eating well without feeling bad!" Right now, the room is only lit up by their tears. "But it's not easy. And every fucking time I relapsed, I ended up here, and who was here?!" *I was.*

They didn't even have to answer their own question.

But they have it all wrong.

Everything I have done has been to comfort them. I told them what they wanted to hear, what made them feel better!

We hugged each other in the dark and made all the pain disappear.

We let go of the world together.

I was in a dark place too.

I still am!

And they knoW it!

I WAS HELPING THEM!

The walls start to move, the room is spinning. They're still throwing things left and right. Screaming.

Tic. Tac. Tic. Tac.

WhyWontThoseClocksShutUp?!

"And it wasn't even enough." Rei lowers their voice, the words cracking. They clench their fists limply and close their eyes. "Because I was getting better, and for one fucking time when I got stressed out and needed to smoke something, I fucked up my entire life again."

"Rei, I…"

"Don't. Say. My. Name." They hiss with hatred through their teeth. "How was I supposed to know you worked at the same shitty hotel I was staying at? I just wanted fire, just once!"

"You WANTED me to follow you!" My words come out louder than I want to, and they flinch, I step back. They shouldn't be scared, they should be happy! "Every single time we met here, you WANTED me! YOU.LOOKED.FOR.ME!"

The ideas, the scenes are stringing together in my mind but they're piled on top of each other.

They let go another piercing scream and the walls crack, the small pocket watches now star pouring out of them.

Tic. Tac. Tic. Tac. Tic. Tac. Tic. Tac. Tic. Tac. Tic. Tac. Tic. Tac. Tic. Tac. Tic. Tac. Tic. Tac. Tic. Tac. Tic. Tac. Tic. Tac. Tic. Tac. Tic. Tac. Tic. Tac. Tic. Tac. Tic. Tac. Tic. Tac. Tic. Tac.

Tic. Tac. Tic. Tac. Tic. Tac. Tic. Tac. Tic. Tac. Tic. Tac. Tic.

Tic. Tac. Tic. Tac. Tic. Tac.

Tic. Tac. Tic. Tac. Tic. Tac. Tic. Tac. Tic. Tac. Tic. Tac. Tic.

Tac. Tic. Tac. Tic. Tac. Tic. Tac. Tic. Tac. Tic. Tac. Tic. Tac. Tic. Tac. Tic. Tac.
Tic. Tac. Tic. Tac. Tic. Tac. Tic. Tac. Tic. Tac. Tic. Tac. Tic. Tac. Tic. Tac. Tic.
Tac. Tic. Tac. Tic. Tac. Tic. Tac. Tic. Tac. Tic. Tac. Tic. Tac. Tic. Tac. Tic. Tac.
Tic. Tac. Tic. Tac. Tic. Tac. Tic. Tac. Tic. Tac. Tic. Tac. Tic. Tac. Tic. Tac. Tic.
Tac. Tic. Tac. Tic. Tac. Tic. Tac. Tic. Tac. Tic. Tac. Tic. Tac. Tic. Tac. Tic. Tac.
Tic. Tac. Tic. Tac. Tic. Tac. Tic. Tac. Tic. Tac. Tic. Tac. Tic. Tac. Tic. Tac. Tic.
Tac. Tic. Tac. Tic. Tac. Tic. Tac. Tic. Tac. Tic. Tac. Tic. Tac. Tic. Tac. Tic. Tac.
Tic. Tac. Tic. Tac. Tic. Tac. Tic. Tac. Tic. Tac. Tic. Tac. Tic. Tac. Tic. Tac. Tic.
Tac. Tic. Tac. Tic. Tac. Tic. Tac. Tic. Tac. Tic. Tac. Tic. Tac. Tic. Tac. Tic. Tac.
Tic. Tac. Tic. Tac. Tic. Tac. Tic. Tac. Tic. Tac. Tic. Tac. Tic. Tac. Tic. Tac.

"Obviously, if I'm dying, and every time these fucking ideas come into my head, you come to tell me they're true. How am I going to react?!"

The room is spinning harder and harder.

"True?"

"I spent too much time convincing myself that I should try to eat, avoiding mirrors, telling myself I didn't need to stick my stomach in and half-breathe." The echo of their voice vibrates against everything around me, echoes and shatters the empty glasses in the kitchen. "Then you showed up to remind me that this place exists and that I'll never be able to escape those thoughts."

"I was never trying to hurt you. Rei," I try to explain, I walk towards them, but they take a step back.

There's nowhere to go.

I reach forward and see something in their eyes.

Panic.

They're shaking their head violently, and their teeth clench.

"Stop saying my name! How do you even know it?! I never fucking told you! Stop. Stop. Stop. Stop. Stop!" Their voice raises and breaks in between syllables.

"You know you were like this before; that's why we met here. Because we're both broken. And only we can fix each other."

They just need to listen to me.

They're confused.

"Do you know what a trigger is? Or are you so fucking delusional that the idea doesn't fit in your brain?" They push my forehead with their index and middle fingers with the strength of a small child and let out a whimper. "You drag me back to the worst I've ever been. And then you have the nerve to chase me down like I owe you something!"

"I was doing what you wanted! You're twisting everything!" I have to make an insurmountable effort to keep my voice down. "You were calling me back. Every. Single. Fucking. Time!"

Tic. Tac. Tic. Tac. Tic. Tac.

I grab one of the mirror fragments from the floor and close my fist around it until it bleeds, until my flesh parts like an opening eye.

The pain helps.

It keeps me grounded.

It helps me not to lose my temper.

They have it all wrong.

They're not okay.

They're so confused.

I have to have patience.

I have to help them see the truth.

"You don't get it! You don't GET it! Every time I got close to being better, you found me." Their voice no longer raises; it can't. It sounds painful. "Like I had a fucking leash on my neck."

They slap their face once, twice, trying to calm themself down.

Then they break down and melt into the floor, crying again, their tears glowing enough to lighten up the whole room.

They have it all wrong.

They have it all FUCKING wrong.

If they listened to me for half a second, they would understand.

But no.

They're too much on their head.

Maybe that's the reason why it was so hard to find them.

They're too closed in, too blind.

What if there's someone else?

Yeah, it has to be it.

Someone who's been putting ideas into their brain. Someone who's making them get it all twisted.

And wrong.

But it's okay, I'm here. I'll help them.

Their eyes are puffy and dazed, I try to wipe the tears from their cheeks but they react like a rabid dog and throw their teeth at me.

"Let me help you! You're confused and scared—"

"I am! I'm fucking terrified. Of you!"

Something breaks inside of me, and my eye twitches.

They're delusional.

They're not okay.

I'll fix them.

I know I can.

I'll be their ally now that I know what's happening to them.

We can get through this together.

But they can't stop crying and the sound doesn't let me think.

Tic. Tac. Tic. Tac.

They start screaming again.

"You only remember what's good for you, don't you?" They're walking toward the bed, but the screaming slowly subsides.

I follow them, hoping they'll sit down and calm down, that we can talk about this together.

"You never even stopped to think, did you? That I didn't tell you my name because I didn't *want* you to find me? I stopped going to the club when I was coming to NIU just so I wouldn't see your face because I knew you would be there."

"Now that I know, I can help you." At least now they're talking normally again, I sigh with relief.

I try to touch them again, but they dodge me.

"Don't you dare fucking touch me! You remember what you want, the little kisses, how being with me makes you feel. Do you have any idea how it makes *me* feel?!" They pause by the bed for a few seconds and then keep going.

Towards the wall.

Towards the window.

No.

No!

"Get down from there!'" I bark, but it sounds like an order. They can't blame me. The situation has gotten me so fucked up in the head. "Let's talk! Why are you being like this?!"

Rei ignores my pleas as they open the shutter.

"I honestly thought ignoring you would trick you into thinking it never happened."

Their voice is steady now, too much to not be alarming. Like they're no longer talking to me, just deciding something for themself.

Like they're already gone.

"I thought they were dreams, until you decided to interfere in my life outside of here."

"You can't mean this. You're just upset. You're overreacting. Rei, you can't imagine how I feel about you. All the times we were together..." I can't finish my sentences, and the shutter is already open.

"Which ones? When we were drunk by the aroma of this hellish place? Desperate for a fake human contact that we are not able to have in real life?" They put one foot up on the bed, then another. I want to run to hold them, but I'm afraid that scaring them will worsen it. "Wake up, Bo. You're just thinking about *the idea of me*, what you want me to be."

"You don't get to do this to **me**! I found you. **I** came all this way for you!" I walk slowly to them, almost kneeling. I don't mind begging them. "I was trying to find you so we wouldn't have to see each other here anymore, so we could be outside together and heal together."

They place a foot on the ledge, their eyes locking onto mine with something way colder than hatred.

"Do one thing for me." They whisper. "Grow the fuck up. And if I ever see you again, if you ever dare to find me again, I will rip your eyes out with my nails."

I lunge forward, reaching for them, reaching for something.

My fingers slice through nothing.

Their body bends backward. Their arms spread like they're letting the void take them.

And then, my perfect White Rabbit vanishes.

No sound. No weight. No trace.

Gone.

And now what?

They'll come back.

They have to.

They just don't understand yet.

I'll make them understand.

GLOWROT

33

Service Unavailable

I look at myself in the mirror and my reflection lies to me, because I shouldn't look like this.

I should look victorious, at last. Relieved. Happy.

I should look like someone who has finally achieved her goal, like the savior.

Although Rei is in absolute denial.

But my eyes are swollen and my lips are raw from biting them so much.

My fingers are trembling. I bring them to my face and touch the skin under my eyes. It is thinner and more translucent, I can see my veins.

I shouldn't feel like this and the worst thing is that **it's not my fault.**

I don't know if it really was someone else, putting ideas in my White Rabbit's head, or their own confusion.

I wouldn't want to blame them but—

But it is their fault.

And that's okay!

I can forgive them without any problem. After all, my feelings are too strong for a misunderstanding like this to separate us.

I blink rapidly. My heart is pounding against my ribs.

I don't know if it was worse to fall asleep in NIU or to wake up in my own room.

I don't know what's real anymore.

"bo,Breathe.YouHaveToBreathe."

At least W is back.

His voice is firm, it reassures me.

It helps me breathe.

GLOWROT

So I do it.

Inhalo.

Exhalo.

My brain is trying to—

The cables, the neurons.

To connect.

They're trying to.

Bzzz

Electricidad.

Qué?

Conectarse.

Connection.

Wires.

My brain is trying to rewire itself, but it's almost impossible when I can't stop thinking about Them.

Where could They be?

I watched Them fade away, never touched the ground. They left NIU like so many other times I did. And if they disappeared from there, they had to have appeared somewhere else, didn't they? And if I showed up in my bed, maybe they did too.

I have to find them.

They said they didn't want me to.

But they didn't really mean it.

They were in a terrible state of mind, overwhelmed and confused. Things would be different if we saw each other outside; they could breathe.

They would realize they want me as much as I want them.

Right?

Right.

"ofCourseTheyWould."

The air is still thick, though maybe it feels that way because I can't breathe. W's fingers trail along my shoulders. Careful. Gentle.

The opposite of me.

"youDidWhatYouHadTo."

One more, just one more.

I bring my hand to my back and bury my nails in my skin, moving my fingers slowly, ignoring the burning sensation accompanying it.

33 Service Unavailable

Rei doesn't understand now.

But they will.

Maybe it's a good idea to go in for another bath, but the hot water is finally gone.

Maybe one last scratch.

I inhale and close my eyes as I feel each line mark on my skin, brushing my fingertips over the swollen lacerations after I'm done. I turn and try to twist my head so I can see the marks in the mirror.

I smile. It feels good.

I obey W and take slow breaths, but it only reminds me how dizzy I am.

I don't want to think again because everything I touch crumbles in my hands.

"youDon'tHaveToThinkAboutAnything.
ICanDoItForYou."

He whispers next to me, and I hug myself.

It's these moments when I feel at least a little peace inside because I can function in automatic mode.

And everything is easier.

Maybe I should just stay here, forever.

Maybe I—

No.

I have work.

I have to function.

I have things to fix.

I push everything down and stand up.

Everything is fine.

It's hard, but I have to give them time. I care for them, they know that. They'll appreciate it, right?

Right?

Right?

Right?

Right?

Right?

Right?

Right?

Right?

GLOWROT

But it's so hard to stop thinking about them.

About their moles, the spider web under their eye, and the rabbit that looked at me every time I followed them.

About that smile and the sound of their voice.

It's hard not to think about their lips and the warm feeling of their chest when I got close.

I could at least try, make sure they understand I hear them and I'm not holding this against them.

Even though they hurt me.

They hurt me so bad.

But I can't stop thinking about how the negative space between their fingers feels like fitting with mine or what the sound of their footsteps is like—

Maldita sea.

I drop to my knees before registering the movement, but it's too late. A sour, yellow liquid is flung from my lips. Bile burns my throat and stomach.

It keeps going.

And going.

And going.

And going.

Like something's trying to claw its way out.

I scream so loudly I feel like I'm going to tear my vocal cords, and when I bend over, all the scratches on my back feel raw.

But the alarm goes off, and I have to get dressed.

"takeItEasy.Everything'sFine.I'mHere."

His voice is a warm hand on my skull. A gentle pressure. A guiding force.

"i'llHelpYou."

He moves my hands, my limbs, my body. I don't have to think, so I don't.

Thankfully.

I look in the mirror. The girl in the reflection isn't me.

When did I leave my bathroom?

I'm dressed perfectly, he's so good at this.

But I can't stop thinking about Rei.

They're not ready, that's all.

33 Service Unavailable

They can't see that they need me to get out of the black hole they put themselves in.

"sayHello," W reminds me I still have to exist.

I blink.

I'm downstairs.

At work.

That's the advantage of not having to think. I can just lay back and breathe.

"How do you feel?" Nina asks worriedly.

I turn to her with a perfectly curated smile.

"I'm feeling better, don't worry," I reply as if I were someone else. "Thank you for caring."

I'm not even aware of the words that will come out of my mouth before they do. But it's okay because they're working. Nina is smiling, so it means they're working.

I'm perfectly fine.

Eric looks up at me from the chair, and I smile without conviction. He squints and tilts his head.

Something is off.

I don't care.

I turn to start arranging the paperwork we'll need for the day.

I need to keep myself distracted because I have to give them some space.

Because they're not ready yet.

They can't see what I see.

But there's a spider web under the desk, and at the sight of it, I have to make an effort to not shove it into my mouth.

Would it taste like Them?

Like Rei?

I open the drawers and start arranging them one by one.

One

by

one,

I sort through the pens, paper clips, and general trash scattered everywhere.

I throw it all away.

GLOWROT

One

by

one.

I have to keep myself busy.

Why do we have blades in the drawer?

Will anyone notice if I take it to the bathroom?

"What the fuck?" Eric's voice pulls me out of my self-absorption.

Ups.

Squeezing the blade this hard was probably not my best idea. I don't think my thumb liked that.

But it's fine.

I'm so fine, perfectly fine.

It's barely a few drops of blood, but enough to make a red mess all around me. Nina stifles a little scream and takes me to the bathroom while Eric holds down the fort.

"i'mFine,IWasReallyFocused.That'sIt."

"I'm fine, I was really focused. That's it." I explain calmly to the blue-haired girl.

She just watches me wash my hands, smiling, with a worried and even a little fearful glint in her eyes.

Nina approaches cautiously and tries to check the wound. She does it with a gentleness that no random coworker would have. She squeezes it gently, just a little.

She brings my hand up to her lips and—

I can't.

Her touch hurts.

It reminds me of things I can't think about right now.

I blink and I'm in the back room now. Losing time has been annoying in the past, but now it feels so comforting.

Finally, I can breathe.

And I start to cry.

Silently, making sure no one sees me.

It's okay, I'm just frustrated.

I'm not crying because I'm weak.

I'm crying because I care.

Because I love them.

It's hard to keep away from them, but I have to giv—

33 Service Unavailable

Unless.

Unless I've been seeing it all wrong.

Unless I'm making a terrible mistake.

Maybe I need to go to them immediately because our conversation is so fresh.

If they see how much they hurt me—

Not on purpose, of course.

They would never hurt me on purpose—

They'll understand.

With a fresh burst of adrenaline, I peel myself away from the door and start rummaging through the mail, searching through the spaces designated for each guest and tenant.

The key to everything.

I shine the phone's flashlight on the lockers.

I need one, just one.

The most important one.

Now that I know what their problem is, I'm sure I can help them fight it.

I can change them.

Fix them.

I search and search for numbers, for the last missing piece of the puzzle.

Things are crawling out from the lockers, but I don't have time to be disgusted.

I grab the <u>caterpillars</u>, one after the other, and flung them to the floor.

A hundred little watching eyes.

They fall with a squish.

They don't matter.

Only Rei matters.

Rei.

Rei.

There.

REI NULL.

731.

"Tired?" Eric's playful tone brings me out of my senses.

He approaches me from behind and starts stroking my back, his fingers brushing the still-fresh scratches and my skin bristles.

GLOWROT

I jerk away and am almost about to send the entire bookshelf crashing to the floor.

He scowls at me, visibly annoyed.

"If you don't want to, you can just tell me," he sounds hurt.

"What the fuck Eric?! Can't you see I'm fucking busy?!" I can't help but blurt out, perhaps a little louder than intended.

"Dude, are you insane?" He savors that last word, like he's been waiting for the perfect moment to throw it at me.

My head twitches, and my fingers follow. My body becomes stiff for a second, and I start breathing faster and faster.

Until I get dizzy.

"What's your fucking problem?" I whisper way too low, because I know my voice is starting to sound less like mine.

And more like something else.

A beast.

"What's YOUR fucking problem? You literally just stuck a razor blade in your finger, you look like a maniac."

I feel the temperature rising, and I continue to breathe.

Faster

and

faster.

My toes are getting numb and stiff, and I have to hold on to the lockers to keep my balance.

I look around for anything that might be useful.

An empty box lies in a corner near me.

I don't think. I don't have to.

I throw it at Eric, and he dodges it, dazed, confused, and furious.
Hysterical.

He's overreacting.

I throw another piece of cardboard, envelopes, whatever I can find.

I know how this looks. Too familiar. Too recent.

The difference is that Eric deserves it.

Besides, it's not like any of it is enough to really hurt him.

"Why are you going through the guest's stuff, you fucking psycho?!" Those words.

They hit something in my brain.

Something fragile.

33 Service Unavailable

Something already cracking.

But I don't want to remember; I don't want to think.

He comes closer to me and grabs my wrist. I shriek.

I hate him.

I hate all of them.

They distracted me and made me forget the most important details of all my encounters with Rei.

Because of Eric and the others, because of work, and because of everyone who tried to bind me to a ridiculous reality that has nothing positive to offer me.

I hate them.

I hate them I hate them.

I hate them I hate them

I hate them I hate them I hate them I hate them

I hate them I hate them I hate them I hate them I hate them I hate them. I hate them .

GLOWROT

"Don't you feel sorry for yourself?" I don't even know what I'm saying, but the words come out like acid. "You can't even aspire to have real emotional connections, so you just crawl over some random girl at work? You're pathetic."

Eric doesn't flinch.

Doesn't react at all.

The door opens behind his back; he doesn't notice, and I don't say anything.

"If I had ever wanted emotional connections, Bo." He steps back and adjusts his shirt. "I wouldn't have chosen you."

It's casual, like a fact.

Like a joke he barely even cares to finish.

Nina peeks in and spits out the gum she had in her mouth.

"Clock me out for lunch?" He says to her, and then he walks out.

What time is it?

My life is falling apart, but at least I have Rei's room number.

That's all that matters.

They're well-rested now.

They'll understand now.

One more time.

That's all it'll take.

34
Caution Falling Debris

I'm finally thinking straight.

It took a while, sure. I had to get rid of the distractions first.

iHadToListenToHim

"Good."

Yes.

W knew all along —even if he didn't really understand— how important it was for me to stop listening to them.

To strangers.

But now I'm ready.

And something inside me tells me They are ready too.

Right now, I can rule the world.

My heels click like metronomes, counting down to something sacred. I walk like a queen returning to her kingdom.

No, her shrine.

MY SKIN FEELS TIGHT AROUND MY BONES, like I'm becoming exactly who I was always meant to be.

The nerves and worries are gone.

My head is clear, and I am no longer worried about not being sure how I got to the elevator.

I can't believe their room has been so close this whole time.

I don't need to practice any speeches because I know that the instant I open the door, I will know exactly what to say to Them.

A couple walks past me, and I smile; they scurry away in terror.

Do I have something on my face?

The cobwebs in the elevator brush my face and crawl up my nostrils. I don't flinch. My smile stays the same.

That has to be a sign, right?

They'll be happy to see me. I was a fool, thinking they needed time. They just needed to get out of NIU, it was messing with their mind.

"maybeItAlreadyDid."

Rei.

Their name tastes like metal on my tongue. Sharp, sacred.

My beautiful, perfect Rei.

My White Rabbit.

My beginning, my middle, my way out.

They just wandered off the correct path, but it's fine.

I'll lead them back.

I know what's best for Them.

Maybe I'll invite them out for a cup of coffee, or a movie.

"maybeYouWon'tHaveTo."

Something to give them breathing room, to remind them how comfortable they feel with me.

This time, I'll listen.

This time, I'll give them choices.

Just not the wrong ones.

I know better now.

The elevator doors open, and I bolt out without even trying to mask my excitement.

"BOLISTENTOME!" His voice slices through the hallway like a fire alarm.

I stop dead in my tracks and turn to look at him. W is standing next to me, more corporeal than ever. Feeling him so tangible reassures me. He's real. Solid.

"What happened? What did I do?" My voice sounds more broken and nervous than I thought.

I'm just so excited to see Rei finally out of NIU.

NIU.

"NIU," he says, moving his lips as if he were someone. His sharp teeth gleam in contrast to his skin shrouded in shadows. **"maybeReiDoesn'tRememberWhatHappened."**

"I wish, but I doubt it because—"

"Bo." He speaks calmly to me and takes my hand, even though we are in the middle of the corridor. **"whatHappensEveryTimeYouDissapearFromNiu?"**

34 Caution Falling Debris

My lips open wide.

W is a genius.

I love him.

He's right; it's hard to remember when you come back from there.

Maybe we'll be able to have a fresh start after all.

"that'sWhyYouNeedMe."

He whispers, moistening my ear with his warm breath.

"youBreakThingsBo. butIDon'tMind."

And doesn't mind either.

I will promise them that I will help them with whatever they need.

To get help, tell them how magnificent they look, and try a few bites.

Little by little, we'll go forward.

Together.

Of course, we will.

"ofCourseYouWill."

The floor flies under my feet until I reach their door. Everything else around me feels hazy, nonexistent.

Because nothing else matters right now.

Just Them and me.

Just us.

ROOM 731

How would Rei react?

If they don't remember, they'll probably cry joyfully seeing I finally found them. They may throw themselves into my arms and ask for forgiveness if they do.

It's okay, Rei, I forgive you.

You weren't yourself.

I love you too much to not do it.

We're together, and that's all that matters.

The carpet under my feet feels softer here. Like it's been walked on by someone lighter.

The hallway hums with something warm.

Anticipation.

I inhale deeply and knock on the door.

Once for the night we met.

Twice for the time we disappeared together.

GLOWROT

A third time for this new beginning.

Then, I tilt my head and listen.

Maybe I'll hear Them breathing behind the door.

Maybe I'll hear Them calling my name like I call for theirs each night.
And wait

patiently.

Everything around me smells clean, the atmosphere feels different than before.

Waiting

More cheerful, fuller of life. I stand there, making sure my hands aren't sweating.

TIME STRETCHES.

I wait. How many seconds have passed?

AND STRETCHES.

I knock again, just in case.

AND STRETCHES.

Maybe they're taking a nap or taking a bath.

Yes.

Of course.

They're probably taking a bath.

That's okay, I can wait.

They'll open the door. They'll open the door. They'll open the door.

And when they do, I'll tell them they're safe now. That they're home.

They're probably taking a bath.

Baths are good, like the ones I take with the pink water. They help me think, maybe it helps them think too.

They'll open the door. They'll open the door. They'll open the door.

They just have a lot to think about.

Like how to apologize to me, for example.

It's okay, Rei, I forgive you.

You weren't yourself.

I love you too much to not do it.

We're together, and that's all that matters.

I smile and drop to the floor, sitting with my back against the door I know will soon open.

I drum my fingers and start checking for anything stupid on my phone.

34 Caution Falling Debris

I can't help but go through their old pictures again. Their cadaverous appearance begged me to save them even years ago, even before we met.

We were always meant to be together.

I bring the screen closer to my face and zoom in on their photos until I can swear I can count his pores. They weren't the same; they were a cheap copy of the Rei I know.

They're perfect now. Their eyes, their silhouette.

Their skin.

I want to peel it back, layer by layer, to see who's underneath.

What's under Rei? How deep do I have to go before they become mine completely?

My sweet, perfect <u>White Rabbit</u>.

Mine.

Mine. Mine.

Mine. Mine. Mine. Mine. Mine. Mine. Mine. Mine.

Mine. Mine. Mine. Mine. Mine. Mine. Mine. Mine. Mine. Mine.

Mine. Mine. Mine. Mine. Mine. Mine. Mine. Mine. Mine. Mine.

Mine. Mine. Mine. Mine. Mine. Mine. Mine. Mine. Mine. Mine.

Mine. Mine. Mine. Mine. Mine. Mine. Mine. Mine. Mine. Mine.

Mine. Mine. Mine. Mine. Mine. Mine. Mine. Mine. Mine. Mine.

Mine. Mine. Mine. Mine. Mine. Mine. Mine. Mine. Mine. Mine.

Mine. Mine.

Mine.

I have to remember to ask them what they do for a living.

It's already that time when most people are getting comfortable for the evening.

What if they open the door already in their pajamas? What kind of clothes do they wear around the house?

I wonder what their voice sounds like first thing in the morning.

Not when they speak to others, but when They speak only to me.

When their throat is still dry, when they forget to sound like anything but their real self.

That's the version I want.

The *honest* one.

The raw one.

The one I can keep.

My version.

Mine.

GLOWROT

Mine. Mine.

Mine. Mine. Mine. Mine. Mine. Mine. Mine. Mine.

Mine. Mine. Mine. Mine. Mine. Mine. Mine. Mine. Mine. Mine.

Mine. Mine. Mine. Mine. Mine. Mine. Mine. Mine. Mine. Mine.

Mine. Mine. Mine. Mine. Mine. Mine. Mine. Mine. Mine. Mine.

Mine. Mine. Mine. Mine. Mine. Mine. Mine. Mine. Mine. Mine.

Mine. Mine. Mine. Mine. Mine. Mine. Mine. Mine. Mine. Mine.

Mine. Mine. Mine. Mine. Mine. Mine. Mine. Mine. Mine. Mine.

Mine. Mine. Mine. Mine. Mine. Mine. Mine. Mine.

Mine. Mine.

Mine.

I knock again, softer this time, like I don't want to scare Them.

Still nothing.

I press my ear to the door.

I want to believe I hear crying.

But all I hear is my own breath.

Maybe they're playing hide and seek with me.

Like rabbits do.

Hiding under the floorboards, behind the wallpaper, in between the seconds.

I'll find them.

I always find them.

My legs are half asleep, so I tap them to wake them up. W is sitting next to me as promised, but he says nothing.

He's just sitting and smiling.

Waiting patiently, like me.

I smile back, he keeps smiling.

Smiling.

Smiling.

S m i l i n g.

S m i l i n g.

I try to match his expression. Maybe that's the trick.

If I smile long enough, they'll come out.

Right?

"They're just shy," I whisper.

W tilts his head. I tilt mine too.

We wait.

I think I hear a sound, a shuffle maybe, or a whisper behind the door. But when I lean closer, it's just the veins behind my own eyes, pulsing too loud.

The lights in the hallway pulse.

I blink.

My phone says it's been half an hour, maybe forty-five minutes.

I look around me. I stand up and check the number, did I make a mistake? Then, gently knock on the door.

Again.

Once for the night we met.

Twice for the times we disappeared together.

A third time for this new beginning.

Again.

I turn around and look at W, he's still smiling.

S m i l i n g .

I'm being so patient.

I've been so good.

The least they could do is oPEN THE FUCKING DOOR.

I knock once more; maybe a fourth time was needed.

Or fifth.

Or sixth.

"Rei? Rei?"

"Hello Rei!"

"Rei?"

"Are you there?"

"Did something happen to you?"

"Rei!"

"Rei, answer me!"

"REI."

"OPEN THE DOOR!"

"OPEN IT RIGHT NOW!"

"They're gone, miss." A voice breaks my concentration, and I almost fall face-first on the floor.

It's strong, heavy, like it could tear through my skull.

I turn to find the cleaning lady. The same one who is always in the same spot.

GLOWROT

"What?" The world is spinning around me, faster and faster each second that passes.

"I saw the guest in that room running out this morning." Her voice is syrupy like it's dripping from my ears. "They looked like they'd seen a spook."

A spook?

Did something happen to them?

Was I late in the end?

"Do you know what time they'll be back?" I try to smile, but W is the only one doing so.

S m i l i n g .

The woman shakes her head.

I feel it.

The urge.

Vivid. Animal. Unfiltered.

Raw.

The urge to grab her by the skull and slam her against the wall until her thoughts spill out.

Would she bleed?

Would her brain leak out in blue dish soap?

Would she split open into something that makes sense?

Bugs?

Caterpillars?

"They were carrying a big suitcase and had one of the security men escort them to the elevator." Her voice feels like it's coming from the walls. "They were looking around. Spooked, I'm telling you. So spooked!"

The last words echo, warped, like they're being repeated over a broken speaker.

Spooked. Spooked. Spooked. Spooked. Spooked. Spooked. Spooked. Spooked. Spooked. Spooked. Spooked. Spooked. Spooked. Spooked.

That's absurd.

She's insane.

That's right, that's why she's been cleaning the same spot every time I see her.

I keep knocking.

And knocking.

A n d   k n o c k i n g .

34 Caution Falling Debris

"They ran! Not here. Do you hear me?" She extends her hand to grab me, but I bat it more forcefully than I need.

She's as fragile as a paper doll.

"You don't know shit," I spit and keep knocking.

A n d   k n o c k i n g .

A n d   k n o c k i n g .

A n d   k n o c k i n g .

"They're." Knock. "Waiting." Another knock. "For me!"

I keep knocking until my knuckles turn raw.

A n d   k n o c k i n g .

The woman stands there expressionless.

A second later, she's a few steps back and struggling to regain her balance. My hands are stretched in front of me.

Did I push her?

In one of them is her keycard.

Did I ever give it back?

That's not important now.

I rush inside and see a less distorted reflection of the room where I had found Rei at NIU, with the same bed and kitchen, with a table in the corner.

There's a faint scent of them left, but it's diluting as time passes.

Skin.

Perfume.

Sweat.

Pain.

I open my mouth and try to swallow it, breathing in every bit they've left behind.

The floor is just a little dirty, and the furniture is in disarray, as if they had run away.

From whom?

I couldn't have been too late.

No, please, no.

I walk to the closet, and there is not a single garment.

GLOWROT

Is it true?

> *Did they leave?*

> *Did they leave me?*

How dare they?!

> **HOW DARE THEY TAKE WHAT'S MINE?!**

Tears burn my cheeks as if they were acid; little by little, they fill my throat until they begin to suffocate me.

I throw myself to the floor and start crawling across the room.

Like something inhuman.

Like an animal.

A beast.

My nails rip against the floorboards. I let out a scream and start checking under the bed, in the cabinets.

They're hiding.

They have to be hiding.

THEY CAN'T BE GONE.

I dig my nails so hard into the cracks that they split. Skin peels. Blood joins the stains they left behind. I press my face into the floor.

I want to crawl into the spaces they used to exist in.

I open every drawer, slam every cabinet, yank open the fridge.

Maybe they're there, maybe they're folded inside of it.

Nothing.

"Rei?" My voice is hoarse. My mouth is barely working now. "Rei?" *It's getting harder and harder to breathe.*

> *The world is blurred.*

>> *It spins, and spins.*

"WHERE ARE YOU?"

My throat is raw now, and I taste something metallic in my mouth. *The world keeps spinning.*

> *And spinning.*

>> *And spinning.*

I belong in this room.

I am what fills it now.

My breath is the wallpaper, my fingernails the carpet.

34 Caution Falling Debris

But it's spinning too fast.

Spin.

Spin.

I look for any point that doesn't move to concentrate, to reestablish my balance.

W.

W is there, standing.

Not in a corner, but in the middle of the room.

And he's still smiling.

S   m   i   l   i   n   g   .

But there's something else.

Something besides his smile, the spinning world.

Sounds, footsteps. The cold floor beneath me.

Did I fall?

"What the fuck are you doing in here?"

I don't move. I can't even lift my head.

My eyes roll back toward the sound.

That voice.

No.

It can't be.

I put my hands over my ears, but the voice drills down until it reaches my bones.

"GOD FUCKING DAMN IT, BO!"

I curl tighter against the floor with my cheek pressed to the dirt they left behind. My body hums like a broken machine.

It beeps.

BEEP. BEEP. BEEP. BEEP. BEEP. BEEP. BEEP. BEEP. BEEP.
BEEP. BEEP. BEEP. BEEP. BEEP. BEEP. BEEP. BEEP. BEEP. BEEP.
BEEP. BEEP. BEEP. BEEP. BEEP. BEEP. BEEP. BEEP. BEEP. BEEP.
BEEP. BEEP. BEEP. BEEP. BEEP. BEEP. BEEP. BEEP. BEEP. BEEP.
BEEP. BEEP. BEEP. BEEP. BEEP. BEEP. BEEP. BEEP. BEEP. BEEP.
BEEP. BEEP. BEEP. BEEP. BEEP. BEEP.BEEP. BEEP. BEEP. BEEP.
BEEP. BEEP. BEEP. BEEP. BEEP. BEEP. BEEP. BEEP. BEEP. BEEP.
BEEP. BEEP. BEEP. BEEP. BEEP. BEEP. BEEP. BEEP. BEEP. BEEP.
BEEP. BEEP. BEEP. BEEP. BEEP. BEEP. BEEP. BEEP. BEEP. BEEP.
BEEP. BEEP. BEEP. BEEP. BEEP. BEEP. BEEP. BEEP. BEEP. BEEP.
BEEP. BEEP. BEEP. BEEP. BEEP. BEEP. BEEP. BEEP. BEEP. BEEP.

GLOWROT

My mouth is open, but no words come out.

Just heat.

Just breath.

Just rot.

Alexia's boots crunch over something. Maybe glass.

Maybe me.

And then, silence.

The kind that only happens right before someone decides what to do with you.

35 Flammable Material

No.

               No.

                             No.

No quiero.

           No quiero seguir.

                        Por favor, no.

Please.

          I don't want to.

                            I can't—

"Are you listening to me?!" Alexia had stopped trying to keep her composure minutes ago.

Maybe hours.

It doesn't matter.

Nothing matters anymore.

I try to swallow the essence that Rei left behind once again, but it has been diluted in the air.

It disappeared.

How could They have hurt me so much?

"Didn't my love mean anything?"

The jolt Alexia gives me lets me know that I said that last thing out loud.

I look around, the cleaning lady has disappeared again but there's a second security guard in front of me.

And W, still standing.

Still smiling.

"You think this is love? They ran out of here shaking. They filed a complaint days ago, Bo."

It can't be.

My Rabbit—

GLOWROT

No.

Surely—

Surely, someone replaced them.

Yes, it's the only thing that makes sense.

But no, it doesn't.

Nothing does.

They dumped me, abandoned me.

Abandoned me like rotten fruit left in the sun.

Something inside my chest caves in, scraping against my ribs.

"youWereTooGoodForThem,Bo."

W says softly, walking towards me.

"weThoughtTheyWouldUnderstand.

ButTheyDidn't."

The words curl like smoke.

We thought.

Did we?

"butNowWeKnow."

Now we know.

"i'mTheOnlyOneWhoUnderstandsYou."

The only one who understands me.

"theOnlyOneWhoCares."

theOnlyOneWhoCares.

"Are you listening to me?"

The floor spins.

I'm being dragged out of the room by my arms, the carpet leaving burns on my bare feet.

Bare?

I imagine tiny red trails left behind.

My heart bleeding the farther away I'm pulled from their last place of existence.

Dragged like a criminal.

Like a wild thing, they finally caught.

"You don't understand. They needed me," I say, almost begging. Bile starts piling up in my throat. "They just didn't realize it yet."

Rei's not okay.

"They were confused. Sick. Lost. I saw it in their skin, in their bones. I only wanted to help. I only wanted to—"

35 Flammable Material

My voice catches.

Make them whole.

Make them mine.

I was just trying to help them.

Help Them be Themselves.

Where are they taking me?

"A complaint was filed by the guest occupying the room where you were found." Her voice is monotone, empty.

Disappointed.

"They were scared when we met. I saw it. I *know* what pain looks like." I say, and my teeth clench until I hear something crack. "They never said no. Not once. Not to me."

"Said guest expressed concern over a member of staff following them—"

"They wanted it!" I scream, my voice bouncing off the elevator walls. "They kept coming back. What was I supposed to think?!"

I'm vibrating and trying to kick everything I find on my way, sobbing, wild.

My knees hit the elevator floor. The metal doors close behind me like a coffin.

The other security guard just stares to the front, completely unphased like he's not even real.

Nothing is real.

Yeah, that's it.

This isn't happening.

GLOWROT

Not real. Not real. Not real. Not real. Not real. Notreal. Notreal.
Notreal.Notreal.Notreal.Notreal.Notreal.Notreal.Notreal.Notreal.
Notreal.Notreal.Notreal.Notreal.Notreal.Notreal.Notreal.Notreal.
Notreal.Notreal.Notreal.Notreal.Notreal.Notreal.Notreal.Notreal.

Notreal.Notreal.Notreal.Notreal.Notreal.Notreal.Notreal.Notreal.
Notreal.Notreal.Notreal.Notreal.Notreal.Notreal.Notreal.Notreal.
Notreal.Notreal.Notreal.Notreal.Notreal.Notreal.Notreal.Notreal.
Notreal.Notreal.Notreal.Notreal.Notreal.Notreal.Notreal.Notreal.
Notreal.Notreal.Notreal.Notreal.Notreal.Notreal.Notreal.Notreal.
Notreal.Notreal.Notreal.Notreal.Notreal.Notreal.Notreal.Notreal.
Notreal.Notreal.Notreal.Notreal.Notreal.Notreal.Notreal.Notreal.
Notreal.Notreal.Notreal.Notreal.Notreal.Notreal.Notreal.Notreal.
Notreal.Notreal.Notreal.Notreal.Notreal.Notreal.Notreal.Notreal.
Notreal.Notreal.Notreal.Notreal.Notreal.Notreal.Notreal.Notreal.
Notreal.Notreal.Notreal.Notreal.Notreal.Notreal.Notreal.Notreal.
Notreal.Notreal.Notreal.Notreal.Notreal.Notreal.Notreal.Notreal.
Notreal.Notreal.Notreal.Notreal.Notreal.Notreal.Notreal.Notreal.
Notreal.Notreal.Notreal.Notreal.Notreal.Notreal.Notreal.Notreal.
Notreal.Notreal.Notreal.Notreal.Notreal.Notreal.Notreal.Notreal.
Notreal.Notreal.Notreal.Notreal.Notreal.Notreal.Notreal.Notreal.

Notreal.Notreal.Notreal.Notreal.Notreal.Notreal.Notreal.Notreal.

Notreal.Notreal.Notreal.Notreal.Notreal.Notreal.Notreal.Notreal.

Notreal.Notreal.Notreal.Notreal.Notreal.Notreal.Notreal.Notreal.
Notreal.Notreal.Notreal.Notreal.Notreal.Notreal.Notreal.Notreal.
Notreal.Notreal.Notreal.Notreal.Notreal.Notreal.Notreal.Notreal.

Notreal.Notreal.Notreal.Notreal.Notreal.Notreal.Notreal.Notreal.

Notreal.Notreal.Notreal.Notreal.Notreal.Notreal.Notreal.Notreal.
Notreal.Notreal.Notreal.Notreal.Notreal.Notreal.Notreal.Notreal.
Notreal.Notreal.Notreal.Notreal.Notreal.Notreal.Notreal.Notreal.
Notreal.Notreal.Notreal.Notreal.Notreal.Notreal.Notreal.Notreal.
Notreal.Notreal.Notreal.Notreal.Notreal.Notreal.Notreal.Notreal.
Notreal.Notreal.Notreal.Notreal.Notreal.Notreal.Notreal.Notreal.
Notreal.Notreal.Notreal.Notreal.Notreal.Notreal.Notreal.Notreal.
Notreal.Notreal.Notreal.Notreal.Notreal.Notreal.Notreal.Notreal.
Notreal.Notreal.Notreal.Notreal.Notreal.Notreal.Notreal.Notreal.
Notreal.Notreal.Notreal.Notreal.Notreal.Notreal.Notreal.Notreal.

Notreal.Notreal.Notreal.Notreal.Notreal.Notreal.Notreal.Notreal.

Notreal.Notreal.Notreal.Notreal.Notreal.Notreal.Notreal.Notreal.

Notreal.Notreal.Notreal.Notreal.Notreal.Notreal.Notreal.Notreal.

Notreal.Notreal.Notreal.Notreal.Notreal.Notreal.Notreal.Notreal.

Notreal.Notreal.Notreal.Notreal.Notreal.Notreal.Notreal.Notreal.

35 Flammable Material

Notreal.Notreal.Notreal.Notreal.Notreal.Notreal.Notreal.Notreal.
Notreal.Notreal.Notreal.Notreal.Notreal.Notreal.Notreal.Notreal.
Notreal.Notreal.Notreal.Notreal.Notreal.Notreal.Notreal.Notreal.
Notreal.Notreal.Notreal.Notreal.Notreal.Notreal.Notreal.Notreal.
Notreal.Notreal.Notreal.Notreal.Notreal.Notreal.Notreal.Notreal.
Notreal.Notreal.Notreal.Notreal.Notreal.Notreal.Notreal.Notreal.
Notreal.Notreal.Notreal.Notreal.Notreal.Notreal.Notreal.Notreal.
Notreal.Notreal.Notreal.Notreal.Notreal.Notreal.Notreal.Notreal.
Notreal.Notreal.Notreal.Notreal.Notreal.Notreal.Notreal.Notreal.
Notreal.Notreal.Notreal.Notreal.Notreal.Notreal.Notreal.Notreal.
Notreal.Notreal.Notreal.Notreal.Notreal.Notreal.Notreal.Notreal.
Notreal.Notreal.Notreal.Notreal.Notreal.Notreal.Notreal.Notreal.
Notreal.Notreal.Notreal.Notreal.Notreal.Notreal.Notreal.Notreal.
Notreal.Notreal.Notreal.Notreal.Notreal.Notreal.Notreal.Notreal.
Notreal.Notreal.Notreal.Notreal.Notreal.Notreal.Notreal.Notreal.
Notreal.Notreal.Notreal.Notreal.Notreal.Notreal.Notreal.Notreal.

Notreal.Notreal.Notreal.Notreal.Notreal.Notreal.Notreal.Notreal.

Notreal.Notreal.Notreal.Notreal.Notreal.Notreal.Notreal.Notreal.

Notreal.Notreal.Notreal.Notreal.Notreal.Notreal.Notreal.Notreal.

Notreal.Notreal.Notreal.Notreal.Notreal.Notreal.Notreal.Notreal.
Notreal.Notreal.Notreal.Notreal.Notreal.Notreal.Notreal.Notreal.
Notreal.Notreal.Notreal.Notreal.Notreal.Notreal.Notreal.Notreal.
Notreal.Notreal.Notreal.Notreal.Notreal.Notreal.Notreal.Notreal.
Notreal.Notreal.Notreal.Notreal.Notreal.Notreal.Notreal.Notreal.
Notreal.Notreal.Notreal.Notreal.Notreal.Notreal.Notreal.Notreal.
Notreal.Notreal.Notreal.Notreal.Notreal.Notreal.Notreal.Notreal.
Notreal.Notreal.Notreal.Notreal.Notreal.Notreal.Notreal.Notreal.
Notreal.Notreal.Notreal.Notreal.Notreal.Notreal.Notreal.Notreal.
Notreal.Notreal.Notreal.Notreal.Notreal.Notreal.Notreal.Notreal.
Notreal.Notreal.Notreal.Notreal.Notreal.Notreal.Notreal.Notreal.
Notreal.Notreal.Notreal.Notreal.Notreal.Notreal.Notreal.Notreal.
Notreal.Notreal.Notreal.Notreal.Notreal.Notreal.Notreal.Notreal.
Notreal.Notreal.Notreal.Notreal.Notreal.Notreal.Notreal.Notreal.

Notreal.Notreal.Notreal.Notreal.Notreal.Notreal.Notreal.Notreal.

Notreal.Notreal.Notreal.Notreal.Notreal.Notreal.Notreal.Notreal.

Notreal.Notreal.Notreal.Notreal.Notreal.Notreal.Notreal.Notreal.

Notreal.Notreal.Notreal.Notreal.Notreal.Notreal.Notreal.Notreal.

GLOWROT

W's hands graze my shoulders, and I swear I can feel him licking my ear.

"noOneElseWillUnderstandWhatYou'reGoingThrough."

He whispers.

I'm the only one who ever saw them.

The only one who ever really *loved* them.

The next thing I know, I'm sitting in the breakroom. Or something that looks like it.

My hands are sticky. My knees are red.

I don't remember if I was screaming or crying or both.

I try to sit up straighter, but my whole body itches, like I'm wearing skin that doesn't fit anymore.

Alexia is still with me, and the useless man is, too. But there's more.

The twins.

Nova is staring at me, and Nina is looking away.

If they're all here, who's at the front?

I don't want to be here; I can't bear their stares.

I sigh and stand up slowly, taking care not to look any of them in the eye, but the moment I try to step towards the door, hands grab my arm and force me back into the chair.

I look at Alexia, but she is leaning against a wall, massaging her temples, and taking what I guess must be a headache pill.

It's the useless man, and now there's another one. They're both holding me and forcing me to stay in the chair. And even though I try to get out of their grip, it's as if their hands have turned into handcuffs.

"SUÉLTENME!" I scream at their faces, but every time I try to focus on them for too long, it seems like they blur to escape my sight. *"Yo me sé sentar sola, imbéciles!"*

Los odio. Los odio a todos.

"Obviamente ninguno de ustedes entiende, porque ninguno de ustedes ha vivido la clase de amor que yo estoy viviendo en este momento y ninguno de ustedes le conoció y no sabían lo mucho que estaba sufriendo y lo perdide que estaba. Y solamente yo puedo ayudarle, y teniéndome aquí prisionera, lo único que están haciendo es joderle la vida y hacer más difícil que yo le ayude. Y Rei no lo entiende, pero aunque no lo quiera, soy la única persona que puede salvarle y—"

"BO!"

"QUÉ?!"

"You're speaking Spanish."

♥ 376 ♣

35 Flammable Material

"I said I know how to sit down by myself," I mumble under my breath and clench my fists, paying special attention to feeling the skin that starts thinning and ripping under my nails.

"Why would you do something like that?" This time, it's Nina speaking; she looks scared and brokenhearted. Her lips are trembling, and her eyes are red and swollen.

Alexia steps forward but can't look me in the eyes.

"You broke into the guest records to get their room number. You harassed a coworker to cover your shifts just so you could follow them around the hotel at night. We went into your room, and you have a fucking weird ass conspiracy shrine covering all your living room walls. That's not love, Bo. That's an obsession."

No, it's not; it's fate.

It's proof.

It's devotion.

Nova laughs, but it's humorless and almost pitying. It's the kind of laugh people make right before they cry. Like she's talking to a version of herself she hates.

"You were telling people you had dreams about them before you even met. You called it fate like you were *meant* to find them here. That's not romantic. That's delusional."

I didn't have dreams about them. I **met them in my dreams.**

But also, I didn't tell anyone—

"You told me they liked it," Nina says, her voice faint, almost disappearing. "That if they cried, it was because they were scared of how much they cared. And I believed you." She shakes her head, disgusted. "You lied to me."

"I never told that to any of you!" I try to be loud, but my throat IS POLLUTED BY NEEDLES.

"I read the things you wrote on the walls." It's Alexia again, this time she approaches me. "You described the inside of their apartment, down to the cracks in the mirror and the mug they always used. They said they never invited you in Bo, so how the fuck did you know that?"

NIU, it was NIU. I saw it there.

Right?

There's a flash in my brain.

Me in the stairwell, looking down. Rei was there, sitting, smoking.

GLOWROT

Diet soda on the floor next to them, half empty.

I was watching. Just watching. Why didn't I—

No, that didn't happen.

I wouldn't do that.

Another one: My hand on their doorknob.

Middle of the night. No reason.

But that doesn't make sense.

I didn't know where their room was until—

I shake my head, hard. False memories. Dreams. W would have told me.

Right?

Right?

Right?

Right?

Right?

Right?

"youDidWhatYouHadToDo."

I try to get up again, but this time, it's she who pushes me down. She looks at me like a sculpture would do. A queen.

Heart.

Heartless.

Shiny, imponent. Deadly.

"You can't leave yet because you have to wait for The Director to arrive." Her voice is firm. Too firm. As if she were making an extra effort not to break.

I feel a chill run through me from head to toe.

The Director?

Surely, it's not so exaggerated as to have to call a man we've only seen once.

"What the fuck does The Director have to do with the fact that you guys are trying to play at being cops with something that doesn't even concern you?" I ask, wanting to spit, but I refrain since my saliva will mix with blood, which won't help the situation.

No one responds.

They all stand there, looking at me and not looking at me.

Their eyes jump from one to the other and sometimes to the door.

35 Flammable Material

The silence is there, but it is not sepulchral because the atmosphere is full of sounds of discomfort, of fury, of feeling trapped, just like me.

Trapped with someone.

No.

Trapped with Something.

"theyFearYouMoreThanYouFearThem"

W whispers in my ear as he strokes my hair.

But I'm not afraid of them.

"notAsMuchAsTheyAreOfYou"

I take a deep breath, pushing away the dizziness so my voice can return to some capacity.

I really have to stop hyperventilating.

I know what happens when I do.

I turn to Nina and smile as gently as I can. If she knew, she would understand. She's always been on my side, after all.

"You've never met them, so you don't know. But they're like a blank canvas. A perfect balance of extremes," I try to reason with her. The words come out calming and soothing. "They're the one thing in my life that makes sense. You don't just walk away from that."

"Oh my God, Bo!" Nina lets out a gasp. "They're A PERSON, not an object!"

Starting to shake is not a decision I make; it's something my body has decided for me.

First, the head vibrations.

Slowly, from side to side.

I only realize it because of how blurry everything starts to get.

Breathe in. Breathe out. Breathe in. Breathe out.

Then the sensation moves down to my neck, my shoulders, my arms, until my hands start to vibrate too.

Breathe in. Breathe out. Breathe in. Breathe out. Breathe in. Breathe out. Breathe in. Breathe out. Breathe in. Breathe out. Breathe in. Breathe out.

I feel how, little by little, the finger bones begin to stiffen, and I lose mobility.

They end up being claws, claws that I'm too used to, even though they haven't appeared for a long time.

I guess it's one of those things you never forget.

GLOWROT

BreatheIn.BreatheOut.BreatheIn.BreatheOut.BreatheIn.BreatheOut.BreatheIn.
BreatheOut.BreatheIn.BreatheOut.BreatheIn.BreatheOut.BreatheIn.BreatheOut.
BreatheIn.BreatheOut.BreatheIn.BreatheOut.BreatheIn.BreatheOut.BreatheIn.
BreatheOut.BreatheIn.BreatheOut.BreatheIn.BreatheOut.BreatheIn.BreatheOut.
BreatheIn.BreatheOut.BreatheIn.BreatheOut.BreatheIn.BreatheOut.BreatheIn.
BreatheOut.BreatheIn.BreatheOut.BreatheIn.BreatheOut.BreatheIn.BreatheOut.
BreatheIn.BreatheOut.

It continues to descend until it reaches my feet.

My toes also tightening.

Claws.

breatheinbreatheout.breatheinbreatheout.breatheinbreatheout.breatheinbreatheout.
breatheinbreatheout.breatheinbreatheout.breatheinbreatheout.breatheinbreatheout.
breatheinbreatheout.breatheinbreatheout.breatheinbreatheout.breatheinbreatheout.
breatheinbreatheout.breatheinbreatheout.breatheinbreatheout.breatheinbreatheout.
breatheinbreatheout.breatheinbreatheout.breatheinbreatheout.breatheinbreatheout.

From there, I know perfectly well what comes next.

My eyes close to prepare.

This is the moment where I lose complete control of my body.

When pretending to be an ordinary person becomes wholly impossible, and I can do nothing but watch.

in*outinoutinoutinoutinoutinoutinoutinoutinoutinoutinoutinoutinoutinoutin*
outioutinoutinoutinoutinoutinoutinoutinoutinoutinoutinoutinoutinoutinoutin
outioutinoutinoutinoutinoutinoutinoutinoutinoutinoutinoutinoutinoutinoutin
outinoutinoutinoutinoutinoutinoutinoutinoutinoutinoutinoutinoutinoutinoutin
outinoutinotinoutinoutinoutinoutinoutinoutinoutinoutinoutinoutinoutinoutinout
inoutinoutinoutinoutinoutinoutinoutinoutinoutinoutinoutinoutinoutinoutinout
*inoutinoutin***out**

An involuntary scream escapes my lips.

One that I recognize perfectly.

Not a scream, a growl.

And I fall to the ground despite my invisible restraints.

Nova takes a step forward to try to help me, but my hand reaches out toward her ankle and scratches her with deformed fingers that are no longer fingers.

She screams and jumps out of my way.

I try to crawl towards her, but at that moment, two soft hands firmly grab my ankles and push me back.

35 Flammable Material

I know there's noise around me, commotion.

Screams probably, whines for sure, but I have lost the ability to translate them into something that makes sense inside my head.

All I can do is lie there with my body moving up and down, my back hitting the ground harder and harder, my head bouncing against it. I open and close my eyes without being able to define what is happening around me.

I can only growl, no, not growl.

Roar.

And

wait

until

this is

over,

not

knowing

if it

will

ever

be.

When I come to, the lights are off, and I'm completely alone in the breakroom.

Well, almost completely because W caresses my hair while my head rests in his lap.

There are more clocks on the walls, but they all point at different times. I can barely see them, with everything engulfed in shadows.

How much time has passed?

I hear distant echoes, overlapping whispers somewhere behind the door.

GLOWROT

I haven't regained control of my extremities, so I can only lie there and try to translate the sounds into words once more.

"Order, order!"

What's happening?

The walls flicker whenever the door opens, and two other security guards come inside.

I still can't distinguish their faces. Like cards on a deck, only different from one another by the number on their backs.

They grab me without saying anything, and this time I let go.

36: Trial in Session

The carpet is wet, damp.

Or at least it feels like it.

The sensation creeps up through my toes as if trying to get under my skin.

My toes?

Where are my shoes?

The two faceless guards are dragging me along. Their grip is protocol, uniform, utterly devoid of personality, of life, of existence. I try to look around, but there is no one else.

No one but us.

The rest?

Where are they?

Who are these people?

They drag me down an endless corridor, one that I don't remember having a direct connection to the break room. There are no doors, just the damp carpet.

It creeps up.

My fingers.

No, not fingers. Toes.

And the flickering fluorescent lights.

They shine.

BEEP. BEEP. BEEP.

They call out to me, but I don't understand their language.

They scream just like I am screaming right now, even though nothing can come out of my throat.

"Where are you taking me?!" I try to shout, but it comes out as nothing more than a whisper.

One of them simply moves their lips; somehow, the words that come out of them make no sense with how they move.

"Meeting," he says in that impossible way.

But the words come from the walls, from the lights.

BEEP. BEEP. BEEP. BEEP. BEEP. BEEP. BEEP. BEEP. BEEP.

I shudder at each beep, not because they are loud, but because they are eerily familiar as if they belong in the same place I do.

The guards stop walking, but my body keeps moving.

Forward, then

d

o

w

n

?

No, not down. I haven't fallen, but the hallway is gone.

The carpet is still damp under my feet.

No, not damp, soggy.

It's swollen like a sponge full of whatever my skin has been soaking up all this time.

I turn to look at the faceless guards, but they are no longer beside me.

I'm sitting now.

This chair.

It's too small for me.

Too small.

I feel chains around my wrists, but when I look at them, they're bare.

"they'rePlayingMindTricks," W says, and I nod.

He knows best, after all.

BEEP. BEEP. BEEP. BEEP. BEEP. BEEP. BEEP. BEEP. BEEP. BEEP. BEEP. BEEP. BEEP. BEEP. BEEP. BEEP. BEEP. BEEP.

The lights are much more powerful here.

They keep flashing, but this time in more organized intervals.

Like a metronome.

Like a warning.

I try to look directly at them, but they dissolve before I can focus my eyes.

I inhale and exhale and try to control my breathing this time. I can't afford another attack like the one I had a while ago.

How long ago was that?

36: Trial in Session

I had forgotten that time had stopped making sense long ago.

We're in one of the hotel's conference rooms, those that business people like Ute use, to do whatever someone like him is supposed to do.

Ute.

My palms itch as if I'm missing holding something. But what?

Something to help me.

Something that glows.

The place is different from what I imagined. The table is much bigger than I expected; for some reason, the walls feel farther away and the ceiling higher.

There's something.

In the middle

A cake?

Tarts?

They smell like something that's been burning for way too long. Right at the center of the table. A hand extends to grab one, and I follow it up the wrist, the arm, and the shoulder until I can reach the face.

Tall. Pale. Red hair that doesn't sit right on his scalp. It's too still, too bright, like a party-store wig glued down too tight. I've seen him before. Once. During orientation.

The Director.

Our boss.

His name.

What was his name?

I try to look at his face, but it fades from my mind's eye every time I blink. My gaze hits a wall there, like trying to stare into headlights.

My lips part. I want to say this is stupid, that it's not serious, that Alexia and the twins are just being dramatic; but the sounds that come out of me aren't words like choking on wet static.

"youDon'tOweExplanationsToAbsolutelyAnyone."

W purrs and strokes my hair to comfort me.

I don't owe them any explanations, exactly.

I did the right thing.

Rei wanted me to follow them, even if they regretted it later.

GLOWROT

"Order, order!"

The words come disembodied, from nowhere in particular. Alexia's mouth is closed, she's sitting next to The Director—

His name.

What was his name?

Sitting next to The Director with her legs crossed like scissors. She looks like royalty in a rental uniform.

Nina and Nova are sitting next to her now. They're wearing matching outfits that remind me how much they look like copies of each other.

But we aren't alone.

More people are here, faces I half-recognize from hallways, elevators, breakroom glances. They look unfinished, as if someone assembled them at the last minute using spare parts.

They all sit in high-backed chairs, scribbling furiously on clipboards. Faster than human hands should.

What are they writing?

"liesAboutYou."

But the meeting hasn't even started yet.

"doesn'tMatter.TheyKnowHowItEnds."

The sound of rustling paper interrupts my conversation with W, and I turn in the direction it came from so fast that I feel like I'm going to break my neck in two.

One of the guards with numbers on their backs is trying to smooth out a crumpled ball of paper.

His face is turned in my direction, but I'm already used to his features being blurred. The familiarity of the situation does not make it more pleasant.

It's terrifying.

36: Trial in Session

The girl of rot, she lost the plot,
She caused our guest so much disrupt.
She learned their name and stole their key,
She watched them sleep, refused to leave.

She stalked the halls, she crept in the walls,
She played with them like they were dolls.
She followed lies her shadow fed,
And kissed the ground where they had bled.

This girl of dread, she cut the thread,
She turned her love into something dead.
Couldn't let them go when they said no.
The girl of woe, by the name of Bo.

I would like to be able to protest, but the words numb me. They anesthetize me to the point of not being able to feel my muscles.

They echo, VIBRATING AGAINST MY TEETH.

One by one.

R_ot_

_gu_**E**_st_

_d_**I**_srupt_

_Λ_**I**_es_

_ki_**S**_sed_

G_irl_

_g_**O**

N_o_

_wo_**E**

Bo

Then, silence.

The wrong kind.

Silence that stretches like gum that has been stuck on your foot for way too long. That drills on your ear until you pass out.

GLOWROT

I heard the same kind of silence all the times the pink water kept me company.

My pulse is slowly disappearing.

Someone coughs.

Glass clings.

The tarts glow.

And then, a voice:

"We'll begin with testimony."

There's motion across the table. A flicker.

Nina stands up and closes her eyes.

Or maybe she was already standing.

"Bo has always been... weird," she says with a trembling voice, looking everywhere except at me. "That's why I didn't realize it right away when all this started."

I open my mouth and—

"No! Wait your turn!" Alexia's voice slices the room until it reaches me. She points her index finger like a blade. For a moment, it really feels like she cut me in half.

"letThemLie,

YouAndIKnowTheTruth."

W growls behind my ribs.

"I thought she was going through something. My sister went through something similar... and she got help. She got better!" Nina pauses before continuing, her voice breaking as if she is about to cry. "I let her use me. She made me cover her shifts so she could... stalk people. Harass them." Her hands shake. "And I let her. I'm sorry. I didn't know."

"Fucking bitch!" I can't help but spit. "You were supposed to be on my side! You were supposed to understand me!"

She's all tears now, they accumulate around her eyes and slowly begin to suffocate her. Stuck. Her body starts to tremble like she's short-circuiting.

"Order, order!" says the disembodied voice again.

Two guards take Nina away and sit her in a corner. She's gasping for air, but Nova stands up before I can concentrate too much on her.

"it'sBetterThatWay,

SheDeservesIt."

She does.

36: Trial in Session

"I know what obsession looks like," she says, her usual relaxed demeanor fully gone. She starts scratching the cherry tattoo on her collarbone. "I know what it feels like. To want someone so much, you think it must mean something. Fate. That you were meant to be in their life, even when they don't want you there."

No.

No.

No.

Coño de la madre.

El cuerpo me emp—

My body starts to tremble again. It's vibrating, but I have to stop.

I can't.

Not now.

"butThatDamnedWoman

IsTryingToMakeYou

LookBad."

I hate her.

She has no right to say anything like that. She's jealous because she's weak, because NIU didn't want her.

Because I'm sure she was absorbed by it and spat out.

Because her own White Rabbit abandoned her.

> *Didn't mine abandon me too?*

No.

> *No.*

> *NO!*

I can't think about that, not now.

"But it was never about love. It was about control. About what I thought I was owed." Her firsts are clenched so hard her knuckles are completely white now. "And what she did," Nova nods toward me without looking directly at me, "is beyond that. It's calculated. It's cruel."

No one breathes. The scribbling audience pauses.

> *The jurors.*

"I didn't see everything. None of us did. But there's no turning back now," she says, clearing her throat. "She's just playing the victim because she doesn't understand no means no."

GLOWROT

"You think you know anything about me?!" I scream too loudly for the size of the room. "You have no idea what it was like! I didn't hurt anyone. I SAVED THEM. THEY ARE UNTOUCHED AND PERFECT. THEY WERE BEAUTIFUL BECAUSE THEY DIDN'T FIT ANYWHERE ELSE BUT WITH ME!"

"Bo!" Nova's voice cracks in the middle of her cry. "You're talking about a person. Not a dream. Not a metaphor. A person! They didn't exist for you to figure out."

"Order! Order!" The voice barks from nowhere. From everywhere.

Desperate.

"I just needed them to stop running." I cry, ignoring the voice and the pain in my ears. "They wouldn't stay still! I would've left them alone if they had just stayed still."

"Unimportant." This time, it's The Director who speaks and the room groans in pain.

"Of course it's important!" I try to move, but the invisible shackles dig into my wrists like needles before surgery.

"Very unimportant," he insists, and I have to hold my ears before they start bleeding.

Important.

     Unimportant.

          Important.

               Unimportant.

                    Important.

               Unimportant.

          Important.

     Unimportant.

  Important.

  Unimportant.

    Important.

      Unimportant.

The scribbling audience tears gashes through the paper until it starts screaming.

It screams.

And screams.

And screams.

"That's enough!"

Alexia's voice bounces off the walls until it reaches my face and breaks my nose.

At least my ears have stopped bleeding by now.

36: Trial in Session

The whole world stops.

The air is trapped in my lungs, it can't escape. I can't breathe in.

Little by little, my vision blurs, and the whole room tilts.

No, not the room.

Me.

"Bo," I hear her say my name, with the same determination as the first time I confronted her when she broke up with me. "You're fired."

I try to laugh, but it's useless.

The absurdity of it all is so great that I can do nothing but let myself fall.

And fall.

And fall.

And fall.

But the world doesn't stop even if my brain has. There are still sounds around me; I still hear words when everything should have gone quiet.

Rules are being read out loud like I'm not even here anymore.

"You are no longer permitted in any hotel guest areas," she continues. "That includes the pool, the lounge, and the gym. You may only come and go from your apartment until you lose it." She pauses, almost as if she is savoring the words. "Which you will, if you can't pay rent."

The carpet has been absorbing Nina's tears all this time, and now it doesn't even feel like a sponge anymore.

It's like a creature feeding off the blood on my toenails.

Like a jellyfish preparing to sting me.

To destroy me.

I wish it would.

Anything would be better than having to face such injustice.

With my cheek resting on the table, I feel like hands are coming out of the wood and starting to sink me at the same time as the walls begin to melt.

It's getting harder and harder to breathe and it's almost impossible to open my eyes, but I try anyway.

I need to see him.

The only one who ever told me the truth.

The only one who stayed.

The only one I should have obeyed.

But when I open them, the lights are off. Everyone has left, and the silence is deathly.

GLOWROT

Cloying.

Rotting.

But I'm not alone.
Someone is looking at me from across the table.

She looks like me.

Her teeth blink at me, her eyes glisten.

Like someone I once was.

Like me, before I became a thing, melting against the wood.
And she is smiling.
And smiling.
And smiling.
And   smiling.
A n d   s m i l i n g .
A   n   d   s   m   i   l   i   n   g   .

37

Do Not Disturb

Void.
Empty space.
Bare walls.
Cold.

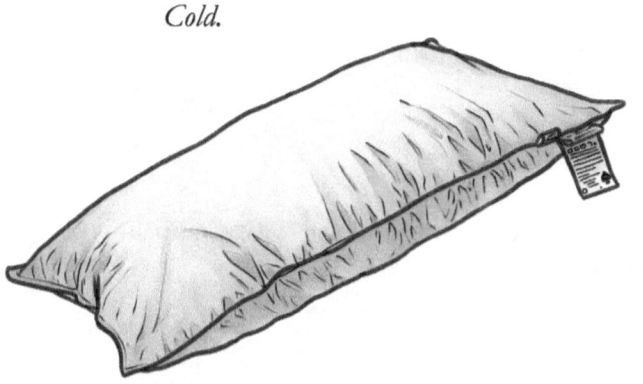

I'm on the floor again, on a carpet of nails that drains me every time I move.

I'm somewhere, I guess, although I can't define where exactly.

Nor how I got here.

My skin—
is vibrating.

It has become A SWARM OF WASPS LIVING INSIDE MY PORES. and little by little, they are starting to sting me from the inside out.

There is no air around me; it is just an invisible treacle with hooves that crush me the instant my lungs decide to expand.

I try to think, to remember how I got here.

Nothing.

Absolutely nothing.

What was the last thing I saw before I closed my eyes?

That smile. That horrible smile.

That was expanding.

And expanding.

A n d   e x p a n d i n g .

A n d   e x p a n d i n g .

A n d   e x p a n d i n g .

GLOWROT

And then?

But—

there's no trace of her.

Or of anyone else, not even the one ~~person~~ I want to see right now.
W?

W.

I need you.

Please don't leave me, not now.

I messed up, I know.

But please I—

I can't.

I can't go on.

Not alone.

The treacle drowns the wasps, and little by little my lungs begin to disintegrate.

M	b	i	u	d
y	r	s	p	o
	a		s	w
	i		i	n
	n		d	
			e	

I'm on the floor again, but this time it's slippery and I can't stand up.
I'm somewhere, I guess, although I can't define where exactly.

I'm wet?

But I don't remember taking a bath

or a shower.

I can't open my eyes, but my eyelids move despite this. The pressure clouds my vision for a few seconds, until finally my sight adjusts to it.
To the light.

Or the lack of it.

"youShouldRelaxALittle,Bo."
W. murmurs next to me.

So close—

almost inside.

37 Do Not Disturb

My body curls up on the floor, now instead of slipping it's like the liquid is welcoming me. My skin absorbs it. I'm no longer wasps.

"**thereYouGo,**" he coos. I can feel his breath against my collarbone. "**youMustBeSoTired.**"

I'm so tired.

The more my eyes adjust, the more I realize where I am. The door, the refrigerator, and the packages on the floor look familiar.

The wall, still with the puzzle pieces.

With the broken mirrors.

I stop on them for a few seconds; I find W's reflection before mine.

Solid.

I open my mouth and see through the glass that he raises one of his now pale hands. He brings it to my lips to shut me up. His fingertips, black claws staining his skin to where his knuckles end, almost brush against me.

So real.

"**AlwaysTryingToHoldYourselfTogether.
AlwaysFighting.EvenNow.**"

His tone is hypnotic, and I'm getting dizzy.

"**iCanHelpYou,IfYouWant.**"

Funny, I thought the lights were on.

I can see his silhouette silhouetted against the beam of light coming in between the blinds in the room; they sneak in only to stop just before they reach him.

"**wouldYouLikeMeToHelpYouRelax,Bo?**"

He places his hand over my eyes, and they close again.

When did he start being so gentle again?

"**youJustNeededToStopRunning,Bo.
YouJustNeededToStayStill.**"

I stop breathing, and he patiently takes my chest and helps me fill my lungs.

At last, oxygen.

Oxygen.

Plenty of it.

It fills my—
The oxygen—

GLOWROT

So much.

Too much.

He then slides the tip of one of his claws from my cheek to my chin, traces a thin line down my neck, and lands on my collarbones. I shiver, but instead of tensing, my muscles relax.

               r   *e*   *l*   *a*   *x*

He's right, I **shouldRelaxALittle.**

He bathes my face with his hot breath and my heart begins to race.
He's so close, too close.
His eyes burn into mine.

> **Relaxing is a wonderful idea,**
> **how had I not thought of it before?**

Release tension.

From the tips of my toes, up my ankles.

Slowly down to my knees and dancing from my thighs to my abdomen. Slowly I let go of each of my senses and give up the control I don't need right now. Until I reach my head.

I exhale.

It's a warmth that makes the hairs on the back of my neck stand on end and gradually makes my wrists feel heavier, so I can't move them.

> *My fingers twitch independently of each other out of surprise.*
> *But it doesn't matter because I don't have to.*

So I let them fall just like my thighs, just like my legs, just like my chest, just like my head.

Because I don't have to.

And I can get away from myself for a while.

"letYourselfGo,Bo.

I'mHere."

My body collapses and—

"iGotYou.

YouDon'tHaveToFightBackAnymore."

My body col—

"letMeSaveYou.Bo."

My—

"letMeLoveYou.Bo."

37 Do Not Disturb

With unprecedented gentleness, the body collapses on the floor, and W takes it in his arms like a puppet.

He deposits it face down on the bed and covers it with the blanket. Protected, at ease. Finally. It lets out a murmur of content, and the face smiles.

And smiles.

A n d   s m i l e s .

I want to close my eyes but can't do that anymore without a body.

The body.

The body.

The body.

It lies there, reacting to the pressure on the mattress next to it, to the claws sliding over its skin. It reacts like it's familiar, like it's used to it.

Like it knows what to do.

The throat closes and gasps when the gashes open up again on its back. The eyes are open but lost somewhere far away.

The brain is focused on the pain.

The pain.

The pain.

The pain.

The weight on the bed shifts from one side to the other, and the body's side is being caressed now. Gently, softly. Carefully.

WithLove.

The lips open slightly, panting. They do so more the second the weight is now in the back, and the skin crawls and writhes when the gashes are grazed again.

But it's okay, he fogs them with his hot breath.

The brain is pleased, the senses sharpen.

The skin stops screaming.

It stretches and tenses, a sound comes out of the lips.

What sound?

Unimportant.

He notices. He always does.

The ankles separate in a tremor, being pulled further and further away. The skin is slippery now, like the floor, like the nails, like the carpet.

But it's okay because it's being held by the wrists.

Tight.

Strong.

GLOWROT

Claws move along, they dig, looking for treasure the body has been hiding for way too long. Slowly, taking their time. They have all the time they would want now.

Another comes out of the lips.

What sound?

Unimportant.

He notices. He always does.

The pressure passes to be around the neck now, and the lip gets bitten in response to it. New gashes. Dripping.

The fingers are long and wrap around perfectly, so they keep squishing it.

Finally.

The mouth opens in a gasp, but the claws help it be closed now, reminding it now it's not the time to exist.

Not now.

But it tries again, so one of the fingers has to fill the void. It pushes until it reaches a wall, and then does it a bit more.

And more.

And more.

And more.

The body vibrates, pants, gasps. The room buzzes. The wasps come back.

He's pressed against the back.

The wrists are caged.

His breath corrodes the skin.

His tongue scratches the jaw.

The claws squeeze. Squeeze.

Until the bones stop resisting.

Until the breath caves in.

The air escapes.

Spasms.

Rustle. Fabric.

Something brushing against the wasps.

They sting.

37 Do Not Disturb

Velvet.

Weightless.

A sound, so loud the ears close up and it becomes mute. It swallows itself.

Liquid, dripping from the corner of a smile. From inside the eyelids.

Air, fresh air.

The claws move to the ribs, and they start dripping too. Blooming.

They meld together into nothingness. Surrender at his feet. At his smile.

The tension that never existed disappears, and the body finds peace.

It shakes.

He hums lullabies through the body's teeth. They blink.

Glisten.

GloW.

The rays of light from the window confess that the night ended long ago. The intense reflection against the white walls is suffocating.

What happened last night?

Crawling into the bed is not an option, the fingernails are now clinging to the indentations in the wall.

The blood is still there,

but it's not dry anymore.

A familiar chill runs down the spine, sharper than a knife against bone.

A breath.

Right now.

Right here.

The body shudders and—

"let'sKeepGoing,JustLikeBefore."

My body shudders, and the air thickens, heavy and damp, like something decomposing and pressing against my skin.

The temperature starts rising.

Suffocating.

Each inhale is sucked out of my chest.

I exhale and collapse backward, my head bounces off the bathroom tile.

The pain is dull, an echo of something I can't quite place.

I can't close my eyes because bugs crawl under my eyelids and pry them open. I bat them away with one hand.

The silence is so abysmal that I feel like it's stepping on me with steel boots.

I hate it here.

But I shouldn't worry.

thingsAreOkayNow.

The clothing feels like someone else's skin, clammy and unfamiliar. It gets tangled with my fake nails, and I end up ripping off a couple without realizing it.

I yawn.

At least I don't have to worry about waking up early to get to work. About the anxiety invading my senses. About my own desire to be irresponsible.

I don't have to worry about not being able to make rent and living on the streets.

I'm taken care of now.

And now the obligatory ritual begins.

Toothbrush, toothpaste, look anywhere but the mirror.

Water, almost choking on the toothbrush and closing my eyes.

I have all the time in the world now.

Hot water is used to rinse; it scratches my gums. No longer freezing.

Thank you.

The bruises run around on my skin, the jump from my arms to my chest, to my legs. I feel them in my back, in my throat.

Maybe I can scrub them away.

But I have to brush first.

I grab the toothbrush and squeeze some toothpaste on it; my eyes dance between the wall and the sink.

My hands feel raw the more I scrub.

Scrub.

Scrub.

My skin dissolves into the mirror.

But I can't look at it.

I can't.

No.

No.

No.

Don't.

No.		No.		No. No. No. No.	
No. No.		No.	No.		No.
No. No.		No.	No.		No.
No. No.		No.	No.		No.
No. No.		No.	No.		No.
No. No.		No.	No.		No.
No. No. No.		No.			No.
No. No. No.					No.
No. No. No.		No.	No.		No.

The word bounces off the walls of my mind; it gets louder with every bounce.

It passes straight through me. I smile at it, in that customer service smile that no one believes in anymore.

**"don'tWorryYourBrain
WithSuchAwfulThoughts."**

I should brush my teeth before I forget.

A blink, another one.
Time slips between my fingers.
But now it's a good thing.

Right?

Right?

I open the apartment door.
White.

The unbearable desire to fill the walls with red CLAWS ITSELF OUT FROM UNDER MY NAILS.

The light from LED lamps bounces all over the polished surfaces, freezing my skin. They flicker colors.

Blue.
Purple.
What else?

*pinkpinkpinkpinkpinkpinkpinkpinkpinkpinkpinkpinkpinkpinkpinkpink-
pinkpinkpinkpinkpinkpinkpinkpinkpinkpinkpinkpinkpinkpinkpinkpink-
pinkpinkpinkpinkpinkpinkpinkpinkpinkpinkpinkpinkpinkpinkpinkpink-
pinkpinkpinkpinkpinkpinkpinkpinkpinkpinkpinkpinkpinkpinkpinkpink-
pinkpinkpinkpinkpinkpinkpinkpinkpinkpinkpinkpinkpinkpinkpinkpink-*

38: SecurityAlerT

pinkpinkpinkpinkpinkpinkpinkpinkpinkpinkpinkpinkpinkpinkpinkpink-
pinkpinkpinkpinkpinkpinkpinkpinkpinkpinkpinkpinkpinkpinkpinkpink-
pinkpinkpinkpinkpinkpinkpinkpinkpinkpinkpinkpinkpinkpinkpinkpink-
pinkpinkpinkpinkpinkpinkpinkpinkpinkpinkpinkpinkpinkpinkpinkpink-
pinkpinkpinkpinkpinkpinkpinkpinkpinkpinkpinkpinkpinkpinkpinkpink-
pinkpinkpinkpinkpinkpinkpinkpinkpinkpinkpinkpinkpinkpinkpinkpink-
pinkpinkpinkpinkpinkpinkpinkpinkpinkpinkpinkpinkpinkpinkpinkpink-
pinkpinkpinkpinkpinkpinkpinkpinkpinkpinkpinkpinkpinkpinkpinkpink-
pinkpinkpinkpinkpinkpinkpinkpinkpinkpinkpinkpinkpinkpinkpinkpink-
pinkpinkpinkpinkpinkpinkpinkpinkpinkpinkpinkpinkpinkpink

The elevator is here.

The doors open, and my heart slows down.

It pauses.

Stops.

GLOWROT

The silence presses in.

Until the doors open up again, and I follow the lead my feet are tracing.

Broken glass on the floor, someone must have dropped some room service dishes.

I know it hurts, but I step on them anyway.

The urge to go to the emergency stairs. It pulls me, inviting.

Like sin.

They're warmer, they feel better than the elevator. And right now I just want to walk, and walk, and keep walking.

ButThat'sOverNow.

I drag my bare feet across the floor, and the little cuts on the soles make me s m i l e .

A phone is ringing in the background.

Faint but—

It gets louder.

Louder.

LOUDER.

Where to?

Someone is calling me.

It's important, it's for me.

I keep running.

And running.

And running.

And running.

And running.

And running.

And running.

And running.

And running.

It rings, it rings.

And I run.

Slip. Fall. Run again.

Run. Run. Run. Run. Run. Run. Run. Run. Run. Run.

Blood on my nose.

On my lungs.

A retch.

That smell.

It's still ringing.

38: SecurityAlerT

The translucent walls show me the way behind desks and chairs.
Behind crumpled papers.

The girl of rot, she—

"stopThatRightNow!"

I shouldn't worry my brain with such awful thoughts.

Awful,AwfulThoughts.

Radios blaring, dancing, screaming.

Photographs blink at me, and their eyelids slowly rot and fall to the floor.

Crawling away.

I know exactly where I am.

I know exactly where this door leads to.

I turn the doorknob and open it slowly, in a welcoming creak.

Until the office swallows me whole.

He's standing there—

Obviamente

He stares at me and drums his fingernails on one of the screens surrounding him. They're engulfed in pink smoke and flicker too many times, too fast.

Like his eyelids.

The screens go back and forth between pink static and fragmented traces of that girl.

The smiling one.

The one that looks like me.

From before.

Then he exhales slowly, drawn out. His shoulders start twitching.

Like he's been waiting for me to catch up.

Like I've already done this before.

Like his patience is melting.

"You took your time," he says without moving his lips.

His sleeves are rolled up, and his shirt is unbuttoned; he is no longer trying to maintain the façade of false eyes from before.

The pupils on his neck, chest, arms, and fingers fly over me and come to rest at a point behind me.

"So, this is how she ended. Interesting."

GLOWROT

Oberon taps one of the screens with his fingernail, and it beeps. His real gaze is still fixed on nothing; the only eyes that rest on mine are the fictitious ones in his face, with nothing behind them.

He's talking about the body.

The corpse.

About the girl.

About me.

I tilt my head to one side.

"She seemed promising at first, addicted to craving," he continues with a sigh. "You got to her before the threshold. That's... ambitious."

"She wasn't herself," another voice chimes in behind me, clearer than usual. It comes from the exact point where all the eyes are staring. **"She was missing pieces, but she's complete now, you see."**

"I can't see," replies Oberon with a chuckle, bringing one of his hands to his face.

Carefully, he pushes the tip of one of his fingers between his upper eyelid and the false eye and pulls it out like a cherry. He smiles, and pink smoke escapes from his teeth, slowly fogging our surroundings.

He takes the eye between his fingers and rubs it against one of the black envelopes on his desk; it squeaks with every touch, and I try to cover my ears, but my wrists don't respond.

None of my limbs do.

When he has finished cleaning it, he puts the eye back with a glassy sound, and his smile broadens.

"When did you notice?" He proceeds to check some of the notes lying on his desk.

I try to speak, but the sound from my mouth is not my voice.

Not entirely.

"It was the emptiness. Something had to leave so it could be filled up again," W's response tickles when it comes out of my lips.

"Filled up?" Oberon responds, the words float in the air and disappear into more smoke. "That's not what the data shows."

He flicks the screen again, and three images glitch back and forth.

BEEP. BEEP. BEEP.

38: SecurityAlerT

A lighter.

Flick me.

A casino chip.

Use me.

A compact mirror.

Look at me.

"These were meant to ground you, Bo." This is the first time his countless eyes look at me. "But you used them to dig instead."

I try to speak again, but nothing comes out.

The sounds curl up in my throat like bile and start leaking through my eyes.

They were keys.

They showed them the way.

They showed me the way.

The images start to distort. The mirror cracks, the chip spins, the lighter engulfs itself in flames.

The screens flicker one more time before they shut down.

"It broke her enough," W whispers with a hiss. **"So I could rearrange the pieces."**

The blood inside me starts to bubble.

I want to run, scream, kick.

I can't close my eyes or lower my head.

I can't pull my hair or ask them to stop.

To stop talking about me as if I weren't here.

I can't ask W what he means or why he feels more human,

and I feel more like a shadow.

I can't breathe, I can't exist.

I can't. I

can't. I can't. I can't. I can't. I can't. I can't. I can't. I can't. I can't. I
can't. I can't. I can't. I can't. I can't. I can't. I can't. I can't. I can't. I

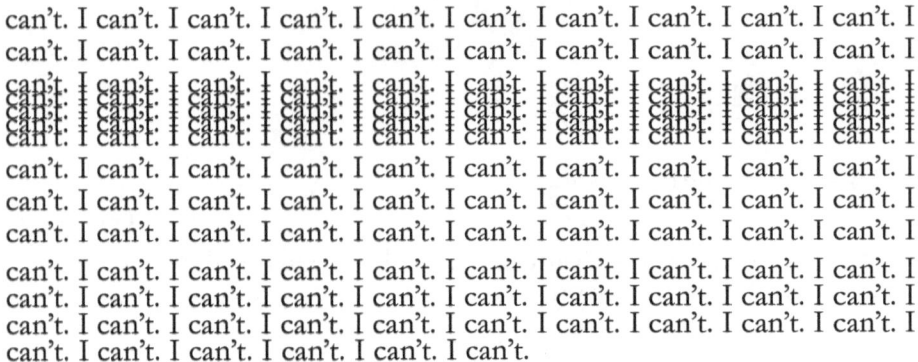

can't. I can't. I can't. I can't. I can't. I can't. I can't. I can't. I can't. I
can't. I can't. I can't. I can't. I can't. I can't. I can't. I can't. I can't. I
can't. I can't. I can't. I can't. I can't. I can't. I can't. I can't. I can't. I

can't. I can't. I can't. I can't. I can't. I can't. I can't. I can't. I can't. I
can't. I can't. I can't. I can't. I can't. I can't. I can't. I can't. I can't. I
can't. I can't. I can't. I can't. I can't. I can't. I can't. I can't. I can't. I
can't. I can't. I can't. I can't. I can't. I can't.

I collapse within myself, unable to even blink.

Oberon stares.

Observes.

Catalogs.

Like I'm a specimen of some sort.

Then he hums, not quite in agreement with what W just revealed, More like...

D I S I N T E R E S T ?!

He was the one watching.

The one leaving me clues.

The one that put the pieces within my reach.

The one that led Ute.

The one that tricked Rei.

He was the one.

The one interested.

He can't **doThisToMe!**

**HeCan't.HeCan't.HeCan't.HeCan't.HeCan't.HeCan't.
HeCan't.HeCan't.HeCan't.HeCan't.HeCan't.HeCan't.HeCan't.
HeCan't.HeCan't.HeCan't.HeCan't.HeCan't.HeCan't.HeCan't.
HeCan't.HeCan't.HeCan't.HeCan't.HeCan't.HeCan't.HeCan't.
HeCan't.HeCan't.HeCan't.HeCan't.HeCan't.HeCan't.HeCan't.
HeCan't.HeCan't.HeCan't.HeCan't.HeCan't.HeCan't.HeCan't.
HeCan't.HeCan't.HeCan't.HeCan't.HeCan't.HeCan't.HeCan't.
HeCan't.HeCan't.HeCan't.HeCan't.HeCan't.HeCan't.HeCan't.
HeCan't.HeCan't.HeCan't.HeCan't.HeCan't.HeCan't.HeCan't.
HeCan't.HeCan't.HeCan't.HeCan't.HeCan't.HeCan't.HeCan't.
HeCan't.HeCan't.HeCan't.HeCan't.HeCan't.HeCan't.HeCan't.
HeCan't.HeCan't.HeCan't.HeCan't.HeCan't.HeCan't.HeCan't.**

38: SecurityAlerT

HeCan't.HeCan't.HeCan't.HeCan't.HeCan't.HeCan't.HeCan't.
HeCan't.HeCan't.HeCan't.HeCan't.HeCan't.HeCan't.HeCan't.
HeCan't.HeCan't.HeCan't.HeCan't.HeCan't.HeCan't.HeCan't.
HeCan't.HeCan't.HeCan't.HeCan't.HeCan't.HeCan't.HeCan't.
HeCan't.HeCan't.HeCan't.HeCan't.HeCan't.HeCan't.HeCan't.
HeCan't.HeCan't.HeCan't.HeCan't.

"You'll get used to it in time," says Oberon before I'm engulfed in a cloud of smoke.

39
ClosedUntilFurtherNotice

Lights.

                                                                    The lights.

They flutter around me.

                              Up,

                              down.

I try to savor them, but it's impossible; THE INSIDE OF MY MOUTH IS BLEEDING TOO MUCH.

The vibration of the music moves the floor like an earthquake, soft but consistent. The whole world is wrapped in neon.

I slide through it and chase down every vestige of light I can find.

                                        Because they are there,
                              but they no longer point towards me.

My knees get stuck in the sticky substances that no longer belong to me.

They wiggle their way in between my pores and burrow where something existed before. Like bugs.

                                                    What kind?

Carve themselves into muscle and pull on the nerve endings they can find. The bugs bite on them but not even they can bear to swallow what's left.

The floor is velvet.

Or skin.

It is impossible to define.

Ideas try to settle in my head, but they go to someone else's.

And I continue to drag myself along while the girls offering syringes tear themselves away from the wallpaper and pass me by.

The points of their heels leave holes in my thorax, but my scream doesn't make its way through the music.

Did it even leave my throat?

They go back and forth, and I'm left on the floor, a thing writhing in a pool of glass.

Because it's no longer my turn.

The nails on the floor pull at my skin until they break it, but I keep crawling.

I go on.

And on.

And on.

Until I reach the corridor with the doors.

The walls are bare again, white.

But not antiseptic.

Everything is the same.

But different.

At least no hands are reaching out to try to grab me. I don't see anyone with my name tattooed on their skin, gleaming.

But I wish they were.

I would give anything.

Anything.

To be seen.

To exist.

At least I no longer feel hungry or sleepy.

I can crawl for an eternity until I reach any part of this place.

Este lugar interminable.

No more eyes are watching me; the caterpillars keep going, and the cameras settle on someone else.

GLOWROT

Someone different,

someone special.

I thought I was special.

The neon pink is now too soft, like the inside of a beast's stomach halfway through rotting.

The nauseating smell floods my senses, but I throw myself towards it with my mouth open, trying to absorb as much as possible before it disappears completely.

Because it's better than nothing.

Better than emptiness.

Better than the echo of something that is no more.

Better than the void.

Even if the music continues to envelop me in the same way, it no longer tickles my gums or tries to whisper secrets in my ear. The air now smells of piña colada, and I end up expelling the little skin that was covering the inside of my stomach.

It dissolves in the ground like acid.

I go on.

And on.

And on.

And on.

I try my luck with the mirrors.

I curl up on the rotating tubes.

I dig my nails into the dying forms I find.

Nothing.

I go on.

And on.

And on.

And on.

And on.

And on.

I look around in a desperate attempt to find any familiar face.

Anybody.

Nick.

Rei.

W.

39 ClosedUntilFurtherNotice

Maybe one of those voices—

The silhouette over there—

Somebody—

Something—

No.

Of course not.

The moment passed, and the vessel broke.

Now there are many more shiny ones, full of life, of craving.

Sometimes I see their faces, but they distort as soon as I get close. They avoid me.

No.

Worse.

They ignore me.

They know I'm here, but they don't care. **There's nothing they can use me for.**

I go on.

And on.

And on.

And on.

And on.

And on.

And on.

And on.

And on.

And on.

GLOWROT

At some point, I pass by a mirror that isn't broken, and my reflection avoids me.

It looks away when it thinks I'm not looking.

A crowd passes by me and continues on its way.

I try to talk to them but my voice stopped being real long ago.

It stopped being mine.

The music keeps playing, it never ends. It never becomes day.

There are no windows.

There are no doors.

There is no entrance.

There is no exit.

Sometimes I think I find Rei, but the rabbit looks different, and the moles are out of place.

Rei.

My angel.

My sweet Rei.

They only had to stay still.

"If only Rei had stopped running," I think, but it's useless.

I stopped running.

And here I am.

And then I sink to the floor.

It starts peeling open under my legs, like hands that finally want to grab me. **Eyes that finally see me.**

Like a stage.

Or a bed.

Or a coffin.

The nails rust against my ankles, and I let myself be dragged.

Finally, somebody.

Something.

The hands reach out, yes, but not in want.

They grab without care, feeling their way without paying close attention.

I don't fight them.

I can't.

39 ClosedUntilFurtherNotice

Al menos—

> *At least they're doing something.*

> *At least they know I'm here.*

A voice says something that thunders between my temples.

"It used to be beautiful."

> *It.*

Someone—

Something laughs.

"What was it?"

"Does it even matter?"

The lights make the shapes melt into each other until they all become one. Fingers press my jaw and mold it like it's clay.

One makes its way between my lips and stretches one side of my mouth.

It stretches, and stretches, and stretches.

And stretches. And stretches.

GLOWROT

Another does the same.
The taste, somewhere between metallic and salty, numbs me.
They shape my smile. They twist my arm in an elegant gesture.

Ridiculous.

Tragic.

The flash and flicker of something that will store this forever, even if time has abandoned this place since its inception.
A melody, a lullaby.

The girl of rot, she's finally caught,
Who she was, we all forgot.
She played a game and couldn't see,
She was never going to be free.

She danced, she screamed, she begged for more,
But she's only worth being ignored.
She tried to keep a moth in a jar,
She tried to take it way too far.

This girl of show, she lost the glow,
Tricked by a beast to lose her soul.
Couldn't stop being vain, couldn't stop the pain,
The girl of shame, who lost her name.

Another round of laughter echoes in my ears.
Another click.
Another smile stretched thin.
They don't ask what I want.
They don't care what I feel.
They just want me still.

So I stay.

39 ClosedUntilFurtherNotice

Author's Note

At first, I thought I was writing Glowrot just because I missed writing dark things. But the deeper I went, the more I realized I was stirring something inside me, a sort of pain I didn't even know was still there until I started poking at it.

When I say this story is based on myself, my life, my traumas, I mean it. Bo is who I could have become in another life. If I hadn't been so lucky. If I hadn't made the terrifying choice to step off a path that wasn't meant for me.

For a long time, Glowrot was a cautionary tale, one I wish I'd heard back then, until I realized I was still carrying guilt for things that were never really mine to hold.

So maybe this is my way of saying: things are not black and white. **People are messy, multidimensional, contradictory. And being hurt doesn't mean we get to hurt others. It never will.**

I don't want to tell you what to take from this. I wrote the story. The rest is yours: to interpret, to rage against, to feel.

Cry if you need to. Laugh. Rip the book. Spit on it. Throw it across the room. It's all valid. The simple fact that it made you feel anything at all is one of the greatest honors of my life.

Thank you for letting me show you the ugly parts of myself.

Thank you for staying.

Acknowledgements

And thank you especially:

Nai (*@naiiphilpotts*), thank you for always being there. For being the brilliant, creative, extraordinary author who has inspired me more times than I can count. Thank you for being my best friend, my sister, my soulmate.

Arkady (*@bibliOdditiesfragrance*), thank you for believing in Glowrot even before we became friends. For helping me craft a respectful, thoughtful depiction of Rei in all their complexity. For creating the scent that accompanies this story, so we can all glow, and rot, just a little. Thank you for being the best mentor and sensitivity reader I could have ever hoped for.

Sabrina (*@thescaredceo*), thank you for making me feel safe with writing again. For building a space and a community that helped me heal, that reminded me my stories are valid after all. Your work, your care, and your presence made this book possible in ways you might not even realize.

The entire team at **StoryForge** (*@_storyforge*), thank you for creating a home for authors like me. Thank you for building and maintaining a safe, magical space where we're allowed to be our full selves, even in a world that keeps getting harder to survive in. I'm endlessly grateful to work alongside you.

To my **Street Team** and **ARC readers**, thank you for helping me share this book with the world. For believing in Glowrot even before you held it in your hands. That kind of faith is rare. You deserve everything good.

To all the **original readers of Nexo**, the first version of this story in Spanish. Gracias por confiar en mí, en Bo, en W, y en este mundo tan extraño. Gracias por sus llantos, sus risas, sus comentarios. Gracias por el fanart, por meterse tanto en la historia, y por haberse quedado cuando tantos otros se fueron.

And last—but never least—thank you, **CJ**. For loving me. For helping me heal all the parts of Bo I still carry inside me. For showing me there's a safe place in the world, and it's next to you. Thank you for reminding me that NIU isn't all there is. That I can want more, and be more. That I don't have to stay still.

Reading guide

If the story is still lingering in your brain, I can't blame you. Words have a very particular way to slither into our ears, like <u>caterpillars</u>. So I made this for you to reflect, either by yourself or with a book club. Don't worry, you don't have to answer them all. Maybe rip this page and throw darts at it? Maybe start your own conspiracy wall. The choice is yours and I'm here to support you on it.

1. Bo constantly shifts her identity depending on who she's with How do you think this impacts her ability to understand what she actually wants? Have you ever found yourself trying to become what someone else wanted you to be?

2. What does Glowrot say about the difference between wanting someone and wanting what they represent? Where do you think Bo crossed that line, and did she ever come back from it?

3. NIU reflects Bo's mental state and deepest cravings. What does NIU mean to you?

4. What is W to you? A voice in Bo's head, a separate being, something else entirely? How does W's presence evolve throughout the story, and what does that say about Bo's relationship to herself?

5. Bo believes she deserves access to Rei, even when Rei explicitly says otherwise. How does this entitlement show up in her behavior, and what real-world parallels do you see? Can someone believe they love another person and still harm them?

6. Bo carries guilt for things that aren't her fault, but also refuses to take accountability for things that are. How does the book explore the difference between guilt and responsibility? Did you find Bo sympathetic, horrifying, relatable… or all three?

7. What's the importance of Glowrot being a retelling? Do you think the story would have been able to exist without Alice in Wonderland elements and references? How many of those did you catch?

8. Wonderland is strange, dreamlike, and constantly shifting, much like NIU. How do the rules (or lack of them) in NIU mirror the chaos of Wonderland?

9. Do you think someone can ever truly "leave" NIU? Is Wonderland something external, or a state of mind?

10. What emotions did Glowrot leave you with?
    Did you relate to anything that made you uncomfortable?

11. If you could say one thing to Bo after finishing the book, what would it be?

About the author

Beatrice Lebrun writes the kind of stories that make people cry, scream, or whisper "I shouldn't relate to this." She's an author and illustrator obsessed with emotional horror, queer longing, and the quiet devastation of being alive.

Born in Venezuela and now based in the U.S., Beatrice grew up living in another world entirely. Dealing with intense maladaptive daydreaming since a very young age, she spent her childhood caught between realities: one mundane and expected, the other wild, dangerous, and hers. When the world demanded she stay grounded, she turned to writing, just to keep the other realities alive.

Glowrot is her debut novel in English. It's deeply personal to her, a love letter to the versions of herself she never got to be, and a cautionary tale she once needed to hear. Her protagonists are raw, flawed, and cathartic reflections of her own wounds. If someone wants to call that a self-insert, she's not offended. It just means they've never needed to write themselves back together.

When she's not writing about haunted girls and broken realities, she's helping others do the same as the Creative Director of StoryForge, where she builds safe spaces for writers and stories that don't fit the mold.

You'll usually find her drawing, dancing, dreaming, or whispering to her characters like they're real people. (Sometimes, they whisper back.)

Keep in touch

Still thinking about Glowrot? You're not alone.

If you're craving more surreal horror, queer longing, and characters who unravel a little too beautifully, I have something for you!

Read the prequel, Sugarlung, for free! A sapphic reimagining of Hansel and Gretel that explores Nova's past and her own experiences with NIU. This story is short but deadly, filled with devotion turned delusion, hedonism as a coping mechanism, and the sweetness of a trap you don't want to escape.

Just scan the code below to dive in:

or visit sugarlung.beatricelebrunauthor.com

You can also follow me on social media (@beatrice_lebrun) and my website (beatricelebrunauthor.com) to stay updated on upcoming releases, secret projects, and maybe the occasional meltdown.

Thank you for reading.

Thank you for feeling something.